Miraval

By the same author

Why I am still an Anglican (Ed.)
The Gnostics

TOBIAS CHURTON

MIRAVAL

A QUEST

WEIDENFELD AND NICOLSON
LONDON

First published in Great Britain in 1989 by
George Weidenfeld and Nicolson Ltd
91 Clapham High Street, London SW4 7TA

ISBN 0 297 79709 3

Photoset and printed in Great Britain by
Redwood Burn Limited, Trowbridge, Wiltshire

Dedication With Love

Anne Brenon
Gerard Lewis
Joseph Ritman
Gérard Zuchetto

This book could not
have been written
without them.

And to all the ladies
and knights of the
Spirit which
never dies:

Stars divided for the sake
of Union

Illustrations by Ian Lowe

Contents

Preface

Some time in the late eleventh century something extraordinary began to happen. Certain men of high and lowly birth began to celebrate Love: a Love which did then as now hang above the earth, seemingly out of reach, impenetrable and mysterious, called down in soft and subtle song to enrich, enliven and initiate men and women into a new life. This was the *Fine Love* of the troubadours and we hear its echoes today in the tormented and joyous loves of our poets of music and of film and, if we are fortunate and true, in our own lives. This *Fine Love* comes to us as a distant and aching melody: a song of the earth and heaven combined, which found its birth in the courts and castles of Aquitaine, Languedoc, Catalonia, Provence and Lombardy and which was to travel as a welcome stranger to the courts and corridors of northern France, Germany and England. While sometimes lusty and mad, the songs of the troubadours more frequently exalted men and women to a spiritual equality in a celebration of the erotic which transcended the purely sexual to a sexual purity which itself seemed to transcend the bonds of the flesh and the bitter ties of the material world. In short, the divinity of the erotic was seized and sometimes understood in a world where a dominant Church saw sex as an inevitable constraint or as a necessary sin. The troubadours celebrated the liberty of Love. But this was not a liberty unbounded by codes of honour. The troubadour-lover must give himself entirely to the dictates of Love, and unfaithfulness invited the scorch of scorn – all the more surprising since the *Fine Love* was always an adulterous Love, both dangerous and demanding. But marriage was not then as we think it now – for by a long and arduous process, many of us now expect marriage to be characterized by precisely those demands which were once the product of romantic adultery. We have the troubadours to thank for that.

At precisely the same time as the *Fine Love* reached its

highest point of development in song, a rival Church to Catholicism appeared in the Languedoc. The Cathars or 'pure ones', not infrequently called 'good men' or 'good women' preached and practised a God who was *all* Love and who also demanded a pure Love which took men and women from out of the grip of the material world. If the *Fine Love* of the troubadour appeared to be perilous and fragile in this world, the Cathar Church provided an explanation of why this was so. Men and women were in truth the fallen satellites of God, enveloped in bodies of pain and restriction by evil angels who had fashioned the world of matter as a tragic counterfeit of the world of God – the timeless world of the Holy Spirit and the source of Love, Truth, Beauty and Wisdom. How many lovers have found themselves to be *contra mundum* – 'against the world' – and have found thereby an Unknown God and paths through life invisible to the unloving and the materialist?

Nevertheless, while Cathar and troubadour lived side by side, sharing a common culture and the highest ideals, the troubadours' emphasis on feminine beauty and the erotic created problems for the Cathars' spiritual leaders who saw all manifestations of sex as being ultimately bonds which kept men and women tied to the machinations of the Devil in the world. Men and women should love God as they should love one another, seeking neither to possess one another nor to set up rival loves to the Divine. For the Cathars the beauty of woman was in its essentials illusory – its purpose to encourage procreation and the enslavement of more divine souls in the prison of the world. However, this division was seldom so clear-cut, for the Cathars felt themselves bound to respect in all Love the vestiges of the source of Love: the *Good God* in Heaven.

The hero of this story, Raimon de Miraval, was a real person, a poor nobleman of the Languedoc who wrote almost exclusively about the *Fine Love*. He was born in about 1165 and died sometime between 1216 and 1229. The ruins of his little castle still stand in the village of Miraval-Cabardès. It was a visit to this place, shown to me by the modern troubadour, Gérard Zuchetto, that first inspired this book. I know of another who, if only he had lived, would have found inspiration there – and had he done so, then I am sure that the whole world would have heard of it.

The story of the book was further inspired by the account of Miraval's life and loves written by his contemporary, the Catalonian seigneur Uc de Mataplana and by the account to be found in a rare book: *Literary History of the Troubadours Vol. II*, Paris 1774 found in the Bibliotheca Philosophica Hermetica in Amsterdam. I am grateful to Jean Gimpel for details of the dam system of twelfth century Toulouse. Mention should also be made of the classic work by L. T. Topsfield: *Les Poésies du Troubadour Raimon de Miraval* (AG. Nizet, Paris 1971). But the greatest insight into Miraval's character must begin with the troubadour's own *cansos* and *sirventes*. I know of twenty-two of them translated from the occitan into French by the late great philosopher and poet, René Nelli.

This is not a history book, however, for the greatest inspiration came to me from trying to live out and live through the tension between the doctrine of the Cathars and the amazing sensibility of the troubadours both in England and in the magical places of the Languedoc to which I shall always owe so very much. Having said that, the greatest debt is due to Raimon de Miraval – a man who really knew how to *turn us on* . . .

Tobias Churton
January 1989
Lichfield

'Spiritual love is wine and fragrance.
But the mysteries of this marriage
are perfected in the day and the light.
Neither that day nor its light ever sets.'

(From the Gospel of Philip. Syria. c.250 AD)

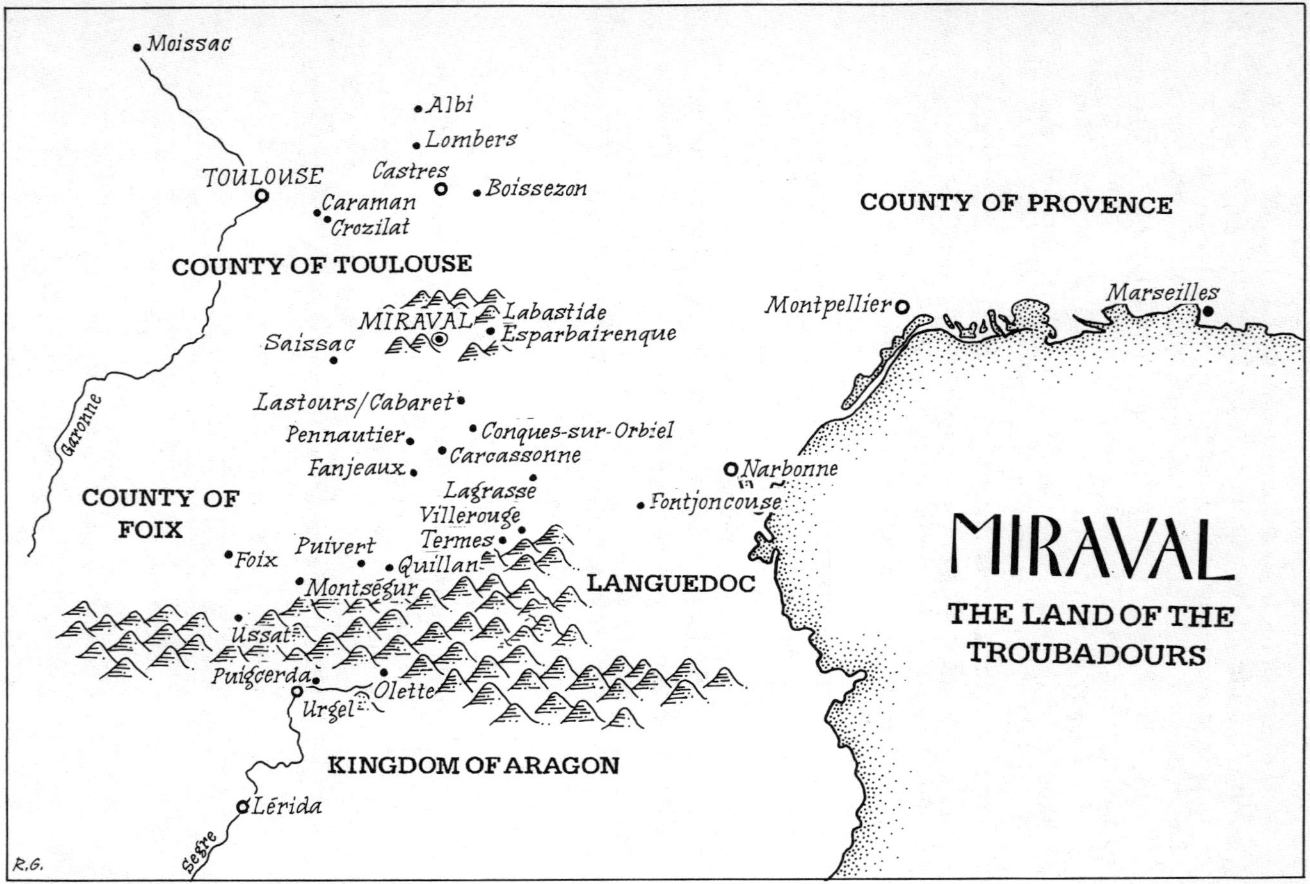
MIRAVAL
THE LAND OF THE TROUBADOURS
COUNTY OF PROVENCE
COUNTY OF TOULOUSE
COUNTY OF FOIX
LANGUEDOC
KINGDOM OF ARAGON
Moissac
Albi
Lombers
Castres
TOULOUSE
Caraman
Crozilat
Boissezon
Labastide
MIRAVAL
Esparbairenque
Saissac
Lastours/Cabaret
Pennautier
Conques-sur-Orbiel
Carcassonne
Fanjeaux
Lagrasse
Villerouge
Termes
Puivert
Foix
Quillan
Montségur
Ussat
Puigcerda
Olette
Urgel
Lérida
Montpellier
Marseilles
Narbonne
Fontjoncouse
Garonne
Segre
R.G.

I
MIRAVAL

I CAN SEE A TRAMP. He looks like a tramp, but he could be a king. The alley is hot. The passage is dark and the place is dangerous. Great pig skin bins are scattered about. Some have fallen over. The shadow of the man shoots like a dagger through the wet wall. He is wearing a turban and it could be a crown. He could be a king. His hands are bleeding and he is fumbling with a lid. He is opening a bin. Inside his head he speaks of what he sees:

—The length of the bin is like a glass for magnifying. The sides are a black extension to a starlit world: silver stars in a black ocean. A globe is advancing toward me. It obliterates the black space and all I can see is this crystal ball, so beautiful: swirling blue and wrapped in swaddling clouds, deeper blues and deep brown spaces. It is the world I've seen floating on the Nile when I mistook it for the moon. It is the image of God and a place of pain. It is a world of men and it has come again.

We are flying across the world. We are light dancing on the oceans. We have feet like wings and wings of mind, beyond the bonds of time. The bars of space expand: over the mountains, over the plains, across the strips of gold and green, beyond the shepherds' fires and the city's face, we come to rest in an ancient place – among the glassy glades of the Cabardès. To Miraval, in Languedoc, in the month of May 1192.

To see Miraval on a day like this, you would think the sun had fallen down from heaven. Raimon de Miraval, twenty-seven years old, troubadour and sometime lord of his castle, would not have missed this for the world. He was out in it, washing in the cool waters of the Orbiel. It felt very good. All about him the branches were dripping with light. Among the scattered beams, Miraval's body was sundered by the creamy haze which hovered about the river. He looked up to the parapet of his tiny castle. She had not arrived. Azalaïs de Boissézon had given her word and Miraval knew better than to question *that*. She still had not come. He felt that twitch of anxiety which robs us of many a fine day.

Miraval looked for inspiration about his magical home and stepped naked onto the round stones at the foot of the little waterfall. There the streams of white light caused the copper streaks of his long brown hair to glow in the hot breeze. His shaven face and ruddy cheeks were shining too. To his right, the wooded mountain rose up a thousand feet: brown-green bushes, bright green trees, light-brown branches flourished among the rocks. The mountain, full of charmed life and hidden depths, fascinated Miraval. The castle with its solitary tower cast a shadow over his green eyes as he turned from the mountain to look up again for Azalaïs. She had still not come. So he sat down by the warm banks of the Orbiel and tried to forget himself. The sound of the stream subsided. His gaze was fixed, not upon the mountain nor upon the image of Azalaïs, but upon another world. This world so transfixed his mind that he was his own no longer, and it was Miraval which spoke through him:

> Now that the days are bright
> And the hard earth opens her eyes,
> Let us not let the summer pass
> As the Joy of Love runs fast!

Miraval dreamt of running water and he felt cold. He came to himself and shuddered. The sun which throughout the day had glided with such ease up the mountain had slipped over the other side and had left Miraval musing in the depths of his own solitary shadow.

Did Azalaïs care? He thought she was like a performer – only singing for the sake of reward – and heaven help you if you begged for more! This was a new experience for a troubadour, more accustomed to passive faces. The ladies of Languedoc were not given to showing their feelings, but their souls were like the mountain and not to be trifled with. Miraval never trifled with women. For him, Love, the *Fine Love* was a serious game and until this year he had lived out this game like a scholar: cloistered within that *Joy* which only a Lady could inspire. His adventures, until now, had all been endured within the space of his own heart. Miraval could not fathom the heart of a woman but he could touch her soul; and although *Fine Love* doubtless meant more to him than it did to her, whoever she might have been, his songs did offer something her husband never could: a glimpse of her self.

Miraval slouched into the main hall of the castle. The room had just enough space for a gaping fireplace and a trestle table which could seat about twenty people. That evening found only Miraval's four minstrels: four wonderful musicians, spaced out on both sides. Ahmed, Berteaux, Gérard and Jacques were drinking wine and cracking jokes about their recent trip to Montpellier. Miraval had sent them there in order to perform his latest works to the lady Agnès, a lady famed for both her beauty and her courtesy. There were many famous women in Languedoc.

'That Agnès ... what can you say?'

'She likes a good song!'

'Easily pleased, though – I was out of tune a dozen times!'

'Easily pleased? Agnès? She didn't miss a thing.'

'No, Gérard, she just looked that way. Truth was, she couldn't understand a word you were singing! It's that Gascon accent of yours – it's so *vulgar*!'

Berteaux got up. He brushed his spiky fair hair backwards and began mimicking Gérard: 'Lurve you like a loidy!'

'You're a bastard! Berteaux the Bastard, that's you!'

'You're all bastards!' yelled Miraval. 'Wasting my time dreaming of sunsets and butterflies and torn hearts so you lot can get pissed for a song!'

The minstrels went quiet. This kind of outburst was not typical. Miraval was a fount of culture to them all and he rarely raised his voice in temper.

He looked to the ceiling, 'Yes, "bastards" ... why else would I love you? Oh, come on! Don't mind me – anyway, where are those women I saw you with last night?'

'That was last night wasn't it? Felt like a night in together tonight.'

'We hoped you might join us, my lord.'

'Not tonight. I had ... well, you know Jacques. I've got something on my mind.'

'A new song, my lord?'

'No, Ahmed. Not quite a new song. Something – well just don't keep me up all night. I'll be hell tomorrow if you do.'

'You know us, my lord. Early to bed – '

'Not when you sleep alone you're not!'

'Sleep well, my lord. We certainly will!'

'Thank you, Gérard.'

'Aye, and good dreams. Don't lose your soul in your sleep.'

'You should know, Ahmed – what you lose at night you always find in the morning!'

'Well said, my lord. There's hope for us all.'

'That's true, that's true,' sighed Miraval as he slipped off to bed. It was not much use, however. As the troubadour turned in his bed, his brain awash with thoughts of his new love, words coalesced at the midnight hour. He could not find the will to rise and write them down, nor could he sleep. But time passed and as the birds began to spring the daylight from the dawn, Miraval finally entered the black space and the world disappeared once more.

Miraval felt a lot better in the morning. He dipped his dry face into a big red earthenware bowl and coolly observed his dripping features as they emerged in the mirror. The mirror had been a parting gift from Loba de Pénnautier. She had told him to keep it until he found a lady who served better. He had been a vain child and, while he had been destined for the church, he had still managed to make his brothers crease up with laughter when he felt like it. Now they were gone, too. Music had changed everything.

Love is all!
Love is all my thought.

The words took him by surprise. He thought they had been lost as so much is lost on the brink of sleep. Now they had returned. Still dripping wet, Miraval reached for some parchment and began to scribble frantically:

Love is Joy,
Spirit of your Joy!

A sunbeam penetrated his bedroom window and lit up the parchment. Suddenly it was a golden flame and Miraval's hand began to shake:

If I had the feeling,
I would suffer for her so long
So long!

Impatient as ever, Miraval thought this enough to be getting on with. He grabbed his shirt and rushed down the cool spiral steps to the hall. His minstrels were snoring, still slumped over the trestle table.

'What's this? Come on! When Miraval is up – nobody sleeps!'

He paced about the table, slapping their backs and banging the table:

'Gérard! Come on! Get to your lute! And Berteaux, we need your flute! Jacques, your rebec! Wake up! The sun is up and it's beautiful!'

One by one, the heavy heads of tousled hair rose from the table. Ahmed looked up, his dark eyes just slits in a Syrian landscape, and smiled that infant smile with a twinkle from his rotten teeth and a glow in his cheeks. Not everybody loved Ahmed – but not everybody had had the chance.

Picture yourself below the little castle of Miraval. The villagers stop their work. The tanner gazes upwards through the ginger haze of his workshop. The milkmaid spills a little milk, the herdsmen wait, Jacquette clenches the salty dough in anticipation and a dog springs to its feet in the musty porch of the echoing church.

As dust is dispersed among the parallel beams of wood and broken light, and music curls about the arcs of stone we glide down to the sound of Miraval:
The drum: a taut skin stretched about a slim glazed body; a tight sound, a rapid pulse, an airy echo of the summer's earth. Ahmed's hot hands: rapid slaps and taps that tease the high melodious flute to fresh ecstasy – an Arabic drift to love. The lute is strummed, caressed, and fills the hall with light, deliberate rhythm and the hint of melancholy. The distant song of Jacques's rebec: his bow arching and bending at each intersection of melody and mystery. The hall of the castle is now a musical prism and all the colours of the Cabardès unite in the

voice of Raimon de Miraval: slow and searching, it plunges and climbs and cries and yearns – he sings with all his soul:

At the bottom of my heart burns a flame
Which leaves my lips when I sing:
Don't let this desire kill me!
Azalaïs, my Lady is cruel to me
And stings me with pride and stony contempt,
But Fine Love will hold me
If I have the feeling!

Was Azalaïs listening now? A doubt flashed through Miraval's mind as he sang. The minstrels looked up to him, smiling. Miraval, reassured, smiled back; with this group he could go anywhere – so what the hell!

All the year my Lady is in the season of beauty
Because she always knows how to be lovable
And when soft words abandon me –
I will always be faithful!
And although from her I don't receive
That Satisfaction which inflames the heart,
Yet am I satisfied – at Miraval!

There was an old woman in the village who said she saw Miraval glow when her lord sang. Not everyone saw it. Not everyone could.

'But, Gérard, two poets in one home is too many!'

The lunchtime conversation had glissaded down from the morning's session to speculation about Miraval's wife, Gaudairenca. The wine helped, of course.

'What would a son of mine have to inherit, anyhow? My brothers' children will fill this castle without any help from me. No, it's better that she's gone.'

'Your brothers may never return from the Crusades. What then?'

'Well, I should think I'll be expected to pay off their debts!'

'But this could be serious.'

'You talk to me of being serious! Look, Berteaux! What can I do about it? What do you suggest?'

'Was Azalaïs listening now?'

'Not for me to say, lord.'

'That's never stopped you before! I'm sure she's happy enough. No doubt some loveless knight is fighting for her favours somewhere. And no doubt she'll be back.' Miraval paused for a moment, 'You remember last year when Gaudairenca held a court here – or what passed for one – and delighted everyone – or nearly everyone – with her bloody gossip and new dance compositions? I'll tell you straight. Raimon de Miraval was bored stiff. If I hadn't met Agnès, I don't know what I'd have done. Without her, I'd never have met Azalaïs de Boissézon. Anyhow, I must tell you that Gaudairenca is not childless for want of effort. I've played my – well let's just say that I've played my part!'

The serious looks evaporated and they all laughed together – except, that is, for Ahmed who was gazing deeply into his goblet.

'What's the matter, Ahmed? Is it empty or something?'

'Nothing's the matter, my lord. That is ... well, the Lady Azalaïs. There's something strange about this lady.'

'For sure, Ahmed. That I know. That I know ... What do you mean?'

'We don't know where it might lead, do we?'

Jacques and Gérard murmured agreement.

'It's not worthy of us to have an opinion,' said Berteaux, inconsistent as ever.

'Well, at least one of you has some courtesy around here. But I'm not sure it's you, Berteaux! Ahmed, my dear man, there is nothing to worry your little head about. We'll always need you. If anyone loses, it'll only be me. I ought to be used to it by now.'

'But you're not, are you?' mumbled Ahmed.

'Listen! I've had enough of all these questions. I can't understand what's got into you! I think –' Miraval leaned back and stretched his arms, speaking to the ceiling ' – I think it's time I saw LOBA!'

'Cabaretz! Lucky man, my lord. Last week in Fanjeaux I heard Peire Vidal call it the castle of Love and that its fame had reached as far as the court of Tripoli.'

'Castle of Love! Vidal is always exaggerating but he could be right. But for myself, I prefer to think of Cabaretz as a kind of school.'

'And Loba de Pénnautier is the professor?' ventured Jacques.

'She's a lot cleverer than most doctors of law, medicine or theology. I've learnt more from her than anyone else alive, or half-dead!'

Soon Miraval was gone and the village was quiet again.

Miraval was well into that afternoon depression which must surely follow a morning's invention and a liquid lunch. He was beginning to doubt – and doubt is a wooden leg to a mental athlete. He thought to himself:

'She cannot exist. I sing about nothing to no-one. I've dreamt of a woman but have never touched her. I've sung of a woman but never seen her. Azalaïs ... who is she?'

Miraval gazed up from the leafy path before him to the forested peaks of the Cabardès. Their mystery, such a dense beauty, bore down upon him with renewed force. Here he was, among the scattered shadows of the Black Mountain which was behind him, making his easy way to the castle of Love, to Loba of Cabaretz, his neighbour and friend. The rocks that pushed and jostled their way through the flaky ferns changed from bronze to pink and from pink to purple. The golden glow of a late afternoon sun caught his purple tunic and warmed his heart. The roar of the Orbiel, a white noise from white water, eased his thoughts out of complexity and into vividness of mind. Surely, he thought, Loba would explain why Azalaïs had become such a problem to him. In less than an hour he found himself beneath the three castles which sat upon the peaks of Lastours. Miraval took a deep breath, spurred his horse, and began the winding ascent to the curling walls of the outer ramparts of that castle called Cabaretz: the castle of Love. The troubadour's heart began to race. Yes, Loba would understand. She always did. Loba was amazing. Everybody knew it – but few knew why.

On the peaks of the ancient Cabardès, a man found coolness of thought and mildness of heart. The wind was beautiful and all that was about him shared in a strange, smooth tone of satisfaction. The cold mirror of winter was finally shattered and the spirit of Miraval ascended to the sky while his horse bore his body past the straining guards as the great gates of Cabaretz were opened.

2
Absolutely Love

The town of Fanjeaux girded a steep hill with brown stone houses and ruddy roofs. This thriving town was dominated by the nobility, and served as an occasional base for some fifty lords of both sexes. Fanjeaux also served as a home to all that was new in the intellectual, artistic and spiritual life of the region.

Around the hill, neat fields and balmy vineyards weaved their way like luminous borders to a fine manuscript. Dusk was gently falling upon the town. The streets were warm and breezy and there was a lightness in the air which promoted a pleasing lassitude in the hearts of the inhabitants.

Outside the house of the Lady Blanche de Tonneins, a group of young girls were huddled together in conference. Their fresh country faces were aglow with the news that Peire Vidal was in town again and would sing at the lady's house to an audience of local knights, ladies and *good men*.

'He's good. So handsome. Such a man!'

'Such a man would do for me! I dream about him all the time. Mother says I have no chance – but she's just jealous!'

'Jealous of what?'

'Well, am I not younger and fairer than she is?'

'Look who's talking! Peire Vidal goes for anyone who pays!'

'Then none of us have a hope.'

'I hear he wants everyone to go to Spain and fight the Moors.'

'Is he going, too? Daddy says troubadours know more about talk than fighting.'

'Your father's only a merchant – what does he know about it?'

'More than you, Garsende!'

A priest spoke as he walked by: 'There's too much fighting already, my girls. There should be more love.'

The girls creased up in uncontrollable giggles, then whispered:

'Did you see who that was?'

'Of course we did, stupid! It's "Randy" Pons – they say he can save neither souls nor a girl's virginity!'

'Perhaps he should become a troubadour. At least then he might save my soul – and maybe keep me intact!'

'Madeleine! Mother says you must never give a troubadour a taste of fanny. You lose all merit with him and become like a wife.'

'I would be his wife!'

'Stupid!'

'I'd be content with a kiss. Just one.'

'No, you wouldn't, Madeleine! Shh! He's started again! Quiet!'

Such sighs as came from the girls were soon lost in the unaccompanied melody of Peire Vidal:

> ... since God has so well endowed me
> it's not right that my price be low.
> I know a hundred ladies who each would
> like to have me for her own, if she could –

The girls outside could hardly contain themselves.

> but I've never been one to boast or pose,
> and I never wanted to talk much about myself;
> instead I kiss ladies and unhorse knights
> – but lovers pay most dearly for their Joy!

The girls, while unprepared for Peire Vidal's lightning exit, each caught a cherished glimpse of the troubadour as he stalked out of the house. This appeared to be enough for them, for as the troubadour raised an imaginary cap in their direction, they scattered – only to reappear from behind walls and wagons as Vidal spurred his horse and set off. They ran after him. Did they know they could never catch him? The clip-clop of the hooves accelerated down the summer's darkening streets and Peire Vidal, fresh from a pilgrimage to the Holy Land, left Fanjeaux to the echoes of piercing screams, tears and pleadings to stay. Who could blame them?

Peire Vidal had good reason to leave so quickly, for notwithstanding Blanche's pretty daughters, he had a date to meet. The date was with Loba de Pénnautier at the castle of Cabaretz, some twenty miles north of Fanjeaux. The 'date' he was to keep was more in the manner of a *deal* and was, in its details, certainly new to Vidal's very broad experience. Loba had informed the troubadour that her husband, Jordan, brother of the seigneur of Cabaretz, Peire Roger, had heard ill of Vidal – though on what grounds he had not made clear. Perhaps he knew of Vidal's recent disagreement with Count Raymond V of Toulouse, at whose behest Vidal had made his propitiatory pilgrimage to the Holy Land. Vidal was in a tricky position, for Raymond V was on his deathbed and so the troubadour was about to lose an important patron. This was apt to make him more impulsive than ever, and if Raymond had informed others of Vidal's 'misdemeanours' he could find himself in deep water very quickly. Furthermore, unlike Miraval, Peire Vidal was not of noble blood. He was a furrier's son and was dependent on his wit and his genius and the patronage that genius sometimes attracts and wit frequently repels. There is always a price to pay.

In this case, Loba had advised Vidal to take special precautions. He had done so. Vidal was fired by his attraction to Loba and was inclined to shrug off his problems. He just had to find new patrons – and that's all there was to it! As he galloped at full speed up the steep and empty streets of Conques, he reminded himself that these problems were 'all part of the course'. He had never expected an easy life and God had made him in such a way that he could cheerfully say 'To stay in any place too long is like being ill.'

He was enjoying the ride. Perhaps this was the best part of his life. Perhaps it was the worst. It all depended on whether he thought of his point of departure or of his destination. At this moment, Peire Vidal was thinking of Cabaretz, the castle of Love. He spurred his horse. As he entered the sandstone gorge where the Orbiel and the Gresillon mingled at Lastours, he reached behind him to feel if a certain bundle tied to his saddle was still secure. The bundle was secure – but was he? The indulgence given by a seigneur to a troubadour who sang well of his wife's virtue was common in Languedoc and in Provence, but there was always an attendant risk. But if truth he told, Vidal relished it. It was good sport.

Nevertheless, he found himself struggling to suppress the memory of a story once told to him when he was a boy by the troubadour Raimbaut d'Orange, while on a visit to Courthezon in Provence. He had heard of a knight who, when dining with his wife one evening, had asked her whether or not she was enjoying the meat dish. She replied that she was enjoying it. It was better than usual. 'That is the heart of your troubadour,' he told her, with an impassivity bordering on insanity. The lady continued eating in silence. She then excused herself, climbed up to the castle battlements and threw herself to her death. As Peire Vidal tried to repress his sense of revulsion, another part of him was reflecting that perhaps the love of such a lady was indeed worth dying for. But he had not yet found such a woman. Perhaps, tonight ...

He dismounted at the foot of the mountain at Lastours and began to sing quietly to himself as he untied the bundle from his saddle. His hands were shaking slightly and his fingers were stiff after the ride:

> And so, old, poor, and needy
> I came among the rich,
> and full of shame – but
> one had better seek protection
> than come to ruin.

There in the silent darkness he began pulling the contents from out of the sack. At first it appeared to be a carpet; but when tufts of fur sprang up in the moonlight, there could be no doubt that this was an animal skin. It was the skin of a wolf, and the head of the wolf was still fixed, stuffed and angry. Loba de Pénnautier had an ambivalent attitude towards men. Peire Vidal looked up to the four peaks of the mountain, to the silhouettes of the three castles: Quertinheux, Fleur Espine and, to the right, the finest of them all, Cabaretz. The troubadour began thinking of what a fine story could be made – with little embellishment – of what he was about to undertake. He tied the wolf skin securely about his body and, on all fours, he began to ascend the vertiginous approach to Cabaretz. A solitary moon observed the spectacle from behind a cloud.

'Damn the thorns!'

Inside the keep: Loba and Miraval. Outside, clutching the mountain for dear life: Peire Vidal; two troubadours, one woman. Did Loba know what she was doing? Loba knew. She was a match for anyone. Widely known for her intelligence, her political skill and her somewhat bizarre sense of humour, still none of her accomplishments could equal the source of her power. She had learned the fascination for the Unknown and the power of it – and no troubadour could afford to ignore her. Thus far the legend. Loba de Pénnautier was Miraval's true friend.

They had been talking quietly to one another in an upper room for over two hours. Beneath the ribbed vault the room was still. A fire was growing in its grate. Loba listened to Miraval as he spoke in half-whispers. She was wearing a blue velvet gown, fastened to the neck. Below her small breasts the figure of a wolf was embroidered in gold. Her fine blonde hair, mingled with a little grey, was bound in braids which fell over her back. She held her head high and her large blue eyes fixed upon those of Miraval.

'But, Raimon, we have had our time. We did all that we could – all that you would allow.'

'Was I too strict for you?'

'Oh, don't worry about me, Raimon. It's you that I'm concerned about. I never did understand your rules of Love – who can profit by them?'

'Profit? In Love we profit by Love – what else is there?'

'You will never understand women, Miraval. We are not what you think us to be.' Loba covered a giggle with a little cough.

'But *you* should understand me, my lady. You have heard my songs. You really listened.'

'Yes, Raimon. I was listening to you – to the sound of your heart; it was beautiful. I am not the only one who thinks so. You flatter us – and we enjoy it. But ... how can I say this? I think you see the best in us – but when you cannot see it, you put it there. You give us what we cannot hold. Everything you do . . . it's all gift, and then you complain that we are unworthy of it. Of course we are unworthy! We can never be worthy of what you bring! You see, Raimon, a woman cannot love with the soul alone – as you can, or think you can. I should say that it is a rare man that would want us to! You, Raimon de Miraval, you are a rare man – and you must search for the impossible. It's your destiny.'

A falling log split the silence.

'How can Love change, Loba?'

'It is not "love", Raimon. It is us. We change. You don't want to change, do you?'

Miraval thought for a moment. 'All I ever wanted was to live in Love. That's all.'

'That's all? . . . *Azalaïs* – now there's a lady. She will change you. You see!'

Miraval looked away from Loba to the crackling fire. He could see *her*. He winced and clenched his fist. Loba took his hand and, opening the fingers one by one, spread them on her lap. On the outside Loba looked serene but inside was jealousy and anger. She did not like Azalaïs de Boissézon. She did not trust her – but she could not tell this to Miraval. He would not understand. Miraval's heart began to melt for Loba again. He looked into her eyes for just a second and tried to suppress a warm smile. Unable to bear this living intimacy, Miraval broke away from Loba's hand, got up, and paced over to the fire. Loba closed her eyes, holding back her true feelings.

'You could have been a knight, Raimon. It could all have been so different.'

'I was going to be a clerk in Toulouse. Imagine it! I dreamed of being special advisor to Eleanor of Aquitaine.'

'She would have loved you Raimon. She eats troubadours like you for breakfast! But you would have made a bad clerk. The bishops would have sat on you for years. They're not interested in what you have to give.'

'That's true!' Miraval laughed, 'Well, you know that we must thank Eleanor's grandfather for saving me from them – or blame him if you like!'

'William, Duke of Aquitaine. There was a man. Yes, he was one of you – but he did manage to combine his writing with some, shall we say, political skill? I should have loved to have met him. We need men like him now.'

'I can remember the first thing I ever read of his. How did it go now?

> I, wish for that which I cannot have,
> and yet the proverb speaks true for me, for sure;
> 'where there's a will there's a way'
> – if one is long-suffering!'

'It could have been written for you, couldn't it?'

'That's what I thought when I first heard it. After that I knew I could be neither clerk nor knight.'

'But you've lost something, too – '

'Of course, Loba. Losing is half of it.'

'That's good, Raimon. Very good. You've got something there. But what I really meant was – well, a knight has his armour to protect him. What has a troubadour to wear?'

'Only the love of his lady!'

'You might get cold that way, Raimon!'

'It is enough, my lady.'

'Is it always?'

'There's Miraval, of course. But for me, Miraval, love and the Lady are all part of one song.'

'But what now? What's to come?'

This remark was unexpected. The thought that things might change, that there might be more for him than his castle and his writing had never troubled him before.

'I don't know what you mean, Loba. This morning I sang "Love is all my thought!" Funny. It seems a long time ago now.'

'Azalaïs de Boissézon is "all your thought" now. Is that not so, Raimon?'

'Yes.'

'She has let you down?'

'She made a promise.'

'A lady's promise is not enough Miraval – not even for you. Sad, isn't it?'

'But, Loba, I don't understand – did she lie to me? I just can't believe this. A lady cannot lie and stay in the court of Love.'

'The court of Love, Raimon, is a game we play when there's nothing more important to do.'

Miraval was shocked but Loba continued, 'Anyhow, how many times have you sung to me that the courts are full of false lovers?'

'It's true! It's true! The false lovers, the disloyal ones – they are the evil. They spread discord wherever they go! If a man and his lady cannot be true to one another, what hope has anyone got? The *Fine Love* is the absolute heart of civilized life! If it should fall, everything else – you can be sure of this – everything else will soon follow! But I'm sure, Loba, I'm sure that Azalaïs is not among them. It must be something else.'

'Everything in this world must fall sometime, Raimon. Even Cabaretz – but we'll fight for it, make no mistake!'

'Oh Loba – you've been listening to the heretics! They have no love for this world. They see only corruption.'

'It's strange, Raimon. Strange that you, you who so craves for spiritual love, always searching for a love beyond time, gazing into space for a glimpse of some other world – yes, it's strange that you should be against the heretics.'

'I'm not against them. I just, well, I just don't agree with them!'

'But aren't you looking for the same thing?'

'But *where* are we looking? Loba, look, the love of a man for a woman, this they condemn. They do not speak of the same Love as I do. For the heretics the beauty of a woman is a trick of the Devil – while I say, the beauty of a woman makes me virtuous!'

Loba smiled, 'Did Loba de Pénnautier bring forth this "Virtue" in you, Raimon de Miraval?'

'Indeed, my lady... "Even when I hear those lies, love never dies, love never dies..."'

'Did I lie to you, then?'

'No, my lady. Not you. You never lied to me.'

'Come here, Miraval.'

The troubadour knelt before her. She clasped his hands and kissed them. A tear fell from her cheek.

'Know this, Miraval. Hear it well. *Fine Love* does not die but there may come a time when we can no longer see it, or feel it. But I have faith in you. While you ride – although you are not an ordinary knight – a greater knight are you because you do not put your faith in a sword but in Love. As you travel, the word of Love will travel and many who know nothing today will know of it tomorrow. Many will tremble at the thought of it and be shamed by it. Many will try to destroy love by trying to destroy you – but, but listen, Miraval, listen to what your lady is saying to you. Listen to what you have said yourself: the real enemies of Love are as you say – those who would sport with Love and play with Love and use Love. Over such people you are a king and have many courts and still more will open to you. And if some close to you, as they will, then you will always have the love of Loba de Pénnautier!'

Miraval was transfixed. It felt like an initiation. He was speechless. He had been blind.

Instinctively he got up, bowed, and began to make his way out.

'Raimon!' Miraval turned.

'Raimon. One last thing – '

'My lady?'

'I have never understood why men had to invent "purity" – but I do know that you will be made fools by it. Adieu, Miraval.'

As Miraval departed, Loba smiled inwardly. She was pleased that Azalaïs de Boissézon had broken the rules. She knew what it meant and to what it would lead.

Miraval was making his way down the path to the valley floor. The sound of uncertain steps began to fade. He began to dream. He was in a town on Christmas Eve. It was dusk. He was sitting with his mother. He tried to attract her attention: 'She's there! There!' Across a street was an eager crowd of troubadours, jostling one another in an attempt to catch sight of something extraordinary. They all carried bundles of parchment and two or three of them were writing on sheets suspended in mid-air. One of them was sitting on a huge orange. In the orange was a face in floods of tears. Miraval recognised the face. It was Raimbaut d'Orange! The face began singing in a strange, slow, solemn voice, 'Lady I ... aaaaaam ... veeeery ... faaaaar ... from YOU!' The Orange screamed, burst and then disappeared! Miraval recognised other troubadours.

There was Guiraut de Borneil dressed in Crusader's costume: a white surcoat emblazoned with a big red cross that dripped with blood. Guiraut was wailing: 'Plunged in thought and gripped by fear! By Fear! By Fear!' Arnaut Daniel pulled apart a vermilion robe to reveal three hearts – all of them broken. 'She slays me!' he cried. 'And damns herself!' Peire Vidal suddenly turned from the crowd and faced Miraval directly. His neck began to extend and wrap itself about a cold pillar. With his tongue drooping out and with the voice of a man strangled, he gurgled: 'I see the whole world in the grip of guile and treachery!'

All of these terrible voices were clashing into an explosive cacophony when, from out of their midst arose the figure of Azalaïs! Her toes glided over the snow-covered cobblestones. Her arms were outstretched and she was hovering like a gull. Azalaïs de Boissézon, more seductive than ever, flying towards Miraval ... He left his old mother to greet her, but something was wrong. Azalaïs narrowed her eyes and looked straight at Miraval. She cocked her head and then it came: a wanton, sinister petulance gave form to a lascivious smile. Miraval reeled back in horror and, with his eyes wide open he began to scream above the weird choir of troubadours: 'This cannot be! This cannot be!'

A great tree surrounded by stars appeared behind the terrible scene. It grew and grew until at last a gaping mouth could be seen at its centre. The mouth began to suck in the troubadours. Azalaïs flew backwards towards it, licking her lips, her hands feeling her mouth, her breasts, her hips, her thighs, smiling snidely all the while. Miraval struggled against the hot waves of attraction which threatened to take him. Someone was laughing. He thought it was Loba. But it was not Loba and it was not laughter. It was Miraval himself, crying out from the depths of his soul, 'I love her! I love her! O God help me!'

Loba was still sitting alone where Miraval had left her. Her face was impassive, her eyes were moist. A sergeant appeared, his chain-mail rattling in the archway. He bowed, wheezing heavily as he did so,

'Madame, forgive me. The seigneur has bidden me to inform madame that a ... that a wolf has been seen among the castle ramparts.'

'A wolf? Sergeant, don't you know there are many wolves in

the Cabardès? There is the wolf which flies on our pennant, for example. There is the wolf who stalks the hearts of our greatest knights. Many wolves, sergeant.'

'Yes, madame. But the wolf is ... the wolf, madame, is climbing the outer wall.'

Loba paused for a second. 'We have a fine pack of hounds, sergeant. Is it not time they were exercised?'

Miraval had never liked the sound of hounds and it was even more irritating to hear them at night. About to quicken his horse, he hesitated. The sound was getting closer. What were they doing out at night? His horse began to shake. 'There, there, Drummer, I'm with you. It's all right.' The stallion began to lose his footing. 'Come on, Drummer. Hold firm now.'

There was a scurrying in the bushes to the right and the sound of skidding to the left. The barking of the dogs grew louder. There was desperate breathing. The hounds were everywhere. Miraval couldn't move. A figure emerged from the undergrowth and looked up to Miraval. In pale terror, the two men stared at each other. Behind the man trailed an animal skin like a serpent's half-discarded scales. He ran off. Miraval heard him fall. The dogs were upon him. They growled. They scratched. They bit and they tore away at the body of the fallen man. He struggled and screamed and scraped the dirt with his bitten feet.

Drummer tried to bolt but Miraval took control and soon they were in the midst of the fight. The hounds glared at Miraval: all teeth and mad eyes bulging and gasping! Drummer reared and kicked and the bully-dogs winced with pain. Miraval took his sword and beat the blade about the bodies of the attackers. A voice from the distance: the sergeant, on foot, was calling after them. Confused, some of the dogs withdrew and Miraval, seizing the moment, bent down and grabbed Peire Vidal's shattered arm. He dragged him to the foot of the mountain. Behind them the dogs barked hysterically but the sergeant, having seen Miraval, called them off. The mad barking subsided and Miraval dismounted. It seemed to him that the man was dead. The victim's face was drawn with grief, his flesh ripped and bruised. There was blood everywhere. Miraval could not tell if the man was a noble or a peasant. A dribble of saliva fell from Vidal's lips and he began to croak, '... Too late ...'

'No, sir. You must not die. Let me help you.'

'Must be gone. My horse – '

Tears were rolling down Vidal's face, mingling in the starlight with the blood, the dirt and the thorns.

'Why sir? Why this?'

'A lady, sir. Always a lady.'

From out of the darkness came Vidal's horse and the broken troubadour got up with Miraval's help. He was shaking with pain.

'My thanks, my lord.'

Peire Vidal mounted with great difficulty and, with one eye closed looked at his helper. His mouth hung open. His right arm drooped low. He raised his left arm and drew his blood-caked hand across his face. Without encouragement his horse began cantering southwards. This strange silent gesture would never be forgotten by Miraval – though its meaning would forever elude him. He felt like a child who had witnessed his first hanging.

He raced back to more familiar sights and sounds, to his castle and his waiting friends. Before he reached home, however, he had come to realise that something had left him. The happy stars which once had served as windows into heaven neither blinked nor winked but shot forth their icy light in blankness and despair.

Losing is half of it.

Azalaïs was there. It was Ahmed who told him.

'Here for some hours, my lord.'

The troubadour did not know whether to laugh or cry, 'Ahmed – you are sure?'

'Of course, my lord. Azalaïs is here.'

'Yes Ahmed. Thank you ... well, go then – go clear everyone out of the hall! No – stop! Announce me to the lady. I'm coming at once.'

He did not. He could not. He walked about the silent village for a while his eyes wide open, his mind in a daze, wondering how summer could be so cold. His heart began to beat louder and louder and he found himself entering the hall. Azalaïs de Boissézon turned from the fire to see him. Miraval bowed. She nodded her head. Miraval stared at her.

'Please don't stare like that, Raimon. I promised I would come.'

That voice! It was like the warm hum of a butterfly on the other side. Miraval felt such a fool. His mind was blank. All he could do was look at Azalaïs. She was so *incredibly* beautiful. Her long, golden-brown hair curled around her face and her shoulders. A lemon-yellow gown flowed about every curve of her slender body in gentle waves. The ermine trim of a white surcoat merged with the firelight. The flickering torches sparkled in her large brown eyes. Beneath an aquiline nose her full lips parted again.

'Lord Raimon, I am late. Say nothing about it. Say nothing anyway.'

Miraval felt weak, so doused was he in the warm mist of his own fatigue and excitement. He could hardly stand up.

'You have been suffering, Raimon.'

'No – yes, my Lady.'

'Suffering is part of Love, Raimon. Suffering leads us to purity. Suffering leads us through the fire. Fire cleanses. We must go through the fire together.'

Miraval blinked. He wasn't sure he was ready for all this.

'I have dishonoured you, my Lady.'

'You cannot dishonour me, Raimon de Miraval.'

'But I have. I doubted you.'

'But you did not stop believing. I know you, Raimon. You could not stop believing.'

'How can you know this, Azalaïs? How can you know me?'

'Oh – I have listened to your music. When you stop believing, you will die – and I see you are very much alive!'

'Now, my Lady – now I am alive. Your beauty has given me life.'

'Oh, Miraval – it wasn't me! I knew you were suffering. Why did I let you suffer?'

'My Lady?'

'I let you suffer, Raimon, so that I could share your suffering and understand you.'

'I don't understand.'

'You think, Miraval, that you know all about Love. You have not yet begun. You will see, I am sure of it – but I will not show you.'

'My Lady. You seem . . . you are so different from when I last saw you.'

'Not different, Raimon. I was at Lombers then and my husband was there. But now my lord Bernart has gone to Aragon to see the king. You see, there's always going to be more that you don't understand, Miraval. The more you learn about me – '

'You are a Mystery, Azalaïs. You are a religion.'

Azalaïs giggled, 'The Mystery of *you*, Raimon. You only see what you know.'

'Then I know what I see.'

'Are you sure?'

'You talk of suffering and Love. You have missed something.'

'Oh?'

'You have not spoken of Joy. You have brought so much Joy to me, Azalaïs. Sometimes I can hardly contain myself!'

Azalaïs giggled again.

'Listen, please, Azalaïs. I want you to know this Joy. I really want you to feel it, breathe it, touch and caress it – be touched by Joy, be caressed by Love.'

'And with the Joy, Raimon, the torment.'

'But Azalaïs – the freedom of Joy – how can I explain? Where there's Joy the suffering ends.'

'Really, Raimon? We shall see.'

'Only if we see together.'

'Well, Raimon, this is all very interesting . . . How was the lady of Cabaretz?'

Miraval was disarmed completely.

'Loba?'

'Yes. How was Loba de Pénnautier?'

'She seemed well.'

'I like Loba de Pénnautier, Raimon. We know each other well. Did you know that?'

'I, I did not know – '

'You see, you're learning already. Yes, Loba is – well, she's not young, is she? Does that bother you?'

'I never think about it.'

'Don't you? But you've noticed that I am young and beautiful. You told me yourself – I've begun to believe it!'

'Yes, my Lady. You are more than this.'

'Yes, Raimon. Much more than this . . . Will you sing for me tomorrow?'

'With all my heart.'

'I believe in you, Raimon. You will survive us all!'

'Then, my Lady, I should be the loneliest man on this hard earth – for I cannot live without you.'

'All right, Raimon. Now listen to me. Tomorrow I must continue to Foix to see the count's sister. Esclarmonde and I have much to discuss. I shall stay for a month. In a month's time, you, Raimon de Miraval and I, Azalaïs de Boissézon, will meet at the cave of the Madeleine at Labastide Esparbairenque. I'll send you a messenger when the time comes. Then, and only if conditions are right and you have been faithful to me, then you may see me undress.'

Miraval slept deeply that night. Azalaïs lay wide awake. She had a capacity for intense thought. She distrusted every appearance and every situation which she herself had not created. But did she know what to do with what she had created?

Azalaïs

Undoubtedly, Miraval had touched the heart of Azalaïs – but he was not the first man to have done so. The first man she had truly loved was a young peasant from Laurac. It had been an endless summer and the boy – for so he really was – had been simple and as natural as the trees which Azalaïs loved so much. His love for her had blossomed without poetry and he had taken her without songs and without protest. It was all so *natural*. They had spoken of the sky and the sun. He killed himself when Azalaïs had had to go back to Boissézon with her parents. She had never returned to Laurac, where the villagers had long memories. She had been twelve and he, fourteen. The experience had taught the young Azalaïs something which she would never forget: that Love is not of this world.

Miraval seemed to sing this message to her again and again – and yet, Miraval could not really agree with her. For him, Love was the world transforming itself, it was the earth giving birth to her own soul but having done so, the world seemed to reject its own living child. Something, somewhere had gone terribly wrong. This was the feeling which united the lovers. After that most beautiful and most terrible summer, Azalaïs had never wanted to change. Everything after it was like a leaden dream. She liked it that way. She hated it that way. She would punish herself.

Her husband, Bernart, the seigneur of Lombers, was fascinated by her. She played the wife but gave very little. Bernart had experienced something very rare. He was afraid of Azalaïs. The truth was that she was more afraid of him – but she despised this fear and was determined, one day, to overcome it.

Then there was Miraval. He was not yet real to her. His coming into her life had more of the character of the arrival of a new idea than that of a living person who might change her life. The thought that she had the power to break his heart repelled her. No person, she was so sure, had any such right. But she had this power and it disgusted her. Why couldn't Miraval see what she saw? Why couldn't Miraval face himself? Azalaïs did not believe that she truly needed anyone. She was wrong. She was wrong to believe, as she did, that life had robbed her of life. If only she could write and sing her feelings as Miraval did. She could not see what Miraval's work was costing him. While he burned himself out with soulful song, Azalaïs bled more deeply, deep down in the labyrinth of her soul.

Ermengarde

When someone says that they want everything it means that they do not know what they want. Ermengarde de Castres was on her way to Toulouse in order to visit her cousin, Jordane de Saissac. She was accompanied by Agnès de Montpellier, a childhood friend. Both ladies were as yet unmarried. Their protection lay in the provision of three unhappy knights from Provence, two of whom rode in front while one brought up the rear. In front of the rear guard rocked a cumbrous wagon which contained several chests and baskets, among which sat two ladies-in-waiting, happily chatting to each other. It was hot and dry.

Having left the court of Montpellier two days previously, the entourage had made a great detour, rattling and bumping its way from the flatlands of the azure coast to the rough mountains of the Corbières. This detour was made so that Agnès could visit a relative, the abbot of Lagrasse. From Montplaisir the party began the ascent to the Corbières. The sky was as blue as the sea they had left. Far above them the mountain of St Victor hurled its way towards the infinite sky. On either side, buckled strata of sandy sediment vibrated along the rusty earth. Great twists and turns of flaky rock bound the foothills together and in the shadows and spaces left, crooked vines lined the way to Fontjoncouse. Here they would rest for lunch, enjoying the hospitality of the monastery there.

Fontjoncouse was a tiny village which gathered itself lazily about a gently cultivated hill, on the summit of which stood, in sandy brown stone, the solid edifice of the squat monastery. This faraway place offered the weary traveller a dry red wine with a peppery air that sank with ease down the parched throat.

Agnès and Ermengarde were sitting on the top of the hill, leaning against a wall in the monastery garden. They were comfortably hot in the warm breeze. Agnès bent her head backwards towards the sun and closed her eyes.

'Oh, it's *so* good to be away from Montpellier,' she said. 'My father keeps inviting the French to the court. He says in times of strife it's best to make unexpected friends! Friends! He's up to something – but everybody is these days. But the French! They despise our Occitan language and they despise us ... I think he's trying to confuse them – '

'In Occitan, of course!'

'Well, why not? But you know, Ermengarde, I don't see how it can work. Each time they come they get a bit more envious. I've seen it in their eyes – so narrow, so jealous, so brusque, so devoid of sensibility!'

'Oh, come on, Agnès, they're not all as bad as that.'

'Well, daddy certainly picks the worst then! Show them a thing of beauty and they close their eyes completely. Open their eyes and what do they say? "How much is it?" Then they narrow their eyes once more.'

'So that's why they can't tell silk from linen!'

Both ladies laughed, patting and hugging each other. 'Oh, but Ermengarde, they know a pretty girl when they see one.'

'You see – there is one saving grace!'

'Oh, Ermengarde! How can you say that? I tell you, my dear, if they ever take the land, they'll take us all!'

'Agnès! Ssh! You'll frighten the monks! But really, Agnès, so long as there are Arabs in Aragon and Saladin in Syria, we'll be safe. The Crusades will drain the hungry barons. No one's worrying about Languedoc now.'

'That's just it, Ermengarde – *we* should worry now, before it is too late.'

'What are you talking about? I – '

'Listen, my dear, haven't you heard the news? Richard of England has retreated from Jerusalem. The Christian alliance is breaking up in the Holy Land while only next door to us it looks certain that Castile and Aragon will unite against the Almohads. So Aragon won't help us if – '

'But Agnès, this isn't for us to worry about. We women – '

'We women, hell! How many dead husbands must there be – '

'But Agnès, there's always plenty of living ones left over!'

'Oh, you're so blind! Don't you see there's war-fever everywhere. Even the troubadours are singing about war now – '

'So what's new?'

'Look, when the blood is up, you don't think they'll stop with the Muslims, do you?'

Ermengarde bit her lip and then looked up to the balmy sky. 'Well, I don't know, Agnès. I really don't. I mean, things always work out. Anyway, what can we do about it? We're away from the city now, so why don't we just enjoy ourselves? Let's have some more wine! Marie! Another jug and, why don't you take a – what do you think, Agnès – for our protectors – a large jug or a – '

'Small!'

'Did you hear that, Marie? – take a small jug to the wagon

for our silent knights!' The two ladies giggled to each other and the tension began to pass.

'I suppose you're right, Ermengarde – but now we're here, I can't wait to be back in the city again. Shall we get up and walk around a bit? There's a lovely breeze blowing about.'

'Yes, Agnès, let's lose ourselves in the breeze.'

The two young ladies in blue and white dresses made a pretty picture, wandering through the monastery garden, avoiding the herbs and distracting a few jovial monks as they held conference on the garden's future. The lives of the monks would go on like this for years – so long as the Arabs could be kept at bay – but the lives of the ladies were more like the fresh wind: touching the petals of flowers, blowing about the bushes and bending branches, but not changing anything. The monks knew that to change things was, if not impossible, certainly unwise, that to allow oneself to be *changed* was sufficient for one short lifetime.

The ladies' conversation resumed its serious pattern.

'Everything was all right until the heretics came, Ermengarde.'

'Oh, Agnès, that's just not true. They've been here for years. I can't remember a time without them – and you know, they've made life more interesting. You should talk to them some time.'

'God forbid, my dear! How can we fight the Arabs if we fight among ourselves?'

'But the *good men* don't fight. I've known lots of them – and so would you if it weren't for your mother! They've hurt no one. They've shown me worlds I never thought existed.'

'Oh, Ermengarde – what do we know of *this* one? There's enough problems here! If people spent more time trying to do good in this world rather than worrying about the next – then, maybe we wouldn't always be hearing of killing and – well, you know.'

'But the *good men* and *good women* do bring peace into the world. They have peace in themselves – and I feel better when I hear them. There will always be war in this world. We will always need the knights to protect us.'

'There you are then, Ermengarde – it would be no good asking the heretics to defend us. They would be frightened of killing for our sakes! What kind of nobility is that?'

Ermengarde de Castres gave out a great sigh, 'I suppose that's true, Agnès.'

'Well, let's hear no more about the heretics then!'

'So what shall we talk about?'

'Well . . . what about music? You know I had the pleasure of being entertained by Raimon de Miraval's minstrels at court some weeks back.'

'Oh, that's funny. I was talking to Guilhabert about the troubadours.'

'Guilhabert?'

'Yes – he's what *you* call a heretic.'

'I thought I said – '

'Just listen a moment. Guilhabert de Castres is a nobleman. He's good and kind and you know – well, when I told him that nothing pleased me more than to hear a troubadour, do you know what he said?'

'I can't wait, Ermengarde – '

'He said that the beauty of woman is an image of heaven – but pity the man who cannot tell the image from the real woman!'

'Hmmm . . . Are you sure that's all he said?'

'Well, there was a bit more about fallen angels and things.'

'I think Guilhabert de Castres is a wise man – but he's still a heretic!'

'What of your troubadour, Raimon de – '

'Miraval.'

'Miraval, yes. I've not heard of him. Is he a fool?'

'Miraval, my dear, is a legend in these parts. Whether or not he's a fool I can't rightly say. I do know that we think he's a great poet – and perhaps there's folly in that. But we dare not tell him what we think for fear that it will go to his head! He is guileless, that's for sure – and some would call that folly! He has sung that in *Love* "folly is wisdom" and . . . He really believes in what he does – unlike some troubadours I could mention!'

'But is he handsome, Agnès?'

'He's not the best-looking troubadour, but he does have a kind of – I suppose you might call it "tragic grandeur" or something like that – gorgeous hair and a smile that could take your – well, you know!'

'Perhaps he is a heretic!'

'Well, now you say it. It's difficult. You know I don't think Raimon is a true Catholic – but he's not a heretic. He seems to come from somewhere else – '

'Now who's talking of other worlds!'

'Yes, Ermengarde ... he frightens me sometimes. He sings and ... Oh I don't know. It's hard to express it.'

'Is he married?'

'I should say that he was too good to marry. But Gaudairenca obviously didn't think so.'

'Who's she?'

'Oh, she's his wife – but it's difficult to say *who* she is. A little mad, I think. Miraval won't even speak of her. There's a mystery there. I'll tell you something, Ermengarde – '

'Yes?'

'Let's sit down again first.'

The two ladies squeezed together on a rock overlooking the village.

'Yes, Agnès. Do tell!'

'It was near here, at Montséret actually, that Raimon de Miraval offered me his castle in homage.'

'You see, Agnès – he is a fool!'

'Yes, but that's what I thought ... I said to him: "Raimon de Miraval, your castle is not your own to give," and he said – I remember his exact words, he said: "Did you think I meant the castle of stone and mortar?" '

'Strange man.'

'Yes, he is a little strange ... I do think of him – quite a lot actually. You cannot forget him. But no one can understand him – if you know what I mean – least of all himself!'

'All right Agnès, let's drink to the troubadour of Miraval, then! Raimon de Miraval, long may he – '

'Love!'

'That's it! ... Oh Agnès, let's take everything that Toulouse has got!'

'And more, Ermengarde. Let's have it *all*!'

The monks of Fontjoncouse were very much amused.

Raimon and Azalaïs

The Peak of the Madeleine at Labastide Esparbairenque had all morning been draped with grey clouds and mist. A July storm was battling overhead for supremacy of the skies and as the clouds fell, the air was filled with fine rain. A million leaves sparkled like lights through the silky mist. The deep green sides of this immense gorge, caked in wet rock, no longer seemed to strain for the distant summit but cascaded downwards like a fairy's bridal gown to the shadows below. Only three miles to the east of Miraval and four miles to the north of Lastours, this extraordinary place had an intimacy and magic all of its own. Deep as the gorge was, the whole effect was one of warm enclosure like a lonely child dreaming on a rainy day. This was an ancient place and its friends were the gentle, ancient dreams of birds and trees. Azalaïs loved this place and the cave where she would meet Miraval was as high up in the mountain as a horse could go. Whirling bands of sullen mist separated the lovers.

Azalaïs was waiting alone in the sandstone cave. She stood at the entrance, her red cloak waving about her bare feet, her hand exploring the crevices of rock. From behind she could hear the echoing rain which fell before her, spaced out in the murmur of the sky and the deep sexual humming of the clouds.

Raimon de Miraval had left the valley of the Orbiel and had just passed the grey, mournful mystery of the St André chapel. From there the slender path began its steep rise to the Peak of the Madeleine. Miraval's horse kept sneezing and snorting as the rain kept rapping on the lids of his eyes. Miraval hardly noticed that he was himself soaked to the skin. His soul and body were bound into one tense paroxysm of anxiety and apprehension. At the same time he felt warmly bathed in the balm of dream and love.

Here was the day. He could hardly believe it. His shoulders shivered with excitement. He felt perfect. Words and poetry were dancing in his head: 'For her ... the shattered life, the broken dream, the flayed heart, the rose that bleeds ... all of my life, my life.' He could hear himself breathing; he sighed and closed his eyes. It was like being a child again. On and upwards Miraval rose. He began to feel terribly nervous and frightened and fragile. What could he say? Would she speak first, or would he?

In the cave, Azalaïs waited. She strained to see through the mist. 'Is he going to come?' she thought to herself. Her fingers were rubbing the sandstone, and little clouds of red dust arose and disappeared. The first glow of a hot sun appeared through the clouds as a great growl of thunder shot across the valley. Miraval's horse bolted. He dismounted and began to lead the animal by the reins those last few hundred yards that seemed so very far. Azalaïs heard the crackle of footsteps. To her surprise, her heart began to pound and she thought she might lose control. Miraval stopped. Her bottom lip was shivering.

'Azalaïs?'

'Come into the cave, Raimon.'

'Yes, my Lady.'

Azalaïs de Boissézon closed her eyes. She took hold of his arms and kissed him on the lips. Miraval fell to his knees and tried to take her hands.

'No, Miraval. Kiss me.'

He looked up to her. Her face was warm, her eyes full of sympathy and determination. His wet hands moved upwards as he rose to his feet, tracing the lines of her body until they cradled her face. His thumbs slowly caressed her cool cheeks. He searched into her brown eyes. She raised her arms and pulled him closer. She opened her mouth and, still shivering, they began to kiss deeply and tenderly. Azalaïs had lost control and Miraval was about to lose himself. No one could find words to express what the lovers were feeling. What can we learn of Love through observation? Miraval was learning. Each infinite second drew him closer to his goal and to his proper end.

How the rain beat down – drenching trees and making them smell, filling the streams and brooks and wishing-wells! Miraval noticed how a single strand of hair began to shine in her eyes. They looked at each other and together, arm in arm, they looked outside. The sun had finally penetrated the clouds and a wonderful feeling was rising up through the dampened leaves and trees, and was spreading over their tops and greeting the sun and the cheeks of the lovers were warm, and there was nothing else in the world but light!

Azalaïs took Miraval by the hand and led him out of the cave. She took him to a waterfall, high up on the mountain. The waterfall was cold and loud. There was a pool on a ledge overlooking the gorge. A halo of vapour was rising from below, and there was an air of transformation and freedom. Miraval unhooked his purple cloak and spread it out at the edge of the pool. He let go of her hand and sat down. Azalaïs, still standing, glanced at him and then slipped off her red cloak. She took the gauze veil from off her head, dropped the pins and the comb and let her long hair fall about her face. Miraval, enchanted, smiled. What would he see beneath the white silken gown?

Lilies and leaves, sewn in gold wire, tumbled over her shoulders. The long sleeves caressed the blades of glistening grass and then she began to undo the gown's golden threads. She stopped for a second and unfastened the belt. The belt fell to the ground. She slipped the gown from off her white shoulders and the lilies and leaves began to fall. Over her soft and pointed breasts the gown fell, along her hips it fell, and so to her cool white feet where it rested. Azalaïs closed her eyes and stepped into the cold pool. Her breasts hovered on the surface and Azalaïs, smiling, bent her head backwards, inhaled deeply and breathed out as she ran her hands through her floating hair. The gleaming water rippled respectfully around her as she floated, and the sun was shining in the deep blue sky.

'Aren't you going to say anything, Raimon?'

Miraval smiled broadly and mouthed the word 'no'.

'Aren't you going to take your clothes off, then?'

'My Lady?'

'Come on, Raimon. It really is beautiful. You can do it.'

'But, Azalaïs, really, Miraval is content.'

'Azalaïs would be content, Raimon – if you would join her.'

'My Lady, really – I ...'

Azalaïs stood up and put her hands on her hips as if to say 'I'm waiting'. It was a good act and Nature helped. Her body was shimmering with silver droplets and rivulets of light. For Miraval, the pool had become a shrine. He swallowed and, his voice trembling, uttered the words, 'You are ... my Lady.'

'That's right, Raimon! You can touch me. Are you afraid of the water?'

Miraval said something to Azalaïs but he did not hear it. His mind had taken him back to that moment when, on leaving Loba, he had heard her say: 'I don't know why men had to invent "purity". But I do know they will be made fools by it!'

'I'm not a fool, Azalaïs!'

'Then come in the water.'

He nodded quickly and began removing his clothes: his leather sandals, his black stockings of dyed Egyptian cotton, his green embroidered belt and lastly, his purple tabard. He was trying to breathe without trying, but he could not. Azalaïs watched closely. His arms were those of a clerk and not like those of her husband. There were no scars. The flesh was white but his shoulders were beginning to brown. A smooth line of black hair descended from his chest to his loins. Azalaïs liked what she saw. She extended her hand and Miraval entered the pool. They looked into each other's eyes once more.

'That's nice,' said the lady tenderly.

'Yes.' Miraval's fingers traced her wet hair from her ear to her shoulder and over her breast to a stiff red nipple. Azalaïs let out a little moan and, as they slipped to their knees in the water, she took his head and kissed his lips and licked his tongue. His hesitancy had vanished and he firmly gripped her back, rubbing her spine with his fingers. They giggled together; their feet slipped from the slippery stone beneath them and they laughed as they splashed and floated and kissed and gasped their way to ecstasy. Were they not above the clouds and was not this place heaven itself? How Joy and Loss will mix when a dream becomes real, when Joy turns to Loss and reality, a dream!

The lovers got out and lay down on the grassy ledge. The air was warm and fresh and their lungs, released from constraint, heaved. Miraval was ecstatic.

'I love you, Azalaïs. It's . . . it's as if the sky was opened and heaven lay beside us!'

'Yes, Raimon. Me too.'

'Do you love me?'

Azalaïs whispered, 'Yes'.

The lovers' feet dangled in the cool water. Dragonflies were dancing on the surface and mating in the air. Long-legged hoppers were walking on water – but Raimon and Azalaïs were not looking. They were into each other, exploring each other, licking, touching, stroking and eating each other. Azalaïs bit the soft skin above Miraval's navel and looked up to him, flashing her large brown eyes. Miraval smiled and pulled her gently up by the shoulders towards him. They kissed and rolled over – and over and over again; wet hair and limbs entwined. Azalaïs felt a great explosive heat in her belly and Miraval lost himself as he entered her. She gripped him tightly to herself, flying in her mind with mouth open and eyes closed. For Raimon and Azalaïs, no joy could ever exceed this moment. As Love made each one the heart of the other, the sun made love to them both, while all about them flowers and trees and all living things strained for the heat and cried for Joy! Miraval had reached the summit of his mountain; he was in the sky inside him; he was in the stars above and he was in the eyes of Azalaïs.

The sun was fleeing from the mountain tops. The flanks of rock beneath them were glowing like embers in the green forge and the lovers began to feel cold. They helped one another to dress. Miraval had tears in his eyes and Azalaïs looked far away. They became aware of time and their hearts slowly sank back into their bodies. A little gap had grown up between them and they looked at each other from the outside. Azalaïs coughed and, nervously, she began to speak,

'I've decided. I'm going to be *consoled*.'

The blood in Raimon's face fled to his feet, 'Um ... I don't understand. What do you mean, "consoled"?'

'Yes, Raimon. I'm going to be *consoled*. I'm going to leave you. I'm going to become a *good woman*.'

Miraval laughed.

'I knew you'd laugh. That's the way you are. But this is not funny, Raimon. So you can laugh to yourself.'

'You want to join the heretics?'

'You can call us what you want.'

'"Us"?'

'It's not question of joining anything. It's a discovery – it's one discovery you haven't made yet.'

'And when did you make this, er, discovery?'

'You can thank Esclarmonde de Foix – you knew I was going to see her. You knew she was a friend to the heretics?'

'She's only a girl.'

'We decided together. And Raimon, *I'm* only a girl – that's all I'll ever be to you!'

'O Azalaïs! That's ridiculous!'

'We've had enough of this life, Raimon. I don't want children – and I don't want to enter a nunnery, thank you very much! And I don't want to make friends with your bed! I'm so sick of it all!'

'This life – today?'

'No, not today. Today is different.'

'"Different"? Is that all you can say?'

'It is not something I want to talk about ... O Raimon, I could talk about it forever but it all comes down to the same thing. I want to stay as I am and – well, I don't want you to change either. We can't go on repeating ourselves. It will always come back to what I'm feeling now.'

'Of course it will, if we stay the same as we are now. But we can grow.'

'That's just it! I want to grow!'

'Azalaïs, my lady, listen to me! I can ... I can never leave this place if we can never return to it.'

'There can be no return.'

'Surely, Azalaïs, we've come too far now?'

'Yes. That's just it. There's nowhere else to go. You of all people should be pleased. Now, Raimon, now we can be true to one another forever.'

'But Azalaïs! What has got *into* you? You are not like Esclarmonde. This holy life – what you call "perfection" – how can it add virtue to virtue? This just isn't you!'

'You are going to have to learn Miraval that there is more to Love than pleasing *you*. We are not the same.'

'No, but, but we are united now.'

'Look again! I will not change.'

Miraval realised it was useless to continue. Azalaïs was more stubborn than he could ever be. He had never expected or consciously desired to make love with Azalaïs. Now it seemed that she was putting herself far from him. But why did eveything have to be so black and white with her? He had shattered his own deeply held code of Love – what was left now? Where could he go? He was too confused, too shattered to think.

But she was right. He should have understood. Azalaïs as a *good woman*, a *parfaite*, should have conformed to his deepest vision of Woman. She had, after all, promised fidelity in Love –

what more could he expect? But this day, this amazing day had changed everything for him. In all eternity, from star to star, from sea to sea, from life to death, this one day could never be repeated. This he could not bear.

For Azalaïs, this day was not one day but a vision of eternity itself and it could never end. Nature had given her all that Nature can give. The debt was paid. Had not Miraval himself taught her that the instant of *Fine Love* was the only fruit of Nature that could transcend Nature? But Miraval was no longer sure. He was filled with doubt. He no longer knew himself.

At the opening of the gorge, before the chapel of St André, they parted. The troubadour vowed that he would never write again. 'Not even to me?' said Azalaïs, smiling. Perhaps Azalaïs de Boissézon was wiser than Loba de Pénnautier. But at Cabaretz, not so very far away, Loba was smiling too.

3
TOULOUSE WITH DIGNITY

MIRAVAL HAD NOT STIRRED from his room in weeks.

'My lord!' Ahmed was knocking on Miraval's chamber door.

'My lord! A messenger has arrived. You must see him, my lord.'

Miraval heard muttering from the other side. Ahmed's voice had sent a ripple across the vast, grey empty ocean of Miraval's mind. He was just a little curious. 'All right Ahmed, I heard you. Bring the messenger to the door.'

'Will you open the door, my lord?'

'Just bring him to the door . . . All right, Ahmed. I'm coming. I'll see him.'

Within five minutes Miraval appeared to be a changed man.

'That's right. Pack at once! The horses! Where's my razor? Instruments! Where's Gérard? Berteaux, find him, will you? We'll take the – what? You've – look, where's that razor? You've forgotten? Nonsense, it will all come back! We're going to Toulouse, my friends – if, that is, someone will find my bloody razor! We're going to our friend Raymonde. Yes! Oh, thank you, Ahmed, I knew it was somewhere about! All right, that's it – come on!'

The little castle of Miraval echoed with life once more.

'Has the messenger eaten? Good. Tell him this: that when he arrived, Raimon de Miraval had already left to see his friend, the count of Toulouse's son. Under no circumstances is the lady Gaudairenca to seek her husband there. Do you understand? Under no circumstances!'

Ahmed, proudly carrying a set of drums, stole up behind Miraval and touched him on the shoulder. Miraval turned round and grinned.

'Yes, Ahmed. New adventures. Miraval may have fallen on the field but Love lives on!'

Azalaïs Prepares

Things had moved fast in the life of Azalaïs. She knew where she was going and she had friends who would help her.

The Cathar Church – the best-organized body of 'heretics' in the whole of Europe – was reaching its height of influence in the Languedoc. The Church of Rome was alarmed but there was not much it could do. There was so much else going on. The Pope would bide his time for a while. Time would tell. Strange times?

The century was coming to a close and expectations of a sudden change in the destiny of Christendom were rampant. Some expected the fiery holocaust prophesied by St John. Others foresaw the fall of Christendom to the swords of Islam. There were those who foresaw the imminent arrival of Jesus Christ who would, at a stroke, vanquish the power of Islam, banish the heretics to the void, thank the Pope for keeping the show going while he was away and so establish his infinite reign on earth. Powers temporal and spiritual shuddered. There were portents in the sky, secret deliberations on earth, and moral panic was sweeping through the hearts of the sensitive.

Wild, perceptive prophets, high on magic mushrooms, were appearing regularly in towns and villages, frequently joining forces with itinerant minstrels, singing boldly of heaven and of love. Accusations and suspicions buzzed from mouth to mouth. Surely the homosexuals were behind it all! The summer of 1192 was particularly hot, and hopes and tempers ran high. There was madness in the air. There were visionaries who saw it all and looked askance – was it not all just one more wave sent out from man's engagement with hot matter in the evolution of the spirit-life? Critics were open-mouthed. For poets, prophets and artists, the green hills and brown mountains of Languedoc began to glow with fluorescent *possibility*. Minds were set free. Children were questioning their parents and some would run away to join the Crusades. And it really did seem that anything could happen.

This was the summer chosen by Azalaïs for her departure from gross matter and the tedium of the past. She had come to join the *spirituals*. She would receive the sacrament of *Consolamentum* from the Cathars: the unpolluted ones, the *good men*, the true Christians. Her true destiny was about to take shape while Miraval played on, blind to all but art. If Azalaïs shared some of the troubadour's blindness, this was soon to pass. Azalaïs was going to change her world and nobody could stop her.

She entered a cellar in the home of Philippa de Foix in the busy town of Mirepoix, nine miles south of Fanjeaux. This house was a house of Cathars, and was used for weaving and for meeting. Azalaïs was in a solemn mood. Nevertheless, after coming in from the hot day outside, it was pleasurable to find oneself in a cool, stony cellar. The only smell was that of snuffed wax and the ceiling was black with carbon. Azalaïs de Boissézon was about to become the centrepiece of a ceremony preliminary to the full rite of *Consolamentum*. Here she would enter into an intimate relationship with God and learn to call Him Father, not because some priest had told her she must, but because she had become aware that she was His true daughter and that her spirit was His spirit.

Waiting for Azalaïs were three Cathar deacons: Raimond Mercier (who would lead the ceremony), Bernard de Lamothe and Guiraud de Gourdon. They were dressed in heavy black cassocks. They were all extremely thin from adhering to strict vegetarian diets, and all three had long hair and beards. Raimond Mercier was the most physically striking of the three. His eyes were large and blissful. A firm mouth and chin added to his look of determination and seriousness. Previous to his induction as a *perfect* of the Cathar Church, Raimond had been a full-time minstrel and had worked with Peire Vidal. He still played an amazing lute when occasion demanded. Azalaïs was pleased that Raimond would lead the ceremony. It seemed right to her that such a thoroughly handsome man should lead her through the portals of a new and infinitely mysterious life.

Three torches were lit in the black cellar and Azalaïs was led in. The torch flames touched her cheeks like water. Her body was dressed in a simple green gown which turned brown in the firelight. Barefooted she stood. Her hair was tied back severely. A single gold ribbon caught the light around her forehead. Raimond Mercier blinked and began to speak to Azalaïs. Flanked by Bernard and Guiraud, her moist hands held together before her, Azalaïs listened intently. The ceremony began easily:

'We have come before God, before you and before the order of the holy Church to receive service, pardon and penitence for all our sins of thought, word and deed, since our birth until now, and we ask for God's mercy, for you to pray to the holy Father for us, that He might forgive us. *Benedicite, Parcite Nobis.* Lord have mercy upon us.'

Guiraud de Gourdon placed a bowl at the feet of Azalaïs. She put her hands before her. Bernard de Lamothe and Raimond Mercier did likewise while Guiraud took a jug and poured its contents over them. The dripping water echoed about the silent cellar. The ritual purification completed, Azalaïs and Raimond began speaking in unison:

'O Lord, judge and condemn the vices of the flesh. Do not have pity on the flesh born of corruption, but have pity on the imprisoned spirit and grant to us on feast days, prayers and preaching, as is the custom of good Christians, so that we might be neither judged nor condemned like felons on the day of judgement.

Benedicite, parcite nobis;
Benedicite, parcite nobis;
Benedicite, parcite nobis.'

Guiraud now placed a bulging book of bound parchment leaves upon a white tablecloth. The book contained the gospel of John. Azalaïs and Raimond each placed a hand upon the gospel.

'Azalaïs, you must understand that when you are before the Church, you are before the Father, Son and Holy Spirit. For the "Church" signifies the assembly, and there, where true Christians are, the Father, Son and Holy Spirit are, as the holy Scriptures teach.

'St Paul wrote to the Galatians in his fourth letter, "Because you are God's sons, God sent His Son's Spirit into your hearts, crying 'Father, Father'." From this we must understand that in presenting you before the sons of Jesus Christ, it is to confirm your faith and the preaching of the Church of God, as the divine Scriptures give us to understand. For the people of God had departed from the counsel and will of the holy Father, following the trickery of evil spirits and because of submitting themselves to their will. You are here before the disciples of Jesus Christ, in this place where the Father, Son and Holy Spirit dwell spiritually, to be able to receive this holy prayer which the lord Jesus Christ gave to his disciples.

'We pray to the good Lord, Who gave to the disciples of Jesus Christ the power to receive this holy prayer with firmness, that He should give you also the grace to receive it with firmness – to His honour and your salvation. *Parcite nobis*.

'Listen to this prayer: "Our Father in heaven" – for it is the true God we are addressing, to distinguish Him from the father the devil, who is a liar and the father of the wicked.

'"May your name be hallowed, may your kingdom come and your will be done on earth as in heaven. Give us this day our daily bread, and forgive us our sins – as we forgive those who sin against us. And lead us not into temptation but deliver us from evil.

'"For the true liberty of man is to be able to do good, and good alone. For the kingdom, power and glory are yours forever and ever. Amen." *Parcite nobis*.'

Guiraud removed the book from the table. Azalaïs and the deacon's hands were by their sides. Raimond Mercier begged an answer from Azalaïs to this question:

'Azalaïs, do you have the will to receive this holy prayer and to retain it all your life with chastity, truth and humility?'

'Yes, I have the will. Pray to the holy Father, that He will give me His strength, Himself, to receive it.'

'May God give you the grace to receive it, to His honour and your salvation. Say the prayer with me, word for word.'

Together they spoke: 'Our Father in heaven, holiness and glory throughout the ages. Amen.'

Azalaïs was alone in her heart as she repeated the words:

'Benedicite, parcite nobis
Benedicite, parcite nobis
Benedicite, parcite nobis'

whereupon she knelt to hear the deacon say,
'May the Father, Son and Holy Spirit have mercy on all your sins.'

She stood up again. Bernard de Lamothe stepped forward and held out the gospel. Raimond continued,

'We give you this holy prayer, for you to receive it from God, from us and from the Church, for you to have the power to say it in every moment of your life, day and night, alone or in company; and that you should never eat or drink without saying this prayer first. If you fail, you must do penance for it.'

Bernard gripped the gospel tightly to his chest. Azalaïs spoke:

'I receive it from God, from you and from the Church.'

She bent her knee and bowed her head.

> '*Benedicite, parcite nobis*
> *Benedicite, parcite nobis*
> *Benedicite, parcite nobis*
> Lord have mercy upon us.

'May the Lord God reward you well for this good you have done to me for the love of God.'

Azalaïs bowed three times and the room was silent. She heard the soft footsteps of the deacons as they made their way upstairs. Azalaïs closed her eyes and, for the first time in her life, she fainted. This was only the first step.

The Mad Seigneur of Crozilat

Miraval's party was only half a day from Toulouse and his minstrels were beginning to feel excited. The riding was easy. Having descended from the heights of the Cabardès, they came upon the great plain which stretched fifty miles westwards to Toulouse in a vast, flat patchwork of vineyards and barley fields. The brown, dusty road was quite busy. Wagons loaded with imported spices, sugars, silks and cotton were heading for the metropolis.

Occasionally, the group would pass a crowd of local farmers who were lending a hand to a stricken wagon stuck in a ditch. If the farmers were lucky, a merchant might pay them for their trouble. The Genoese, always in a hurry, were the most generous. This was perhaps surprising because they tended to be the richest merchants, able to afford horses to pull their wears. Most people used oxen.

There were many hot, sweaty faces stinking of dung. Young men from the scattered villages came to the roadside to talk and drink wine. It was too hot to fight but sometimes, the country girls, sticky and bored, would try to whip their boy-friends into jealousy by flirting with passers-by. Miraval's tired minstrels were often amused by what they saw going on at the roadside. Their laughter echoed around Miraval's giddy head – for without any effort on his part, sad and hopeful words came pirouetting out from the depths of his brain:

'No sky above
No hands laid in anguish
No fervent mix of meaning
No loneliness intense
No folly or fear
No more this madness of intent
No more the memory
No more delightful hills
No hell
No more the fool alone

But all around in all I see
Beauty dwells eternally,
Today the love, tomorrow's curse
What's good today could get much worse!'

Ahmed rode up to be beside Miraval.

'My lord is dejected again?'

'Oh ... yes, Ahmed. It's the same old thing, I'm afraid. Do you think I shall ever get out of it?'

'You must. We all depend on you. And we're not the only ones.'

'But Azalaïs ... it seems that she can do without me – and that is all that matters to me now.'

Ahmed thought for a moment. 'I once knew a lady, my lord.'

Miraval turned to face Ahmed. 'Ahmed! You surprise me!'

'She was ... she had a mother. Her father was always away. Her mother hardly ever spoke to her. If the mother loved her, she did not show it very much. Not enough, anyway. Well, this lady secretly hated her mother. She never wanted to risk – she was afraid of love. She never trusted me – and in those days, I was so innocent and open-hearted.'

'Don't worry Ahmed. You have not changed.'

'But more so.'

'All right, please go on.'

'Well, she never wanted children. I wanted to marry her but she was so afraid. It took me a long time to understand.'

'What happened to her?'

'I don't know. I left. She wouldn't come with me.'

'That's terrible, Ahmed.'

'Yes, my lord.'

'What do you mean when you say "It took me a long time to understand"?'

'It just did. You see, her mother had never really softened her daughter's heart with love. And her daughter – her name was Damsin – she had wanted many times for her mother to speak to her of the heart. But in the end she had decided that it wasn't worth it. Her mother wanted secretly that her daughter be strong. The mother thought she had been weak to marry Damsin's father. Damsin had somehow grasped this. She was too afraid that I would hurt her, too.'

'You know, Ahmed, it really is better to love from afar. Your love remains constant that way – and the lady may enjoy it. Azalaïs and I – we came too close. Too close, Ahmed. Be warned!'

'I don't think so, my lord.'

'Please, Ahmed, not now.'

'But, my lord, you are in love with this lady.'

'I know that, Ahmed. But she's found something she loves more than me.'

'And what is that?'

'I think she's found God.' There was a moment of silence.

Ahmed laughed, 'Which God my lord? Allah? Jesus Christ? Which God?'

'The *Good God*, Ahmed, the God of the heretics.'

'"Good" God, my lord? Is there really a "good" God?'

'You're too clever for me, Ahmed. You'd better argue this out with Azalaïs, not me. She knows what she's doing ... Maybe I need this Good God, too.'

'You have found this God, my lord.'

'Really?'

'Your God is Love. That is why Miraval is so special.'

Miraval thought deeply about what Ahmed had said. It disturbed him greatly. Ahmed seemed to have seen something in Azaiaïs which had eluded him. He had seen her suffering. Miraval had seen only his own. But now it was too late and Ahmed was giving him something which was too painful to live with. Ahmed offered him hope. But hope frustrated can turn to bitterness, and he was afraid of this. A troubadour with bitter songs would needs go a great distance to find a hearing. He was convinced that a lady could find sympathy for a dejected troubadour, but would be repelled by a bitter one. Agony can be sweet. Agony may find a melody. Bitterness is bare rhythm. As Ahmed had said, a great deal was expected of him. He would do his best – and if that was not enough, who could say?

It was time to rest for lunch. Miraval chose a clearing in a wood a mile from the town of Caraman. Through the silver pillars of trees, the party could just discern the outlines of a castle. The sky was blue and the air was warm.

'Gérard, have you got the bread there?'

'Yes, my lord. You'd better ask Berteaux for the cheese.'

'Aye – and the wine,' mumbled Jacques.

'It's good wine, my lord.'

'Is it, Berteaux? Then I'm surprised there's any left!'

Everyone laughed. 'Let's play before we eat. What is this place? Does anyone know?'

'Crozilat.'

'How do you know that, Berteaux?'

'Well, my lord, the château of Crozilat is famous.'

'I've not heard of it.'

'Well, famous to those who know.'

'Berteaux! For goodness sake – famous for what?'

'The seigneur of Crozilat is said to be – well, a little mad.'

'How's that?'

'Well, my lord, of course I've never met the er ... gentleman myself, but it is said that he has ... strange affections.'

'Trust Berteaux to know!'

'Sod off, Gérard! You never listen to anything!'

'All right, you two! Just let Berteaux tell the story!'

'Story, my lord?'

'Of course, you spiky-headed git! If there's madness, there's always a story.'

'What is it, Berteaux? What's the story?'

'I don't know, my lord.'

Gérard threw a piece of wet bread at Berteaux. 'You bat's arse!'

'*I* know it.' Everyone turned to Jacques who was removing his rebec from a leather case tied to his saddle. Jacques turned round and blushed. He scratched his neck and began to speak.

'Speak up, Jacques!'

'Ahmed, quiet! Jacques, would you care to speak up a little.'

Jacques started stroking his thick black beard while his bulbous eyes gazed heavenwards. This rotund minstrel began to tap his stomach with his thick fingers and at last spoke in a tone both sonorous and aristocratic: 'It is very simple – and yet, very strange. At least to me. Not to put too fine a point on it, the seigneur of Crozilat has gathered together a collection of village girls.'

'Is that all? It's his right, isn't it?'

'Yes, but there's a catch. The seigneur of Crozilat chooses only the ugliest of girls.'

'Then he's doing the village a service!'

'Shut up, Berteaux! – but Jacques, may we ask what it is he does with these girls?'

'Indeed, my lord. It is said that he has a large copper bath.'

'A copper bath?'

'A *large* copper bath my lord. He fills it to the brim with a mixture of – um ...'

'Don't be shy, Jacques!'

'Dung, Gérard. He fills it with a solution of dung and milk. Quite mad.'

The group reflected a little on this revelation.

Gérard began to choke on his food, 'You're ki- ki- kidding, Jacques!'

'Really not, Gérard. Dunks them in the bath and then dresses the girls in the finest silken gowns. He then inspects them – they have to stand in a line – and kisses each one on the lips. Then he chooses the most grotesque girl he can find and leads her to his room.'

'Shit!'

'Aren't you going to say anything, Raimon?'

'That's the word!'

'Shut up, Berteaux!'

'Well, when this evil-smelling girl enters his chamber, the seigneur takes a small whip and begs on his knees that the girl beat him, with passion and severity.'

'Oh come on, Jacques! You're joking.'

'I don't joke.'

'We've noticed!'

'Shush! My dear Jacques, is this ... all?'

'No, my lord. When he has been beaten to a state of satisfaction ...'

'State of what?'

'Satisfaction. You know!'

'Blowed if I do, Jacques! I've never been whipped by an old hag stinking of shit and dripping with milk!'

'You mean you've forgotten!'

'All right, all right – at least I didn't beg for it!'

'If you gentlemen would like to hear the remainder of the story ...'

'Get on with it, then!'

Jacques coughed and continued, 'The poor girl – for so we must think her to be – is next required to take a wash in a bath of brass. And while she does so, she is constrained to echo a litany composed and sung by the seigneur.'

'What are the words?'

'They are in Latin, my lord.'

'Pity. I thought there might be a song in it.'

'But Jacques,' begged Berteaux, 'does he actually get to ...'

'No, my friend. The wretch is dried off with an altar cloth and ...'

'Altar cloth! Wonder what the priest would make of that ...'

'The seigneur of Crozilat *is* the priest!'

'Fuck me! How old is the old bastard?'

'The "old bastard" is nineteen.'

Gérard coughed out his wine-soaked bread onto the grass. Ahmed giggled as Berteaux rolled around, kicking the jug of wine as he did so. Miraval caught it just in time. 'Well, gentlemen. I think we have cause to remember our sojourn here at Crozilat. Thank you, Jacques – and, may I just say how well you told the story! We salute you!'

'Thank you, my lord.'

'Jacques.'

'Yes, my lord.'

'Put your rebec away again. I don't think we'll play here, somehow.'

'Oh but lord – maybe ths seigneur needs a song – to cheer him up!'

'Do we know that he is in need of ... further entertainments?'

'For ourselves, then. Let's sing a comic song!'

'What about that one about "loving her in secret"?'

'Seems appropriate. Are you all sure?'

'Yes, let's do it!' Miraval looked to Ahmed. The boy – for so he would always seem to Miraval – the boy from Tripoli grinned and nodded.

'Very well, my friends. Just for ourselves, then!'

The musicians tuned up while sitting cross-legged on the grass. The rhythm was jaunty and happy. Gérard relaxed into the beat and smiled, his right hand making lightning strums upon his lute. Berteaux's flute and Jacques's rebec played the melody in unison and Ahmed drummed for all he was worth, hoping with each hard beat to raise the sunken spirits of Miraval. For a few minutes, Miraval put his troubles behind him, loosened his throat and sang an ironic song with a tongue so lively that were it not so busy stretching and fixing the vowels of Occitan, it would most certainly have been lodged firmly in his cheek:

'How can I count your qualities?
The best woman in the world?
But you put a high price on your love!
I am tormented by sadness – though you never promised
Softness.
She's made my heart timid and discreet,
I pray for myself – and she gets the benefit!
But really I've got nothing to hide –
She doesn't care to love me – but at least she never lied!'

Gérard began playing a lively solo. The lute strings seemed to merge into the green grass and the grass into the bodies of trees. Miraval looked away from the group to the woods around them. He was sure he could see two pairs of eyes looking out from behind a great oak tree. Was he dreaming? He looked back to Gérard. The solo was over and he nodded to Miraval. Bang on beat, Miraval sang:

'And I really don't love her any more – it's just a habit,
A just habit!
People think because I criticize her in public
I love her in secret,
How right they are!
But really I've got nothing to hide,
She doesn't really love me!
A song, when there's no one to hear it
Isn't worth very much,
But folly, among lovers, is wisdom
And so, without reward or satisfaction
I will wait another year!'

As Gérard hit the closing chord and Jacques faded out on a staggered note, the group heard a distant clapping. They all looked at each other and their shoulders tensed. Gérard whispered: 'Shit! It's the seigneur!'

'No ugly girls here!'

Gérard and Berteaux laughed through their noses and wine fell dripping from their nostrils.

'Seigneur Raimon! Raimon de Miraval: a star in our dark world!' said a distant voice.

'Thank you, troubadour. Thank you, brothers. A very clever song,' said another.

'Very clever, seigneur. Allow us to introduce ourselves,' said the first.

Miraval stood up to see two *good men* making their way from out of the woods towards the group. That they were *good men* was impossible to mistake. Their thin faces beamed with some otherworldly wonder. Their hair was long. Their beards were thick. Their cassocks were black and they moved with purpose. Miraval spoke: 'Welcome, sirs. You are most welcome. We can only offer you bread and wine.' The two *good men* smiled to one another. ' – and a little cheese.'

'We do not eat cheese, seigneur. But we are very happy to join you. Will you share a prayer with us before we share the bread and wine?'

The group looked at one another, a little embarrassed.

'We understand, sirs, if you do not choose to share our prayer. We are grateful to share your bread.'

'Sirs, you must understand that I, Raimon de Miraval, and these my friends: Gérard, Berteaux, Jacques and Ahmed are not members of the Cathar Church. But I think that I can speak for all of us when I say that we are not against you. We all have reason to admire you but not – if you understand me – to join you. So let us share these crumbs together. Please seat yourselves amongst us.'

The *good men* laughed heartily. 'Oh, seigneur Raimon! You talk of us as if we were from a foreign country. I was born here.'

'And may we know your name sir?'

'I am Guillaume de Caraman. My brother here is called Raimond Mercier. He comes from Mirepoix.'

'Our pleasure to greet you.'

'Aye, welcome!' Berteaux led the chorus of minstrels. The two *parfaits* sat on the grass, closed their eyes and prayed for a minute.

The troubadour and his friends were silent. Guillaume de Caraman began to speak: 'You, seigneur, and your minstrels, are justly famous in this region.'

'May I ask how you know my name?'

'Ah! The purple tunic. The voice ... I suppose we could have been mistaken but it was a reasonable – guess.'

'And I was hoping to lose myself!'

The *good men* laughed. Raimond Mercier spoke: 'How can a man lose himself among the lost?'

'Very easily, sir. He need only forget himself.'

'If you forget yourself, you may find yourself. How long did it – '

'O Guillaume de Caraman! Please, save yourself. I've thought about all this long enough. I beg you not to disturb what little peace I enjoy here.'

'Are you in a world where peace may be enjoyed?'

'You see, friends – there's no end to talk when the *good men* get to work on you. They have an answer for everything. But you'll notice one thing – they keep clear of the love of women! This explains their peace!'

The minstrels laughed, as did the *good men*.

'You are right, seigneur. We have an answer for that. But we should not offer it without invitation.'

'All right my friends, the day is still young. Give us your answer.'

'The love of women is illusory – and the illusion makes you blind.'

'Well, that is certainly concise. I notice you refrain from calling such a love a sin, as the Catholics do.'

'Not as the Catholics do, sir.'

'What do you mean Guillaume?'

'You sing of women. This is pleasant, even goodly at times. Then you sing of Love – and the Love you sing of bears much of the character of Divine Love. You confuse, I think, Love and her darkest shadow: lust.'

'Then, sirs, I am afraid I must say that you do not understand what I am singing about!'

'Please enlighten us, seigneur.'

'When you speak of Love as lust, I agree with you. These are different things. Lust is of the body. But beauty! Beauty is not something you can touch or hold. Beauty is of the soul and Nature can barely support her.'

'But you sing of real women, seigneur. Flesh and blood. You deceive yourself. You experience anguish when you cannot hold her close to you, or kiss her or touch her. You sing of how you wish to be in her arms. Your lust will not settle until it is so.'

'But this, sirs, this is only an outward sign of an inward and spiritual love.'

'And by this sign, seigneur Raimon, do you change the body? Is flesh transformed?'

'Of course not.'

'Of course not, seigneur. The body is corrupt and will return to nothingness.'

'This is so. The body may be of corrupt substance but it is the soul which gives it life. I could never sing in praise of a corpse!'

'Likewise, seigneur, the *Good Christian* cannot worship a dead Christ.'

'Well, let's not get into all *that*. If we could stick to the point.'

'The point is simple, seigneur. If you wish to be a *Good Christian*, then you must come to renounce your *Fine Love.*'

'If I were to do that, sirs, then I should lose all contact with Virtue whatsoever! The beauty of a woman makes me virtuous. Can you not see that? Her beauty makes me kind, generous, sometimes chivalrous, heroic and even, yes, it has even led me to the love of God. How can you corrupt beauty in this way? How, sirs, how can you give account of this Virtue?'

'The *Lord of this World*, seigneur – you may call him the Devil – the one who made this world of corruption and who imprisons immortal souls within it, binding them to passions, diseases, hunger and death, he – '

Raimond Mercier interjected, 'Let us just say that he had little imagination of his own.' The minstrels laughed. 'Being a liar and a thief he could only imitate what he stole from the realm of the *Good God* in Heaven. He fashioned the bodies of women after observing the angels of the second heaven. That is why one sometimes sees some – '

'Some fugitive Light in a face, a smile, a word, a gesture. It is this Light which brings you to the Spirit. But in this world everything is confusion. Things are seldom what they appear to be – '

'For sure, sir. On that we can agree!'

' – and from this confusion comes your *Fine Love*. Or are you content with a look? Do you see a woman as you might a pretty brooch?'

'Like a brooch, I have seen the beauty of a woman shine like firelight in the darkness – and it has given me hope!'

'We suspect that your *Fine Love* is really a kind of sickness, a fever of the head!'

Miraval looked to the grass and thought of that extraordinary day at Labastide; he thought of Azalaïs and he thought that, yes, it was a kind of sickness. The *parfait* continued, 'You see, seigneur, what your eyes see and what your heart yearns for are not the same. There are days in Love when it is perfect joy to be alive – '

'Yes! Yes! That's it! *Joy*. That is what we are about!'

'It is easy to rejoice in the summer sun and when the vintage is good.'

'But this *Joy* – it makes up for the suffering, and sirs, if I understand you properly, how could this Love ever be perfectly at home in this world? It comes to us like a promise of tomorrow. Yes, it does make me hot-headed and feverish – for Love to survive, there must be suffering in a world which destroys itself over and over again with every passing season, century and age! I have known of holy men and women who crave only for God – and they feel melancholy in this world, too. All who seek the good things must suffer!'

Guillaume de Caraman looked at Raimond Mercier and both raised their eyebrows as if to say 'This troubadour has found something which we did not expect to find in him.' Guillaume began to rise. Miraval quickly got up. The *parfait* extended his arms, gripped the arms of the troubadour and leant forward to kiss Miraval upon the cheek. Miraval felt a great force in the body of the *parfait*. Guillaume looked into Miraval's eyes with a strange and startling look of recognition and understanding. Miraval blinked.

'We thank you, seigneur. We thank you, Gérard, Berteaux, Jacques and ... Ahmed.' Raimond Mercier got up too. 'Raimon de Miraval, I do believe we shall meet again.'

'It has been a pleasure,' said Miraval without thinking, so taken was he by Guillaume's amazing eyes. The *good men* turned and walked silently back into the woods.

'Well, I think it is time to be moving on.'

The pensive minstrels all nodded and began to tidy up. In a few hours they would ride into a very different world.

Toulouse

The sun was still blazing when at six o'clock the party passed through the St Etienne gate. The brown walls of the great fortified city were glowing invitingly. The minstrels looked to one another in anticipation. The gateway itself, but for the guards, was almost deserted. Even the ubiquitous money-changers had closed shop.

'I can smell dinner.' said Gérard.

'I can smell lots of dinners!' added Berteaux.

'All right then. Let's stop a moment,' said Miraval. The party came to a halt beneath a great web of wooden scaffolding. The great church of St Etienne was encaged behind wooden beams, rope, leather buckets, baskets, intricate pulley systems, trays of mortar and piles of stones. The crisscrossing of scaffolds cast weird shadows over the hot faces of Miraval's party.

'Now, my friends, we had better sort things out. I'm going straight to the keep to see Raymonde, the count's son. That is, if he will see his old friend! I'm sure he will. Now listen – there's a decent tavern on the Rue de Courteliers. It's almost next door to the church of Notre Dame-de-la-Dalbade and I've heard well of it. I'd like you lot to pop along there and fix up some space.'

'What's wrong with the usual place?'

'Berteaux, there is *some* difference between a tavern and a brothel. But what you do after I return is entirely your own concern. Now get on – '

'My lord.'

'Yes, Ahmed?'

'You haven't told us what it's called.'

'The tavern? It's called *The Ferryman's Lady*.'

The minstrels trotted off with their tongues hanging out.

It was possible to see the castle keep rising above the city to the north if you gazed above the round, red tiles of the merchants' quarter. But Miraval was looking at the street life – not that there was much going on outside. The streets were quietening down. The barking of dogs echoed about. Now and then he could hear the screaming of infants and the cries of parents calling their children in to supper. He would nod a 'good evening' to some traders who were packing up their stalls and gathering their wares into baskets: olive oil, pottery, glass, honey, dyed woollen cloth, furs, candles and haunches of meat.

He was passed by several knights on their way from the castle, rattling along. It was strange, he was thinking, now that he was in sight of the castle, that he could not really remember his reason for visiting Raymonde. All of a sudden, bells began to ring out across the city: first the Basilica of St Sernin to the northwest, then the Augustinian convent in the city centre, the little bell of the church of Notre Dame-du-Taur and then the muffled bell of St Etienne came heaving out from beneath all that scaffolding behind him – and Miraval remembered how there was always more happening in the world than in his own part of the Cabardès, and that, perhaps, this was why he had come to Toulouse. He smiled and looked up. Two young women were leaning over a carved balcony in the shade of a holm-oak tree, their red dresses peeling from off their soft shoulders,

'Hey, troubadour. Give us a song!'

'Don't go! We're open late!'

Miraval waved to them as he passed. 'Honest women,' he thought to himself. 'For them love is simple.' Then he reflected on this thought and mumbled, 'What do I know about it?'

'What was that, seigneur?' said a fat merchant who was leaving the bordello.

'Nothing sir,' replied Miraval. 'What strange things happen in cities!' he thought. 'It's like going through a forest of moving trees – and they're all listening.'

Again, an odd paradox for 'Are not cities the places where great secrets are kept?' Miraval did not care much for secrets. If you couldn't sing about it, then it was probably not worth knowing. Then he thought of Azalaïs and of what secrets she might keep and how she was still like a secret to him. His life had become more secretive since meeting her, and now here he was, going to the centre of secrets: to the court of Raymonde V, the old count of Toulouse.

> All about me it goes on and on
> No Spirit in Space or Time
> Timeless Love and Joy are mine!

Miraval's encounter with the *good men* had begun to affect his lyrical experiments. He dismissed them: 'Not real enough.'

The troubadour passed the smart stone houses of the solicitors and merchants. On his left, as he began to head northwards, a quarter of a mile from the St Etienne Gate, he was struck by the Romanesque beauty of the Augustinian convent. Beneath two slender pillars of an upper window he passed a crowd of townsfolk waiting to be invited into the convent hospital to see their sick relatives.

At the capitals of the slim pillars, freshly carved souls in torment awaited the redemption of Christ amid palm-tree leaves which flourished in the hovering stone of the early evening sun. The convent had been the recent recipient of large sums of merchant money – guilt-money from those too rich to go on the Crusades. Some of the visitors, observing the unfinished carving of an illustrious bishop in elliptical lines, were complaining that while new building work went on unchecked, there had been no new hospital bed for twenty years. 'City life!' thought Miraval. 'Never satisfied – in the Cabardès we suffer at home!'

Some quite noxious smells were beginning to blow down the streets from the river Garonne in the west of the city. The tavern he had chosen was even closer to the river. Miraval laughed to himself as he imagined his minstrels' reaction to a deep inhalation of the restless Garonne. A new smell began to mingle with that of the river. As he turned left onto the rue du Taur at the foot of the castle keep, he could smell the animal market. There was ox dung all over the street but the oxen were nowhere to be seen. The gutter which ran down the centre of the cobbled street was overflowing with thick blood of a deeply crimson hue. It was a long way from Miraval. There were guards attending the portcullis of the outer wall. They had small piggy eyes and appeared all but featureless in their heavy head-mail.

'Here we go,' thought Miraval. The guards crossed their pikes and one of them called to Miraval, 'Who goes there?'

Miraval, tired and feeling a little supercilious, answered,

'Raimon, lord of Miraval. Troubadour. Come to see the count.'

The guards looked at one another, shrugged their shoulders and uncrossed their pikes.

'Nice of you. Good evening.'

'Yes, my lord.'

On his way up to the keep, Miraval noticed the new herb garden which had been planted on the slopes and, yes, were there not roses too? 'That is good to see. Somebody must be optimistic.' There were ladies strolling about the roses, their white veils drifting in the warm breeze and the echoes of chattering and gossip bouncing off the thick walls of the keep.

'Raimon!' one of the distant ladies called to him. Miraval waved in the general direction of the garden and saw a figure come running towards him. It was Raymonde.

'Mi-ra-VAL! What a joy! What a joy! What brings you from out of the woods? Surely not to see me?'

'Oh come on, Raymonde! What else could it be?'

They gripped one another's arms, looked closely at each other for a few seconds and then launched into an instinctive hug. Miraval snapped out of his introspection and responded to Raymonde's insistent patting.

'You've noticed Raimon? We have a rose garden. Imported from Picardy. I was *so* upset that we had to copy from the north, but then I thought – roses are roses! And the ladies adore them. And I adore them – and what with that damn butcher's yard down there – we need all the pleasant aroma we can muster! If my father weren't such a stick-in-the-mud, I'd have them creeping up the walls of the castle, too! And look at the walls! So aggressive! I tell you, things are going to change when I... Look, did you know that father's trying to marry me off – '

'To whom?'

'Richard of England – '

'Richard!'

'No, his sister Joanna! Of course it'll all take years to arrange. Until then I can't get near the girl!'

'Do you love her?'

'Raimon, come over and have a look at the garden – there's so much to talk about. These ladies are making my head *giddy* with gossip! Sergeant! Take care of the seigneur's horse – only the best for the troubadour!'

Off they walked, arm in arm: soft talk on a summer's evening. Raymonde was resplendent in a bright red cotton surcoat with a golden sun embroidered upon it. It was trimmed with golden leaves that came down to his feet. His animated face was thin but looked quite bold, set off as it was by his thick black hair with a curly fringe, cut straight about the neck. The hint of an attempted beard bristled upon his prominent and deeply dimpled chin. He looked the part. His eyes were cold blue but could look deep and warm when he chose to smile. He chose to smile on Miraval and the troubadour was so excited that he was at a loss for words. Raymonde had no such difficulty.

' ... And what about all those heretics? Delightful chaps! Father doesn't know what to do about them. The Pope keeps sending his legates to force his hand and all I keep saying is, "Look Daddy, why do anything?" Some of my best friends are

Cathars. They're always fascinating and they fit right in here. Father says he doesn't like to see me round them – so he'll be pleased to know I'm seeing you. I say, you're not one, are you?'

'No, but – '

'The whole world is going crazy, Raimon, and some of these Papal people are absolute shits! They just can't see the joke at all. Funny, it's all going mad and yet it's just the same. Do you know what I mean?'

'It's like that song of Raimbaut – '

'That's the man – Raimbaut d'Orange! You know I've been trying to think of that blessed man's name all day. Now don't tell me the name of the song, Raimon, it's, it's "The Inverted Flower". Incredible song!'

'Yes, I remember, "Thunderclaps are to me songs and whistles."'

'It's the last line that gets me: "I have sung – "'

'"Gone", Raymonde. It's "I have gone – "'

'" – gone like a thing inverted, searching crags and vales and hills, distressed like one whom frost torments and tortures and cuts."'

'It's his best, Raymonde. No doubt about it.'

'Tragic death, Raimon. Tragic. Damn plague. Devil's work. And I was only a boy ... '

The men heard the group of ladies giggling close by.

'Did you hear that, Raimon? Ladies! What do they know of higher things? I ask you, do they deserve – Yes my lady, you are indeed perfect!'

'Thank you, my lord' said a lady. The voice was familiar to Miraval and he was thereby distracted from what Raymonde was saying: 'What was it? Yes. Miraval, are you listening?'

'Mm.'

'Tell me, you know all about *Fine Love*. I'm just an amateur – better with a sword than a song – and not much good at that! So says the great count. Do you think, Miraval, that a woman's head has any right to inhabit such loveliness? It's a trick of the Devil, to be sure – the old bastard!'

'Well, Raymonde. I know a lady who is attempting to separate the two.'

'What? Body and soul? God preserve us, Raimon! Really? But that would spoil all the *fun*!'

'Tell that to her.'

'And who is this poor, misguided lady?'

'The wife of Bernart – '

' – de Boissézon. Azalaïs! Up to her games again. You should have seen the mess she made of the king of Aragon's son. He's given himself over to war completely now. Good thing, too, with all those damn Almohads on the warpath again. Can't have – '

'Raymonde. Please!'

'Ah! Then it's *true*. It *is* serious. I am sorry. I shall speak no more of it.'

'Thank you.'

'I'm sure your songs will tell all, Miraval. Will you sing for us?'

'Can't make it tonight, Raymonde. The minstrels need a good night's rest and I – '

'What *you* need is a bath! I have a new one from Bourdeaux – maybe not as good as your river but it's a damn sight better than the old tub you had to use last time you were here.'

'That wasn't a tub. That was a privy!'

The two men cracked up in laughter. From out of the corner of an eye Miraval glimpsed a lady's blush. She looked to the ground and curtseyed. Miraval bowed immediately. Raymonde was watching.

'Yes, Raimon. Of course, you know Agnès. She's come all the way from Montpellier with her friend, Ermengarde. Agnès, my dear, where is the delightful Ermengarde?'

'My lord, she is dining with her cousin, Jordane de Saissac, in the town. But you need only send – '

'No, no, my dear Agnès. But please invite her to the court banquet tomorrow night.'

'Banquet, my lord?'

'Yes, in honour of the re-emergence (Miraval blushed) of our good friend and brilliant inventor of words and situations, Raimon de Miraval. And if that is not enough to encourage the lady, tell her that it is also in honour of the new Pope's accession.' Raymonde looked at Miraval with a tongue in his cheek, ' – and that it is a *religious* duty that she simply *must* perform!'

'My lord.'

'My lady?'

'I don't think I ought to mention His Holiness to Ermengarde.'

' – don't tell me, Agnès,' Raymonde whispered conspiratorially, 'She's a *Cathar*? Has the lady been *consoled*?'

'No, my lord.'

'Then, my dear Miraval, there's hope for us yet! Very well, keep the Pope out of this. After all, between you and me, I've been trying to do that for years! How do you like that, Raimon? What did I tell you? Heretics everywhere! It's all such *fun*!'

'Raymonde ... '

'My dear friend.'

'Really, I must go and see how my minstrels are settling in.'

'You're not staying here?'

'Not this time. I hope you're not – '

'Not at all. I'll have the bath all to myself! Now do come tomorrow. We shall be waiting. And Raimon, a word in your ear. Watch out for the *delicious* Ermengarde de Castres. She'll knock this Azalaïs thing right on the head!'

Miraval grinned warmly at Raymonde, 'That would be – '

'Don't you worry about a thing. Coming to Toulouse is going to change your life. You mark my words. And don't be afraid to let yourself go a bit now that you're here. I'm sure you'll find plenty to do.'

'You're a friend, Raymonde. I'll do my best.'

'We know that – don't we, ladies? Hear that, Raimon? Nothing but giggles. Take my advice. Give them your body. Keep your mind for your real friends.'

The Ferryman's Lady

Sixteen water-powered mills, newly constructed on the right bank of the Garonne, were fed by the Château Narbonnais dam. The dam was also of recent construction and the city engineers were proud of it. They had reason to be. It had taken a lot of work and a lot of money to see off the old floating mills. The old mills had had a habit of breaking off from their moorings in times of flood and thereby crashing into boats and generally wrecking the vital thoroughfare of waterborne trade between the Mediterranean and the Atlantic.

The dam straddled the upstream Garonne in a diagonal line more than twelve hundred feet long. Thousands of oak piles of eighteen foot had been sunk by piledriver into the river bed. The spaces between the parallel lines of stakes had been filled with gravel, earth, wood and boulders, while breakwaters had been positioned before the dam so as to save it from floating debris.

The Château Narbonnais dam was the first of three. Less than a quarter of a mile downstream, a little beyond the Ferryman's Lady, the dam of La Daurade fed the churning wheels of fifteen mills. A quarter of a mile downstream again brought you to the Bazade dam. Twelve mills took their power from La Bazade. The dams of Toulouse were big business – and the source of cut-throat financial struggle and industrial espionage.

Raimon de Miraval was very impressed by this titanic technology. He was riding upstream along the smelly river-bank, being happily distracted from the stink by the shards of light which came sparking off the tumbling water that roared and echoed about the empty embankment. He came to the last mill of the Château Narbonnais section, a demonic silhouette against the red sky, and watched the ferry come in from the Lombers road. The ferry disgorged a few late stragglers onto the main thoroughfare to the St Etienne Gate.

Miraval followed this road a little and then turned first right at the little church of Notre Dame-de-la-Dalbade and found himself in the Rue de Courteliers. It had not changed much since he had been a student nearby, but the tavern had gone slightly upmarket in his absence – and it had changed its name. The tavern had been called the Old Mill – but that would no longer do. The 'Ferryman's Lady' was clearly an attempt to attract the kind of custom who enjoyed the fashion for the new music. But Miraval had heard the city troubadours before and was none too impressed. They stole lyrics, sang them badly and fooled about with an artlessness that offended the artist in him. Nevertheless, the cities did provide a style of music which was well-nigh impossible to obtain in the country. Going under the general term of 'heavy minstrelsy', it explored bawdy themes with a great deal of rhythmic inventiveness and visceral intensity. Not surprisingly, Ahmed loved it too. Miraval, ever on the lookout for new ideas, had told his minstrels to watch out for it as well, but as he entered the plain scrubbed archway of the Ferryman's Lady, he was having doubts as to whether they would find any *heavy* minstrelsy there.

The Ferryman's Lady was absolutely packed. Miraval could hardly breathe. He was beginning to think he had made a mistake and glanced about for his friends. He could hear the tinkling of faint music permeating the talk and shouting. At the far end of the hall, there on a raised platform were his minstrels – *his* minstrels playing in a place like this. They were wearing their best outfits: long yellow tunics with black cloaks and red breeches. They looked so glum, sweating away.

'What could have happened?' thought Miraval. He began pushing his way through the packed house. He was not used to being ignored in a crowd and his patience was stretched. As he penetrated the mêlée, he could not fail to notice how the crowd was effectively divided between the ordinary townspeople, many of them mill-workers, on the left and the rich merchants and burghers on the right. This was not at all the tavern he used to know. He heard an unfamiliar voice,

'O Seigneur! Seigneur de Miraval. Welcome! Welcome! The Ferryman's Lady is honoured.' In a moment, blocking his way, stood a young man, smiling profusely. His green eyes were wide and he was coolly dressed in a pink tunic with a black belt. He looked to be about twenty. His hair was cropped and red. He did not stop smiling. He had to bellow at Miraval in order to be heard: 'Yes, great isn't it? I took it over from the miller's wife who used to run it. What a shambles! Really, we've had the workmen in on it for weeks! Fantastic, really – don't you think? Look, sorry 'bout the minstrels but they – Hey, do you want a drink? Marquésia! Wine for our guest.' An exceedingly pretty girl with long curly black hair and endless legs wrapped in a tight black gown blew a kiss at the host. 'Sure, Arnaud! Pot or glass?'

'Glass for the troubadour. Anyway, what was I saying?'

'Not much so far.' Arnaud looked blankly at Miraval and then resumed.

'O yeah! Your group arrived and I said "Who are you?" and they said:

"From Miraval with the lord of Miraval." Amazing! So I

said, "Look lads, you can stay for nothing if you play for me tonight." And they looked at each other and said, "We can't speak for the Seigneur." So I said, "Who could? I mean, er ... of course you can't." So how about it then?'

'How about what, sir?'

'A song. You can stay as long as you like.'

'I shall consider your offer. Now do excuse me.'

Miraval started to press on. Arnaud's mouth was wide open: 'Er ... Seigneur. Look, sorry about the music but they were playing a bit too loud so I said, "Come on! Make it soft and sweet – like the Ferryman's Lady." Get it?'

Miraval reached the stage. The minstrels looked at each other, somewhat embarrassed and stopped playing. Nobody seemed to notice.

'Ahmed!'

'My lord?'

'What is all this?'

'Pardon us, my lord. But well, we know how short you are of money and we thought ... '

Miraval looked extremely hurt. He *was* hurt. Ahmed registered this straightaway: 'We shall play no more.'

'No, Ahmed. On the contrary. You accepted the man's offer and you will play. Nobody will ever say that my minstrels are thieves, do you understand?'

'Yes, my lord.'

'But, Ahmed ... '

'My lord?'

'Since tonight is the only night we shall be spending in this place, let us please leave them with something they will not forget. Gérard! Berteaux! Jacques! Ahmed! – a little *heavier* then usual, please.'

The minstrels grinned. Ahmed pulled out his large hand-drum from a leather bag, placed it in front of him and took two ivory hammers. He began to drum slowly, inaudibly at first and then built up into a thunderous roll. Jacques began playing a counter rhythm on the thin glazed drum. Gérard hit a chord on his lute and Berteaux hit a high note on the flute. This caught the attention of Arnaud, the young host. His mouth quavered. Marquésia looked to him for guidance. Arnaud looked at Miraval. Miraval smiled and extended his hand as if unveiling the sounds. Arnaud looked at Miraval, blinked and gave a nervous smile.

The tavern began to go quiet. Some of the burghers left. Some others moved to the front where the millers were sitting and tapping their feet and clapping in time. The young women began to smile and Miraval sat down at a table and quaffed a deep draught from his glass of wine. Miraval was indeed content. He listened to the millers' talk. Over it all came the chorus and the young women joined in:

'Say nothing of love but good!
Say nothing of love but good!

Drink the water, don't die of thirst.
We hunger for her love.
She is whiter than ivory
And bolder than brass.
Say nothing of good but love!'

And the young men joined in. And the old men. And the burghers and the merchants and the millers and their sons. And their daughters kissed and hugged and screamed and the new, dead tavern exploded into life. And Miraval would have dreamed but for what he overheard.

'That's right. Not what it was. There's hardly any of us left now.'

Miraval leaned over to the miller who was shouting to his friends. The miller had eager blue eyes which flashed in the firelight and golden-brown hair covered with grease. He wore a thick brown moustache – something of an eccentricity in Toulouse – and the hairs of the moustache vibrated over his old lips.

'Excuse me, sir,' said the troubadour.

The Miller's Tale

The miller looked straight at Miraval and, noting the troubadour's obvious rank, covered his mouth and coughed. 'Can I be of service, seigneur?'

Miraval spoke directly into the miller's ear: 'You said that there's hardly any of you left. What did you mean?'

The miller turned to his friends and shouted: 'He's asking what we're talking about! What d'you think?' The friends pushed out their lips and nodded. The miller turned to Miraval: 'Can you hear me?'

'No problem there, sir. I wrote this music! I can't live without it but I can certainly live with it – if *you* can!'

'Years of working near a millwheel, seigneur! This is nothing! All right, what did I mean when I said we were few? Simple, really. We're all millers here. I expect you can see that. And we used to own our own mills, see? You probably don't remember but there used to be, ooh – upwards of sixty-three mills on the Garonne here. Floating mills. Good, most of the time, but you know how it is – you get a flood and they break away, cause damage. I mean, I always said it would have to change some day. But when they built the dams – great dams they are, make no mistake – well, something happened. Then there was forty-three mills, see? Bigger mills, marvellous, really, but everyone had shares in their own mill. One share is worth an eighth of a mill. You couldn't have all the shares – fair enough – because the changes were so expensive. Things worked out. We worked it out in places like this. Together, talking to each other like we are now. Well, the first big thing came because the mills were divided up into three so we millers were in competition with one another. All right, we'd always been in competition – but we controlled it ourselves. Then the city people with the money started buying up all the shares. I mean, they even started setting up latticework on the tops of the dams to net the jumping salmon. So then there was the question of fishing rights. What do you think? Do the millers get a share? Not likely! Sold off and the cash given to the shareholders at an annual banquet. Many of my family helped to design the new mills. The new people weren't interested in technology. Talked a lot about it but knew nothing. I mean, we're all just employees now. It's all gone mad. There's too much money about. I hope I haven't bored you, Seigneur.'

'No, sir. Not at all. I'd like to know more.'

The miller looked around to his friends again for reassurance. They nodded. 'These boys on stage. They with you, then?'

'Yes, sir.'

'May I ask your name, Seigneur?'

'Miraval.'

'Very pleased to meet you. We've heard of you but we never get to hear you.'

'Well, I tend to sing at home or at court, that sort of thing.'

'And why not? I mean, most people here wouldn't appreciate what you do. I mean, most can't tell the difference. *I* can. Music is music.'

'That's right, sir! That's true!'

'Look, see those men over there?'

On the right hand side of the stage in a corner sat a group of men gathered about a table. There was money on the table and parchment spread out, too.

'The thin bloke, the little bloke, the sullen one. He's a solicitor. Don't know his name. Notice his clothes. Cheap. He's rich as Dives. Gives money to the Church. Know what I mean? The other man, the merchant. His name's Flamel. He's got most of the shares in the Bazade dam. He was up in court last year for closing the *navère*. Couldn't get a boat through in two days! Said it was for "building work". There was a riot – and he blamed the *Straight Jesus* – said they was fighting the *Juice Tramps*.'

'I'm sorry. The who?'

'*Juice Tramps?* Oh, they're from Gascony. Come riding in, about a dozen or two of them. Some of them are *Waldensians*, you know, live communally like Christ; don't like the wealth of the Church. Some come looking for whores, a good time. Some come for the music. Salt of the earth, some of 'em. Really good. They get blamed for most things. The Bishop says they're the result of heresy – calls them *Hell Demons*. Bishop says heresy sends 'em mad. Bullshit! Life sends people mad. Some of the *Juice Tramps* used to live on the banks of the Garonne north of here, fishermen, but the old Count had them cleared off. Said they were obstructing the river.'

'Interesting.'

'Well, this fat bloke, Flamel. He's doing "repair work" again. We all know he's raising the dam to get more power for the mills. 'Cause every time a dam's raised downstream, the pressure's down on the upstream dams. It'll end in court and the richest man will win. Could take years. The old count's too dependent on the merchants to interfere. It's chaos.'

'The old count is on his deathbed.'

'What? Again? No, he's just tired of fending off Aquitaine and Anjou. I mean, it stands to reason, doesn't it, Seigneur? Staying in bed creates uncertainties. Political capital. He's a clever bastard and he likes his money.'

One of the miller's friends nudged him in the ribs.

'Oh right, well, you see the other guy? He's Olivier de Saissac. He's a knight, but he's been in the city too long, if you know what I mean. His sister's a heretic. Common knowledge. She hangs out with the Mauran family. They're Cathars, too. Good family. Very rich. They've been trying to help the millers by buying shares and giving them back to us. There'll be hell to pay for that one day. It's just a matter of time. But you've got to watch what you say. You understand me?'

'I understand.'

'This Olivier de Saissac. You wait. He'll be selling shares in the Daurade dam for a price soon – probably to some of us. You see the problem? Then the dam at La Bazade will be raised and shares in La Daurade will go down and he'll buy into La Bazade. As for Château Narbonnais, they'll bring out the knives. We used to love it here. Are your minstrels going to play here again, seigneur?'

'I doubt it, sir. It's not our kind of place.'

'You're right there. I think we'll start looking for somewhere else.'

'Good luck, sirs. I shall see what I can do. But who really listens to a troubadour?'

'O Seigneur de Miraval. You'd be surprised. You'd be surprised. Just look *around*. May the *Good God* go with you!'

Miraval did a double-take. '*Good God*'? Was that not a phrase used by the heretics? He recalled what Raymonde had said: "Wonderful chaps!" and he thought of Azalaïs, of how she was joining them, leaving him between the devil and the deep blue sky. He was looking forward to seeing Raymonde again. The young count-to-be was certainly overbearing on occasions but Miraval trusted him. Raymonde was no fool, though he could play the part to perfection. Life could be safer that way. Miraval thought of what the miller had said: "You've got to watch what you say." Nobody ever said this in the Cabardès. Miraval missed his home but his friends were close and gazing on them, he knew . . . something or other. He had fallen asleep.

Between Two Desires

It was the night of the banquet. The hall was stony vast beneath the flanks of beams. Bright golden torches hushed the warm evening air to the ceiling in waves, and the audience of many-coloured courtiers looked up in apprehension. They looked to the figure of Raymonde, who had risen from his seat on the high table at the far end of the hall so as to address the court before him.

'One moment, please, ladies, seigneurs, knights, everyone! Firstly, I must apologise on behalf of my father, who cannot be with us tonight. We are assured by the finest doctors in the country that he will rejoin us soon. Until then, you must be content with me.' The court started cheering and banging their goblets upon the polished tables which lined the walls of the hall. 'Thank you. Thank you. I'm sure the count would appreciate your feelings for him. As I do. Now, we have all enjoyed a fine feast – even the geese were well stuffed! – and before we receive admonishment from our lord Bishop, who has *insisted* on taking this opportunity to address us – that is, if the gentleman can still stand up – I want to bring before the court someone who surely is no stranger to anyone here but who has been, shall we say, *indisposed* for some time in a *most* distant region of our country. I do believe he has distilled this epic experience, refined it and joined it to music, for us to hear this evening. Please welcome the lord of *Fine Love*, eloquence, beauty, sound proportion, devotion and of Miraval itself, now, by our influence, firmly established as a light in our present – ' Raymonde looked round to the old Bishop, ' – darkness. So before his Grace begs you to leave to crusade in Spain, here, to remind you of what you might be missing is our dear friend, Raimon de Miraval!'

As the hall erupted into the most enthusiastic applause, the doors at that end of the hall facing Raymonde and his immediate family were opened and in strode, with infinite aplomb, the troubadour and his minstrels. Miraval held his head high, his face impassive, his eyes upon Raymonde. As he reached the centre of the hall, he stopped and smiled at the count's son. He instructed some servants to bring cushions for his minstrels. He would stand. His feet would not move but his arms, hands and head would express that which his words could not. Miraval was dressed in a full-length purple cloak which fell square from off his shoulders and skirted the smooth stone floor. The minstrels wore yellow shirts and black hose. As the court quietened down, Miraval made an introduction.

'My friends – and enemies – of all places and kinds, let me offer you the chance to meet halfway the skills of my four friends. Playing the *organistrum* this evening is Gérard. On flute, Berteaux. On rebec – that's the one with a bow – is Jacques. My faithful drummer, is, as he is always, Ahmed. I am Raimon de Miraval and I come with *Joy* from the Cabardès!

'The song you are about to hear is completely new and I trust that Toulouse will not be offended by its originality. It is not only new but is entirely true. And if it is true for me, then it may also be true for you! The song is dedicated to a lady who, like our good count, cannot be with us this evening, but whether through illness or some more unearthly cause I cannot honestly say.'

The court began murmuring amongst themselves. Miraval noticed, to his left, Agnès de Montpellier as she whispered something to Ermengarde de Castres. Ermengarde's eyes widened and stared straight into those of Miraval. He looked away, to his minstrels. Miraval nodded to Gérard. Gérard began turning the handle of the *organistrum* before him and pressed a key over one of the three strings. The string, vibrated by the revolving mechanism set in the carved body, built in the shape of a large latticed shoe, began to produce an eery, faraway drone, like a single organ tone might make in the wind-blown dome of an empty mosque. Berteaux began playing an exquisite melody which advanced up and down a scale in swift three-note melismas. It sounded so magical that you could almost smell the mellow green fields of a late spring! Jacques began playing the deep notes of the principal melody on his rebec. This combination induced a special alertness within the court who discovered, in spite of bodily satisfaction, some fresher space in the dimension of their collective Soul.

Miraval's voice came as if from nowhere, rising in the minds of the listeners. Miraval sang slowly, never rushing to a line but instead curling and curving, chopping and chafing each hint of irony and meaning, so bringing the whole to such a pitch of emotion and spiritual clarity that Miraval would lose all sense of where he was and to whom he was singing. As the music left his material body to bounce from wall to ceiling and on into the warm night air, Miraval had to restrain his spirit from leaving him altogether. Something had already told him that this might be his last performance.

'Between two desires I remain a dreamer,
Because my heart tells me "Sing no more!"
While Love will not let me abstain,
  so long as I am in this world.
O I have reasons, nonetheless
to compose these songs no longer,
But I will sing because Love and Youth
restore all that Measure and Reason have made invisible.

And if ever I strove
to be an artful man, courteous and gay,
I must now apply myself with yet more eagerness
to saying and doing things which please her;
now that I've put all my hope
in a lady whose precious and cherished favours
would be unmerited by an ill-mannered man,
whether he be rich, powerful or handsome.

Beneath such honour and nobility
I have always shown myself to be a sincere lover,
in spite of sorrow, distress and anguish,
I have never sought escape from the worst of it.
They say that from a hidden love
it is impossible to derive satisfaction,
But they lie! I have known the pleasures and the benefits
As much as I've suffered the shame and deceit of it.

In all that matters concerning this noble lady,
I am demanding of her,

lest she do anything which lowers her Value;
but if it is a lady of small virtue who betrays me,
is that any cause to become party to unpleasant quarrels?
No! She would be too happy
if, thanks to me, she were made the subject of gossip.
The bad ladies of this kind, their faults inflict injury,
and they only feel important when the centre of gossip
and dispute!

But my lady belittles the pretentious types
Since her honour increases as she shows it least:
She is like the rose and the gladiolus
which becomes more beautiful when summer returns
But my lady is all year in the season of beauty
Because she always knows how to make herself more lovable,
With her charming manners and her gracious gestures
which heighten her merit and all her ways.

It's thanks to her that I love the fountain and stream,
the wood and the orchard, the coppice and the hedge,
the ladies and the wicked ones too!
the wise and the mad and even the simpleton
Of that noble region in which she lives.
My thought is so attracted to this place
that I cannot imagine it ever beholding
another country or another race.

My lady Azalaïs de Boissézon
renders her merit supreme, when it was but good
And God will come to miss some respect due to Him
since she so gently entered my life.

It is a new love which invites me
to serve her in such a manner
that at Miraval let there be firmly established
all the goodness of love and of sincere accord.'

The clapping began quietly but grew and grew until the hall was like the heart of a thundercloud and Miraval was overwhelmed, eyes bright with large tears which fell over his hot cheeks, so full of joy was he. Raymonde stood up and applauded the more. He stepped down from his high table, dashed over to Miraval and shouted into the troubadour's ear:

'Absolutely out of this world, Raimon! Amazing! Really amazing! But look, get Gérard and the others to play some dance music! If we get the court dancing before the old bishop starts his sermon, we can save the evening for Love and leave war until tomorrow!'

Miraval, wiping his eyes, nodded and gave the appropriate instructions to Ahmed, who informed the other three minstrels. The court began to move to the centre of the hall as the minstrels struck up a gay dance tune. Raymonde ran up to the bishop, only lately awakened from sleep.

'Come to dance, bishop? Seems that events have got the better of us! It happens all the time. Do enjoy yourself and we'll save the Crusade till the morning, all right?'

'My lord Raymonde has outmanoeuvred his bishop. But tomorrow may come sooner than he thinks.'

'Now, now, my lord bishop. Don't let's get nasty. How about a little Courtly *Love*? I'm sure the Lord Christ would approve!'

The bishop, accustomed to a cat-and-mouse game with Raymonde's father, was unwilling to make an overt enemy of the count's son and so swallowed his anger. 'Do not think me a bore, my lord. I much appreciate the works of the troubadours. Perhaps you could invite Bertran de Born to the next banquet. He sings most eloquently of Love – Love for Christendom which even this very day is threatened by Ya'qub and the whole Almohad dynasty in Castile, Aragon, Navarre and León – a love which would direct the noble heart to arms against the heathen!'

'Hold fast to the Faith, your Grace. *Faith*. And now, you must excuse me, I have *serious* business to discuss.'

The bishop nodded and then looked to the joyous scene before him. He had never been able to make up his mind about public gaiety. On the one hand, he could see Christ at Cana, turning water into wine, while on the other he saw the Whore of Babylon drunk on the blood of the Saints. He took a gulp of wine himself and licked his lips. The blood of saints could never taste as good as this.

'Raimon, my dear friend. Shall we go outside? Up to the battlements, say?' Miraval perceived a conspiratorial air in what his friend was so casually suggesting. They climbed a spiral staircase, turning a full 360 degrees in only five steps. One hundred and eight steps brought them to the battlements.

'O dear, no red sky tonight Raimon. Looks like tomorrow will be miserable. A perfect day, however, to listen to the protestations of the clergy.'

'What is it this time, Raymonde?'

'Things have become very complicated. But I want you to understand the situation.'

'I'll try, Raymonde.'

'Now I know, my friend, that beneath your artistic life lurks a mind not only sensitive but sensible – politically sensible. Were it not so, then I am quite sure that Trencavel would have had your castle years ago. Since you officially owe allegiance to him, and by extension to the King of Aragon, I know that your coming here carries certain risks.'

Miraval thought this a most strange thing to remark upon, as though Raymonde were trying to implicate him in some network of circumstances of which he had been hitherto unaware. 'Not at all. I never think of it. My parents lost most of the family inheritance to the Trencavels. I'm of no interest at all. I don't think Trencavel looks much beyond Carcassonne and Béziers.'

'Not so, Raimon. It is your relationship with me that temporarily guarantees your small estate.'

Miraval wanted to say, 'I don't wish to know all this'; but contented himself by gazing southwards over the city instead. He could see how the glittering river penetrated the city walls. He could see firelight all over the city, but particularly concentrated in the merchants' quarter near the church of St Etienne. He could see ... Ermengarde de Castres: two wide eyes in the torchlight downstairs. Miraval felt Raymonde's hand on his shoulder. 'Are you listening Miraval?'

'Yes. Every word. Did you know about the scam being pulled by Flamel on the Bazade dam? How the millers are being – forgive the pun – sold down the river?'

'Oh, yes I know. All about it. Not much you can do, I'm afraid. Not much I can do, at any rate. My father is thinking of setting up an investigation. But, Raimon, there are more pressing matters. We'll deal with the merchants later.'

'You'll never deal with them. They're always there. They'll have us all some day.'

'That day is far off, Raimon de Miraval. Can we return to the purpose of our conversation?'

'Yes, Raymonde. What was it?'

'You know that in the past year Christendom has acquired a new Pope?'

'Celestine III, I believe.'

'Formerly Cardinal Hyacinth, papal legate, co-founder of the Christian military Order of Santiago, much distinguished at the relief of Huerte. The man's main interest in life is the defence of Spain from the Almohads. Their king, Ya'qub I, has recently defeated his internal opposition in Tunisia and Majorca and has pursued the *Jihad* with growing – how shall we say? – ardour. He has, I believe, given up all interest in art and music – subjects in which he more than distinguished himself in his youth. This Holy War, no doubt further encouraged by Saladin's defeat of Christian forces at Hattin five years ago, is, in the opinion of the Pope, not to be confined to Spain but sees as its ultimate objective, the total defeat of Christendom.'

'I had gathered as much.'

'So you do not think only of *Love* in the Cabardès? That is good, if sad. It is the Pope's fervently held view that Christendom stands to fall to the might of Islam at any moment.'

'Does he not believe in the providence of God?'

'No doubt, but he is convinced that we – the rulers of armies – do not. God's providence, in this case, is demonstrated by the provision of weapons to defeat God's enemies. The kingdom of God on earth must, apparently, be defended like any other kingdom and I, for one, do not disagree with him on this point. First comes the sword, then the theology! My heretical friends do not agree. But on one thing we are in accord: it is a wicked world, Raimon. Only the love of your lady can make you see it otherwise. But that is another story.

'The Pope, in his wisdom (which is great) has sent his nephew, Gregorio, to Castile as a legate. His mission is to reconcile the Christian rulers of Castile, León, Aragon and Navarre while Ya'qub recovers from some illness in Morocco. My information is that Gregorio has been most successful in this. Alfonso of Castile has made a truce with his namesake in Aragon and they have agreed to a ten-year truce with León. Negotiations with Navarre are still under way. Now I know that Ya'qub's troops are presently held back as far south as the Tagus but I believe there is some substance in the Pope's view.

'What I do not appreciate is a lateral mission currently in motion whose object is to get the king of France and therefore, since we are his vassals, Toulouse to join in an almighty Crusade against Ya'qub. That, in effect, we fight Holy War with Holy War and let God and the force of battering rams decide the result. All very admirable, no doubt. And hasn't Richard of England, Duke of Aquitaine, already set a most splendid example to us all? He has made us look like cowards. I don't like it at all. We are constantly being reminded by bishop and legate of that expedition of three years ago to Portugal. Do you remember?'

'I have some dim memory.'

'The Church has not forgotten. A fleet of uncouth crusaders from Dartmouth in England decided to make a detour from their appointed destination, namely Jerusalem, in order to besiege the Arabs at Silves. They are praised as every kind of good Christian when we all know that the English *enjoy* war. A phenomenon which the Pope finds only rare occasion to condemn.'

'So the question is, "What are you going to do about it?"'

'Precisely, Raimon. Here lies the problem.'

'And the answer?'

'It's in the pot, Raimon. We're working on it. But there are many ramifications. Let us say, for example, that I raise an army now, on my father's behalf, and head off, banners waving, to Castile. Several things could happen. Firstly, Aquitaine has constantly claimed Toulouse as its own. Henry of Anjou, Richard's father, attempted to take the city in '59. He failed – for once! But if Richard were to return from Aquitaine to the Holy Land? He already holds some of our lands in the Quercy ... Well, we don't know. Personally, I like Richard but you never know. Secondly, there's Viscount Trencavel down near you in Carcassonne. He is absolutely itching to get his hands on some of our territories to the east of here and in Provence. While he may be a vassal of Aragon, and no doubt we would be in league with Aragon for any projected Crusade, Trencavel is somewhat independent minded. It's too risky. Thirdly, what if we lost the war – unthinkable I know – but we must consider the possibility. That would leave the Pyrenees and the rest of France open to Almohad invasion. Not a comforting thought. Surely it's better that we present a second line of defence should Aragon and Castile fall.'

'So what is the problem?'

'Very simple. The Church does not agree. The Church, of course, has other interests – and I do not mean those of a spiritual nature. The Pope is of the opinion that only a totally united Christendom will dissuade both the Almohads in the west and Saladin in the east from pursuing their Holy War. Control of the Holy City itself is still on the table but at the present, the Church is on the defensive. This is a passing phase, no doubt. Of course, to unite all Christian princes behind a cause directed and controlled by the Catholic Church has been the ambition of Rome since time immemorial. Naturally, the Church's political power increases every time they can persuade a prince to do their bidding.

'The whole thing about a Crusade as I see it, is that initially it serves to harmonize otherwise divergent interests: the interest of kings, barons and knights in making war, taking booty, land and pursuing a material Grail, while the Church increases its political control of the countries concerned and, indeed, their economies as well. Not all princes see the issues so clearly. But whatever the Pope is selling, I don't buy it, Raimon. I don't buy it at all. I believe that the dangers from the Almohads are being vastly overstated at present. As I said, Ya'qub isn't even in Spain at the moment. The Church knows how many barons lust after a good fight and they know the appeal of suspending a knight's debts should he go on Crusade. It's a set-up.'

'I know. My brothers haven't been seen in years.'

'Exactly. And you worry about the millers down there! The thing is that this marketing of Crusade destabilizes the power and organization of lawful rulers. This can be in the Church's interest. It is not mine.'

'So where is the solution?'

'You are wise enough, Raimon, to know that most serious problems are not resolved by envisaging one major solution, but by working step by step to some dimly perceived goal. The goal is the thing.'

'What is your goal?'

'First, security for our land and our people. And then ... '

'And then?'

'And then, my dear Raimon, joy, music, spiritual liberty! Things like that. But Security first. Nothing more and nothing less will do. It's an expensive game.'

'So the question arises, if I read you correctly, how to appease the Church while not doing precisely what they demand of you.'

'That's it. And there is a way, Raimon. But there is also a great problem.'

'And that is?'

'They are both the solution to the problem and the problem in the solution. I refer, as I'm sure you've guessed, to the *Good Men*. The Pope regards the Cathars as worse than the infidel. To him they are an insidious fifth-column, rotting Christendom from the inside. I, as you might expect, do not agree. Heresy is a living tradition here. But since two years ago, my father is supposedly bound, as a Christian ruler, to burn all unrepentant heretics.'

'And he has not been doing so?'

'Well, from time to time, an unlucky Cathar ends his earthly life in flames. But no, it has not been policy to actively pursue them. Of course, you can see how all this looks: Islam at the door and we can't even extinguish our own heretics! Especially as it is common knowledge to the Church authorities that I am friendly to the Cathars – encouraging public debates with them and so forth. The Catholic Church feels that it is losing control over Languedoc. And they are right. And I don't care. My father, however, is inclined to be occasionally alarmed by this development. Consequently, he frowns on my fraternizing with them – can't have anyone saying his son's a heretic – '

'And are you, Raymonde?'

'That's my problem. It is presently in my father's interest to help the bishops in extirpating heresy. It's a complete failure, as you might expect, but at least it looks as if we are doing *something* in these "dark days" and all that! Nobody wants a bloodbath. Just a demonstration of will. Father's been pressurized by Philip of France – and that bothers him more than the Bishop of Toulouse. Philip has never forgiven father for doing homage to Henry II of England and his sons nearly twenty years ago. So you see the position.'

'Indeed. But why are you explaining all this to me?'

'Raimon, you would help me, wouldn't you, if I was in desperate need?'

'Of course. No question about it.'

'Good. Because there's something I want to ask you to do for me.'

'Yes?'

'Listen, Raimon. What I am about to tell you is of the utmost secrecy. The utmost secrecy. I want you to swear an oath that you will never divulge this information to anyone unless I or a representative of mine says so.'

Miraval felt a cold shiver go right up his spine. He blurted out, 'No! Raymonde. Please don't drag me into this. I know it's something terrible. I just know it. Not now. I'm not ready for this. Please don't ask it – I've never sworn an oath to anyone but a lady. I cannot, really, I'm sorry.'

Raymonde changed his tone completely. He became jovial and playful once more. 'Not to worry Raimon! Just testing the water. We'll talk no more about it. Let's rejoin the party!'

Miraval led the way back down to the hall. As he neared the bottom of the dark staircase, he noticed that he could no longer hear Raymonde's feet behind him. He stopped and looked round. The shiver returned. He saw two white eyes in the blackness and heard Raymonde's voice: 'Just think about it, Raimon. That's all I ask. Good night.'

Miraval re-entered the hall, feeling most peculiar. Suddenly he was in the present. Everything that had been bothering him for months felt distant, the subject not of anxiety but of nostalgia. He saw Ermengarde and Agnès sitting on a long bench, obviously enjoying themselves, pointing out particular nobles and knights as they danced in line with fabulous ladies with long, long hair. It was 'now' all right, but 'now' felt like a super-vivid dream. He walked straight over to the ladies.

'My lady Agnès, my lady Ermengarde. I'm so delighted to see you here.'

'You are most gracious, seigneur Miraval. We had rather wondered what had become of you.'

'My lady Agnès, I suppose you might say that I had been detained by "reasons of state" – something quite beyond my scope.'

'You surprise me.' Miraval looked at Ermengarde. Raymonde had been right. Ermengarde was captivating: large brown eyes, innocent and seductive by turns, black wavy hair with long brown streaks, warm round cheeks, soft shoulders and inviting breasts.

'Why do I surprise you, my lady?'

'Oh well, I've heard so much about you. I had been given to think that nothing would be beyond your scope.'

Miraval was thoroughly abashed. Ermengarde was offering herself to him. He was sure of it.

'That is ... '

'What Ermengarde means, Raimon, is that judging by your performance tonight, you are clearly able to paint pictures of all feelings and situations.'

'Oh yes, well, I've been working at it a long time.'

Miraval felt so stupid. Why was he always so lost for words when he found himself directly questioned?

'Only on parchment, seigneur Miraval?'

'I write and sing about what I experience. No more than that, lady Ermengarde.'

'Then your experience is very great.'

'Thank you, my lady. And how do you find Toulouse?'

'Oh, it's marvellous. We're having a lovely time, aren't we Agnès? We've seen all the sights and tonight really sets it all off. What an extraordinary man is the count's son! Is he a friend of yours?'

'A very great friend. He listens to all my works.'

'I was so sad,' said Agnès, 'that you were unable to be in Montpellier recently.'

'I hope my minstrels gave you full satisfaction?'

'Oh, they were marvellous. I do simply *adore* your little drummer. Where did you find him?'

'I did not find him. Ahmed found me. He comes from Tripoli, in Syria. He was brought up as a Christian but he could pass himself off as a Muslim if he had to. And indeed he did have to. Ahmed narrowly escaped conscription into Saladin's army. He fled to Constantinople, I believe, and thence via the Danube he made his way to Languedoc. He assures me that our music is known even in Syria. His ambition is that some day we will perform in the Holy Land and in North Africa.'

'That's quite a dream, given present conditions, is it not?' said Agnès.

'Yes, it is. We need to dream, don't we?'

'Mmm.' Ermengarde smiled at Miraval – not an ordinary smile; it was a sign of promise and Miraval understood it very well. He was so taken by her. The only word to explain it would be magnetism. It was purely sexual. But Miraval could never bring himself to see this. He knew he had to see her privately. There was no question about it.

'I heard, lady Ermengarde, that you were staying with a cousin, Jordane de Saissac, if I remember correctly.'

'You remember very well. Yes, Jordane and her brother Olivier.'

'Olivier?' Miraval recalled his conversation with the miller from the previous evening. Olivier de Saissac was involved with the Flamel swindle. Miraval had cause to feel that special sense of superiority which comes from intimacy with a secret. This was new to him and he was enjoying the *frisson* of conspiracy. After his conversation with Raymonde, he felt very much up to it.

'Olivier de Saissac. I've heard of the gentleman.'

'Yes. He's all right. Quite a character, really.'

'A character? Yes, I've heard something of that.'

The conversation had started to go dead – not because they had nothing to say but because there was too much. Agnès began to gaze over to the far side of the hall. Miraval looked to his minstrels. There was nothing to worry about on that score. They were having a wonderful time, inviting feminine glances and feminine approval. Ermengarde looked to her hands, clasped upon her knees, and then at Miraval. Miraval looked at her but was too full of the moment to smile. He looked away. Agnès was troubled. She cared deeply for Miraval but knew in her heart that it was no use. She wanted to stay but could see the attraction between Ermengarde and the troubadour. Had she not encouraged it, in spite of herself? She found herself getting up. 'Excuse me, Raimon. I think I can see an old friend. Do you mind, Ermengarde?'

Ermengarde felt suddenly exposed and caught in a dilemma. She knew that if she stayed with Miraval she would have to make love to him. There was nothing else to do. 'Yes, Agnès. It's all right. We shall just watch for a while.'

Miraval rose and bowed to the departing lady of Montpellier. He was a little sorry to see Agnès go, because something told him that he was saying goodbye to a friend and that Ermengarde, for all her charms, could never be that. Ermengarde was something else: solid gold temptation, and Miraval was sorely tempted. So there they sat: Ermengarde de Castres and Raimon de Miraval, full of feeling, their bodies warm and tense. Who would speak first?

'So you know Olivier?'

'I didn't say that.'

'Then you know of him?'

'Not much.'

'What have you heard?'

'He loves money.'

'Not only money.'

'He has been in the city too long.'

'Whatever do you mean?'

'He's a knight.'

'Yes.'

'City's no place for knights.'

'Is it a place for a troubadour?'

'Depends.'

'On what?'

'Who he's with.'

'And who are you with?'

Miraval paused for a second. 'I'm with you.'

'Yes. Shall we go?'

'Yes. Where to?'

'You're staying here, aren't you?'

Miraval thought of his minstrels. He had promised to join them for a drink in their new-found taven after the banquet. 'Look, just a minute. I must speak to my friends.'

'Please go ahead.'

Miraval got up, bowed, and made his way to his friends. He

called Ahmed, who got up from his drum. 'Look, Ahmed, I've got to stay here tonight. Do you understand? Have a great time without me.' Miraval reached for his purse. 'No, my lord. We're fine. Really!'

'All right then, well, I must go.'

'Go well, my lord.'

Miraval came back to the bench. Ermengarde was not there. 'Damn!' thought Miraval. He looked to the main doors. She was there, talking to Agnès. He rushed over, 'Ermengarde! I thought you'd gone.'

'Not yet, Miraval.' They excused themselves and walked out together on to a torchlit landing. Great retrievers were moping about, looking for scraps.

'Well, it's near here, if you'll follow me.'

'Mmm. All right.'

They walked up a stairway, their steps becoming louder as the sound of the banquet subsided. They found themselves in silence, outside the door to Miraval's chamber. Ermengarde opened the door and walked in.

One thick candle illuminated the small room. Miraval followed Ermengarde. She stopped in the centre of the room. Miraval closed the door, wincing at the creak of the old hinges in the still silence. Miraval stood with his back to the door. Ermengarde gave a nervous smile and looked down over her body. In Miraval's eyes the night air began to shudder with love. The vibration became like a deep beat, a heartbeat. There was a rhythm and the lovers joined it.

She began untying the rough cord which ran from her neck to her navel. She picked the cord with delicate fingers, spreading the material as she did so. Goose-pimples rushed down from her collar bone to her belly. Ermengarde was breathing heavily and opened her lips. Miraval caught her heady scent. The green velvet dress unfolded before his eyes, slipping from her shoulders to the floor. Now Ermengarde looked at Miraval, a look of innocence and longing. Miraval marvelled before warm brown skin, large brown nipples, a soft belly which flowed into a forest of black hair. Ermengarde felt every pulse in her body as her eyelids faltered and waited. He lifted off his surcoat and approached her. He placed the warm cotton garment over Ermengarde's flesh. She sighed as it pulled her hair and drifted over her breasts.

He began to smother her hair and her forehead in kisses, sucking her cheeks, licking her ears and penetrating her wet mouth. Their breath was loud and heavy. Ermengarde imagined Miraval singing in the banquet hall and felt her spirit loosen and flow about her skin. She felt down Miraval's spine to his arse. She rubbed hard and kissed his neck, pulling his shirt off from his waist as she did so. Miraval was mad for her, grasping her shoulders and forcing her head downwards over his chest.

Candlelight kissed his belly and so did she as she tugged at the cotton hose and revealed a white linen loincloth which was carefully unwrapped. She tenderly gripped his awakening penis and began to stroke and suck it. The sensation was quite sublime and Miraval inhaled as much air as he could. His tense body began to relax. His skin felt alive and cool. Ermengarde pulled back in a hot movement that had the troubadour utterly transfixed. She looked up to him and began to rise. They wrapped each other in their arms and kissed deeply.

For Ermengarde this was a spiritual exaltation which for her transcended her material self and released her passionate soul. For Miraval this was a descent from the mind which creates to the body that hinders. But for the moment, he shared the liberation which Ermengarde was offering him. But as the kiss went on, he did begin to feel separate from the event and when Ermengarde lay down on the great pillowy bed, he had the distinct awareness of one going through the motions of love. And as he tugged and pushed his body into hers, and as she cried and gasped in profound delight, he thought of Azalaïs.

But Ermengarde was a match for this thought; and when he looked down at her, his feelings changed and the excitement resumed. He would lose himself in Ermengarde and forget the past. Ermengarde twisted Miraval onto his back and he began to smile. She tried to speak to him.

'Raimon ... Raimon ... I know you've been suffering. I can feel it. It's all right now ... please hold my breasts ... that's good.'

'Oh what the hell!' thought Miraval. 'What the hell! This is good. This is great! Thank God I came to Toulouse!'

He would not be a slave to Azalaïs forever. She had hurt him. He thrust deeper into Ermengarde. She had damaged and belittled him. Harder he pushed. Had he no rights to Joy any more? Ermengarde began to moan louder and louder. Miraval was moving with the lady's heat. She was expert. Raised as a Cathar believer – taught to reject the body! Miraval marvelled. Ermengarde had found her own way to spiritual knowledge and Miraval was receiving a taste of it. She loved Miraval. She would love him to death if she could. She was riding him, hands flowing through her sparkling hair, feeling her breasts, his stomach and hands. Tender touches and driven delight combined with airy minds and rippling skin until the lovers growled and cried their earthly souls into one ripe, bursting orgasm!

Miraval lay flat out on the bed, his chest rising and falling – or was it the room? She lay beside him, too excited to sleep but happy to caress his wet skin as the cool, grey dawn rose over the rooftops of Toulouse. The banquet was over.

Everyone's a Loser (Except Me)

When Miraval awoke it was raining. The chamber was dark and shadowy. What a comforting sound, thought the troubadour, is the swell of heavy rain splattering over a window ledge: the drizzly droplets jumping madly like children upon the old stone. Ermengarde had gone. Miraval had some memory of the door being closed some time earlier. He was not hung-over. He had been sober all night and knew perfectly well what had happened and yet, strangely, he felt no shame as he should have done.

He recalled Raymonde's saying that meeting Ermengarde would 'knock that Azalaïs thing right on the head'. Raymonde could not have seen the depth of love which Miraval felt for Azalaïs. Far from obliterating his yearning for her, the night's experience had served only to intensify the obsession. Perhaps this was why he began to feel contempt for Ermengarde. But he knew a hypocrite when he saw one; and on realizing his own hypocrisy, he did start to feel shame. Azalaïs was beginning to appear more holy than ever. He perceived that the love for Ermengarde's body had led him to understand the incomparable superiority of the lady of Boissézon – and he felt grateful for that. It seemed that *Fine Love* had triumphed over lust after all.

He got up to look through the slit window, carved out of the stone in the shape of a cross. He could hear distant thunder – a sound which always excited him. Black clouds were battling with bare sunlight in competition for the chance to paint Toulouse in its own colours and shades. How could anyone be foolish enough to imagine that they were in control of their own destiny when so much that is seen depends upon the battles fought out in the sky above us in frightening analogues of the soul's anarchy? '*Vanity of vanities. All is vanity*, saith the Preacher.'

There was a note. Why was it that the heretics always seemed to be better educated than anyone else? Ermengarde had a neat, sexy style. On the torn parchment was written: 'Come for dinner this evening. Meet Jordane and Olivier. Ermengarde.'

He decided that he did not wish to go. The thought of Olivier de Saissac alone was enough to put him off. Secondly, he had a strong feeling of futility and fatality about Ermengarde de Castres. But as the day drew on beneath a cosy sheet of grey sky, he found it difficult to avoid thinking of Ermengarde. Her image seemed to be everywhere, inhabiting every shadow, grinning through every reflection. So at eight o'clock he found himself riding along a side street off the rue de Carcassonne, a short walk from the merchants' quarter in the south of the city. It had started to rain again and Miraval was huddled beneath a bright red cape in the blue light. He observed the flow of fast water coursing down the street, bearing the unhappy burden of old turds and vegetables. He arrived at the Saissacs' city house thinking of vegetables. How perverse it was, he thought, that the innocent food had never appeared in any song he had written! The Saissacs' house had two floors and was constructed in yellowy-brown stones with a plain arched window downstairs blocked by heavy wooden shutters and a rectangular window upstairs, from out of which Jordane de Saissac was leaning. She held a large red bowl over her head and did look a charming sight as the rain rushed over the gently sloping tiles and splashed over the bowl and about her crazy red hair! Miraval could hardly see her face behind the cascade of running water.

'Seigneur de Miraval! Is it you?'

'Yes, it's me. Good evening, my lady.'

'I'm just coming. There's a little stable opposite. You can leave your horse there.'

'Thank you, my lady. You are most kind.'

'Pardon?'

'Most kind.'

'Oh, I'm just coming.'

Miraval liked the sound of Jordane. How could she possibly bear to live with her brother? Perhaps she had no choice. Olivier beat her to the front door.

'Seigneur. We are most privileged. We are almost ready. Do come in.'

Miraval felt repelled by Olivier's false humility and snobbish manner. Nor did the troubadour look favourably upon the knight's appearance. Olivier's black hair was cut very short while his cropped beard bound his spare features into a grizzly image of deception and greed. His blue eyes were narrow and analytical. His reluctant smile was weak and distant. On his chest was a large red ruby, set in mother-of-pearl, which hung from an elaborate silver chain around his long neck. 'If ever a man looked like a villain!' thought Miraval.

'We are not used to music at our house. We find that it disturbs the spiritual atmosphere in which we like to live. Is that not so, Jordane?'

Jordane was busy laying the table, 'What's that, Olivier?'

'I was just saying to Raimon that we prefer to live quietly.'

'Well, I don't know. I was so sorry that I was unable to come to the banquet last night, but Olivier wished me to write some letters for him.'

'Yes, business is booming at the moment and there's so much to do. It's so difficult to overcome the constraints of material existence. I gather that you, Raimon, have no such difficulties.'

'I'm sorry. I don't understand you.'

'O come, come. You write songs, don't you? You must live in the spirit all the time.'

Miraval was baffled by the contradictions in what Olivier was saying. He did not wish to give himself away to such a man. Staring at the plaster ceiling, Olivier continued, 'Of course, I suppose we have all wished at some time or another for the kind of life you lead – but we just don't have the time.'

'If *we* don't have the time, Olivier, who does?'

'Time, Raimon, is of the Devil. But how can we beat the Devil?'

'I thought that Christ had already accomplished this task.'

'Yes, yes, of course. Christ did beat the Devil – by deception.'

'By *deception*? How could Christ *deceive* anyone?'

'I should have thought that was obvious, Miraval! He tricked people into thinking that he was an ordinary man. He tricked the Devil into thinking he had been crucified. He said that we must be "wilier than serpents".'

One thing that Miraval had not expected was to find that Olivier de Saissac was a religious crank. This was heresy of the strangest kind.

Saissac continued: 'It's like all those parables. They're riddles. Take the one about the Good Samaritan, for example. Christ was asked, "Who is my neighbour?" and then Christ made it clear that the Samaritans were good neighbours in his eyes. And why the Samaritan? Because the Samaritans were despised people. Because they were rich, no doubt, and could afford to help the poor – and we know that Jews want to be richer than anyone – so the parable means that you must become richer than the Jews in order to reach heaven. You have to pick up the '*rejected stone*' and build your fortune upon it. You must, in short, deceive the Jews because they are accursed people. The whole thing's a riddle! The Catholic Church has got it all wrong. But where would they be if people like me didn't give them money – I say "people like me" but naturally I myself refrain. I give money elsewhere.'

'I see, well . . . '

Jordane interrupted, 'Now, sirs, Ermengarde and I are ready to serve dinner. With all that talking you've been doing, you should have worked up a real appetite!'

'An appetite for Truth, dear sister.'

'Yes, dear. That too.'

Ermengarde sat opposite Miraval at the table. She hardly seemed to notice him.

'And how is the lady Ermengarde this evening?'

'Quite well, thank you, Raimon.'

Jordane spoke: 'Well, I'm so very pleased to meet you at last. Do take some vegetables. We have radishes, beans, peas, cabbage and carrots, and a lentil soup to start with. We have a lovely wine, too. It's – '

'Please don't tell me, Jordane. It's made from – '

'No, it's not made from vegetables, Raimon! You are cheeky! The wine is from Minerve, actually.'

'Excellent choice and I may say – '

Olivier butted in: 'Don't think we drink wine as good as this every day. Only for special occasions, you know. Anyhow, Raimon, what, if anything, brings you to our great city? I thought you hated cities.'

'What gives you that idea?'

'Something Agnès was saying yesterday.'

'Really? And, by the way, where is Agnès today?'

Ermengarde looked to Jordane. 'Well,' said Jordane, 'she felt rather unwell today and is, I believe, resting at the castle.'

'I suppose the food at the banquet was rather rich.'

'Very rich,' said Ermengarde.

'So it should be with all the taxes we have to pay,' interjected Olivier. 'Richer the better.'

Ermengarde laughed.

'What's so funny?' said Olivier.

'Oh nothing ... *you*, I suppose. You're so pompous, Olivier!'

Miraval looked to Jordane and gave a secret smile. Jordane's eyes darted to Olivier who was staring at Ermengarde, thinking of something to say.

'I've got a right to be pompous. Business going well. God helps them that helps themselves, you know.' He began to warm to his theme: 'D'you know something extraordinary, Raimon?'

'And what is that?'

'I'll tell you. Heard last week that the Germans were exporting pivotal windmills to the Holy Land – first ever to be seen in Acre, apparently. I'm going to see if we can't undercut them. Problem is: the difficulty involved in getting the damn things over with the way things are. Panic's on. The Devil knows how the Germans managed it. Clever. They might not get Jerusalem but they're sure to get treasure in heaven!'

Jordane, conventionally pious with the gift of tolerance, coughed and the table went quiet but for the munching of vegetables. Olivier farted. Only Miraval seemed to notice. 'And how long is the lady Ermengarde staying in Toulouse?' he asked.

'Well, that depends.' Ermengarde looked to Olivier who offered a smile on one side of his face. 'It depends on – oh, all sorts of things. Maybe a month, maybe longer. My sister's running the estate at the moment. She enjoys it more than I do.'

'And have you met anyone interesting since you arrived here, Raimon?'

'Well, Jordane, present company excepted, of course, I did run into some fascinating people at the Ferryman's Lady a couple of nights ago.'

'The Ferryman's Lady. Is not that the new place you sometimes frequent, Olivier?'

'Sometimes, Jordane. Yes, I *sometimes* go there.'

'And who did you meet, Raimon?' Jordane asked with wide-eyed eagerness.

'A group of millers, as a matter of – '

'*Millers*!' Olivier exploded. 'Don't come here and talk about bloody millers! They're absolute scum! Always wanting something for nothing! All thieves and layabouts. They think of nobody but themselves. Always causing trouble! Won't knuckle down. Trying to get rich – ideas above their station. Ah ... but we've got them sorted out now. Oh yes, we've got them!'

'Olivier, please! Calm yourself! I must apologize for my brother – '

'Don't you apologize for me, sister! I know what I'm saying. You troubadour!'

'Olivier!'

'You troubadours! Soft-hearted, soft-headed, bleeding-hearted fools! Don't think I don't know what you're implying, Raimon de Miraval. Think you're clever, do you? No doubt those irreligious bastards told you that we were stealing their mills. *Their* mills? We own the dams. We paid for them. Where would the damn mills be but for the dams? Down the bloody river, the lot of them! I know what they're up to – trying to interfere. They want to organize a strike! Do you call that *honourable*, Miraval, do you? That's the real trouble with this city – people don't know their place! Got high expectations. Scum! All they think of is their little mills while I dream of heaven. They've no mind for spiritual things – just think of their bellies and their vile children! Everything's gone mad. Lords and knights reading poetry and writing songs when there's *real* work to be done!'

Miraval got up from the table, 'Excuse me, my – '

'Don't think that you can leave my table just like that!'

Ermengarde started laughing, 'Oh Olivier, do sit down and eat your dinner!'

'I'll eat my dinner when I'm ready to eat. I'll eat when Raimon de Miraval has the simple *courtesy* to eat what a lady has had cooked for him!'

This was too much for Miraval. How dare this grotesque idiot question his *courtesy*? 'You, sir! You, Olivier de Saissac! You speak of *courtesy*? You don't know the meaning of the word!'

'No, maybe not. But as God is my witness I know the meaning of this: "I come not to bring peace but a sword!" – at which he reached for a broad sword standing in the corner of the room and, drawing it out, threw the scabbard on to the table with a violent slap.

'O dear God!' cried Jordane.

'What do you say now then, troubadour? Going to give us a song? I'll make you sing!'

Saissac made a lunge for Miraval across the table, his belly crashing into the table's edge. Miraval grabbed Saissac's head and pushed it into a bowl of fresh vegetables. The knight then made an attempt to lift the sword but Miraval seized his wrist. Both were scrambling jerkily upon the rumbling table, squashing harmless radishes, carrots and peas. Miraval reached for a fork. Olivier head-butted Miraval, who instantly fell back, plunging the fork deeply into Olivier's inner thigh as he did so. He screamed out, as did Jordane: 'Oh dear God! Raimon! What have you done?'

There was a banging at the front door as Olivier de Saissac fell like a dead weight from off the table. 'For pity's sake, who's that at the door? Can't a family fight in peace?!'

Ermengarde opened the door and in rushed Ahmed and Gérard.

'Give us a hand, will you?' cried Miraval. 'He's gone mad!'

Saissac sat up and reached on to the table for his sword. Ahmed jumped on to the table and with one foot pressed the blade fast to the table-top and with the other, kicked the knight clean in the face. 'Wog! Filthy wog!' Ahmed picked up the sword and aimed it at Saissac's throat, 'Kindly say that again, sir. Just once more.'

'Get out of my house, you scum! Get out!' Ahmed slapped Olivier on the head with the flat of the blade. The knight fell backwards, banging his head on the enamelled tiles.

'That's it, Gérard! All right my lord, shall we go?'

'I think we'd better!' As they all backed out of the house, Miraval bowed. 'Terribly sorry, ladies. These things happen, don't they?'

Ermengarde ran after Miraval into the sodden streets. He was already on his horse so she grasped his leg and looked up to him, her face dripping wet. 'I'm so sorry about this, Raimon. Really, it's all my fault. I should have listened to Agnès. I just wanted to see what you were like together.'

'Are you satisfied now? Have you seen enough?'

'Look Raimon, we'd better let things cool down for a few weeks. If you're still in Toulouse, I'll get a message to you. Will you be with Raymonde?'

Miraval looked to Ahmed, who slowly shook his head. 'No, my lady. I shall stay closer to my friends here. Where are you now, Gérard?'

'We're staying at the Drum.'

'Are you serious?'

'Best place in town for people like us.'

'Did you hear that, Ermengarde?'

'Yes, Raimon. I won't keep you waiting long, I promise you.'

'Don't promise. Just come.'

Miraval loosened the reins and gave Drummer a nudge.

'Farewell, Ermengarde.'

And off they galloped, leaving Ermengarde standing in the rain, weeping and waving.

'Good Lord, Ahmed!' shouted Miraval through the rain as they sped through the empty streets of Toulouse. 'How did you find me?'

'Had a visit from Agnès de Montpellier. Said she thought you might need some support!'

'Clever Agnès. That's all I can say!'
'That's all you need to say, my lord! No regrets, all right?'
'Everyone's a loser, Ahmed!'
'Except me!' said Gérard. 'I enjoyed every minute!'

At the Drum

The Drum was everything a good tavern should be: a fair mix of people, a tolerant and open atmosphere, and a jovial and intelligent host; which is to forget the ale which should not be forgotten, for without the ale, brewed on the premises, the place could not exist. Miraval's minstrels were particularly enamoured of it.

'Suzanne, come 'ere!'

'Who's Suzanne?'

'A new slag upstairs. Terrific girl, down from Tours. She's done us a lot of good.'

The host, Thomas, about thirty-five years old displayed a discerning candour and a disarming sincerity. He had longish brown hair and wore a moustache. When he had had a bit too much to drink, he would lean on the bar, gaze directly into his interlocutor's eyes, widen his own and, more often than not, say something like: 'What's the problem? Too pissed to drink?' He had a great dislike of all pretensions and the Ferryman's Lady definitely came into that category. He loved his job and understood the true value of it.

'These are the people you should write about, seigneur de Miraval. Like that Arnaud bloke at the Ferryman's Lady, the ones who try to rip you off! It's all right. I'll get you the next one, Gérard. Your boss had a hard time, then?'

'Oh, the Saissac household.'

'Saissac? Arsehole. Rip-off merchant. I remember Olivier when he was training for his spurs. Shy boy. Little did we know! But that's it, isn't it? It's the times. Some years favour a shit like him. Next year it'll be someone else. No, you've got to stay true to yourself. It's the only way.'

'That's right, Thomas. That's right.'

Miraval soon began to feel at ease. He looked about him. The Drum was built around a space forty feet square. Three long trestle tables ran parallel to the bar. The second floor was accessible by means of a stone staircase, which took you to a wooden balcony that extended round all four sides. Three or four buxom whores leant on the balcony, picking up on odd bits of conversation going on beneath them.

'You've had no problem with the Juice – '

'Juice Tramps? None whatsoever. Salt of the earth. Isn't that true, Jeanne?'

Jeanne had been living with Thomas for some years and their relationship, though unblessed by the Church, was very much respected by the regulars of the Drum. She was small with short, curly brown hair and good brown eyes. She did not say very much but should she ever observe a patent injustice, whether in a game or in a dispute, she was very quick to speak of it. Embarrassment could not deter her, but she was often seen to be shaking afterwards. She was so shy. Thomas cared deeply for her. He had been married but his wife had gone off with a Provençal boat-builder who had made a fortune out of the Crusades selling sailing tackle for Christ.

'I like them,' she said.

'Yes, that's right. Always welcome here. Never cause any trouble – unlike some of the better dressed customers who come in. While it's on my mind, seigneur, may I ask you as to the health of the count?'

'I think he's fine.'

'The son used to come in here – well, still does but not so much. He's very popular. Charming fellow. Real class.'

'He's got his work cut out for him, that's for sure.'

'You mean the Pope?'

'What do you know?'

'Well, we hear things. We had some of the Papal Legates' servants in recently. It's clear that the count's son is none too popular in that quarter. Personally, I think that's why the old count keeps getting "ill". Keeps them on their toes. They're never quite sure who they're going to have to negotiate with next! So, listen ... No, come out the back a minute.'

Miraval walked through the bar to the cellar steps. 'Listen seigneur. I think that – well, since your minstrels came here, I've noticed some odd characters coming in, too – and even a couple of *good men*. Some of these types are here tonight. Look around you – and seigneur, watch what you say. I don't know what you've done but someone's on to you.'

'Thank you, Thomas.'

Miraval was no fool. He knew immediately that the problem must surely revolve around his visit to Raymonde. *Secrets.* He was glad he was not party to them. What had he to do with all of this? 'Love is all my Thought,' he had sung – so long ago. He felt a tremor of excitement as he realized how close he had come to the centre of a vortex, a political vortex whose reverberations extended into realms and associations with which he was altogether unfamiliar. It was also a little frightening, and he felt a paternal concern for his minstrels, especially Ahmed. Ahmed was acceptable in Languedoc but outside, what would become of him? But what was he thinking? This was crazy. Why should he ever have to travel further than the land he knew so well?

Days and nights piled up on one another as Miraval stayed put in the Drum. He was enjoying himself, slipping into a regular drinking pattern which dulled anxieties and gave him flashes of hope. He enjoyed the food too. The speciality of the tavern was a unique faggot dish: a combination of pork, liver, onions and lamb's brains, chopped fine, cooked in red wine and then dried out for a day. They were cooked to order and Miraval ordered them twice a day. The days were dreamy and interesting. Thomas had a fund of good stories and the ladies of the house were kind. Gérard, Ahmed, Berteaux and Jacques were well fixed up but Miraval slept alone, his mind a confusion of images and feelings. He took a special interest in something Jeanne told him one late evening in one of those moments of revelation that come when the ale is flowing nicely and the company is good, when the outside world is quiet and the soul is bright. 'There's nothing I haven't done. You name it, I've done it.'

Miraval could not help but make the comparison between her openness and evident understanding and the craziness of the women who attracted him and were attracted by him. A woman like Jeanne would never fall for him.

There were moments of great humour. Thomas and Jeanne had a perverted dog called Brun. He would follow the men to the privy outside and sniff their backsides with unaffected relish. Somehow, Brun encapsulated the spirit of the place.

Occasionally, Miraval would put pen to parchment and try to write. It was difficult at first. People would gather round to watch. Since none of them could read, Miraval wondered what it was they expected to achieve simply by watching. Then he recalled the Mass. People did not participate directly as the bread and wine were miraculously transubstantiated into the body and blood of Christ – but that did not stop devout Catholics from turning up on Sundays, just to catch a glimpse of a Mystery.

Miraval began to realize how hungry people are, how desperate people can be for a little holy magic and, one evening, he realized how desperate he was, too. Was it Azalaïs or was it Ermengarde? Or was it something else altogether? If he could be a voyeur to a Mystery, what Mystery would he choose? Perhaps there was no choice. He was grateful for the presence of his friends. They kept him down to earth. It was warm and cosy in the tavern. The sweeping sky was too much for him now.

At the bottom of my heart is born the flame
which leaves my lips when I sing,
and with it I set ablaze the ladies and lovers.
And my melodies are gentle and grave,
lovable, gracious and courteous;
and that is why one can learn them gladly.
So the one who is slow to love
on hearing my beautiful words
will hurry towards love.

At the Basilica of St Sernin

Late one night, a messenger arrived at the Drum.

'A message for the seigneur de Miraval.'

'Seigneur, a message for you!'

Miraval's head was cradled in his arms. 'What's that, Thomas?'

'A message.'

'Who is it from?' he asked wearily.

'Lady Ermengarde de Castres.'

Miraval got up quickly and strode over to the bar.

'It's private,' said the young messenger.

'All right, let's go out the back.'

'The lady requests that you see her at the Basilica of St Sernin at eight o'clock tomorrow morning. How do you reply?'

'Is that the entire message? There's no more?'

'That is all, seigneur.'

'Tell her that I shall be there.'

The great Basilica of St Sernin had stood in the north of the city for a little under a century. Surrounded by rough land rented out by the Cluniac Order of Benedict to the townsfolk, it rose to a height of over fifty feet by means of a stunning new four-tier octagonal tower, largely paid for by pilgrims visiting the tomb of St Saturninus. This latter saint had been dragged to martyrdom by a bull in Roman times and the city had never been allowed to forget it. The octagonal tower, whose every storey was pierced by slim Romanesque arches, was supported by a vast nave and apse three hundred and seventy-five feet long. The Basilica of St Sernin was undoubtedly the architectural pride of the city and the city burghers vied with each other for the chance of enriching her many glories.

Miraval arrived a quarter of an hour early, having walked the city's dawning streets in an attempt at collecting his scattered thoughts. Long pink streaks were beginning to vanish into a cool white sky as he arrived to see hints of sunlight catching the white cornices and window frames of the pink stone basilica. Miraval thought how gentle and peaceful it all looked.

The message which he had received had failed to indicate whether he might see Ermengarde inside or outside the basilica. He waited outside a while, his arms folded, gazing about him, watching the beams of sunlight penetrating the morning haze. The basilica bell began to chime the hour, whereupon Miraval began strolling around St Sernin, nodding to busy Benedictines, trying to appear as normal as he could while he checked behind every buttress in the hope of finding her there. He was beginning to feel quite agitated when at last he came to the great double-arched door, the Porte des Comtes, which gave entry to the south transept. Miraval entered the cold basilica. The door closed suddenly behind him. He turned round with a start and in the echo which thudded into quietness, his attention was gripped by a series of carvings made in the capitals above the door. The sharp gnashing teeth of an infernal beast were poised to devour the rich man Dives in Hell. In the sculptor's sealed vision, there could be no exit from the destiny of the pitiless rich. Lazarus, the poor man, looked down upon the former magnate with a look of benign expressionlessness. Miraval was again distracted by muffled footsteps, shuffling, voices. He moved from out of a shadow and looked to his right. There, beneath a great marble altar, stood a priest while kneeling before him were a man and a woman.

'Do you, Olivier, lord of Saissac, take this woman, Ermengarde – '

Miraval's eyes widened as he tried to maintain his footing. A hard kick in the crutch could not have been more painful than this blisteringly bitter sight. He wanted to speak but his voice had disappeared. Ermengarde's and Oliviers' hands were joined before the priest. Miraval began to step slowly backwards as all his nerves fused into the blank tranquillity of emotional inertia.

'Excuse me, sir, there is a marriage taking place. Pilgrims may enter just as soon as it's over.' The low whisper of a Benedictine canon broke the spell.

'I'm a dreamer' said the troubadour in a low, faraway monotone.

'Yes, well, perhaps if you dreamt outside for a while.'

Miraval looked into the well-fed face of the smiling canon, wondering what this man was doing in his mind, 'I'm sorry. They're not even Catholics, you know ... '

'They must be Catholics, sir, because this is a Catholic wedding. Do you know of another kind? Heretics don't marry in church, you know. They don't marry at all ... Are you a friend of the couple?'

'No. No, I don't think so. I was just ... looking.'

'Well, as I said, sir – ' Miraval started to flee the basilica. But where was the exit? Weird plastic light was breaking through stained glass as Miraval ran about in terror like a rat in a labyrinth. From pillar to pillar he ran, grabbing the smooth surfaces, desperate for a hold, while all the time above him, beside him, inside him and around him whirled the images of Christ in Majesty, seraphim, saints, bishops and cherubim, sinners and angels, demons and virgins: all the legions of the damned and the damnable glared down from the capitals, cornices, windows and walls! A booming voice echoed down the nave from the chancel:

'Who in Heaven's name is that? Who is it?'

Miraval was completely confused, his stomach was churning, his mouth agape, his hands were feeling maniacally for a door. Suddenly he felt the vicious grip of two large hands digging into his shoulders, squeezing into his neck.

'I might have known it would be you! You'll pay for this, Miraval! Ruin this holy day, will you! I'll see that you never sing again as long as you live! Now get out, you damned fool!'

'Please seigneur de Saissac!' cried the priest.

'You get out, too, priest – out of my way! Ermengarde! Is this your doing?'

While Miraval was manhandled out of the basilica, Ermengarde sobbed loudly: 'Oh no! No! It wasn't me! Really it wasn't! It wasn't me! Please Olivier, please leave him alone! Olivier!!' she screamed.

The next thing Miraval knew he was plunged head-first into a muddy puddle outside, feeling Olivier's foot on the back of his neck, his face being forced into the foul water.

'Now try singing, troubadour!'

Ermengarde was pulling at Saissac's white shirtsleeves. 'Please Olivier! Leave him be! We're married now! It's all over!'

Ermengarde was on her knees tugging at her husband's leg, 'Oh please let him alone ... you'll kill him! Stop it! Stop it!'

Miraval felt the pressure of the boot lessen. He was gasping for air, unable to move.

'All right, Ermengarde. You defend him. He has ruined our wedding day – but all right, whatever you desire, wife! But some day, I shall get what I desire and no one will stop me! Come on, let's be gone from this damn place!'

Miraval spluttered the dirty water from out of his mouth

and nostrils, unable to think of anything. Two canons came to his aid.

'Oh sir, sir, we are so sorry for this. Come sir, please rise.' Then one spoke to his colleague: 'Are there any pilgrims waiting?'

'No, it's all right. It's still clear.'

'Thank Heaven for that!'

They helped Miraval on to his feet and walked him to the rue de Taur at the foot of the castle. 'Farewell, sir, and good luck.'

'Yes, thank you. May God go with you.'

'And you, sir. Good day.'

With that, the canons returned to the basilica in order to prepare candles for the day's intake of pilgrims while Miraval, heavy-footed and sore, made his way back to the Drum, wiping the mud from out of his hair and clothes and skin as he did so. A gang of children followed him, giggling and shouting: 'Hey, sir – got any money?'

Back at the Drum

'You!'

'Me, seigneur?'

'Yes, you. What's your name?'

'Garsende, seigneur Miraval.'

'Let's go – and please, bring the wine.'

'Yes, seigneur.'

Miraval took the whore's arm and pulled her upstairs. Garsende gave a faint smile to Thomas, who raised his eyebrows and looked over to Ahmed. Ahmed closed his eyes, inhaled deeply and started tapping his fingers on the table.

'Ale on the house, Ahmed.'

'No, thank you Thomas. We've had enough.'

'You had too much?'

'Not too much.'

'Then how do you know what is enough? Come on, let's all have a drink!'

Two *perfecti* got up from the table and left. An ill-looking Catalan in a brown tunic covered his mouth and started slowly fingering the rim of his tankard. Brun looked mournfully up at Thomas and walked outside just as Berteaux burst in.

'Hey, lads, it's great outside – the Count of Foix has just arrived with his sister, Esclarmonde! There's fifty knights just crossed the river by ferry. Incredible sight! Come on – we can't miss this. What a sight!'

'No, thanks, Berteaux,' said Gérard. 'We're not in the mood.'

'All right,' said Berteaux, somewhat crestfallen. 'Where's Jacques?'

'He's still asleep.'

'I'll ask him, then.'

'I shouldn't go upstairs, Berteaux,' said Ahmed.

'Why's that? . . . Look, what's the matter with you people? It's an absolutely fantastic day out there and everyone's so miserable. Come out, enjoy yourselves!'

'Berteaux.'

'Yes?'

'He's back.'

'Who? – Oh, the boss. Where is he then?'

Ahmed and Gérard pointed upwards.

'Ah . . . well . . . well I'll see you all later then. *Adios*!'

The old Catalan got up, nodded to Thomas and followed Berteaux out of the tavern.

'That Catalan,' whispered Thomas to the two minstrels, 'I'm sure he's spying. He's watching the seigneur. He has a friend who comes in sometimes. But they're never together long. It's like they're on some sort of shift. I'm sure he knows I'm on to him.'

'Who'd spy on us?' enquired Gérard, 'and why follow Berteaux out like that?'

'I don't know. But either he or his mate will be back soon. You can guarantee it.'

'Who's spying?!' It was Miraval from the balcony, 'Spies! You're all spies! Where's Suzanne?'

'She's out shopping, seigneur.'

'Tell her to come and join me and Garsende when she comes in. We're not worried about spies. We're going to have a good time. I tell you, Ahmed, these ladies really understand what love is all about! They're good girls. No lies. No lies. No games. They don't play games, do they, Gérard?'

'No, my lord. Straight as a string on my guitar.'

'Yes – and good to strum and pluck.'

'They make fine music, my lord.'

'For sure. Get Suzanne up here as soon as she's back. I'm going to – ' he belched, 'pardon me, *they* can sing for a change. I shall beat the drum – know what I mean, Ahmed?'

'No, my lord.'

Miraval closed his eyes, took a swig from a bottle of wine and looked at his friend. 'Well, Ahmed, it's about time you learned! Now just get Suzanne and I'll be satisfied. I don't want to hear any more arguments. Everything's simple. Just enjoy yourselves. Drinks on the house, Thomas!'

'Very well, seigneur.'

'*Very well, seigneur*. Very well. I'm very well, thank you. Well, carry on, don't let an old troubadour stop you.'

Miraval withdrew again into a chamber and banged the door closed. Thomas blew the hair from off his forehead. 'Is the seigneur often like this?'

'Never. I've never seen him like this. Something's badly wrong.'

'Well, I guess we'll all find out soon enough. Something will break. Poor bastard's being torn to pieces – and I don't mean Garsende! She's a gentle girl. Just seventeen – or looks seventeen, anyhow. She'll look after him. Probably wants some feminine sympathy. Doesn't look like he's been getting any in the quarters he's been mixing in.'

'Strange, isn't it?' said Ahmed.

'What's that?'

'Well, he'll probably get more understanding from the house whores than from all the landed ladies put together. But he would never write a song about one.'

'That's his problem, though, isn't it? I mean that he's got this lofty idea of women and it's all wrapped up with good manners and what they call "breeding". My girls charge only a few *écus* for their services. Some of these "ladies", I'll bet, will make him pay for the rest of his life! I know that some of these noble women really deserve the title. That Esclarmonde who's just ridden in with her brother. She's a lady. She doesn't toy with a man's feelings.'

'Yeah,' interjected Gérard. 'But she doesn't toy with any part of a man. She's a Cathar. She wouldn't fuck even if you threatened to burn her.'

'Pity she didn't meet your boss, then! Sounds like the kind of woman who wouldn't disappoint him.'

'But he's learning, isn't he?' said Ahmed. 'It takes time, doesn't it?'

'I guess so' said Thomas, 'but you can never learn enough about women. Jeanne is still a mystery to me – and she never even tries.'

'It's odd, though' said Ahmed, 'that whenever you talk about women, you never reach any kind of conclusion. We love them, fuck them, please them, beat them, smile and shout and all the time we hardly know who we're talking to.'

'Things used to be simpler,' said Gérard.

'Maybe, Gérard – but then it was more cruel, too.'

'Ahmed, you're a fool. I know a lot of women who like a bit of the rough stuff – makes 'em feel, I don't know, a bit contented. Know who's in control. Problem with these women the boss meets is they've got too much power. They don't know what to do with it. They have to employ men to do their fighting for them. Until they can do it for themselves, they'll be unhappy. Since there's no chance of that, it's easier to pick on troubadours and poets who get on their knees before them as if they were peasants. They're easy game.'

'What of *Fine Love*, Gérard? Don't the women suffer, too?'

Gérard grunted, 'Another one, please, Thomas.'

'Just coming up. Ahmed?'

'Yes. Why not? I've seen enough glittering knights. Why don't we play some music, Gérard?'

'Let's wait for Jacques.'

'Let's wait forever, then!'

Meanwhile ...

The Light Shines in the Darkness

The torches were lit in a cellar at Cabaretz. Jordan and his brother, Peire Roger, the seigneur of Cabaretz, were there.

Loba de Pénnautier, Jordan's wife, stood at the back with Bernart, Azalaïs's husband. The *Consolamentum* would be administered by Bernard Raimundi, the Cathar bishop of Toulouse, and his *filius major*, Guilhabert de Castres.

Azalaïs entered the cellar. Never before had her mind been so concentrated upon the object of her life. The weeks of preparation, deep prayer, study and consultation with the *perfecti* combined in her eyes as they beheld a single Light, a light neither present in the cellar nor absent from the assembled company. That Azalaïs de Boissézon, the flighty and the flirt, should have come to *this* was simply astonishing to all those who knew her. Her meeting with Raimon de Miraval had changed everything – but *he* did not know it. Had he done so, he might have found the courage to separate himself from the crucible of lust into which he had fallen. *God moves in mysterious ways* – but rarely had a conversion been so sudden or so unexpected! Azalaïs stood before the wisdom of the old bishop and the great spiritual and physical strength of Guilhabert. The rolling folds of the white cotton smock which Azalaïs wore over a black gown curled up like flames in the still torchlight, giving emphasis to her clear facial lines, now honed into sharpness by a week of fasting. Bernard Raimundi, dressed, like all the *perfecti*, in a black woollen cassock, held the gospels to his chest and turned to the small assembly, commencing that ceremony whereby the living soul of Azalaïs would be reunited with the immortal, divine Spirit:

'Brothers and sisters, if I have done or said anything against God or my salvation, pray that He will forgive me.'

Guilhabert spoke: 'May the holy Father, the just, true and merciful One, who has the power in heaven and on earth to remit sins, remit and forgive all your sins in this world.'

'Amen,' said Bernard and, continuing, 'Let it be done to us, Lord, according to your word.'

The assembly spoke in unison: 'Bless us, have mercy on us.'

Azalaïs was then handed the gospels, whereupon she knelt with her head facing the hard stone floor.

Bernard questioned her: 'Azalaïs, have you the will to receive the spiritual baptism of Jesus Christ and the forgiveness of your sins, thanks to the intercession of good Christians, and the laying on of hands, and to keep it throughout your life with chastity, truth and humility?'

'Yes, I have the will to do so. Pray that God Himself will give me His strength.'

'May God give you the grace, the consolation, for His honour and your salvation.'

Guilhabert now spoke: 'Azalaïs, you want to receive spiritual baptism, by which in God's Church, the Holy Spirit is given to us, with the holy prayer and the laying on of the hands of the *good men*, this holy baptism is the spiritual baptism of Jesus Christ; and the baptism of the Holy Spirit as John the Baptist said, in Matthew's gospel: "For I baptize you in water, but the One coming after me is more powerful than I, and He will baptize you with the Holy Spirit and with fire." This holy baptism, through which the Holy Spirit is given, the Church of God has maintained from the apostles until now; it has come down from one *good man* to another, to us here, and the Church of God will maintain it to the end of the world.'

Guilhabert took the gospels from Azalaïs and Bernard resumed: 'Azalaïs, do you have the will to receive this holy baptism of Jesus Christ and to keep it all your life, with a purity of heart and mind, and not to fail in this commitment for whatsoever motive?'

'Yes, I have the will to do so. Pray to the good Lord, that He may give me His grace.' She rose from her knees and curtseyed three times before the *perfecti*.

'May the Lord, the true God, give you the grace to receive this gift for His honour and your salvation.'

Bernard Raimundi turned again to the assembly. '*Parcite nobis*. Good Christians, we ask you, for the love of God, to grant to our friend here present this good which God has given you.'

Azalaïs knelt again, saying, '*Parcite nobis* – for all the sins I have ever committed in word, thought or action. I ask God's forgivenness and yours also.'

'By God, by us and by the Church, may they be forgiven you. We pray to God for you. Receive the consolation.'

Azalaïs felt the weight of the gospels as the book was placed upon her head and the weight of her commitment as the *perfecti* laid their hands upon it. But with the gentle laying on of hands, the sensation of weight simply disappeared and her spirit rose in a timeless moment to greet the unknown and unexpected God. The cellar was so peaceful that she could hear music, an inner music which rained upon her, upholding her and releasing her. She heard, for the first time in her life, the sweet echo of that divine gift which Raimon de Miraval had heard since childhood and to which only now had his ears become deaf.

From some distant and yet absolutely intimate place came the voice of Bernard Raimundi, speaking words whose plainness contained those infinite but elusive possibilities of an eternal life; absolutely unconditioned by Time and Space:

'*Benedicite, parcite nobis*. We adore Father, Son and Holy Spirit. Holy Father, welcome your servant into your justice and put your grace and Holy Spirit upon her.'

Bernard and Guilhabert intoned together, 'Our Father in heaven. May your name be hallowed, may your Kingdom come and your Will be done on earth as in heaven. Give us this day our supersubstantial bread, and forgive us our sins, as we forgive those who sin against us. And lead us not into temptation but deliver us from evil. For the Kingdom, Power and Glory are yours forever and ever. Amen.'

The gospels were then removed from her head and, holding them before him, Bernard began the following recitation:

'In the beginning was the Word, and the Word was with God, and the Word was God. He was with God in the beginning. All things were made by Him; and without Him was nothing made that was made. In Him was life; and the life was men's light. And the light shines in the darkness.'

Azalaïs rose to her feet and Guilhabert put a dark cloak over her shoulders, signifying that she was now a 'clothed' or full Cathar, one supremely significant step beyond the believers and sympathizers who made up most of the assembly. She then received the gospel book from the large hands of Guilhabert de Castres and having kissed the book moved to face the assembly. The assembly bowed three times and one by one stepped forward to Azalaïs and kissed her on both cheeks.

This final sequence was especially hard for Loba and for Bernart, but they did it nonetheless. It was unheard of for a consoled Cathar, a *parfait* or *parfaite* to retract his or her *Consolamentum*. Azalaïs was now bound to the elect of the Cathar Church and would depart not with her husband to Lombers but to the mountains of the Ariège with Guilhabert de Castres and Bernard Raimundi.

The torches were left to burn out in the cellar.

And the Darkness Did Not Comprehend It

Miraval was sitting with his minstrels in the Drum.

'So it's back to Miraval, then?'

'Looks like it, Gérard. I can't see much profit in staying on here any longer.'

'We could give another concert,' offered Ahmed, hopefully.

'Raymonde is very busy at the moment. Anyhow, it really doesn't feel *right* any more. No, I think we've had our fill. It's back to Miraval and start again.'

'Start what again?' asked Berteaux.

'Yes, Berteaux's right for once. We don't need to start again. We just go on. Getting better all the time.'

'Maybe, Gérard. But, I don't know, I feel we ought to change some things. I don't know what yet. We'll work on it.'

'My lord . . . '

'Yes, Ahmed.'

'Couldn't we play here tonight?'

Miraval found the suggestion interesting. He thought of the miller he had met in the Ferryman's Lady. He thought of what he had said about only singing at court and at home. 'Ahmed, you know that might just be the best way of our going out. Thomas, do you mind?'

'*Mind*? Certainly not, seigneur. I couldn't think of anything better.'

'That's it, then. We'll play for the ladies upstairs and Ahmed, you – '

'My lord?'

'If it is not too inconvenient, would you mind going round to the Ferryman's Lady and asking the millers there if they'd like to come to a free concert in their honour? Tell them nine o'clock.'

Ahmed, thrilled at the idea, jumped off his stool and ran out of the Drum into the streets of Toulouse.

'Now, Gérard, Berteaux – fetch Jacques from upstairs and we'll tune up and arrange a stage. What about a stage, Thomas?'

'No problem, seigneur. Take the trestle tables and put them alongside one another. We'll take the old tapestry from upstairs and lay it over. The punters can sit on the floor for this one! Garsende! Get the tapestry from off the wall and bring it downstairs! We've got something special happening tonight.'

'Oh, what's that, then?'

'The seigneur is singing for you.'

'For me? Fuckin' 'ell! What have I done to deserve it?'

'Well, I don't know, Garsende! Can't you guess?'

'Guessing's for scholars, Thomas. I'm just a slag.'

'Not to us you're not – now get on with it!'

Miraval and his friends were just completing the stage when the ripening bonhomie was rudely shattered by an unholy noise.

'MIRAVAL! Time for you and the others to pay a debt.'

Olivier de Saissac had arrived in full body-mail and helmet, accompanied by four armed retainers. He looked to them, 'All right men, I'll take care of the troubadour first, then you deal with those damn musicians!'

'Perhaps, Olivier, you have observed that I am not armed.'

'You!' he called to a retainer, 'Give the troubadour your sword – he won't have it for very long.' The retainer unsheathed his sword and threw it with a clang at Miraval's feet.

'And if I refrain from taking it up?'

'No more than I'd expect from a coward. I'll kill you anyway. What's one dead troubadour?'

'You leave me no choice, Olivier.' Miraval picked up the sword. Saissac advanced toward him, blade in hand. He took a swipe at the troubadour. Miraval ducked and began edging his way backwards around the floor in the direction of the exit.

'No exit, troubadour. We're not in the basilica now!'

Saissac took another sweep, splitting the air as he did so. Miraval met the blade with his own, his hands gripping the sword for dear life. Sparks flew. Thomas broke a nail on the bar. Miraval, no match for Saissac in swordplay, knew that his only chance of survival was to get out and fetch help from the castle. He tried a desperate gambit. Screaming as loudly as he could, he ran straight at Saissac, using his sword as a body shield, and managed to push Olivier over with a pommel to the gut. The minstrels made a start but their way was blocked by the retainers, itching for a kill. This movement left the entrance clear for a second and Miraval ran to it, opened it and jumped outside. He looked to his left and felt a finger on his right shoulder. He started round to see a young man who grinned and then spoke in an unfamiliar Gascon accent: 'Are you looking for some help, sir?'

'I might be – '

'Pleasure. You're not interested in music, are you? All right, we'll waste no time. All right lads!'

About eight men piled into the Drum, dressed in black leather tabards and breeches, adorned with little embroidered patches and steel studs. They wore daggers and carried clubs. Hot on their heels came the miller whom Miraval had met at the Ferryman's Lady, closely followed by his friends. Miraval was stunned. 'That must be – '

'That's right, sir. The *Juice Tramps*. And I'm Fabien. Good to see you again, seigneur – care to join us?'

'Yes, of course.'

Miraval followed Fabien and three other millers back into the *Drum*. The place was in absolute uproar. The *Juice Tramps* were making short work of Saissac's retainers, clubbing their kneecaps and generally sticking the boot in, their arms linked about the shoulders in a crazily violent dance. The millers were helping Gérard, Berteaux and Ahmed, who were using a fifteen-foot bench to pin Olivier de Saissac to a wall. Jacques lay unconscious on the floor after having taken a blow from Saissac. Olivier's face was a positive delta of exposed veins. One of the *Tramps* grabbed a jug and threw it at Saissac. The jug smashed into pieces just inches from the knight's head. The knight pushed the combined weight of the millers and of the minstrels back in an agonized movement of blind rage, reaching to the ground to pick up his sword as he did so. He began swinging it about in great windy cuts to the air. 'Watch out!' One of the *Tramps* went straight for Saissac. The knight lunged forwards and cut the *Tramp* across the neck. Blood started spurting out from under his rippling jaw. 'Christ!' cried Fabien. The other *Tramps*, putting the finishing touches to the retainers' demise, looked round: 'Get the bastard!'

'Just try it!' Saissac was insanely slashing the space before him. Miraval realized he was still carrying a sword. Now was the time to use it. 'Olivier, the argument's between us.'

'Not any more it isn't!' shouted one of the *Tramps*. Olivier's eyes were darting about from left to right and back again. 'Miraval! Come for me! Show me, Miraval! Show me now! Come for me! Coward! Woman's man!'

A club came flying through the air. 'Get down Miraval!' It collided with Saissac's skull, which cracked as the club fell to the floor. Olivier moaned and followed the club to the floor. Miraval moved forward to seize Olivier's sword.

As he did so, the knight began swinging his blade upwards towards Miraval's unprotected crotch. The troubadour hopped sideways and plunged his sword into Olivier's kidneys. 'Aaaaaaagh!' The scream became a submissive gurgle and Olivier dropped his sword. The millers jumped on top of the knight and began thumping and kicking him. One of the *Juice Tramps* joined in, reached for his dagger and slit Olivier de Saissac's throat. He then ran out into the street, leaving Saissac to slump backwards and die.

The tavern went quiet. Two of the retainers were dead, one was unconscious and the other was groaning. Thomas helped the wounded *Tramp* onto the stage.

'Garsende! Suzanne!'

Garsende ran downstairs. 'Is it all over?'

'Just get some sheets and some water – bring a blanket to throw over the dead. Shit! Seigneur, there'll be hell to pay for this. You *Tramps* had better go. The blame's bound to fall on you.'

'Not this time,' said Miraval. 'This is my fight and I take responsibility.'

'Don't look too solemn, seigneur.' Miraval turned to see the sweaty face of the young *Tramp* he had met outside. 'My name's Brian.'

'*Brian*?'

'Parents from Brittany. You should be pleased. You've just seen off one of the biggest bastards Toulouse has ever seen.'

'Maybe, Brian, but – '

'You can stay with us, seigneur, if you'd like to lie low for a while.'

'Brian, I hope we meet again. But I must stay. I'll deal with all this. Thomas is right. You'd better go – and Fabien, you'd better go too.'

'Question is,' said Gérard, 'who killed Saissac?'

'Who cares? He came to kill. He got his own. Seigneur de Miraval, if ever you need us again, put the word out to Fabien here. He'll know where we are.'

'Yes, Brian. Now do go. But – wait a second, Gérard, Berteaux, Ahmed – what do you want to do?'

Gérard looked to Ahmed, who spoke for the others, including the unconscious Jacques. 'I think, my lord, that we had better go too – with the *Tramps* for a while. The count's son will protect you – but us? Call us when it's all blown over.'

'I think that's wise, Ahmed. You'll have to carry poor old Jacques here. May God go with you all.'

'Don't mention it' said Brian,' grinning broadly. 'We'll meet again some day – I just know it. This was no accident. Or else everything is – Adieu!'

Into the Labyrinth

'Dear, oh dear, Raimon. What *are* we going to do?'

Raymonde was pacing up and down his sunny apartment while Miraval sat by a slit window, looking down over the rose garden.

'You have put me in a very *tender* position, Raimon. *Very* tender. Saissac's family are demanding recompense from my father. Father has asked me to deal with the problem – so you have some hope. You're a great man, Raimon, and you deserve it. I know what these shits are trying to do to you. But there are difficulties.'

'What difficulties, Raymonde? We are innocent.'

'That's a big word, Raimon. We like to apply it to children. But children we definitely are not. You see, Raimon, the trouble is that your witnesses do not agree with the witness of Saissac's retainers – those two who are still alive, that is. They are saying that you were already with those weird chaps – the er . . . '

'*Juice Tramps.*'

'Yes, *Juice Tramps*. Where *do* you find your friends? If only you'd stayed here, this would never have happened. No matter, I know you're an honest man. Not innocent, Raimon, but honest.' Miraval nodded. 'Yes, well they say that you were already with them when the late Olivier de Saissac entered the tavern. They say that Olivier had heard from his wife – *poor* Ermengarde! – that you had cooked up a plot to "do him over" – charming expression! – in some kind of sentimental effort in support of the millers of Toulouse. They say that Olivier had come out to deal with you personally, and not by force of arms.'

'Why, then, bring the soldiers?'

'Oh, of course that was in case you should set your friends on to him. Look, Raimon, what I truly fail to see is why you found yourself feuding with Saissac in the first place. I mean, we could all see that you were in love – or something – with Ermengarde.'

'I did not know that she was engaged to the man.'

'Yes – that surprised us all. But life is so full of surprises like that, isn't it? It's difficult to keep up with them all. *Who'd have thought it*? How many times have we all said this?'

'Raymonde, do you believe the retainers' testimony?'

'Of course not, Raimon. It is quite obvious that they are being put up to it by Saissac's family – a very nasty bunch indeed! But it doesn't look good, does it? Even your jolly minstrels have fled the city.'

'On my instructions.'

'There you are, you see? Makes it look even worse, doesn't it?'

Miraval was thinking back to the message he had received begging his presence at the basilica of St Sernin. What if Ermengarde had not sent it? What if he had misread the whole situation? Who else could have sent the message – and why? Miraval looked up to Raymonde who gave him a smile, a smile of pity. Raymonde shook his head slowly. 'Raimon, the family want blood. In particular, *yours*. Pardon me for being so blunt but that's how it is. I must ask you, Raimon, who killed Olivier de Saissac? Was it you?'

'I certainly helped. There really was no choice. It all happened so terribly quickly – '

'These things often do.'

'The man was quite insane.'

'Apparently the poor man's throat was cut. That doesn't sound like you.'

'No, that wasn't me. The fellow who did that fled the tavern before the fight was over.'

'Would you recognize him again?'

'That's difficult. They all look pretty much the same to me.'

'Somebody's got to pay the price, Raimon.'

'I shall stand as a witness, Raymonde.'

'Most noble, Raimon – and no less than I should expect. But what of the other witnesses?'

'I shall call them back to the city.'

'And cause a riot? The millers are getting very testy about this matter. We can't start slaughtering the millers – the whole economy will go up the spout.'

'I see what you mean by "*tender*" now.'

'I'm glad you do, Raimon. It *is* all very tender.'

'Like a woman?'

'Quite, Raimon. Couldn't have put it better myself! We had hoped, both of us, that *Fine Love* would civilize us all and lead us to peace and understanding. Trouble is, Raimon, that while we ... cuddle each other, what are the villains like Olivier de Saissac doing? You, as a troubadour, are not compelled to cope with this dilemma. That unhappy burden falls on my shoulders.'

Raymonde left Miraval to feel this 'unhappy burden' for himself for a few minutes before continuing, 'Now, Raimon, you've got to help me. Not only for your own sake – there's your friends to think about now.'

'Yes, that's true.'

'I think,' said Raymonde as he fingered the window ledge, looked down below, and, blinking, gave a false shudder, 'I think that you had better disappear.'

'Disappear?'

'On an affair of state, Raimon. Secret mission, that sort of thing.'

'Oh ... I see.'

'Well, you haven't really got much choice now, have you?'

'But how can I disappear? Saissac's family will be out looking for me.'

'Then they must find you, Raimon.'

'Find me? I thought – '

'Dead. They must find you dead.' Miraval shuddered. 'Not you, of course. Headless corpse on a river bank, your clothing, that sort of thing.'

'No, Raymonde. It can't work. I'd never be able to return to Miraval – '

'Price of fame, Raimon – '

'I can't live the rest of my life in secret. It just won't work.'

'Hmmmm ... it might prove inconvenient I suppose.' He paused, glancing at Miraval's eyes as he did so. 'I suppose we could put those *Tramp* people on trial along with a brace of millers. Cause a stink, though – but we might get away with it.'

'Not the *Juice Tramps* again – they get blamed for everything!'

'Not surprising, is it, if you go around cutting people's throats?'

Miraval felt himself being pushed into a corner with every possible exit being systematically closed to him.

'It's a pity you never did become a priest. You could have appealed to the Pope!'

'Very funny, Raymonde.'

'I'm sorry, my friend, but if you can't help me – what can I say?'

Miraval closed his eyes and thought for a moment.

'How could I help you, Raymonde?'

'Do you remember our little conversation on the battlements some time ago?'

'I can't say that I recall every word. But I got the gist.'

'Good. That's enough for starters. Raimon, I want you, if you would, to go down and have a little walk in the rose garden for an hour. Clear your thoughts – then come back and see me. And then, I'll make everything clear to you from my end.' Raymonde patted Miraval on the back and took his hand to help him from off his seat. 'We're getting there, Raimon! I do believe we're going to find a way out of this mess. See you in an hour. And do enjoy the roses! The rain's done them a world of good. I do believe they've never looked or smelt lovelier!'

Miraval, disturbed and dejected, left Raymonde's apartment. The count's son sat down by the window, stroking his beard with his thumb, waiting for a knock at the door.

'Come in, sergeant!'

'My lord. We have him.'

'You've found the guilty *Tramp*?'

'We have him in the dungeon. We caught him at the ferry. His friends had taken the Bourdeaux road.'

'Don't bother about them. Let them go. This is the man we want. How are the two retainers doing sergeant?'

'Settling in nicely, my lord.'

'Have they found the courage to retract their false witness?'

'Very close to it, my lord.'

'It's just as well they were covered in bruises when they came to us, isn't it?'

'Yes, my lord. The lads have done a really good job.'

'And sergeant, have these two unfortunates recognized the *Tramp* as the killer?'

'Their memory is improving, my lord.'

'I'm *so* glad sergeant. I'm so glad. When they have sufficiently recovered their wits, send a message out to their employers, saying that the count urgently requests the Saissac family – senior members only of course – to consult with him in Toulouse. And sergeant – '

'My lord?'

'If you wish to advance in my service, you will maintain absolute secrecy in this matter. Understood?'

'Fully understood, my lord.'

'Very good. Now run along – there's some land deeds I must examine. Can't have a worthy family like the Saissacs going off without a sign of our pleasure and trust in them, can we?'

A rose can mean many things. To look at the flower is to forget the thorns; but to look at the thorns and then to the fruit of the thorns is to obtain wisdom – and Miraval was getting wise. Was he not impaled upon the thorns of Love? He looked deeply through the wet red rose and saw that all was not lost. The thorns, for all their outward appearance seemed inward-looking, insecure; but the flower was like the unexpected opening of a lady's lips, kissed by the sun – so beautiful and so secret. Miraval knew that he would accept whatever Raymonde was offering. There was nothing else left to do. The thorns had led him on.

'Very well, Raymonde. I'll do it. Whatever it is.'

'You're a great man, Raimon. I knew I could rely on you. What I am about to tell you must go no further. Those who already know the secret will make it clear to you without your asking. Now, do sit down and please try to concentrate. If you remember our last conversation on this matter, you will recall how that in order to avoid participation in a crusade against the Almohads, we need to take some action on the home front.'

'Against the Cathars?'

'It must certainly *look* that way, Raimon. But apart from the odd burning, we have another card up our sleeves.'

'Which is?'

'This may seem quite fantastic to you, Raimon, and yet, as I think about it, you of all people should accept the truth of the story. I have told you of the Papal Legate Gregorio's mission to Castile?'

'Yes, indeed.'

'Before he crossed the Pyrenees, he met with my father and me to discuss the situation and how we might be of help. Apart from the usual stuff about the Pope being *so* grievously disappointed in us and how we should repent of our peaceful ways and go forth to war, he said there was yet a *singular* act which would cost us little but would earn us the favour and understanding of Pope Celestine in "these times of difficulty" – an act which would indicate to Holy Church where our Catholic hearts really lay. My father expressed his willingness to comply and, knowing me well, thought that such an act might even earn for me *his* favour. If I could please him in this matter, he could please the Pope and the Pope would be pleased in us both.'

'It all sounds too good to be true. What is this singular act?'

'Strange, Raimon. It seems such a small thing to ask. Even . . . painless.'

'Well, what is it, then?'

'Books.'

'Books?' Miraval felt somewhat let down. He had expected a secret of more arresting dimensions.

'Yes, books. Not your average manuscripts, mind. These

books are special. I shall be as brief as I can. Holy Church has received intelligence regarding the existence, in Languedoc, of a set of ancient manuscripts containing words of the Lord Christ and whose message – how shall I put it? – whose message fails to support the claims of the Roman Church to be the One True Church. Interesting, no?'

'Interesting? It's unbelievable! Absurd!'

'Why, Raimon? Why absurd?'

'Well, the books of the Bible ... I've read them – you've read them – the Cathars have read them ... all heresies are based on them and all Church teaching is based on them.'

'So?'

'Well, take the Cathars, for example. They find enough to deny Rome in the gospels. I can't see how the existence of false books makes any difference.'

'How do we know these books are false, Raimon? Anyhow, you're missing the point.'

'And what's that?'

'The point is *doubt*. Sow doubt in a great enemy and the "great enemy" soon becomes so many weak units. Doubt could crack the universe. I've heard it said and I believe it.'

'So why aren't these texts being used already by the heretics?'

'All sorts of reasons, Raimon. For a start, very few people can read. Of those that can read, they can only read Occitan, Latin or French. The books in question are, I believe, written in an unknown language.'

'Well, what use are they, then? How does anyone know what's in them?'

'To be frank, my dear, I don't know. But I'm pretty keen to find out! And so is the Pope. I suppose it is a petty matter in many respects but in the "wrong" hands and used judiciously and politically, this material could be the cause of the most extreme embarrassment to the Church. What, for instance, do you think would happen if the Almohads or Saladin got hold of them?'

'But *they* deny the Christian scriptures anyway. They don't ask for further proof that we're all infidels.'

'I don't think you understand this business at all, my dear Raimon.'

'What's in the books that's so amazing? I need *some* clue.'

'I've already tried to explain that we don't really know.'

'So what am I supposed to do about it?'

'The Papal Legate has requested that we obtain these books and surrender them to the bishop of Toulouse for public burning.'

'Why public?'

'So that if anyone should afterwards produce copies, the authorities can say that they must be wicked forgeries, and that "all the world" has seen them properly, and with ceremony, destroyed. Naturally, the public will only ever hear that these wicked books are used by the heretics to imperil their souls, that they are inspired by the Devil and so on. The plan is simply to sow doubt in the minds of those attracted to the Cathar faith, to discredit their leaders as being liars and perverters of the true gospel and to re-establish the Roman Church in Languedoc as the proper body, commissioned by Christ, to interpret the Gospel. It's a good plan and, as I said, used at precisely the right time, could be most effective. In short, its aim is to turn doubt upon the doubters.'

'It all sounds quite mad to me.'

'It is mad, Raimon. They're all bloody mad!'

Miraval reflected for a few minutes. 'You know Raymonde, it's strange. I don't know about you, but when I was a student here I often wondered what had happened to all the other books written about Christ referred to in Luke's gospel.'

'Well, I don't know about all that, Raimon, but I do share some of your fascination. If there is any truth in all this, I'm quite determined that the Church doesn't snuff it out. The Cathars have made many things clear to me and though I will never commit myself to their teaching, I do have a kind of concern that the county should inherit and pass on all that is good, interesting and true. Do you understand me?'

'Yes, I do. I know exactly what you mean. Even hearing about these books sends a shiver up my spine. But what can I do? I don't want to help the Cathars – they've got enough supporters, many not entirely unknown to us. I should prefer to stay on the right side of the Christ my mother taught me about. It's hard enough trying to understand *Fine Love* – never mind the universe!'

'That is well understood, Raimon. Look, it's quite clear that you have come to the end of one tether of your life and that you need a new beginning. It is also clear that you've got to get out of Toulouse. All I ask is that you be a courier of sorts – a man I can trust.'

Miraval thought for a moment. 'I think they're on to me.'

'Who?'

'When I was at the Drum, Thomas – he's the publican – said he was sure I was being spied upon.'

'Oh damn! Then there's really no time to lose. Listen to me now and please, Raimon, listen carefully. I want you to go back to Cabaretz. You will meet a man called Mercier.'

'Raimond Mercier?'

'Yes. How did you know?'

'Incredible, isn't it? We met him at Crozilat. He came out of the woods – or out of the blue! Amazing!'

'These Cathars aren't stupid, you know. You'll come to see that – in time. So you'll know Mercier when you meet him. That's good. He will put you in touch with the books. I can't tell you now where they are. I want you to ensure that these books are taken to a place where they can be copied – forged if you like. I shall require two copies. I shall then stage a raid, obtain the forgeries and then hand over one set to the Church. This will please me, my father, the Church and – '

'What of the original books?'

'I want them translated – don't ask me how – that's your job, and then I want them out of the country completely, back where they came from, wherever that is.'

'Sounds easy enough.'

'Hmm . . . it's up to you to make it work, Raimon. Are you up to it?'

'Yes, I am. But what of Ahmed and the others?'

'You will have to live without them for a while. I'm sorry, but that's how it is. I shall put about the story that you've gone to join them, precise whereabouts unknown. I suggest you leave for Cabaretz at first light tomorrow. I dare not risk disclosure of any part of this plan to anyone else, so you must travel alone. And remember, Raimon, you owe me no formal allegiance in this matter – you go as a trusted friend and I rely on you as a friend.'

'I am your friend, Raymonde. You can count on me.'

'Then I think we must now bid one another farewell. We must not meet again until the affair is over. Raimond Mercier will be the only intermediary. Farewell Raimon de Miraval! God speed and God's Grace go with you – and above all, my friendship, my love and my trust!'

Raymonde took Miraval by the arms and kissed him on both cheeks.

'Farewell, my friend.'

'Come back in one piece – and I'll find you a lady whose praises you will one day sing all the way to the stars!'

'Adieu, Raymonde!'

4
Nothing Guarantees Love

What a weird place Toulouse was, thought Miraval. All his thoughts had been turned topsy-turvy like three dreams happening at once in a sleeper's brain. How good it was to be out at last!

He rode hard for Cabaretz, thinking he would go via the great fortified city of Carcassonne, expecting to arrive at the Castle of Love in time for a late dinner. He did not notice the scenery – there was not much of interest on the south road between Toulouse and the Trencavel stronghold. In the event, he bypassed Carcassonne and headed south for Conques and then north to Lastours.

It was still light when he arrived below the four peaks. Rather than encumber his unwitting hosts with the burdens of hospitality, he took dinner at a tavern in the village, the Black Tabard. Finishing a good bowl of pork in a wine sauce, he began to feel dreamy and inspired. He went out into the darkness and reached to a saddlebag for his writing materials. He sat himself down in a shadowy corner of the tavern and began writing:

Nothing guarantees Love
There, where Love asserts his strength
He accepts no other law
than this: that he must accomplish his desires!
Thus does he exercise his lordship;
and those who sulk, resisting him
Will in the end be obliged to beg mercy of him,
unless he would renounce Love entirely.

That is why the wicked are terrified
at the idea of running love's adventure;

but he who concerns himself with his greater glory
embraces that loving service which makes him more valiant
and more noble and more proud.
It is Love who renders a man celebrated
for his gifts, his courteous manner,
for his boldness and for his generosity.

Also I have longtime been
a faithful lover and without falseness,
for a lady who keeps me accordingly more in doubt,
that I show her more obedience.
And I will do well in seeming to protest,
for she knows well that, as long as I will live,
I could not separate myself from her,
such pain have I undergone from it!

This contrariness is to me so bitter
that I'm feeling almost resentful,
for she has made me endure such long suffering
that it makes me want to be avenged of her,
or else with beautiful words I could please her ...
And henceforth, any accursed gossip
will speak such evil of her, that I will take her in hatred;
not that I would return to Love the good merit my songs have won him.

Beautiful lady, soft and charming,
you who are of a nature so noble and so kind
and more gracious than any other
Why won't you pay me any attention?
The heart burns me like a hot cinder;
I am colder than a stream;
Make me pine no more, since I love you
– and you don't want me to die entirely!

Now that the air is so good
and the new leaf comes to life again,
before the cold returns
I would have much need of pleasure;
for the exaltation of love soon dies
and if one lets the summer pass

without any recompense, without any satisfaction
It would make it easy for a slanderer to destroy everything.

When he had finished, the tavern, warm in an amber glow, was empty.

'Have you a room?'

'Most certainly, seigneur! Will you –' the landlord was nervous, 'will you be wanting anything else?'

'Not for now.' The landlord backed away, hands clasped and bowing. He was puzzled as to why Miraval should not be sleeping at his castle, only a few miles away.

Miraval ascended the wooden steps to a landing. There was a low square bed, covered in furs, and there was a bowl of water there. Miraval slept for twelve hours.

After All This Time

During these twelve hours, Miraval dreamt a hundred dreams: vivid dreams of dislocation and pain. He saw Azalaïs being carried away from him. He saw burnings and breakings. He saw Ermengarde cursing in a whirlwind of sand. His heart beat fast and his legs assumed a life of their own. He was crying out, 'Love is nothing! Azalaïs is nothing! Aza- Aza! Aza! Aza –'

'Seigneur! Seigneur! Are you well?'

'Gone! Here-love-her-gone!'

'What's that? Something about a glove? The seigneur must be ill,' said the landlord to his wife. 'Go get some water!'

'There's water there already.'

'No, it's all over the place. He's tipped it all over.'

'All over!' Miraval came to, suddenly. He knew exactly where he was and spoke with amazing clarity: 'Ah landlord, don't trouble yourself. Lastours is beautiful. I see the dawn rising. Everything's going to be fine today. You know something?'

'Seigneur?'

'You don't know what you've got until you lose it.'

'Lose *what*, seigneur?'

Miraval slumped back and disappeared under the fur covers.

'Uracca, you can leave the water. Just a nightmare! Better let him get more sleep.'

'Sleep ... sleep ...' thought Miraval to himself, 'how sweet is sleep.'

He finally awoke in a state of anxiety and tension which froze him to his bed. Uracca, the landlord's Navarrese wife, wrapped tightly in a linen dress, smiled over him. 'Seigneur. Bread and soup. Please take some.'

Miraval smiled sweetly and took the bread and bowl. He was stunned to find himself waking up in such a strange place at midday. Was he not in Toulouse? He got up, pulled himself together, paid his host and mounted his horse. Beyond the stark castle turrets behind him, a deep blue sky was brimming over the mountain. Miraval took a deep, fresh breath of summer air and began the ascent to Cabaretz. He retraced those steps he had last taken when he had rescued the strange man from the castle hounds. He could hardly believe it had ever happened. It was such a splendid day and he felt reborn. Music and rhythm was flowing through him again. It was so good to be home, back in the Cabardès where he belonged.

Loba came to the battlements above the main gate.

'Raimon!'

'Loba! I'm back.'

'After all this time! Where have you been?'

'Don't know, Loba. Crazy times.'

'I'm coming.'

Loba and Miraval walked around the small courtyard together.

'It's so exciting to be back, Loba. I don't know where to begin.'

'Well, calm down a bit first, my dear.'

'I love the breeze here – right over the mountaintops. It's superb. I've missed you, Loba. I didn't know it until now.'

'Missed you, too, Raimon. You look older. What's been happening?'

'Don't know where to begin. I'm on a mission from Raymonde.'

'A mission? Raymonde? What's new?'

'I've got to meet Raimond Mercier. Is he here?'

'Yes. He is. How did you know?'

'I've got to do something. Something about a – '

'Shhh. All right Raimon, I know what it is. Come inside. Raimond Mercier's there. How on earth did you get involved?'

'Had no choice, really.' Miraval grinned, cheekily. 'No choice at all.'

Loba's husband, Jordan, a striking redhead, entered the courtyard. He was accompanied by Peire Roger, the seigneur of Cabaretz, and by Azalaïs de Boissézon. Miraval's mouth dropped. His legs weakened. Azalaïs! What was she doing here?

'Raimon de Miraval! It's been so long.'

Miraval bowed, 'My Lady. You ...'

'Raimon. It's so good to see you. Please come inside and meet our friend.' Miraval hardly recognized the new, calm and confident tone of Azalaïs. She seemed to have gathered at least a decade in wisdom since their last fateful encounter at Labastide Esparbairenque. Time stopped still. There she was! Azalaïs, the absolute love of his life. He felt confused and strange, helpless and happy. It was like greeting old friends after the smooth passage of death.

Loba looked towards Miraval. She saw his wide-open eyes and ready lips. She knew love when she saw it and she respected it. Azalaïs looked to the ground and smiled briefly. She then resumed a serious, businesslike expression.

'Raimon, do come inside.'

Miraval was imagining her standing in the pool by the waterfall, naked, not dressed in this off-white linen robe.

'Yes, Azalaïs, how are you?'

'Never better, Raimon. Life is so good now. I've learnt so much since we last met. I wouldn't know where to begin.'

'No. Me neither. All this time...'

'All things must pass, Raimon. The sunset doesn't last all evening. We have new things to discover.'

'I don't understand.'

'No. But you will.'

Jordan and Peire Roger laughed and put their arms about Miraval's shoulders. The troubadour was absolutely thrilled by it all. What a welcome!

'Special times these, Raimon. Glad to have you here!' said Peire Roger.

'Glad you could get here!' said Jordan. 'Come, come and meet the *good man*.'

The party walked up an enclosed stone staircase to the lodgings by the keep. Seated in a foyer, surrounded by colourful tapestries depicting the exploits of Lancelot du Lac, hunting scenes and the Wedding at Cana, was Raimond Mercier. He was as handsome and earnest as ever. He rose to greet the party.

'Raimond Mercier!' cried Miraval, 'Raimond, how wonderful to see you again!'

'Seigneur, this is a rare pleasure. How was your stay in Toulouse?'

'I have to say, Raimond, that it was something of a mixed bag.'

'Of course. You were trying to lose yourself, as I recall.'

'Is that what I told you?'

'Yes. And now you find yourself back at Cabaretz!'

Everybody laughed at this. Jordan scratched the back of his long neck and turned to Peire Roger, a large man, dressed for the hunt: 'Well, I think we had better leave you two to discuss your affairs.'

'Come Azalaïs,' said Loba quietly, 'let's talk to the children. They wish to meet the holy lady of Boissézon.'

Miraval, somewhat startled, looked round. Loba was guiding Azalaïs out of the foyer. She turned to Raimon and smiled for a second. For Miraval, that one smile made everything worthwhile. His spirits raised, he turned to the Cathar deacon, 'Very well, Raimond Mercier. To business, then. Where are the books?'

'There is only one, seigneur. It appears to contain a collection of several different works – all of them quite undecipherable.'

'May I see the book?'

'Yes, seigneur. But we must wait until after dark. The whereabouts of the book is, as you can imagine, a matter of some necessary secrecy.'

'I take the point. But in the meantime, can you tell me everything you know about this book. Where did it come from? Who brought it? And – most of all, if you say that it is impossible to understand, why all the fuss?'

'I believe, seigneur, that the book was brought by one of the brethren from Constantinople to Chartres. There is a great theological school there, as you probably know. Now it happens that this school is running into some trouble with the Catholic authorities. There is a scholar called Amalric de Bène – he has been accused of stirring things up there. I believe he's fled to Paris now.'

'Heresy?'

'There have been accusations. The study of Plato and Aristotle is, I believe, at the root of the problem. Then there is the Hermetic book of Asclepius – a copy of which we have, by the way. Quite amazing! You should read it some time. Oh, and then there are works from the East: Al-Fārābī, Abu Ibn Sina, Ibn Bajja, Ibn Tufayl – a veritable host of ideas, seigneur, none of them, as you might expect, in accordance with strict Catholic doctrine. Very deep, seigneur, very full of spiritual knowledge; knowledge of the divine intelligences, the spheres of creation, the nature of the soul, the nature of man. In short, seigneur de Miraval, the eternal gospel of the spirit.'

Miraval's head was reeling. The deacon was enjoying himself. The very mention of the names of these philosophers sent his mind into a vision of bright silver stars in heaven.

'What's so threatening about all this?' asked Miraval.

'Using philosophy to support Catholic dogma, seigneur, this is all very well. But what happens when the mind takes the philosopher to places proscribed by the Church?'

'Heresy, of course.'

'So it is said.'

'Raimond, I must make it clear to you once again that I am not a heretic!'

'What are you, then?'

'Me? I'm a – well, funny to hear the question put so directly. I'm a troubadour.'

'But what do you believe in?'

'Love, sir. Only Love. The *Fine Love*.'

'Then you are a "heretic" too.'

'But Raimond, to be a heretic, you must contradict or pervert some point of dogma.'

'Yes.'

'Well, I contradict nothing – nothing except lies, false lovers, hypocrisy, ignoble behaviour.'

Mercier thought for a minute. 'Where do your songs come from?'

'My life, my dreams, my experience – the whole tradition. From my hopes, I suppose.'

'You are not being very specific, seigneur.'

'It's rather difficult. I sometimes have to ... to look through the world of the senses – '

'Away from the body?'

'Yes. If you like. To look through things, to sense the music and poetry that moves in ... in another world.'

'What is the nature of this world?'

'It's imaginative. It's – well, it changes when you bring it back here ...'

'Is it material?'

'Not at all. Not material. It's bigger than that.'

'Who made this world?'

'Must be God.' Miraval looked troubled. He looked to the tapestries for inspiration. 'Daily life; it's like water: thin, passing, difficult to grasp anything for very long, but ... sometimes you go further. It's a richer world. But it's connected with this one. Look, Raimond, look at the tapestry behind you. It's Christ turning water into wine, isn't it?'

'Yes, seigneur. It is.'

'Well, that's it. The troubadour turns the water of life into the wine of song!'

Raimond Mercier nodded enthusiastically. 'Pity the Church does not approve of your love of women.'

'It's not a question of "love of women" in the general sense. Anyhow, if I recall our last meeting correctly, you yourself were not very approving either.'

'I didn't think your *Fine Love* went far enough. But now I'm not so sure. The world you speak of, when you're inspired – I believe this world to be real.'

'Oh, it's more real, somehow. Beauty in nature is like the gateway.'

Miraval looked far away, drifting as he tried to grasp the essence of his meaning but, on touching it, it slipped away again. It always would. He looked directly at Raimond and said abruptly: 'This is all very fascinating but I don't see what it's got to do with the writings you've told me about.'

'You don't?'

'No, not really, no. I don't understand all your stress on absolute purity. I think it's destructive. It's impossible to be like Christ. You can starve yourselves, surrender your attachment to the flesh, give up meat and do good works – but you can never be like *Him*. Why bother?'

'It is possible, seigneur, to be very close to Him. Closer than the Catholic Church will either admit or allow. Many of their priests don't even try – they enjoy the material benefits of the job and do no spiritual work at all. He, seigneur, is within us.'

'So why don't you people work within the Church?'

'Why should we? Why don't the sincere Catholics work within *our* church?'

'Because, I suppose, they came first.'

'How do you know?'

'I – I believe it is so.'

'It is not so, seigneur. There was always more than one church. There was the church of matter and there was the church of spirit. Which church do you belong to?'

'The Church of my fathers, Raimond. I know it's not perfect but it's the Church I know. You must choose for yourself.'

'I have.'

'To be honest, I can't say I think all that much of any church. I don't think yours is really the church of spirit – it all looks fairly material to me – and you rejected *Love* when we first spoke. I don't see that you know any more about the world than I do.'

'You must see for yourself, seigneur. I can only point the way.'

'I'm here to do a job, Raimond. I'm doing it for a friend. Could we keep the theology to a minimum in future, please?'

'As you wish, seigneur. Now I must retire for meditation. Let us meet here again at midnight. I will show you the book – and then you must leave tomorrow morning.'

'I must speak to Azalaïs de Boissézon.'

'That's none of my business, seigneur.'

'No, well, thank you, Raimond. I'll see you at midnight, then.'

'Midnight. Good day, seigneur. Thank you for a most illuminating talk. I hope we shall have more discussions like this. Incidentally, seigneur, I used to play the lute for Peire Vidal.'

Miraval did a double-take. 'Peire – '

'Vidal. That's right. Perhaps we could play together sometime?'

'Um, yes, surely. Good day, Raimond.' Miraval's head was still reeling. And he had failed to express himself.

Miraval looked at the tapestry again. Christ was standing in the midst of a wedding party. There was a castle behind. It could well have been Cabaretz. Yes, it was! Christ in the Cabaradès! Christ held a large cup in one hand and with His left hand pointed to seven standing jars. The group around Him were laughing and joking. Children were scampering about the people's feet. Miraval heard a step. He looked round to see Azalaïs. He rose from his seat.

'I've brought some wine,' she said.

'My Lady!' He knelt before her and took her hand. He kissed it.

'Thank you, Raimon. You never wrote to me.'

'I didn't?'

'No.'

'I didn't know where you were.'

'True, Raimon. I've been everywhere.'

'How does it feel?'

'Being a *parfaite*? Peaceful. I've never known such peace before.'

'That's nice.'

'You don't see it, do you?'

'I've known no peace since we parted.'

'I didn't expect you to. I am free now – and you are still bound: a captive of Love.'

'Yes.'

'You must walk freely in Love, Raimon. You shouldn't be so attached to me. You'll spoil everything for yourself.'

'It's too late for that, Azalaïs. I've spoilt everything already. There's no easy way out for me.'

'Do you think this was *easy* for me?'

'I didn't mean that.'

'What did you mean?'

'I can't do what you've done. I cannot renounce the world. Even if this world is only a window – it's still a window. I don't belong on the other side of it. Maybe you do. You were always there, really. To me, at least. I never expected to touch you.'

'You wanted me so much, Raimon. Loving you as I do, how could I refuse you the once?'

'It would have been a lot easier if you had, my Lady.'

'Life cannot be *easy*, Raimon.'

Miraval was determined to enjoy every single second of Azalaïs's presence. Even in her plain robe, her blonde-brown hair tied back, she was still beautiful. She was still his Lady.

'Azalaïs, do you really believe the Devil made the world?'

'Someone made it.'

'And you with it?'

'The Spirit is of God, Raimon. Flesh is of this world. Since it cannot last, it cannot be of God. The Father of Light is eternal. Everything of Him lasts forever. Time is of the Devil.'

'And *Love*, Azalaïs? Does Love last forever?'

'If it is of the Spirit of God, yes, I believe it does.'

'I don't know who made the world any more, Azalaïs. It just seems stupid to say "The Devil made it" – as if that answered everything.'

'Good and evil cannot come from the same source.'

'There is suffering in Love, Azalaïs. Some say suffering is evil.'

'Love is only painful in this world. Love has taken you beyond yourself, has it not?'

'Only to Oblivion, my Lady. That is my new home.'

'Not *home*, Raimon. Your pain will not last forever. One day you will see.'

'I . . . I only want to see *you*!'

'Oh Raimon, really! You can "see" me any time. This is not enough for you. You want to own me.'

'No! That's not true! Oh, Azalaïs, can't you see that I don't know what I'm doing any more. I don't know what to believe in. Everything is confused. Once there was me, there was Miraval, there was *Fine Love* and Cabaretz and you, and Loba and, I don't know, the birds, the mountains, the morning and the stars. It was enough.'

'You are not telling the truth, Raimon. These things were never enough for you. The world cannot satisfy you. That is why you are here. That is why we are speaking now. In spite of yourself, your vanity and delusion, you have found a quest.'

'Found? I never asked for it. It was thrust upon me.'

'By what?'

'Circumstance.'

'Circumstance? What does that mean? Was it Circumstance that brought you to Crozilat to meet Raimond Mercier – yes, I know all about it. Was it Circumstance that made it possible for Raymonde to persuade you that you had no choice? No, Raimon, you always had a choice. You made your own destiny – but it was destiny, nonetheless. The *Good God* moves in mysterious ways. Do you think that you have reached the end – that you can reflect on what it all means? We none of us know. Of course I don't know "who made the world"! How could anyone know for sure? I only know that I was brought out of the world, its corruption and blindness, by a loving hand. You, Raimon, you played your part. You loved me. I know that you still do – and I love you, Raimon de Miraval. But not only you. Not only you. Oh Raimon! You have a long way to travel yet before your eyes will be opened – and all the while you will think the end is close – but it isn't. It is true – you don't know what you are doing. Because, dear troubadour, you don't know yourself!'

'I should like to hide away at Miraval.'

'It's too late, Raimon. Miraval cannot hide you forever. You must do what you have set out to do. It's not a matter of choice any more. I will always love you – I will never love another in the same way. But I cannot let you hide away. There is work to be done. And you can do it, Raimon. Please, never doubt yourself. I know that the *Good God* loves you too. He loves you in ways I shall never know or understand. You thought everything was lost – and you were wrong. Everything is waiting for you. Everything. You have hardly begun. True Life is eternal, Raimon. We shall always know one another. I will always be your Lady. Never despair dear troubadour!'

Miraval fell to his knees again.

'Oh Raimon, it's not necessary. You can stand by my side now. You are not my servant. You are my friend. Now I must go. We shall meet again. Be kind to Raimond Mercier. He is not all-knowing you know! Be tolerant of him. He is not a bad man. Adieu!'

'Adieu, Azalaïs! God bless you.'

'And you, my darling. Take care.'

Miraval was alone again. But he was not alone. He felt warm inside as if he had gained entry to a body of loving friends. He could not see them with his eyes, but he felt their presence in his heart – and, for once, this was enough. There were no guarantees. Nothing guarantees Love.

The Book

IT WAS A WARM MIDNIGHT in August. Raimon de Miraval met Raimond Mercier in the upstairs foyer as planned. They could barely discern one another's features in the silence and the moonlight. The Cathar put his hand over Miraval's mouth and led him outside by way of the enclosed staircase. In the courtyard, the stabled horses snorted. The hounds scratched the dirt as they slept. All else was perfectly quiet. The two men tiptoed their way to the round tower to the north of the castle. Mercier took a large iron key from his belt and silently inserted it into the lock of a door at the base of the tower. Inside, a recently lit torch cast a bronze glow about a landing. Mercier unlatched a wicker door. He opened it on to a set of wooden steps which led to a dungeon. He pointed to the torch and Miraval took it from its bracket and began descending into the darkness. The steps creaked lightly beneath Miraval's soft shoes. Stepping off the stairs, the men found themselves in a small stone room. It was the same room in which Azalaïs had undergone the *Consolamentum*. Miraval wondered what he was doing there. The room was completely empty. As he shone the torch about him, he noticed a carving of a dove made in relief on the east wall. This splendid dove, so simple and so effective, was the only decoration. Miraval looked to Raimond Mercier.

'The Holy Spirit, seigneur.'

Miraval nodded, his eyes intent and wide. Mercier bent down to a stone slab in the floor below the carving. He took two long files from his belt and slid them into the grooves around the slab. Miraval shuddered. The Cathar looked up to him and whispered, 'Nearly there, seigneur.'

He began to ease the slab upwards. Miraval bent down. Mercier raised his hand. 'Please don't move, seigneur.'

The slab was removed. Miraval moved the torch so that he could see what was there. Mercier began to withdraw a large lead box from the hollow. He placed it on the floor. The box was a half-metre square and bound up with rope, gathered together in a peculiar knot.

'This is the book, seigneur.'

'No, Raimond. This is a box. Where is the book?'

'We mustn't open the box, seigneur. The book is inside but is, I believe, exceptionally delicate. Please do not try to open it. You can see it after you have taken it to its destination.'

'Which is?'

'Puivert, seigneur. You will be welcomed there by Bernard Congost, the seigneur, and his brother-in-law, Raymonde de Péreille. Bernard's sister, Alpaïs, will take care of everything. May the Holy Spirit be your guide.'

Miraval nodded and took the heavy box from Raimond Mercier, 'I will leave at first light.'

'We trust you, seigneur.'

'And I am trusting you, Raimond Mercier.'

The two men smiled at each other as the adventure of Miraval's life began.

5
The Blood of the Earth

Miraval had begun to hate himself. As he made his lonely way southwards some fifty miles from Cabaretz to Puivert, he felt overcome by self-disgust and nausea. What was he doing, playing the part of a courier in a plan fixed by another? Surely he had better things to do than to help the Cathars. All life had lost its savour since Azalaïs had turned heretic. The whole business sickened him. Everything had become such a mess. He wanted time to stop still. He wanted to start again. Years before he had been interested in magic and mysticism and holiness and God. Now all he wanted was the simple life in Miraval – or so he told himself. He tried to convince himself that he hated the very idea of destiny and of hidden values. Tired of himself, Miraval was emotionally exhausted. The whole thing was like a charade; and what new nonsense might lie in wait for him at Puivert, he dreaded to think.

Some ten miles south of the massive walls of Carcassonne, he stopped by the river Aude so that Drummer could take a drink. He sat by the river, glaring blankly at his own miserable reflection. There was no revelation, no sudden grasp of meaning, no poetry, no sense. Drummer snorted and stepped back from the waters. Miraval mounted again and continued on his way. Just before he reached the little town of Quillan at five o'clock, he turned westwards into the bleak forests of the Ariège. The path wound up and up the Col du Portel and then wound its way downwards in dizzying spirals that called forth all Miraval's skill as a horseman. Above the dark green trees, the fierce sun shone with unnatural brightness. Now and again he would pass by some shepherds leading their flocks of goats to better pasture further up the mountains. Those mountains to his left were certainly impressive and yet they left Miraval peculiarly unimpressed. To his right, the forest of Espezel looked sombre and horrible: regiments of winged beetles with a taste for blood were blown out from the trees by the breeze to oppress and annoy the casual traveller. Miraval passed through the village of Nébias but could see no one to whom he might ask the way to Puivert. He knew that it must be close.

So it was. Passing out of the empty village, he heard a distant trumpet sound, and in the distance saw a tall, flat tower and around it, in soft, light-brown stone, the battlements of Puivert. The castle was shining in the evening sun. Miraval felt a frisson of excitement, but suppressed it.

'Not *more*!' he thought to himself.

He rather hoped that his arrival there would be greeted with nonchalance, that all his efforts on Raymonde's behalf would end in a damp squib of inconsequence, that he might yet wake up in Miraval and that his regular life as a troubadour of taste might be resumed once more. But the closer he came to Puivert, this odd castle sitting squat upon a hill, the more excited he felt. There was no doubt that this castle had a special atmosphere. It was very still and balmy. The battlements about the keep were touched by the rosy sunset. Miraval's eyelids grew heavy and he began to slump over his horse. Quite suddenly, the drawbridge was falling before him with the sound of oiled chain uncoiling in the night.

'Seigneur de Miraval. We've been expecting you.'

'Seigneur Bernard Congost?'

'Before your very eyes! And this lady is my sister Alpaïs.'

Miraval looked to Congost's left. Alpaïs de Péreille was a beauty to behold. The lady wore a yellow satin dress joined below the neck by a triangular cotton vest, her slim waist emphasized by a purple belt of velvet. Miraval felt her presence and her presence awoke him from lethargy. Her thin, delicate face, framed by curly red hair, broke into a smile,

'Seigneur de Miraval. We do so appreciate what you are doing. Will you come to join us for supper?'

Miraval bowed, 'It would be the greatest of pleasures, my lady.'

'You have a talent for exaggeration,' said Alpaïs with a laugh.

'On the contrary, my lady. I have an exaggerated talent!'

Bernard Congost roared with laughter, 'I can see we're going to learn a great deal with you about!'

Congost, a thick-set man with a full-set beard, still dressed in a stout leather hunting robe, beckoned his servants to take care of Miraval's horse and to assist the troubadour get off it.

'Seigneur Raimon, you have the ...'

'Yes, I have it. It's tied to the saddle.'

Congost's eyes lit up on seeing the lead box. He clicked his thumb and a shaven-headed clerk appeared in a heavy brown robe.

The clerk gave a quick grin to Miraval (whose eyes were fixed upon the face of Alpaïs) as he loosened the harness which fixed the box to Miraval's saddle. Miraval could hear music.

'Yes, seigneur, we have music here. Not entirely "cut off", you might say! I hope it is up to your standard. Will you join us?' Miraval was not entirely sure, but he suspected that there was a certain tone of sarcasm in Congost's ample voice.

The troubadour ascended with Bernard and Alpaïs to the second floor of the ancient keep. Bernard Congost pulled back the curtain to reveal the banqueting hall. The hall was vibrating with energy and expectation. To the right of the high table, four musicians were playing a sad melody with a strong Hebraic flavour. There was a lady harpist in a plain long gown of brown, over which was a loose, white cloak. There was a boy dulcimer player and a fair-haired man in a striped cloak playing bagpipes. A wild-looking man with flaming red hair was playing an overgrown flute. But what was most strange of all, apart from this otherworldly group, was that the banqueting table was unmistakably *round*. This Miraval had never seen before – but of course he had heard of such things.

Seated around the table were nine people, all of them drinking red wine from silver goblets. At the centre of the table, surrounded by twelve candles, was a piece of rough stone. A concave bowl had been carved in its centre and lined with beaten gold. The light coming from the stone, surrounded as it was by the twelve candles, was quite fantastic. Miraval observed a mirror which had been suspended from the vaulted ceiling above the stone. This arrangement served to cast out streams of silver light which lit upon the assembly as the mirror hovered above the stone. Sitting alone at the high table was Raymond, the seigneur of Péreille, whose own castle was only eight miles away to the west, a little beyond the Val d'Amor. Alpaïs was Raymond's wife. Around the banqueting table Miraval could observe three *good men*, beaming joy from every pore; an eager young man, possibly a troubadour but perhaps a little too scruffy for that; three knights in mail with yellow surcoats; one knight in a white surcoat emblazoned with a red Celtic cross – clearly a stray Templar; and finally, without any doubt at all, there sat Azalaïs de Boissézon.

Miraval heard whispering behind him. Bernard Congost was confiding something to Alpaïs. As Miraval turned round, Alpaïs left the hall. Miraval felt a trifle disappointed but did not show it to Congost as he was eased in the direction of the high table. Four more places were set besides Raymond de Péreille's. Péreille looked up and then stood up. He was a formidable-looking knight. His face was stern. He looked straight into Miraval's eyes. Miraval smiled warmly, forming an instant respect for this man.

'Well done, Miraval! Well done. The lady Azalaïs assured us that we could rely on you. She was right. I'm pleased to make your acquaintance. Please sit down.'

Miraval was utterly fascinated by the people around him. There was an almost visceral atmosphere of seriousness and high spiritual endeavour among them. But for all that, perhaps, there was a strange absence of *humanity*. He cursed himself for his former lack of interest. Here was a world he had only imagined. It was vibrant, engrossing – even delightful, but definitely *odd*. Miraval dared not speak. Instead, he gazed down at Azalaïs. She was talking with warmth and fervour to one of the *good men*: a rotund, muscular man with full, round cheeks, a man given to humour, irony and, it could be discerned from the depth of his gaze, a certain genius. Azalaïs glanced up at Miraval and smiled quickly before resuming her conversation. It was a select gathering, to be sure, and he, Raimon de Miraval, troubadour of Love, was a part of it. What had he done to deserve this? His mind was full of rainbow wonders!

'Venison for our guest!' called Bernard Congost to a servant.

'And for you, seigneur?'

'The usual vegetables.'

'Certainly, seigneur.' The earnest servant hurried off to the kitchens below.

'Do you like our castle?' asked Congost.

'Oh, really Bernard – it's . . . fascinating, marvellous.'

'We tend to keep ourselves to ourselves, you know.'

'You have some extraordinary guests.'

'You have not seen our most special guest, Raimon.'

'Oh?'

'But you will, of course. Do you see the young man down there?'

'Yes. Is he a troubadour?'

'The boy can't sing, Raimon – but he writes exquisitely. He's supposed to be an escaped monk. His name is Robert de Borron.'

'Why "escaped"?'

'From his vows, Raimon. He's writing a masterpiece.'

'He's very young, Bernard.'

Raymond de Péreille looked over to Miraval. 'You're no great age yourself, Raimon de Miraval. What has age got to do with it?'

'To do with writing? A great deal, Raymond. You learn in time what *not* to write. When I was younger, I wanted to say everything. Had I continued like that, I should have written nothing at all!'

'De Borron is different, Raimon. If you'll pardon me, the boy is a master. *He* found us. We did not commission him. He came here a year ago. He said he was looking for the *Great Theme*.'

'And did he find it, Raymond?'

'Oh yes,' said Raymond, nodding his head as he gazed about the hall. 'He found it. He came to the right place, you see.'

Miraval reflected for a moment, somewhat sceptical of the implications.

'The right place?'

'Puivert!' said Congost. 'Puivert is where it all started. Or didn't you know that, Miraval?'

'I've heard something or other, Bernard. Childhood stories, that sort of thing. It was a long time ago – something about the Holy Grail, was it? And there was something else – Mary Magdalene?'

Congost looked at Raymond Péreille, a look of jovial conspiracy.

'Yes, well, the legend is rich enough. Rich enough for anything.'

'Please remind me, Raymond.'

'There's time enough for that, Miraval. First, enjoy your food! You have come such a long way to find us.'

'A day's ride, that's all.'

'A *long* way, Miraval. It's often like that. Robert de Borron said it had taken him all his life – but as you have said, that's not very long really, is it?'

Miraval was most disturbed at the tone of the conversation. In fact, he felt quite out of his depth. 'I suppose not. What's in a life?'

At the round table, meanwhile, Robert de Borron was indulging in a friendly argument with the most imposing of the *good men*, Guilhabert de Castres:

'But seriously, Robert, this notion of yours that the Grail is a vessel to carry the blood of Christ. Can you not see that this is a materialistic conception? It is quite carnal, Robert. There can be no mystery in this.'

'But, Guilhabert, Christ Himself said of the wine drunk at the Last Supper, "This is my blood of the new testament, which is shed for many."'

'But that was poetic analogy. He was not referring to the blood itself – for if he was, any stone on which he had cut His foot would become precious. The Blood is an *image* and you must think of it as such in your book. There are enough fairy tales obscuring the Truth, Robert – please don't add to them!'

'But, Guilhabert, what if the Blood had some more profound and yet more obvious significance?'

'Oh *that*! You refer, no doubt, to the legend of Mary Magdalene coming here with Christ's family, and with Joseph of Arimathea. That the Blood should signify also the descendants of the House of David – the Holy Family. What family was ever truly "*holy*"? No, we cannot take this seriously. It is a legend for little children. Are you writing a children's book?'

'Did not Christ Himself, Guilhabert, on seeing the little children, say that "unless you are as these, you cannot enter the kingdom of heaven"?'

Guilhabert laughed loudly: 'The boy knows his scripture!' He then looked intently at Robert de Borron and said firmly and quietly, 'We preach the *spiritual* gospel – that gospel which saves us from the corruption of our flesh and blood. And we have become a new family through this – bound together not by blood but by the Holy Spirit itself. For I tell you Robert, if you leave red blood long enough, it will soon become discoloured and earthy; but should you give the Spirit leave, you may create a heaven in which to live. We, we for whom the Spirit is an encircling wall, we have no need of Blood.'

'Then what, I wonder, brought me to this place?'

'You came here to seek the Truth, Robert – not to manufacture a counterfeit. These Grail stories which are so much the rage nowadays, I do believe that I can understand the idea behind them. I think it is this: that there is always a hidden cause, an unknown principle, a vital and inward symbol which, if men feel it has been lost, will become like the image of a Lost King. The 'blood' is the inner spiritual meaning of Christ. Every man and every woman could be its guardian. *Who does the Grail serve*? Then there are those people who are without a living principle, those who are prey to all the fantasies and nonsense which, for their protection, their fancies may create, these people become desperate for the Grail and will take up, not the flaming sword of intellect, nor the armour of Love, but will take up the cudgel and the shield of War and carry themselves off to their doom. There is no Grail in Jerusalem, as the Crusaders think there to be.'

The Templar looked up from his goblet. 'The *good man* is right about this. I have lived and fought in Jerusalem. There is no Grail there. The place stinks!'

Guilhabert continued, 'How can I put it to you, Robert? Listen! The Grail is the spiritual life itself. Christ had no interest in his family. He saw that in order for us to follow Him, we should be prepared to "hate our mother and father" – that is to say, our birth in flesh and this, mark you, came from a man who is said to have revered the Ten Commandments! Now this Grail story – no doubt it is inspiring at the first, but ultimately, my dear Robert, it is too ambiguous an image to serve the spiritual life. Cease your game, Robert, before future generations, reading your work, misunderstand your intention and proceed to take your work as fact!'

'I cannot, Guilhabert de Castres. There is something that remains unseen. I have barely touched it yet, but I – '

The stray Templar interrupted: 'There was always a secret gospel. This gospel the Church of Rome has ignored – for, if it were ever found, the Church of Rome could not exist. Robert de Borron's Grail is the symbol of this.'

Miraval, excited by the fragments of talk which he had overheard, shouted down to the round table, his earnestness both surprising himself and alerting his fellows at table, 'But what *is* this secret? Why can't we have it out, now, once and for all – *what* secret?'

'These things cannot be spoken of!' retorted one of Raymond de Péreille's knights. 'Not here nor anywhere!'

'If not here,' added Bernard Congost, 'then where? For it is certainly true that the Magdalene came to this place and did here preach the true Mystery of Christ. And *that* is why the Cathars came to this place a century ago. They too were looking for the secret. The secret *is* a secret, Raimon de Miraval. It will always be so. No one can hear it and speak of it. It is the Truth itself.'

Guilhabert had been listening intently to the discourse. He turned round to the high table. 'There is something in this. You cannot *speak* Light. That is true. You can only live *in* it or point *to* it. The Light of Truth is itself. For man, it is always sercret.'

Miraval's head was spinning again. If he was honest to himself, he would have to confess that he could understand little of what the assembly was discussing. In exasperation, he blurted out, '*Love* is all my thought! And let that be an end of it! Forgive me, but I'm thinking that you're all quite mad!'

'Bravo!' cried Guilhabert de Castres. 'This man is a true Christian!'

Miraval was surprised to hear this. He turned to Raymond de Péreille. Péreille said, 'I'll drink to this brave troubadour. Love *is* all! Raimon, your songs celebrate the quest of true men for the perfect Love. You yourself have written that to the true lover, folly is wisdom. This folly we celebrate here. For us, the Magdalene is Wisdom Herself – threatened by a world who would stone her to death. But the wisdom of the world is indeed Folly. And the True King loved the Magdalene.'

'And did the Magdalene love Jesus?' asked Miraval.

'As only the truly redeemed can, Raimon. Wisdom had been lost in the earth, made prostitute to the guile of men. And

Christ brought her forth again and loved her. She proved herself wiser than the wise. And she came here, Raimon. She really did.'

Miraval squinted. Péreille continued, 'And now you too have come. What, my dear Miraval, what is it that you can do for *Her*?'

Miraval looked away from Péreille, down to the round table. All was hushed. All faces were upon him. Miraval was completely speechless. Even the music had stopped. The stone was shining from the table. The air was pure, and perfectly so. But still Miraval could not speak. This extraordinary moment ended only when footsteps were heard from behind the high table. Miraval shivered. A door behind him was closed. He could feel a lady's hand upon his shoulder.

'Seigneur de Miraval,' Alpaïs said softly, 'this man is Eugnostos.'

Miraval turned round with a start and saw a tall man in a black cloak, his face smiling from beneath a black damask turban, his sharp, long nose framed by a thin, black moustache and a goatee beard. The man bowed. Miraval got up, his features quite frozen at the sight of this mysterious man.

'Eugnostos is a Copt, Raimon.'

'From Egypt to Puivert?'

'Yes, there are good Christians in Egypt too, seigneur.' What a startling voice the Egyptian had! He seemed to speak through the ages: a deep, sandy voice of forgotten wisdom. There was an understanding in his voice, surprising in one so alien from the life of the Languedoc. His dark brown eyes were full of humour.

'I, I never doubted it, Eu – '

' – gnostos, seigneur. Eugnostos. It's merely a pen-name but natives of this region find the more intricate names of my country rather difficult to express. Anything that is strange to us must pass through translation. If you have finished your meal, would you care to follow us?'

'Follow you?' asked Miraval.

'Follow us to the book which you have brought. You may desire to see its contents. I am here to translate the manuscript.'

'Yes, yes of course, Eugnostos. What of Bernard here and the seigneur of Péreille?'

Bernard Congost rose from his seat and put his arm round Miraval's shoulder. 'No, Raimon. You see it. The room is very small. We have waited long enough. We can wait another night. You see it before you sleep. It may be your only chance.'

Eugnostos the Copt had taken a tiny upstairs room in which to make the copy and translation of the manuscript. Alpaïs and Miraval were shown into the little room. It was no more than eight feet square and the air was thick with candle smoke and incense. A rough cotton picture was nailed to the wall by the narrow window. Flickering in the candlelight, painted in the late Byzantine style, it depicted a shepherd standing upon a cloud. Behind the cloud, the rays of a yellow sun reached out like wriggling serpents.

'We all need an image from time to time, seigneur,' said Eugnostos to Miraval, apologetically. 'It helps me concentrate. Look!'

Before Miraval, spread out upon a large, heavy table, were the manuscripts. On the left, sitting upon a thick leather binding, were a pile of papyrus leaves. They were about a foot square, but the papyrus was broken down the middle. On either side of the golden papyrus, in neat rectangular blocks, were pages of writing. To Miraval the writing looked like lines of continuous, thick black squiggles. This, no doubt, was the 'unknown language' of which Raymonde had spoken in Toulouse. On the right was a pile of parchment leaves, an ivory inkwell and a reed pen.

The Copt spoke again. 'I have translated some of the passages for you. The language is an archaic Coptic but not too difficult. If the lady Alpaïs would care to read from this parchment, we might hear some passages I have been working on for the past hour.'

'Just one thing, Eugnostos.'

'Seigneur?'

'How old do you think these pages are?'

'I should say that this is the most ancient writing which can be seen in France at this time.' Miraval raised his eyebrows and Alpaïs began reading from the translation:

'Jesus said, I have told you that these priests and scribes are blind and deaf. For many will accept our teachings in the beginning and they will turn away from them again by will of the Father of their error, because they have done what he wanted. But he will reveal the sons of the Word in his judgement. But those who become mingled with them shall become their prisoners, since they are without perception. And the guileless, good and pure one they shall push to the worker of death, and to the kingdom of those who praise Christ in a restoration. And they praise the men of the propagation of falsehood, those who will come after you. And they will cleave to the name of a dead man, thinking that they will become pure. But they will become greatly defiled and they will fall into a name of error, and into the hand of an evil, cunning man and a manifold dogma, and they will be ruled heretically.'

What a lovely voice Alpaïs had, thought Miraval as he tried to grasp the subject of her recitation.

'But many others, who oppose the truth, and are the messengers of error, will set up their error and their law against these pure thoughts of mine, thinking that good and evil are from the same source. They do business in my word, and they will propagate harsh fate. The race of immortal souls will go in it in vain until my Appearance. And there shall be others of those who are outside our number who name themselves bishop, and also deacons, as if they have received their authority from God. They bend themselves under the judgement of the leaders. Those people are dry canals.

'But he who is father of Mammon is also the father of sexual intercourse. But he who is able to renounce this shows that he is from the generation of the Son of Man, and has power to accuse them. But the baptism of Truth, not water, is something else; it is by renunciation of the world that it is found.'

That sexual intercourse was the basis of marriage and not of Love, Miraval had decided long ago. But it was Azalaïs, the *parfaite* who had made him question this – while now she herself, the *pure one*, had come to understand Miraval's former conviction. Truth inverted itself in Miraval's mind and reason slipped away from him. What did it mean to 'renounce the world'? Which world? Whose world?

'I'm afraid that this small passage is all you can hear for now, seigneur, madame.'

'How long will – '

'I shall need at least three months to translate and copy the entire book. But I am sure, seigneur de Miraval, that you will not be at a loss for – '

'Things to do? No, Eugnostos' said Miraval, smiling at the lady Alpaïs. 'No, I can fill the time quite well.'

'You are our guest, Raimon. Please feel at home.'

'I shall try, lady Alpaïs. Perhaps I shall write again.'

'You never know!' said Alpaïs with a glint in her eye.

Climbing into his bed later that night, Miraval began to dream of all the wonderful things that might happen in a place like Puivert. Azalaïs was there. What could be more perfect? Perhaps the renewal of his powers was only a breath away. He took a last sip of his wine. His new friends had told him that the wine bore a special name. It was called the *Blood of the Earth*.

6
The Pool beyond the Veil

Early in the morning, Miraval felt a tug at his shoulders. He heard Azalaïs voice.

'Raimon, wake up. Wake up!'

'It's so early ... ' He opened his eyes, 'Azalaïs, what is it?'

'They've gone, Raimon. Gone!'

'Who's gone, my lady?'

'Everything. Eugnostos has gone. The book. All gone. Not a trace left. All gone!'

'Oh Azalaïs – not the *book*!'

'I'll see you at breakfast. Come quickly!'

Azalaïs left Miraval's chamber, leaving him to sickening thoughts of personal failure. What a disaster! What would Raymonde think? So much had been depending on him. He had failed to concentrate on the task in hand. Of course he should have suspected Eugnostos; of course he should have slept in the same room as the manuscripts. Why hadn't he thought of it before? He had been thinking of Alpaïs – or was it Azalaïs? No, he had been thinking of himself. No, it wasn't true. It was the banquet. The odd assembly had deranged his senses. It was Puivert. It was the strange Egyptian. No, it was the wine. 'Damn! Damn! Damn!'

Miraval re-entered the hall. The assembly of twelve got up from the round table and turned to him. They stared at him, icily.

'Come forward, Raimon,' said Raymond de Péreille.

'What's all this? A court of law?'

'We're waiting for you.'

'I ... I had no idea. I thought Eugnostos was a friend of yours.'

'A most trusted friend, Raimon.'

One of Bernard Congost's knights offered Miraval his seat at the table. The twelve sat down.

'You've sent out a search party, of course?'

'I don't think that will change the situation, do you?' said Congost.

'Well, you must do *something*.'

'We shall take breakfast, Raimon.'

As soon as they were seated, the assembly began indulging in trivial conversations about the weather, the collecting of dues from merchants, the necessity of building repairs and such like. Miraval ate his bread and cheese in gloomy silence. From out of the chatter, the voice of Azalaïs rose and called for Miraval's attention.

'Raimon, there's really no need for you to stay here any longer. May we suggest that you return home until we have further news? Our agents will inform the count of Toulouse of the new situation. There's nothing more to be done.'

'No, nothing,' added Raymond de Péreille. Everyone but Miraval nodded in assent. Miraval looked around him: to the two knights of Raymond de Péreille; to the disgruntled Templar,. to the three *good men*; to the conceit of Robert de Borron; to Bernard Congost; to Raymond de Péreille; to Alpaïs and to Azalaïs de Boissézon. Miraval was quite unnerved. In his mind he heard himself say clearly, '*Leave now! You are not of them.*'

He got up and backed away. The assembly stood up and spoke in unison: 'Farewell Miraval. May the spirit of wisdom come upon you.'

'Yes,' said Miraval, involuntarily. 'Yes, thank you. Goodbye.'

Bernard Congost nodded slowly. The troubadour did not hear another word from the castle as he quitted Puivert in almost complete silence. He spurred his horse and galloped away as fast as he could, wondering, as he did so, what on earth, or in heaven, was going on.

By the time Miraval had reached Quillan, at the foot of the Col du Portel, his mood had completely changed. Now that he was out of the harsh Ariège, he found himself swimming in an air of freedom, filled with new hopes. He would not return straightaway to Miraval. Never mind the fact that Gaudairenca was likely to be in residence, he resented the idea of doing Azalaïs's bidding. How completely she had taken on her new role staggered Miraval's credulity. Instead, he would ride north-east, to some old haunts – to that place where he had offered Agnès de Montpellier the citadel of his heart, to the region about Fontjoncouse among the languid heights of the Corbières. Back he would go to his past and to the memories of familiar things.

Passing beneath the heady peak of the castle of Termes at eleven o'clock, he made his way up the sandstone col around the town of Villerouge-Termenès and then skirted by innumerable serated escarpments until, sweating in the warm wind (which never seemed to stop blowing from off the sea), he arrived at the old monastery of Fontjoncouse. The monks were still in their herb garden where Agnès and Ermengarde had left them and all was quiet. A cooler wind swept over Miraval's face as he sat in the garden, drinking wine, chatting to the monks and thinking of the opal sea only ten miles to the east. How good it would be, he thought, to get away completely, perhaps to discover fresh inspiration and simpler feelings. *Africa*, he thought to himself – now there was a place! Thinking of Africa threw up the friendly image of Ahmed to his mind, and he realised how much he missed his Syrian friend.

The troubadour decided to take a walk in the afternoon. As he strolled through the balmy village, he passed by some village girls in bright red cotton robes from which there extended from the knee the most delightfully long, brown legs he had ever seen. The girls looked to each other and then stared at Miraval, the stranger. He smiled back to them and bid them good afternoon. The girls blushed with cheeks as red as their dress. Their warmth and natural feeling kindled some hidden place in Miraval's expansive soul and he began to laugh: a beautiful, conceited laugh that loosened his every limb as cool waves of joy swept up his hot body.

He felt the peculiar pleasure of breathing as his senses began to blend into the ethereal atmosphere of deep summer. He became part of what he was seeing, which is to say, no doubt, that he *was* what he was seeing; while all he saw existed in his own infinite imagination. More than this, he had the distinct sensibility of walking through his own mind. And this mind was truly the mind of the creator and his eyes were lights within the body of God. All in all, this sudden sense of *vision* was quite amazing! He had not felt this way since he was a little boy. All of Nature was singing within him and, as a man, he could only love every little thing on which his eyes did alight. He was feeling the hand of *Providence*, which is to say, *the eyes that see before we see*. How could anyone, he thought ecstatically to himself, be so blind as not to feel this flow of infinite life?

He laughed when he considered the Grail-seekers, feeling pity at their making new crosses for themselves and, locked tightly into their own fantasies, were half-blind to the divine life about them.

'They'll *never* understand!' he said to himself with a chuckle.

He felt so light and airy. A subtle peace flowed within him and without him. The cicadas sang a chorus of Joy and Miraval contemplated all those past who had felt this Vision and who had been made to suffer for it – and he was grateful to all those unknown and unsung who had carried the flame of life through the bars of the blind. In one thing at least the Cathars were right. It was indeed necessary to be separate from society a while so that the hope might be rekindled, time and time again. If this world could appear so divine, then it was surely because the spark of divinity still smouldered within the heart of man. But if this world was as dark as Azalaïs maintained it to be, then the Devil lived in our own minds – for the Devil was neither more nor less than the Fear of Vision and the resistance to Love. And if man had fallen then so might he rise again – and the key to it all was Love. There was no other way.

Miraval felt moved to follow a path out of the village. Surrounded by chalky plates of buckled rock and twisted vineyards, he walked on. He had just passed over an ancient stone bridge, its walls hidden among the speckled branches of two great oak trees, when he realized that he had passed something which he should not have passed. He traced back his last few steps. There was certainly something there, or someone ... Yes, someone was calling him. There was no sound, but someone was definitely calling him. He could see nothing through the webbed branches of the tree. He was sure that something special awaited him. The leaves were like a still veil. Something was sparkling beneath him. Miraval looked deeper into the branches. There it was! – a pool some ten feet below him, an ancient pool by a forgotten bridge, veiled by time from worldly eyes. The pool looked impossible to reach, the branches being so thick, but, Miraval knew that he would reach it. Carefully, he seized hold of a branch of the tree and swung himself downwards to the bulbous trunk. From there it was just a jump to the soft banks of the pool. Landing, he was immediately seized by a sense of magic, of feminine enchantment.

'*Everything is within us*,' he said to himself.

He had gained entry to a most secret place. The green waters were crowned by a crystal haze. He looked up but could not see the path, only the glittering canopy of green branches. The scent of the place was quite dizzying. Two broad beams of sunlight penetrated the leaves and were received by the water. At his feet, the pool's edge was made up of the caverns and arches of twisted roots. It did seem that some pact had long ago been made between the pool and the oak tree. Now the oak embraced every part of the soft banks.

Miraval, his eyes full of wonder, his mouth agape, had the most powerful feeling of being in the presence of a lost, feminine spirit, dwelling sadly in the water. The lonely spirit was calling him. Miraval felt pity as he accepted the spirit's invitation. He began to remove his clothes.

'Come in' the pool seemed to whisper. 'It's good. I love you.'

As he slowly entered, his bare feet sinking into the virgin sand at the bottom of the pool, he could feel the ice-cold water rise up his warm white body as the pool embraced him. He inhaled deeply, his lips shivering. The pool was, at its deepest place, not deep enough to swallow him entirely. Little clouds of sand rose like clouds to the surface and mingled with the reflected light which danced upon the fragile surface. Standing, the water caressing his shoulders, he let his head slip backwards and his toes began to rise. Floating in the pool, he was touched by the light and peacefully overcome by the beauty of it all. Even the flies were friendly! The tree roots welcomed him too. Among themselves in the light of the water, the many spirits sought to join themselves to the troubadour as delicious sensations flowed about his skin. He began

'Everything is within us'

to swim around. A helpful branch seemed to extend itself to him and he grasped it and pulled himself through the cool water, singing out, 'Sister spirit ... what joy! *Joy! Joy!* I am reborn!'

Where was *time* now?

For a second, Miraval remembered that he could not stay there forever, and he was truly sorry. But it seemed to him that whatever lonely, lovely spirit dwelt in the pool, she would come to speak to Miraval in his dreams and forever remind him of their love. For a few moments, he had made her come to life again and Miraval now knew that he would always, wherever he might go, carry a feminine soul within him:

> 'Love is all my thought:
> Love is all I care about
> The malicious gossips will say
> that a knight should be occupied elsewhere
> But me, I say they know nothing of it,
> For it is from Love, no matter what they say,
> that the greatest value proceeds, in folly as in wisdom;
> And all that is done through Love is good!'

'And it is through Love, my dear troubadour, that man has divinized the world.' Miraval, amazed at the voice, swung round in the water with a great splash. Before him, standing astride the little waterfall that fed the pool, still dressed in black, was the Egyptian.

'I don't believe it! Eugnostos! How did you get here?'

'How did *you*, seigneur?'

'I ... I found the way.'

'Quite.'

Eugnostos sat himself down upon an adjacent sun-kissed boulder, gazed upwards to the sky, and inhaled deeply.

'Seigneur Miraval, I shouldn't intrude upon this moment. I know that it is special for you and does not concern me at all. Further along the path, to the left, you will see a waterfall – that is to say, you will hear it. There are a series of delightful rock pools there. I shall be waiting. Come when you are ready.'

The Egyptian removed his sandles, pulled up his robe to his bony knees and made his way, quite eccentrically, up the brook which fed the little waterfall which fed the pool in which Miraval was swimming. There was nothing else Miraval could do now but to get dressed, say farewell to the lady of the pool and go and find his way to where Eugnostos was waiting.

Eugnostos was soaking up the sun while his feet dangled in a clear water rock pool. Bluebottles were buzzing about the butterflies while dragonflies united in the clear air – unknown ecstasies filled the afternoon, somewhere between sunset and imagination. Miraval joined him on the golden rock which, having been carved by flowing water over the ages, flowed about them in soft waves. The two men shared the bliss of the day.

'Tell me, "Eugnostos", what's your real name?'

The Egyptian took the question in his stride, 'My "real" name, as you call it, is Raghib Abd-as-Ṣīna. Don't you care for "Eugnostos"?'

'I thought it a trifle portentous.'

'Yes, I suppose so. They liked it at Puivert.'

'That doesn't surprise me.'

Raghib laughed, 'No, no ... I can see that. They are *very* serious, aren't they?'

'Did you take the book?'

'Yes, I took it.' Raghib seemed to find the whole business a cause for mirth. 'I took it away for a while. I hated that little room. And I didn't much care for the castle. Not open enough.'

'It's a pity for me, Raghib. I'm supposed to have a copy or two of it. I mean to say, some people regard the whereabouts of this book as being of some *political* importance.'

'Yes, I suppose they do ... But that is not important.'

'Not to you, maybe. I have a debt to repay, Raghib. I must have the copies.' Miraval was not enjoying the repartee, not because he objected to Raghib, but because he liked him.

'What a pity about your debt. What about your debt to *yourself*?' Raghib laughed to himself.

'Why, Raghib, why did you come to me? How did you know – ?'

'Oh I shouldn't worry about that if I were you. Who can truly understand the *Necessity*?'

'Necessity for what?'

'Surely, seigneur Miraval, your being a poet, surely you have felt the force of the *Necessity*?'

'Miraval reflected for a moment on the events of this extraordinary day.

'Maybe, Raghib. Maybe I did today. It feels quite lovely, really. Just you and me and the bubbling stream and the hot stone.'

'There you are then. You are feeling the *Necessity*. Nice, is it not?'

The two men sat in the sun, in blissful quietude for another hour. Suddenly Raghib let out a great burst of laughter, splashing the water about his feet like a little boy.

'What's so funny?'

'Oh . . . you know I spent the whole of last night working on the translation.' Raghib chuckled. 'You know I do not think the Cathar Church is going to like everything that is in the book.'

Miraval, at first somewhat shocked, then began to laugh. 'Why, why ever not? It's, it *is* their book, is it not?' Raghib looked round to him, his eyes moist with good humour. He shook his head. Miraval began to feel the tide of an incoming joke. 'Come on, Raghib, what's the joke? I know you've got something up your sleeve.'

'May I be permitted to read you a portion of the translation?'

'Please do.'

'First, I should tell you that this so-called "book" is not a book at all. It's a collection of extracts from other books – put together for I don't know what reason. But nobody will believe this now. Did you not observe how Raymond de Péreille said that he and his friends could wait another day until seeing my translation. Did you not think this a little *strange*?'

'Well, Raghib, your room was very small.'

'I could have brought the book to the hall. You know, it really is very simple. They had *already* seen the book!'

'How so?'

'In their *minds*, seigneur. They have already composed their own secret book. Anything which I can translate will only ever be used to fit in with their original notion. Of course, the same principle applies with equal – or even greater – force to the Cathars' enemies as well! Why does nobody ever see things for what they are? Don't try to answer, seigneur, there's a mystery in it!'

'Or is there?'

'Exactly! You've got it! I'll wager that even if the book were to be destroyed, it would always exist. It must exist so long as men think as they do.'

Miraval started to laugh. Whereas before he had felt like a pawn in another's game, now he felt like a prince of jokers. The divine humour of the ages fell upon his head and he collapsed in tears of laughter, wiping the flies from around his eyes. Raghib grinned broadly and, closing his eyes, nodded gently. 'Yes, seigneur, I'm afraid there's nothing we can do to change it. *Necessity*, you see!'

'But . . . but Raghib.'

'Don't fight it, seigneur!'

'Very well, my friend, let me hear your translation.'

'Promise not to laugh?'

'I will not. I promise.' Miraval tried to keep a straight face as Raghib reached for a sheet of parchment from out of a bulky leather satchel.

'Now, where are we? First, seigneur, do you recall the last translation I read to you?'

'Yes, of course. It was about renunciation of the world and its pleasures, was it not? Especially the erotic pleasures.'

'That's the idea. Now listen to this: "It is a truth to be accepted as sure and evident above all other truths, that by God, the Master of all generative power, has been devised and bestowed upon all creatures this sacrament of eternal reproduction, with all the affection, all the joy and gladness, all the yearning and the heavenly love that are inherent in its being. And I must needs tell you of the compelling force with which this sacrament binds man and woman together, were it not that each one of us, if he directs his thought upon himself, can learn it from his inmost feeling. For if you note that supreme moment when, through interaction without pause, we come at last to this, that either sex infuses itself into the other, the one giving forth its issue, and the other eagerly taking hold of it and laying it up within, you will find that at that moment, through the intermingling of the two natures, the female acquires masculine vigour, and the male is relaxed in feminine langour. And so this sacramental act, sweet as it is, and a thing that must needs be done, is done in secret, lest, if it were done openly, the ignorant should mock, and thereby the deity manifested in either sex through the mingling of male and female should be put to the blush, – and the more so, if the act is exposed to the eyes of impious men."'

'But that's beautiful!'

'So it is, seigneur, so it is. But the Cathars won't like it.'

'I wish Azalaïs could hear it now.'

'Yes, that is a shame. For her body speaks this wisdom constantly to her. But, alas, she has learnt to deny this wisdom.'

The two men paused for a minute to reflect on the confusion engendered through higher aspirations.

'Well, seigneur, as you can see, the stone is turning pink and I must be on my way.'

'Why, Raghib? Where can you go to?'

'Forwards, Raimon de Miraval. It is the only way.'

'But the copies! I must have the translation and copy!

'Why? Is the book yours?'

'No, but – '

'You will see the book again, seigneur. In good time – or maybe ... bad. Farewell!'

Miraval looked to heaven, closed his eyes, and looked back to Raghib.

'It has been a marvellous day, has it not?'

'It has.'

'Do you know, Raghib, I cannot say that I care what you do with the book. But please take care of *yourself*!'

'It shall be as it must. *Necessity*, you know! God be praised!'

'Yes, Raghib, God be praised!' Miraval looked back to the water. A glowing pink orb was hovering on the water. He looked back to Raghib but the Egyptian was gone. Miraval felt a little chilly and smiled to himself, thinking, 'Best ride back to Miraval. Come what may, it has been a day to remember!'

With that, he rushed back to Fontjoncouse to collect Drummer from the monastery stable, and, having paid the monks for their trouble – a gift they were loth to accept – he galloped off into that space between the sunset and the emerging stars, over the Corbières and on homewards, to Miraval.

Azalaïs is Not Forgetful

Something was bothering Azalaïs de Boissézon. She fretted over it for days, secretly and silently. What could it be? She would take walks around the battlements of Puivert at sunset and at sunrise. She would seek spiritual guidance from Guilhabert de Castres. She would involve herself with the maintenance and development of Catharism in conference with Raymond de Péreille, Alpaïs, Bernard Congost and a host of visiting *perfecti*. And yet, after all, it still did seem that her precious sense of inner peace was disturbed. Guilhabert told her that she must never look back; that Miraval, 'though without any doubt a noble and talented man,' did not have 'what it takes' to be a full Cathar. He could never be a part of them. So long as the troubadour continued to praise the beauty of women and desired to be in their embrace, he would be firmly bound to the diabolical *Lord of this World*.

Azalaïs started scratching herself, involuntarily: long scars appeared along the length of her arms. Sometimes she drew blood. The more she scratched, the more the image of Miraval quitting Puivert entered her mind. Had she been cruel to him? Yes, she had, but she *had* to, did she not? She had put him down. She had used him badly. Azalaïs began to feel guilty and no amount of Lord's Prayers would put the guilt to rest.

One afternoon in autumn, she found herself crying. Robert de Borron discovered her on the top of the keep, her long hair untied and blowing in the wind beneath a leaden sky.

'Azalaïs, you are crying.'

'Go away, Robert, please.'

'Something's the matter. Don't you like it here any more?'

'Yes, of course. I've never been happier.'

'Why are you crying?'

'Please, leave me Robert. There's nothing the matter.'

Robert began to walk away but returned to Azalaïs, 'Raimon de Miraval. You are in love with him.'

Azalaïs turned to him, large tears falling upon her cold cheeks.

'You love him greatly.'

Azalaïs nodded.

'You must do something.'

'I don't have any choice, Robert. I must stay and help

Guilhabert. We are travelling soon: Ussat, Montségur, Foix, Fanjeaux, Carcassonne, Lastours, Tarascon, St Félix, Toulouse. There's so much work to do. There's the preaching, the consoling, the fasting, the praying, the – can't you see there's so much left to do? I said I would help and I will. It's my life now. I must write to my husband. Bernart is so lost now. I don't know what to do. I've messed up everything I've touched. I . . . I . . .' Azalaïs collapsed in tears. Robert held her tight.

'No, no, my little Azalaïs. Don't cry. Don't cry. I know something will happen soon. Please believe it will.'

Azalaïs sniffled and whimpered as the sun began to fall behind a cold, dark cloud, hard-blown and icy-fresh from the Pyrenees.

Virginity Can Kill

Ahmed was bored and stiff with cold. He was standing by a fir tree in a damp wood on the outskirts of Moissac, a wealthy town in Gascony some forty-five miles northwest of Toulouse. The *Juice Tramps* had established a camp there because it was close to the Garonne river and because the wood afforded ample opportunities for shelter and for hiding. Behind Ahmed, huddled about a crackling fire, Gérard and Berteaux were cooking salmon with Brian, the *Tramps*' 'leader' (for they did not believe in leaders). Jacques was expected to return from town with bread at any moment. Large droplets of rain were falling at irregular intervals from the trees above their heads below, and the group was feeling glum. How long would it be before they had news from Miraval? Gérard and Berteaux tossed damp sticks onto the fire but the fire stubbornly refused to consume them. Ahmed was dreaming of Syria and of the departed summer. The long drizzly winter of Languedoc was fast approaching and Ahmed had developed a nasty cough. There was a sound of crunching leaves and heavy breath. The *Tramps*, scattered about the small enclosure, reached for their knives.

'Jacques?' called Ahmed.

'Yes, it is Jacques,' came the reply. Ahmed nodded to the *Tramps*.

'Good morning, sirs. Jacques has brought bread for all! I see the fish is almost ready.'

'Many thanks, Jacques,' said Ahmed. The rest of the group grunted in the affirmative. Jacques looked about him at the downcast faces, sunk into a collective gloom.

'Sirs, I have a story for you. Would you care to bend your ears in my direction?'

There was no response.

Jacques coughed and continued, 'Gentlemen, the story concerns the fate of a virgin.'

'Come on, Jacques!' said Gérard. 'That's easy to work out. We know the fate of a virgin. Is this another "mad priest of Crozilat" tale?'

'Not quite, Gérard. I heard this story in Moissac this morning. The baker there was most concerned that all should hear it. This story is as fresh as the bread!'

Brian spoke up: 'Jacques, consider us to be your captive audience. Give us the bread and tell us the story! Come on, lads, come closer to the fire. If we don't hear the story now, we may never get another chance.'

'Quite so!' said Jacques. He proceeded to distribute the few loaves of bread and Ahmed divided the four salmon amongst the eight of them. Gérard poured the wine into the home-made earthenware mugs. The smoky smell of damp and burning leaves filled the air as Jacques coughed violently and, at last, began to tell his story.

'Some months ago in Lyons, a cleric set eyes upon a pretty girl who was carrying a jar of wine across a field, close to his church. The maid looked at the cleric and began to walk faster, away from the priest. The cleric began to run and soon fell upon the girl and made the nature of his *interest* apparent to her. She struggled with all the dignity that was in her until she was forced to cry out, "I am a virgin! I will not know a man. Leave me in peace!" The priest was shocked. He was suspicious – for it is the common custom there that the priest may sleep with any girl he fancies – and some count it an advantage to comply with his wishes, thinking that thereby they may come closer either to his God or to his purse! The frustrated priest reported the incident to his abbot and the abbot declared that the priest must trace the girl and question her. This the priest did and by doing so, discovered that the girl was one of twenty men and women who had chosen celibacy and who met regularly in the house of one of them to hear the gospels and to pray. The girl was arrested and accused of heresy and of unnatural practices. Her friends were rounded up, too. They were burned last week. The girl had a relation in Moissac. The home of a priest in Moissac was stoned last night.'

Everyone sat quiet, munching their breakfast. Gérard struggled in his mind for an appropriate quip but could find nothing to say.

The silence was finally broken by a loud whisper which came from out of the trees: 'Brian!'

Brian turned to Ahmed and Gérard: 'I know that voice ... Fabien. It's Fabien the miller!'

Fabien stepped from out of the trees. 'Brian! Ahmed! Gérard! My friends! I thought I'd never find you! What's going on in Moissac? The atmosphere's terrible. There's a riot going on. Someone's started a fire. The monks have locked themselves into the monastery. There's fighting and shouting and I don't know what. The place is in uproar!'

Brian got up from the fire and embraced Fabien. 'It's so good to see you!'

'But what's happening?'

'Oh, it's another burning. Not here, thank God. In Lyon. A girl – a relation of someone in the town. Sit down, Fabien, join us for breakfast.'

'What girl? What had she done?'

'Refused a priest his *daily bread*.'

'What a bastard! When will these mad priests just lay off?'

'God knows, Fabien. Not in our time, I think.'

'What brings you here, Fabien?' asked Ahmed.

'I've received a message from your seigneur at Miraval. You minstrels are respectfully invited to return at once to Miraval.'

'At last!' cried Gérard.

Brian said, 'Had enough of us, have you?'

'Of course not, Brian, it's just that – '

'Don't bother apologizing. I'm glad for you. Now, Fabien, is it safe to go to Toulouse?'

'Is it ever safe for you in Toulouse?'

'You know what I mean. Is the count or the Saissac family going to get us if we go back?'

'I don't think so. They got Guiraud instead.'

'We'd guessed that.'

'He's dead. They hanged him. I'm sorry, Brian. Sorry, lads.'

'He should have stayed with us. He should never have run off.'

One of the *Tramps* spoke up. 'There's no justice in this world, Brian.'

'He killed a killer. What would God think of that?'

'Now he's dead.'

'Now he's with God.'

'Lucky Guiraud! Are you listening up there, Guiraud?' Brian looked up to the dark sky and cried out, 'Lucky bastard, Guiraud! ... This life is Hell. How can the priests threaten people with Hell? We're there already.'

'Aye, that's true.'

A heavy rain began to fall and the little fire gave up the ghost.

'We'll return with Fabien,' said Brian. 'Don't forget us, will you?'

'Never,' said Gérard.

'And if your seigneur ever needs our help, we'll be ready.'

The minstrels hugged the *Juice Tramps* and everyone left Moissac to the rain and the riot.

7
Together Again

'Azalaïs!'

Miraval ran up the bank which led from the waters of the Orbiel to the mound upon which his little castle sat.

'Azalaïs, I can't believe it!'

She was mounted upon a black horse, flanked by two *good men*.

' – And you've brought Guilhabert and Raimond Mercier! Please, all of you, please come in.'

'No need, Raimon. Guilhabert and Raimond are going back to Lastours.'

'Are you sure, Guilhabert? You are most welcome here.'

'You are, as usual, Raimon, more than kind. But I'm afraid we must refuse. I do believe,' Guilhabert had a sparkle in his eye, 'that Azalaïs would prefer to be alone with you. So we shall leave you with our good wishes and our love. May the *Good God* bless you, Raimon de Miraval. Farewell!'

Mercier and Guilhabert reared their mounts and left Raimon and Azalaïs looking into each other's eyes. Miraval was shaking his head in disbelief. 'I don't understand it, Azalaïs. I thought I would never see you again.'

'I hope you don't mind my coming here to see you.' Azalaïs's voice had changed. There was a suppleness and sweetness there. Gone was the old tone of insistence and stark candour.

'*Mind*? It's absolutely wonderful! Ahmed, Gérard, Berteaux and Jacques are here, too. What a gathering! I just can't believe it, Azalaïs – it's incredible!'

'And Gaudairenca?'

'Provence. She has new friends.'

'And you, Raimon, how are you?'

This was one question Miraval hated being asked. His moods changed so fast that if ever he felt very good he would remember some recent sorrow and the bliss of the moment would vanish.

'How am I?' He thought how good he had felt since the encounter with the magical pool at Fontjoncouse. But then he recalled how much he had missed Azalaïs and of how he had failed in his mission for Raymonde.

'I'm well. Very good *inside* ... but now you've come – pure *Joy*, my lady. Pure *Joy*! Azalaïs, come and sit with me by my little river.'

'By your little castle?'

'The very same – the best place in the world. Here, Love *is* King!'

Raimon and Azalaïs sat huddled together by the Orbiel. It was cold. The Orbiel, filled with fallen leaves, was very cold. Azalaïs was wrapped in a bearskin cape but Miraval hardly noticed the chill. He was filled with new ideas and thoughts which hit off one another in fiery flashes that brought fond memories to Azalaïs's mind and warmth to her heart. This was the Miraval she had first encountered. She looked at him adoringly, her cheeks cool and pink, her hair blowing in the breeze. Miraval's eyes looked firmly into some imaginary space as he gestured wildly about fresh observations and ideas for new *cansos*. Occasionally he would glance at Azalaïs and smile. The afternoon was filled with promise. Before Azalaïs knew what she was doing, she found herself in a warm, passionate kiss as the cold water rushed over the rocks, flushing leaves away from the banks which floated on down the river to Lastours. Lying on the bank, looking over Azalaïs, Miraval whispered.

'I don't think Guilhabert would like to see this. Looks like backsliding.'

Azalaïs giggled, 'I know. It's quite unforgivable, isn't it?'

'God is Love, Azalaïs. This I know. Only this I know.'

'I know.'

They kissed again. Azalaïs was now sure of her love for Raimon. Miraval had never doubted his love for the lady of Boissézon.

'What are we going to do now? I doubt whether you can ever forgive me for the way I've treated you.'

'I do forgive you. You are my lady. Our love is stronger now. That's all that matters.' He thought for a moment, 'Will you go back with Guilhabert?'

'I don't know yet. I need some time to think about it. May I stay here for a while?'

'Of course. Miraval is yours, my lady. Do you know something?'

'What's that?'

'I can hear the river singing your name! Can you hear it?'

Azalaïs listened. She put her hand to her mouth. 'I can hear it, Raimon. It is singing both our names.'

'I do believe you're right – I hear it too! I love you, Azalaïs.'

'I love you. Forgive me?'

Dinner that night was unforgettable. Miraval got the big fire at the centre of the hall going and everyone sat round it, joking merrily. The minstrels played and looked to one another and then to Raimon and Azalaïs, arm in arm. Miraval was ecstatic and told stories of his childhood and of all the extraordinary people he had met. Everybody sang and reminisced and then it was dawn and Ahmed saw that Berteaux, Gérard and Jacques were asleep – Jacques snoring loudly – and that Raimon and Azalaïs were still awake, nose to nose, lost in each other's eyes. Ahmed was so happy. Everybody was happy. As daylight began to creep into the hall and the many birds began to sing, Ahmed wished that the evening would never end, that they would always be like this. But with the oncoming day would come the questions of the day, the questions of the day . . .

Breakfast at eleven was mellow. The weather could not make up its mind.

'What are you going to do, Azalaïs?'

'What are *we* going to do?'

'You mean it?'

Azalaïs nodded.

'I think the future is written for us.'

'What future, Raimon?'

'That book. We've got to find it, haven't we? It must be somewhere. Eugnostos told me that I would see it again.'

'Eugnostos told you that? When?'

'Oh, we met.'

'You didn't tell anyone?'

'Why should I?'

Azalaïs laughed, 'Raimon, you're incorrigible!'

'I do hope so.'

Azalaïs put her elbows on the table and started to finger the crust of a piece of bread. 'Raimon, I'm going to tell you something that I promised Guilhabert I would never tell. But before I do, I need to know how important finding the book is to you.'

'The book? The book isn't important to me at all. I really don't need it. But it is important to Raymonde – and that means that it's important for the county. Let me put it another way – I think your Church will be under less threat if Raymonde succeeds with his plan.'

'The true Christian is never under threat from men, Raimon.'

'Do you want to go to the stake?'

'Of course not. But if it must be, then I am ready.'

'I can't understand you, Azalaïs!' Miraval got up from the table and began pacing about the hall, 'Are you all mad? You must see that Raymonde is on your side? Of course you must help him. I had been under the impression that you were trying to help him – what's going on, Azalaïs?'

'I'll tell you, Raimon, if you'll just calm down for a moment.'

'I'm sorry, my lady. I am very impatient, it's true, but the thought of you – '

'Being burnt to death?'

'Yes.'

'I am with *you*, am I not? You won't let that happen, will you?'

'Never!'

'Then just listen! After you brought the manuscripts to Puivert, there was a meeting.'

'I was in bed, of course.'

'Of course.'

'Dreaming of better things.'

'Were you?'

'Oh yes, what a wonderful time I was going to have with you all!'

'You were wrong.'

'Again.'

'Again.'

'Am I often wrong, Azalaïs?'

'Not often – but when you are, it's hard to convince you of it.'

'Must be pride.'

'Can I get on with the story?'

'Please!'

'While you were in bed – '

'Dreaming.'

'Shut up. While you were in bed, we had a meeting. At the meeting Raimond Mercier explained the plan whereby a copy would be put into the hands of the bishop of Toulouse – for public burning.'

'I know all that, Azalaïs! What did you all decide? That's what I want to know.'

'You are a very mischievous man, Raimon.'

'I know. Can I have a kiss?'

'No. Listen a minute! It was decided that not even a copy of the book should be burnt. It would be quite wrong, and a faithless act, to burn something which was so sacred.'

'But right to burn the woman I love, I suppose?'

'A body may be burned – that is only hastening the end of what must die anyhow.'

'Painful, nonetheless.'

'To destroy holy books – that is like spitting in the face of the *Good God*.'

'He prefers books to people, does he?'

'We decided that the book must never come into the hands of the Church of Rome in any form – not even a copy.'

'I see. It's not really a question of a burnt book but a question of who burns it.'

'If you like.'

'This is incredible, Azalaïs! Do you all want to commit suicide as well? Raymonde did not want to take your precious book away from you! He wanted to read it for himself. Only a forgery would be destroyed. Even *I* was ready to become party to this plot – and remember that I am a Catholic! It was a favour to a dear friend, and a service to our country – and, when all is said and done, it was for you and your friends! Can't you see how much pressure Raymonde is under to destroy the heresy in these parts?'

'He can never destroy the Truth, Raimon. No one can.'

'Are you serious, my lady? I grant you, a few may be preserved – but what of everyone else? You and Guilhabert de Castres, you have been travelling the length and breadth of the country, preaching your gospel of light and your hatred of the Church of Rome – '

'No, Raimon. That's not true! We do not *hate* anyone. Love is King in the true Church as much as he is here in Miraval.'

'I'm sorry, Azalaïs – but the point is that if the count of Toulouse should so choose, he could make it almost impossible for you to practise your religion.'

'I doubt it, Raimon. Half of the nobility are sympathetic to us.'

'Today, perhaps. But things change.'

'Yes, they do. More of them become our friends every day. The count cannot afford to persecute his own supporters.'

'So why make it harder for him to tolerate you? There must be some give and take. Love *is* like that, is it not Azalaïs? You don't get everything you want.'

'*Losing is half of it*?'

'Yes, exactly. It is important to surrender sometimes.'

Azalaïs went quiet. 'I shall have to think about it.'

'You have as much time as you need, my lady. I shall be rehearsing today. Do me the honour of hearing you when you are ready.'

'Yes, Raimon. Thank you. I shall walk about.'

Miraval bowed and Azalaïs left the hall.

The day was filled with song as Miraval and his minstrels filled out the verse and musical structure of *Nothing Guarantees Love*. The theme of '*running love's adventure*' gained fresh poignancy in the new circumstances. The insecurity of Love filled Miraval with excitement as he gazed out of the hall windows into the skies and thought and felt that *good love* does all the while hang above the earth. Even the dark earth itself seemed to be yearning for the sky and the light of the stars beyond. Miraval was excited by thoughts and feelings that could hardly find expression – something about the tension between earth and heaven; of how this tension was itself the source of song. Everyone can touch love, he thought; everyone could, if they would, kiss the sky. Miraval no longer hated himself, feeling, as he did, the full dignity of his calling. To be a troubadour was to be blessed with wings; and if he had wings, the fantastic and limitless wings of the spirit, he could go anywhere and do anything! He would carry the spirit of Miraval across the world!

'Raimon, you want to know where the book is. I shall tell you. Eugnostos has – '

'I say, Azalaïs . . .'

'Yes?'

'Did you know that his real name was Raghib?'

'No, I – are you really interested?'

'Profoundly so, my lady.'

'Eugnostos has a translating house in Tripoli. Greek and Coptic into Arabic is, I believe, his speciality. He earns quite a lot of money that way.'

'Perhaps he could translate my songs.'

'Ask him.'

'Where can I ask him?'

'In Tripoli, of course.'

'Which Tripoli, my lady?'

'There's only one, isn't there?'

'Well, as Ahmed would happily tell you, there is a Tripoli in Syria and there is a Tripoli in Africa.'

'Oh, then it must be Africa, because he told me about the Almohads.'

'Castile is at war with the Almohads. We're all supposed to be at war with the Almohads!'

'Exactly. Tripoli is on the furthest borders of their territory. The point is that it is still possible for a Christian merchant to travel there if he his reasonably discreet.'

'Reasonably?'

'*Very* discreet.'

'I see.'

Miraval experienced a terrifying vision of being sold into slavery by the Berbers of the African coast, never to see Miraval again. 'You mean Azalaïs, that if we, that is, I – '

'No, Raimon, *we*.'

'If the book is to be retrieved, it will be necessary to go to Tripoli to find it?'

'Yes, Raimon. Are you still interested?'

Miraval paused for a minute. 'I hear they have good music in Tripoli!'

'We're going, then?'

'It will take some planning.'

'Yes, it will.'

'We shall need to take Ahmed, of course.'

'Of course. What of the others?'

'Perhaps you had better ask them.'

'Very well, my love. I will.'

And she did.

Tripoli It Shall Be

The weeks passed while Miraval waited for his bailiff to collect the rents from his land and for Gérard to return from Marseilles with information about transport to Tripoli. Occasionally, Azalaïs would lie with Miraval but the lovers remained celibate. Erotic restraint was the order of the day – and night. Azalaïs wanted the 'best of both worlds' but was certainly not prepared to sacrifice the disciplines of one for the fleeting pleasures of the other. Miraval was deeply satisfied by the arrangement and his love for Azalaïs grew and grew. Indeed, his love for her grew to such an extent that he became hourly concerned for her safety. His thoughts began to dwell upon the rigours of a sailing expedition to Africa and the countless risks involved in the adventure. Lying together one cold night, Miraval began to tell Azalaïs of his worries for her.

'They say that men will give five camels for a Christian noblewoman in Marrakesh, Azalaïs.'

'Is that all, Raimon? I should have thought they might offer more.'

'Perhaps for a virgin.' Azalaïs giggled. 'How can you laugh?'

'What's the matter, Raimon?'

'I'm afraid for you.'

'Don't you want me to go?'

'Of course I do. It's just that – well, did you know that there is no privacy on board a ship?'

'Is that true for all ships?'

'True of the *barcas* which trade with Africa, certainly, yes.'

'It's only for a month, though, isn't it?'

'If all goes well.'

'Well, then, I'm sure we can rig something up.'

'It won't be up to us.'

'I'm sure the crew have seen a woman on board ship before.'

'That's just it.'

'What do you mean?'

'Some crews won't have women aboard. They think it will bring them bad luck. Silly, of course.'

'Then I can prove them wrong, can't I?'

'I suppose you're right.'

'Only "suppose", Raimon?'

'Some of these crews are pretty rough, you know.'

'What are you saying?'

'Pretty *rough*. You know. As for Tripoli ... this is all very risky. I'm not sure if ...'

'If what?'

'Perhaps it would be better if you stayed here. I do need someone to look after things.'

'Do you want me for a wife, Raimon?'

'No, no, of course not.'

'Then don't treat me like one.'

'Pardon me, my lady.'

The conversation trailed off into sleep.

When Miraval awoke, Azalaïs was gone. On reflection, he was not terribly surprised. He would have to admit to himself that he had driven her away. Now he could dream of her every day. It was sure that Azalaïs was a far stronger force in his life when they were physically apart than when they were together. This subtle interplay between the spirit of the heart and the attraction of the body fascinated Miraval.

Azalaïs herself was quite disappointed in him but she had all along known in her heart that she would return to Guilhabert and her fellow *perfecti*. Joining herself to them had, perhaps, been the one genuinely free decision which she had ever made. She never expected Miraval to understand this fully. A woman keeps her philosophy in her heart. Miraval liked to see it written in a person's face. Nevertheless, the expressionlessness of Azalaïs was a welcome mystery to him. He knew that in her heart she must be free. Raimon and Azalaïs both wanted the best of both worlds.

In the spring of the following year, Miraval and his friends glimpsed the city of Marseilles. From the high hills about the city, they saw the fine and famous harbour, full of ships: from large galleys to forty-five foot *caravos* from Tunisia – and behind their swaying mastheads, the deep blue waters of the Mediterranean. On the eastern side of the habour, behind the great abbey of St Victor, they could see over a hundred ships, packed tightly together. These empty, battered ships were regarded with a certain awe, for in these Richard of England had, three years previously, led his Crusade to recapture the Holy Sepulchre in Jerusalem. Having seized Acre, Jaffa and Ascalon, Richard's army had been unable to take the Holy City itself from Saladin's dispirited garrison. It had been a near-miss.

Now, having been sailed from Venice in the past month, the fleet was up for sale and buyers were turning up from Genoa, Pisa, Barcelona and even Africa; Jewish merchants were acting as necessary middlemen for Islamic shipping fleets. As for the heroic King Richard, he had been taken prisoner by his fellow Christian, Leopold of Austria, vassal of the Holy Roman Emperor. With the Crusading spirit suffering a temporary relapse, the merchants were moving in to pick up the pieces. For Miraval, this was a fortunate development. Trade between Syria, Egypt, Africa and the continent was opening up again, if only tentatively, and the city was feeling the benefits of a prosperity dampened only by a sorrow at the failure of a Christian enterprise which propriety demanded from Christian merchants. Jewish merchants, understandably, kept quiet about the affair.

The Benedictine monks of St Victor and the canons of the cathedral of Notre-Dame-de-la-Major looked askance at the new trade. Some merchants were moving towards the Cathars, who did not prohibit the practice of usury among their rank-

and-file members. Others salved their consciences by making rich endowments to the abbey and the cathedral. Although the Church's policy on usury and trade with non-Christians was strict – if almost completely ignored – the monks continued to thrive on gifts from the pilgrims who came from Italy, Spain, Germany, England and from all over France.

The pilgrims came to adore the jawbone of St Lazarus, believed to be the brother of St Mary Magdalene. The monks told the pilgrims how, after having been raised from the dead, Lazarus had become bishop of Marseilles. The abbey of St Victor also offered the pilgrim proximity to one of the ribs of St Lawrence the Martyr, some of Martha of Bethany's bones, and the preserved corpses (it was said) of a hundred and forty innocent Christians slaughtered for their faith in Roman times. The abbey was also proud to possess several of the rods used in the scourging of Christ before the Crucifixion.

Miraval had not been long in Marseilles when he heard that Peire Vidal was in town, singing at the court of his new patron, Barral, the count of Marseilles and vassal to the king of Aragon, Alfonso II. Miraval had not (so he thought) spoken to Peire Vidal for about four years. On that occasion, there had been a summer gathering of troubadours in Fanjeaux and at Cabaretz. Miraval had been greatly impressed by Vidal's compositions and was keen to hear him again.

A Political Song

When Miraval arrived at Barral's court, the whole place was in commotion. Servants were dashing through archways in the oblong courtyard. Flags waved from the battlements above the steep, stout walls of Barral's castle. Ladies in flowing gowns were making their way between knights and richly dressed merchants to the trestle tables laid out in the courtyard. The tables were covered with bowls of fruit: oranges and lemons, dates, olives, peaches, grapes and apples bulged from the great marble bowls spread out at regular intervals along the tables. These Syrian bowls, exquisitely carved in interweaving floral patterns with cursive Syriac script decorating the broad rims, reflected the warm, golden beams of an early evening sun. Boys in short woollen robes carried carved crystal ewers of glittering wine to the tables, and everywhere there was hubbub and chattering.

Suddenly, trumpets sounded from the battlements and in walked Barral: a short man with the broad grin of a practised hedonist, accompanied by his wife, a shy and attractive Catalan lady, dressed in a red silk dress, embroidered in gold with stylized pineapples, stars and thistles which sparkled alarmingly about her heavy, brown breasts. From out of the hush which followed Barral's arrival, the count rose to speak in a rushed and somewhat flat tone, his bulbous eyes staring all about him. 'The court of Barral welcomes Peire Vidal.'

Into the centre of the courtyard strode Peire Vidal, who proceeded to sing, without accompaniment, a new *canso* which combined, as was his style, a review of current political events with a searching look into his own heart's adventures:

'For a little I'd give up singing
because I see Youth and Valour dead,
and Merit too finds no pasture –
everyone repels and rejects it;
and I see wickedness hold such sway –
it has conquered and overcome the world –
that I can scarcely find a country which
has not caught its head in its snare.'

'What a voice!' thought Miraval. Without doubt, Peire Vidal sang better than anyone in the world.

'Now, how the Pope and the false doctors
have cast Holy Church into such confusion
that God Himself is grieved!
It's because they're so foolish and sinful
that the heretics have sprung up;
and since they're the first to sin,
it's hard for one to do anything else –
but I don't want to be their advocate!'

At these words the knights cheered, the ladies laughed and the bishop frowned. Others rolled their glazed eyes and wondered what the troubadour could possibly mean. Several priests shook their heads but could not take their eyes off Vidal, so bold and forthright was he.

'And all the trouble comes from France,
from those who used to be best,
for the king is neither noble nor true to Merit,
nor true to Our Lord; and he's quit the Sepulchre,
and he buys and sells and haggles or just like a pleasant or
townsman,
whereby his Frenchmen are put to shame.'

Miraval was intensely excited. What control Vidal exercised over his audience! He stared at Peire Vidal who was gesticulating only twenty feet away from him. The troubadour was wearing a long robe of royal blue with long, black boots which extended a little beyond his toes into points. Over the blue robe, Vidal wore a white silk surcoat with blue arrows embroidered up the sides. His long brown hair was crowned by a curious blue cap which sat like a dome upon his head and which was folded up at the sides and decorated by ogee arches in white dye. Peire Vidal hardly moved his lips as he sadly sang that:

'All the world's coming to such a pass
that yesterday we saw it bad and, today, worse;
and ever since he broke God's command,
we hear not of the Emperor increasing in Merit or virtue.
And yet if henceforth he leaves Richard to his fate,
now that he's in prison,
the English will vent their scorn on him.'

Peire Vidal closed his eyes, hung his head low and waited for the applause. There were certain people in the audience who were shocked at the content of the song and the applause was muted, an embarrassment further emphasized by those ribald cheers which came from the back. Miraval rose from his seat and began clapping hard. Peire Vidal slowly looked over to him and smiled with a slight nod of the head. Miraval stared at him, his eyes widening in increasing amazement. He saw a deep scar in Vidal's face which ran from just below his left eye to his dimpled chin, hitherto in shadow and out of view. Miraval was suddenly brought to the recognition that here was the man who, many months before, had been savaged by the hounds of Cabaretz. He sat down abruptly in a state of complete astonishment. This scar was the work of Loba de

Pénnautier and the hounds had been those of the Castle of Love! As the old Barral rose from his feet to express a guarded word of praise for Peire Vidal, Miraval's mind was filled with the image of another Vidal, mounted upon his horse on a dark night at Lastours, his bloody hand passing over his blood-caked face, never to be unmarked again.

He nudged Ahmed, 'Do you see that? It was Peire Vidal!'

'Of course, my lord.'

'No, Ahmed, don't you remember my telling you about the poor man – the one running from Cabaretz with a wolfskin trailing behind him?'

'Yes, my lord. Now I – it was Vidal?'

'It was him. I must find him and speak with him. Excuse me, Ahmed.'

As the assembled court began attending to the food and wine, Miraval got up and went looking for Vidal, who had left the courtyard.

He found him leaving the privy on the first floor of the castle.

Vidal said: 'I saw you, seigneur. I thank you deeply for your appreciation. I think I've just lost another patron! Raimon de Miraval, is it not?'

'Yes, and I'm sure you haven't! Barral is not the man, I think, to let something of quality slip through his great fingers.'

'I hope you're right, seigneur. This last year has been pretty tough.'

'I know. I saw you at Lastours last year.'

Peire Vidal thought for a moment and, as he did so, his face changed into delight and wonderment. 'It was *you* who helped me! I thought I recognized you, but it was so dark – and the wounds ...'

'But I didn't recognize you!'

'Is it any wonder? I was lucky.'

'Lucky?'

'Always lucky, that's Peire Vidal! Alfonso of Aragon put me up for six months until I was fully recovered – to "put one over", you might say, on the count of Toulouse! Amazing how many times envy and hatred finds itself in the service of Love, have you not noticed?'

'Oh yes!'

'Well, it was Alfonso – tiring of me, I suppose – who wrote

to Barral on my behalf – so there's another reason why Barral must put up with me! But, you know, seigneur – '

'Please call me Raimon. We do share a calling; and thus far we share a rank – at least between ourselves.'

Vidal bowed and smiled, 'Most kind. You know that – Oh! I've forgotten what I was going to say!' Peire Vidal continued, breathlessly. 'It's such a wonderful life we troubadours lead, don't you think? I mean that we can sing anything we want to – that is, so long as we have a fast horse! Some things just have to be said, don't you think? But who'd have thought it? When I first felt this scar on my face, I thought my career was over – but no! People think I won it fighting the Moors! And why should I contradict them? I simply say that I won it on the field of Love!!'

'Or mountain – '

'Near enough. But striving for a lady and fighting a Crusade. What's the difference? Both things make me want to sing and write! It's never easy whichever way you choose – and we have no choice, do we?'

'I do believe, my dear Peire, that you are right. I've learnt to accept it.'

'Accept with open arms, my dear Raimon. We're the luckiest men alive! I tell you, just before the Lastours incident I had – at the instigation of the count of Toulouse – been on pilgrimage to the Holy Land for my sins! I found myself in the county of Tripoli – '

'In Syria?'

'Yes, of course – I wouldn't go to that cesspit in Africa. Lose my head in no time there, no mistake!' Miraval swallowed. 'Do you know Tripoli, Raimon? The one in Syria, that is?'

'I'm afraid not – but my drummer comes from there and I've heard a bit about it.'

'Unbelievable place. Unbelievable! I met the most extraordinary lady there. Black as pitch she was. A beautiful princess – and how she danced! Try and imagine this lady, scarcely a bead on her black body – it was like rippling silk by a waterfall! I was completely in her power, and I would have given her everything – only I've nothing to give! So I gave her a song, "To her I yield myself with sure and guileless heart, for I am wholly hers ...'

'Only *hers*, Peire?'

'But of course. Hers ... and a hundred others! You should see the love-letters I receive. Everywhere I go – they would make even a priest blush!'

'That is saying something!'

'Indeed it is. Such ladies as you would never believe existed. All wonderful! All magical! Peire Vidal loves them all! It seems to me, Raimon, that amidst all the evils of our times, the only thing left to venerate – besides Our Lord, of course – is the sweetness and beauty of our ladies: whatever their husbands' religion, they are our friends the world over!'

'Couldn't agree more. Will you join my friends and me?'

'To be sure, I should love to – but, alas, there is someone – '

'A new love?'

'As new as tomorrow and as fresh as spring! Yes, from the Carcassès. Oh, how I love this Provençal air! There's pure *joy* here and nobility as nowhere else. Who could ever leave it? But one must, alas!'

'I too must leave.'

'Where to, seigneur Raimon?'

'Strictly between you and me, I am bound for that African dump you spoke about.'

'Tripoli? You must be mad! You'll never make it. Just listen around town here for a few days. Africa is completely wild. Every religious madman has been let loose to spread his madness. The whole place is in turmoil. Killing Christians is sport to many of these people – and religion to others. No, really, you must not go, Raimon – not if you want to see Miraval and your lady again.'

'I simply must go, Vidal. it is a debt of honour.'

'Is there *Merit* to be won?'

'Who knows?'

Peire Vidal scratched his head, 'Look, Raimon de Miraval, you did me a great service beneath Cabaretz – '

'A Christian duty, nothing more.'

'You might be surprised how many think they can be Christians without performing such duties! No, listen, I shall introduce you to a sea-captain whom you can trust, Joseph Abulafia. A great storyteller. He trades with Tripoli – but you must be disguised. Do you speak Arabic?'

'My drummer. He does.'

'Good. Then, Raimon, you must become a Jew.'

'A Jew?!'

'If you want to live, Raimon. As a living Christian your life won't be worth a single mark. But your severed head would win Paradise for an Almohad. You just can't be too careful. I shall take you to Joseph. He is well known at Tripoli docks. He will not give you up. Please accept this service, Raimon. It is the least I can do for you – and the most!'

'What of your rendezvous?'

'She will have to wait. It will increase her *Joy*!'

'And *yours*, Vidal?'

'Spoken like a true troubadour! I almost wish I was coming with you – but *Tripoli*!'

A Barca

Miraval returned to the courtyard and collected his minstrels – a rather difficult operation involving many abject apologies offered to friendly ladies. 'Come on you lot! We're going to sea!'

Peire Vidal pushed his way grandly through the thickening crowds and darkening streets which led to the harbour. The pungent smells became quite overwhelming: exotic mixtures, musk and cowdung combined in a swell of impenetrable filthiness. Knights, thieves, merchants, beggars, salesmen, sailors, pimps and prostitutes bustled in the crowd, flashing in and out of gauzelike beams which flicked and flickered in shafts and shades, sometimes flooding in crowded squares and market places.

Miraval almost lost sight of Ahmed, who was doing his best to keep up with Peire Vidal. Berteaux, Gérard and Jacques kept looking to one another in looks of wonder and confusion. The whiff of sewage was soon replaced by that of sea air and the tang of salt. Standing at the dockside, the group was astonished by the size and number of shifting ships. The squawk of diving gulls broke the skyline and soon the group found themselves hopping over bollards and hooks, cranes and cargo, knots and lines; dodging hardened sea-faces with craggy jaws, wild eyes and pulsing muscles flexing in the sun, sweat and sorrow. Every face told a story but it would take a thousand and one nights to hear them all ...

Peire Vidal stood breathless before a *barca*. Its timber body creaked up and down the dockside. Great hempen ropes bonded the ship to land, stretching and squeaking with the waves. The ship was called the *Merkabah* and weighed about fifty tons. She was square-rigged with two sails, now lashed to the beams. Half of the deck was occupied by a long thatched cabin, on the roof of which two sailors, stripped to the waist, were working hard to reweave the rushes which made up the only shelter from the elements. One of the sailors was applying thick slurps of tar to provide some insulation. But for them, the *barca* appeared to be totally empty. Peire Vidal called up from the dockside, 'Joseph! Joseph! It's Vidal! Peire Vidal! Come out – I've got friends to see you!'

The sun finally touched the horizon and the light changed. A rosy glow hovered upon the beams of the ship and the two sailors who were working on the cabin began to assemble their tools and to climb down.

'What y'want?' asked the younger of the two.

'Joseph Abulafia. Tell him, please, that Peire Vidal is here with passengers.'

The sailor shrugged his shoulders and went inside the cabin. Peire Vidal grinned at Miraval. 'He'll come. He's probably looking over charts. He's very serious about his work.' Miraval raised his eyebrows, wondering what other sea captains must be like – did they do it all by the stars? From out of the cabin walked a tall man, dressed in a long, black overcoat which was cut like an angular hourglass and bound at the waist by a red sash. The man had powerful features and would have looked extremely handsome but for a huge pointed nose which seemed to rise from out of his face like a volcanic peak. It was simultaneously funny and frightening. His shiny brown face was garnished by a long black beard, speckled and sparkling with a myriad stray grey hairs. He walked to the prow.

'Joseph! So good to see you. Did you win?'

'Vidal!' Joseph had a thunderously deep voice, 'Vidal!', the greatest troubadour that Tripoli ever saw!'

'Don't forget Provence, Aragon and Toulouse, Joseph!'

'How could I, Vidal? They've all been home to me. Now, what can I do for you, my dear friend?'

'Will you take passengers, Joseph? I have here the most noble troubadour of the Languedoc.'

'That's generous from you, Vidal! Then this man must be ...' Joseph looked carefully at the hopeful Miraval, 'Miraval! Raimon de Miraval, I am so pleased to meet you. Come aboard! You are my honoured guest. And please, bring your friends – musicians no doubt.'

The group walked up the gangplank. Joseph eyed them all and then frowned. 'Vidal, I have room for only three passengers. No more. I already have a crew of eighteen and – I'm sorry Miraval – I have a large cargo of furs for Tripoli. Only three. Twenty marks for the return journey, provisions provided – and safe-conduct.'

Miraval looked to Vidal as if to say, 'That's twice what I expected.'

'Privacy too. That is, I don't want to know your business.'

'He's the best, Raimon,' said Vidal.

'Jacques, Berteaux – I need Ahmed – and Gérard is good with a sword. I'm sorry.'

'I'll take them!' said Vidal, 'Yes, I need good musicians. How about it, Jacques, Berteaux? Will you play for me? I tell you – there's nothing for you in Tripoli. *Terrible* diseases, that's all – better the pox you know, eh? But stay with me and together we shall play the greatest music to be heard anywhere in the whole world! Am I not right, Joseph?'

The captain nodded.

Miraval looked regretfully at his two loyal friends, 'To play with Peire Vidal. I admit it's a good second. Do you accept his offer?'

Jacques and Berteaux accepted the offer.

'But listen, Peire,' said Miraval, 'Don't take them out of Marseilles. I want to rejoin my friends here when we return.'

'How long must we wait?' asked Jacques.

'I should think ... no more than three months?' Joseph nodded in agreement.

'We shall be here,' said Berteaux, 'with or without the illustrious Peire Vidal.'

'Good. That's settled then. When do we sail, Joseph?'

'We sail for Sicily at dawn. Get drunk now if you're not used to the sea.'

Miraval and his companions hugged each other and the

troubadour shed a tear as he saw Peire Vidal disappear into the crowd with his two friends.

'Well, that's that,' said Gérard. 'I've never been to sea.'

'You will love the sea,' said Joseph. 'I can tell just by looking at you. You must all promise me that you will get on with the crew. I want no arguments. We have Moslems, Christians and Jews here. The sea is no theologian – she will swallow anybody. We talk about drink, women and the weather. If your desire is for deeper intellectual nourishment . . . talk to me! I've heard it all – but I'm always ready to learn! Good. You had better go and collect your luggage. Not too much mind – just enough to sleep on. And remember, the sea is wet. Only the wit is dry on this ship. Welcome aboard Miraval!'

8
The Stars

MIRAVAL LEANED ON THE SIDE of the deck with Joseph Abulafia as the *Merkabah* sailed out of Marseilles and headed eastwards towards Italy. This was Miraval's first time at sea and his eyes were moist with tears. A grey ribbon had begun to emerge along the horizon and, as it rose into the dome of the sky, it slowly absorbed the bright silver stars. Ahmed and Gérard were somewhere in the cabin, sleeping off a heavy night's drinking. Miraval could not sleep. Joseph spoke to him.

'Different, eh?'

'Oh yes, very. I've only dreamt of this before – but to *be* here. To hear the slap and splash of the waters . . . yes, it's very different. Just look at the sky. One is so exposed here. It's like being in the eye of God.'

'Yes, Miraval. The Eye of God. Yes, we are in the eye of God. Now you know God has blue eyes!'

'Swimming in the eye of God . . .'

'We are not swimming. We are enthroned here. *Merkabah* means "throne". It means the Throne of God.'

'You're a poet, Joseph.'

'Of course, Miraval. You cannot ply these waters without poetry. Nobody writes our verses. The wind hears them. The sea swallows them. The air carries them. The sun destroys them. And then we start again . . . My father sailed this course before me – and his father, and his father before him. Thank the Lord. He abides with us. His face is on the waters.'

Miraval could only listen. He had never met anyone like Joseph before.

'I like to read, Miraval. I read a lot. There are always new things to read on this journey. The sea carries knowledge. I love the sea, Miraval. She bears knowledge. She is our mother. Mother Sea.'

'Joseph.'

'Swimming in the Eye of God'

'Yes, Miraval.'

'Sorry to bring you down to earth – '

'Earth?' Miraval got the joke and the two men laughed. 'You were saying, Miraval?'

'It's just that Peire Vidal said I should be disguised as a Jew.'

'It might help you. Do you want to?'

'I don't know. I don't like disguises. Will it make a difference?'

'Seigneur, I don't know your business but I know this. A Christian stranger is going to attract attention.'

'How can I become a Jew?'

Joseph laughed. 'How much suffering can you bear? How to become a Jew? Just say you are a Jew.'

'Will they understand me?'

'Not in Occitan, no. You will need a necklace. Buy a Star of David necklace in Sicily. Buy a skullcap. Look rich. Grow your beard. Wear my clothes. Get your friend Ahmed to translate for you. Make it appear that Ahmed is in charge.'

'Are Jews so safe in Tripoli?'

'No, not always. The holy book of Islam is a most extraordinary work. But its attitude to Jews and Christians is not always clear. Let me give you an example. It is written in "The Table" of the Holy Koran: "You will surely find that the most violent in their opposition to the faithful are the Jews and the idolators, and that the nearest in friendship with true believers are those who say: We are Christians. That is because there are priests and monks among them, and because they are free from pride. When they listen to that which was revealed to the Prophet, you will see their eyes fill with tears as they recognize its truth. They say: Lord, we believe. Count us among your witnesses."'

'I never heard this. You know the Koran well.'

'It pays to know the mind of the man with whom you do business. It builds respect.'

' – And understanding?'

'That, dear Miraval, takes much longer – and we may never have the time.'

'The Cathars say, "Time is of the Devil."'

'And they are right! Now excuse me, Miraval. There is work to be done. Enjoy the stars! They are our only true guide.'

Miraval looked up to the dawning sky and wondered, as

only those who are at sea in a little ship can wonder, whether he would be lost in a world where waves, and not words, were the builders of destiny.

For a week the *Merkabah* had sailed peacefully along the coast of southern France before swinging south towards Calabria. After two weeks the *Merkabah* docked at Messina in Sicily. There it stayed while Joseph ordered in fresh supplies and did some minor trading in dyed woollen cloth and honey. Miraval, Ahmed and Gérard were encouraged to go ashore to obtain the costumes which, they hoped, would make Gérard and Miraval indistinguishable from many other Jewish trader in Tripoli.

It felt incredibly strange to be back on land after two weeks at sea. In fact, the sensation was quite unreal. This sense of unreality was heightened by the strangeness of the environment. Sicily was governed by a Norman-French monarch: Tancred, who was, in the truest sense, an 'ugly little bastard'. It was said that he looked like a crowned monkey. He owed his throne to King Richard who just over two years previously had ensured that the rival claimant, King Henry VI of Germany, remained out of Sicily while the Crusaders consolidated and prepared for the next leg of their journey. There was still a lot of talk about the Crusaders in the town. There had been rape, rioting and wrangling of every kind.

The Crusaders, for their part, had been shocked to find themselves in a flourishing Norman kingdom, set in a landscape of quite astonishing beauty, in which Arab, Greek and Norman managed to live together without killing each other. Only the arrival of Crusaders had stirred up trouble. The biggest problems had been caused by the inevitable price rises which came when two hundred ships full of famished troops had arrived, leading to almost instantaneous scarcities. Many soldiers had got themselves into gambling debts. Peace finally broke out when Richard, in a deal with Tancred, had regularized the price of a loaf to a penny and set a fixed price on wine. A few Crusaders had decided to stay, opening up the odd tavern and marrying local Christian girls who, Miraval was astonished to sea, had embraced a fashion for wearing Arab-style veils. Miraval was, of course, intrigued by the idea and wondered what Azalaïs would look like in one! Oh Azalaïs! What was she doing now?

Miraval and his friends followed the crowds around the town and managed to pick up the requisite costumes: long cotton robes in red and white stripes, little white skullcaps and some cheap jewellery. In spite of the fun they were having, and the anonymity which they were enjoying, Miraval, especially after such a long time at sea, soon began to find the crowds oppressive. They returned to the *Merkabah*.

'Joseph, I should like to explore the coastline, where it's quieter. How long do you intend staying in Messina?'

'I shall leave the day after tomorrow. If you're not back ... too bad.'

'Any ideas where we might go to?'

'Yes. You could ride to Cefalù. If it's quietness you're looking for, there are great rocks and cliffs and views there. Splendid places for meditation.'

'You know it?'

'Of course, Miraval. Many times. I have a business contact here who will, for a small fee no doubt, lend you horses. Cefalù is fifty miles west of here – so you don't have much time. Remember, we depart at dusk on Friday. I should hate to leave without you.'

'We'll be back!'

'And by the way – '

'Joseph?'

'I like your costumes. I think they'll do. Be humble. Be good.'

Cefalù

Miraval was sitting on the top of a twelve-hundred-foot-high promontory, overlooking both the changing sea and the town of Cefalù which fanned out below him. The warm air of spring was delightfully fresh and creamy and Miraval had begun to feel that distinctive mode of happiness creeping up his spine. It was good to be alone. He had let Ahmed and Gérard go wandering about the thriving town, currently home to bands of Armenian, Calabrian, Greek and French builders and sculptors. These wealthy artisans were in the process of completing the town's new cathedral, which had arisen upon an eminence below the edge of an overhanging cliff.

Above it, Miraval was sitting upon a huge boulder, one of many strewn about him, in the shade of a Persian nut tree, thinking about Azalaïs. He had experienced a great fear aboard the *Merkabah* but he had not shown it. He had felt cut off from home, exposed and terrifyingly isolated, caught up in a tense, sickly maelstrom which had threatened to overcome his tired mind. He had been aware of the immense scale of the creative power within him and, in the vastness of the open sea, had begun to be aware of that dark and evil side that forever lurks in the human breast. There were times when it had become almost overwhelming and he had felt driven to throw himself overboard. He missed Azalaïs terribly and this powerful emotion had combined with the fear within him, the fear of darkness and of loneliness, of the sheer power of the creative spirit, to produce the sensation of lost control and nausea: a vacant mind of fleeting forms and departing spirits.

Now, firmly on land, close to the distinct and lovely forms of nature – enormous geraniums, huge daisies, oak trees, olives, oranges and lemons, cotton plants, corn and sugar cane – he began to feel safe again. He was driven to reflect on the problem of evil – that dark side of his nature which, in the throes of amorous enthusiasm, he had denied and which, somehow and in spite of 'himself', had got out of control, in the terrible débâcle which had resulted in the seduction of Ermengarde de Castres and the murder of Olivier de Saissac. He would have to admit that Love was not *all* his thought. Having made this startling admission to himself, he did feel some genuine relief and he begun to look about him. He observed how to the west, some fifty miles away, a line of hills ran into the sea. To his right, beyond the groves of oak and of olives, a great rock precipice also plunged into the sea. Indeed, not one nor two but all of the mighty pinnacles of rock, those many silent bastions against the waves, were tumbling slowly but inexorably into the sea. The thought did not terrify him. As his own little river, the Orbiel, had washed him, the sea could be said to wash the world.

He looked again to the distant hills and laughed to himself, 'A woman is like a landscape – best seen from a distance!' He knew he could amuse his friends with this line but, on deeper reflection, he began to find it had a hollow ring to it. The hills only looked distant because he was so small! He remembered the spirit in the water at Fontjoncouse and he felt her close again. And he looked to the sea and he saw her there: Azalaïs! And in his mind, Miraval embraced the sea and loved her. He was part of her. She was part of him. There was no part of Her where Love could not reach, no matter how profound her depths, how powerful her waves of destruction – there existed no darkness where Love could not reach! And Miraval came to a conclusion that perhaps only Joseph Abulafia would comprehend: that without evil, there could be no Love! And without darkness, there could be no Light – and without the Lady, there could be no Raimon de Miraval! He was ready to go back to sea. The *Merkabah* was waiting.

It was dusk at the port of Messina. Miraval could see Joseph's silhouette against the vanishing sky. The captain turned round as Miraval approached him.

'Come here, Miraval! Yes, yes I can see you have been to Cefalù. It was good, was it not?'

Miraval, shining with sweat after a long ride and a fast run to the docks, just nodded and smiled and, with that sweet, lilting charm which he had hitherto hidden away in his voice, replied, 'Ah yes, Joseph. Cefalù!' Then he shook his head with near disbelief and evident delight. 'Thank you, Joseph! How can I ever thank you?'

'You have thanked me enough! Just seeing your face is sufficient!'

'Why? Is it so different?'

'Your soul is healing itself, Miraval. You are – how can I put it? – you are coming together!'

'Land and Sea, Joseph!'

'Land and Sea. Can't have one without the other, can we?'

'That's right! That's right! Why didn't I see it before?'

Joseph laughed. 'Oh, we all lose sight of it sometimes. We forget. Being in the world is mostly like being asleep. The Sea wakes us up. The Sea breaks down the walls. The best crewmen feel the freedom of the Sea. That's why the landspeople fear us. But we don't fear them, do we, lads?'

'No, sir! Not us!' cried the crewmen, who were unfurling the great square sail and securing the rigging.

'Ready to cast off?'

'Aye, Aye!'

'Aye to that!' said a happy Miraval. 'Gérard! Ahmed! Are you ready?'

'We're ready!'

'Cast off!' called Joseph and then, whispering an aside to Miraval, said:

'There's no going back now.'

'That's fine by me!'

A Rose by Any Lover's name

LOBA WAS IN THE COURTYARD at Cabaretz. 'Hurry up! It's started raining – shit! Look at my hair! No, don't look at my hair – look over there! Yes, that's it – get the roots in before the rain washes the soil away. Good, that's lovely! Now go inside and get something to eat. Thank you, gentlemen.'

Loba stood looking at the new patch of rosebushes lined up by the outer wall, wondering whether that was the best place for them. She looked somewhat doubtful but it would do for now. Why was nothing ever the way she wanted it? Sometimes it was just too much and nobody could understand the way she felt about it, least of all her husband. But they did look rather sweet. No, they looked beautiful. She had been right. If only people would listen to her more often! Then they would not get into such a mess!

The rain on the petals made the bushes quiver. Loba looked closely at the deep pink flowers. They looked as if they were weeping but they smelt wonderful. Her fine fair hair dripping wet, Loba cupped a rose in her thin hands and, closing her eyes, kissed it. In her mind was a picture of Raimon de Miraval. 'Where could he be now?' she wondered. Loba had started to worry about him. Bringing the rosebushes to the castle was supposed to take her mind off him but it didn't.

She wiped a little tear away. 'Oh! He's such a useless man! He's not worth crying about.' But that did not stop her. 'Silly man wants a mother to look after him! Shit! That's another dress ruined!' She looked up to the purple sky.

A mighty crack of thunder swept up from the horizon and echoed about the sea. The waves responded in kind and began to beat about the *Merkabah* with a vengeance.

'All hands on deck! Miraval! Gérard! Ahmed! Join the men at the tiller!! We're in for a big one! May Heaven protect us!' The whole universe came alive in Miraval's mind as its breath roared and beat about the big sail.

'You, boy! Come down from the nest quickly! Help furl the sail!'

Miraval looked over to Joseph at the helm. Joseph nodded. 'Give your heart, Miraval! Give your heart to the *Merkabah*! She needs you all! Hold firm! Hold firm!'

A terrible black phalanx of angry cloud was advancing towards them. Miraval was totally exhilarated. This was marvellous! This was really living! Live or die, it did not matter! The rain slashed the faces of the crew. Some of them began to retch. The *Merkabah* rose up on mountainlike waves and then plunged into walls of water thirty feet high. Sheets of rain rushed across the deck like cold flames. Soon Joseph's commands were lost amidst the mad chorus of the heaving ocean.

Miraval began to sing – or rather shout at the waves. He would sing to the Sea who was screaming at the ship:

> 'As the rose among a thousand branches
> is more gracious than the flower of any other seed!'

Gérard and Ahmed began to join in:

> 'So among the false and treacherous posers ...

Whoosh! Down flooded the waves! Up bobbed the *Merkabah* into the blackened sky

> does my lady stand within her tent ...

None of their false oaths can harm her!'

A bilious wave knocked Ahmed across the slippery deck.

'Ahmed!' Miraval could not let go of the tiller to help him. 'Ahmed!'

Ahmed was sliding about the deck in complete terror. Another wave knocked him to the far side and Miraval could not see him for mist.

'Keep singing!' cried one of the sailors.

'I can't! Where's Ahmed?'

'Sing, you fool! Sing!'

'Her Merit has grown under friendly stars
I pray that, due to them, it is not lowered!'

'Carry on! Don't stop!'

'I can't remember . . . I . . . Ahmed! Come back!'

One of the Arab sailors began repeating: '*Muhammad rastel allahi. La ilaha illa-llaha*!'

Miraval felt a touch on his shoulder. Surely it was a ghost – but no, it was Ahmed! 'Oh Ahmed!'

As Miraval thanked God for saving his friend, the entire cabin roof came flying towards them.

'Duck! Duck!'

'Fuck! It's the roof!'

'Get down! Down!'

'*La ilaha illa-llaha*!'

'Hold! Hold!'

'Unbelievable!' cried Miraval.

Down went the *Merkabah* again and again until it was so dark it did seem that Hell had finally opened its mouth. Then again, up flew the ship.

'Watch the mast!'

One of the crossbeams began to slip down and scrape across the deck, throwing up great splinters. The sailors looked at Miraval in panic.

'You take the tiller! Hold it for, the sake of Allah!'

Miraval was screaming with Joy, 'It's up to us! Let's show them!'

The sailors took the ropes and began heaving back the spar. Miraval, Gérard and Ahmed held tight. The sea came crashing in.

'Secure the ropes! The ropes!'

The cabin boy was swinging from the mast, gripping the rope with his teeth, his hands and his feet. Round and round he went.

'Don't let go, boy! Hold the mast! Your feet! Around the mast!'

The poor boy swung round and round the central mast until he was flung hard against it. He let go of the rope and slipped down the mast, coming down to the deck with a crack and a slap. The rope above was flying around like a stray hair in the head of a windswept giant.

Joseph crawled down from the helm, 'Hold the spar! I'll get the rope!'

As the mast rose and fell, the brave captain climbed upwards from bracket to bracket and then on to the rigging.

'Don't look!' cried Gérard.

Down slid the captain, gripping the rope. 'Now bind it well!'

'Incredible! The man's incredible! I love him! I love him!' screamed Miraval.

Joseph scrambled over to the great tiller and joined Miraval. The latter put his arm round Joseph and smiled.

'Don't you dare take your hands off that thing!'

'Pardon me, Joseph!'

'Later! Later!'

And so the crew held firm through the storm and as the tumult began to subside, Miraval became aware of a deep bond of affection shared among the crew for their master, for their ship and for each other – and, most surprisingly, an equally profound affection and respect for their mistress, the Sea. The hot sun came out again and before long, the sodden deck was dry once more.

And Loba slipped inside the castle and out of the rain, making her way to the chapel to say a prayer for Miraval. As the sun burst through the window of the empty chapel, Loba knew that Miraval was safe.

Amid tremendous spirits the *Merkabah* sailed on southwards to Tripoli. Five days after having passed the island of Malta, and only eighty miles from the African coast, the lookout sighted a ship sailing straight towards them and alerted the captain.

'Did you hear that, Miraval?'

'He said it was a dhow.'

'Yes, Miraval. A dhow. Yusuf! What is our speed?'

Yusuf, a burly Arab with a split nose and long black hair bound at his neck, ran to the prow and threw over a wooden block attached to a rope. He counted the evenly spaced knots in the rope as they passed through his hand until the block had passed the stern of the ship.

'Six knots, master!'

'Thank you, Yusuf. Open the armoury. Swords and bows for every man. Quickly!' Joseph looked grimly at Miraval and nodded. 'Yes, Miraval. One of the many joys of the Sea in these parts is the pirate. Are you good with a sword?'

Miraval raised his eyebrows and looked quizzically at Gérard. 'The seigneur can take care of himself,' said Gérard.

'But is he good with a sword?'

'I'm not good,' said Miraval, 'I'm evil!'

'That's good!'

' – And I'm better!' said Gérard.

'With any luck, we won't have to put your *gab* to the test.'

Ahmed began to shake. He had heard stories about the pirates of these waters. He had heard of the sheer delight they took in slaughtering the unprotected voyager.

'Oh come on, Ahmed' said Gérard. 'These people aren't invincible, you know. This is the *Merkabah*! I've been talking to some of the sailors. This is nothing new for them. They've all been through this before.'

'I'm frightened, Gérard.'

While the crew was hastily armed, Joseph approached Ahmed. 'Now, Ahmed, I can see from looking at you that you have fire in your eyes. This is good. Very good.'

Ahmed gave a nervous smile.

'Yusuf. Fetch the mandragora!'

'Now, Ahmed, because you are so brave and so intelligent, I have a special task for you to perform. Ah – thank you, Yusuf.'

'What is it?' enquired Ahmed, with one eye fixed on the approaching dhow.

'Don't look at that, Ahmed – look at this! This is mandragora. You see it is rooted in the pot. You see the leaves? In the soil is buried a curious root. It is thought to have magical properties – and you will see that it does. Now listen to me carefully. You must be very precise ...' Joseph whispered his plan into Ahmed's ear. Ahmed soon lost the quiver in his smile.

As the dhow drew nearer, out of the sun's glare, it became clear that the entire ship, including its lateen sail, was coloured bright red. The pirates themselves could not be seen. Apparently it was their strategy to show not more than a few of their number on deck but to lie in hiding beneath old sails. The crew of the *Merkabah* could expect to have to face as many as thirty pirates, crammed for short periods into a single dhow and all thirsty for blood.

Although the dhow was smaller than the barca, it was much faster, and in addition to speed and manoeuvrability, the pirates enjoyed an even greater weapon: a psychological one, for the Berber pirates attempted, with each successive expedition, to surpass themselves in acts of atrocious physical barbarity. They were the stuff of which nightmares were made. Joseph, however, was no fool. He encouraged an offensive and active attitude in his crew. Each member had a specific task to perform in such situations and was expected to excel in self-discipline and knowledge of the appropriate 'drill'. Joseph stood upon the prow and addressed the anxious crew: 'This is the *Merkabah*. There is the enemy. The *Merkabah* does not fail.'

Then, to Miraval's astonishment, Joseph retired within the newly reconstructed cabin. Miraval clenched his sword, wondering why Ahmed was sitting cross-legged on deck with his arms wrapped around the pot containing the mandragora. Yusuf approached Miraval with a very long dagger, smiled, and in one stroke cut Miraval's robe from the feet to the crotch. 'You may need to jump! Now, you and Gérard, please stay at the back.'

Yusuf took his place on the line of nine crewmen, armed with daggers and bows and spread out along the bough facing the approaching dhow. The remaining nine sailors placed themselves upon the spar behind the sail, further up the rigging and behind the cabin – all of them armed with the sharpest and deadliest of mattocks. The dhow was now clearly visible. Not a sound emerged from its decks. Suddenly the dhow erupted into a loud hooting sound. The sound came from a battered trumpet and was immediately followed by a high-pitched cacophony: an irregular chanting, like a hundred mad muezzin swooping round a minaret.

Yusuf looked round toward Miraval and Gérard, both of whom were having difficulty finding their footing. 'To the tiller! Join those men there. If they destroy the tiller, we're finished!'

The pirate vessel began to close in on the *Merkabah*. Miraval saw three dark figures emerge on the enemy's deck. They were swinging grappling hooks. The *Merkabah* was dropping speed when, quite suddenly, the chanting stopped. The dhow was now within twenty feet of the Merkabah and was closing in fast. It seemed to hover by the boughs. From behind the sail of the scarlet dhow, a tall figure emerged: dressed from head to toe in a spotless white felucca, the man cried out: '*La ilaha illa-llaha*!' 'There is no God but Allah!' and then made gestures to the men with grappling hooks.

At this precise moment, Yusuf called back: '*Muhammad rastal allahi*!' 'Mohammed is the prophet of God!' – at the sound of which the defenders of the *Merkabah* all fell to the deck.

Ahmed stepped forwards. He held out the pot containing the mandragora. He gripped the leaves. The pirate captain stopped dead still. A great wailing scream came from the *Merkabah*'s cabin. It grew louder and louder until it became a blood-curdling roar. At its highest pitch, Ahmed pulled the mandragora from the pot, and with all his might threw the phallic root on to the deck of the pirate ship. A great gasp came over the enemy vessel. The entire crew of the *Merkabah* shot up and the pirates were suddenly faced with a column of bows, poised to fire. The pirate captain smirked and shrugged his shoulders. Warily, he bent down to pick up the root. He looked at it, fingered it and began to laugh.

Immediately, Joseph stormed out of the cabin, dressed in a blue silk robe and proceeded to march at great speed to the prow of his ship. From a star-studded scabbard Joseph drew a long Castilian sword and in five separate sweeps made out the figure of a pentagram in the air. Joseph stared into the dark eyes of the pirate captain and repeated the act, only this time, with each sweep, he cried out the words:

'OLAM HA-TOHU! GEBURAH! GEBURAH!'

Straightaway the pirate called off his men, gave orders for departure and, with a sickly smile, bowed his head at Joseph Abulafia. Miraval was impressed and the *Merkabah* was safe.

The ship was in sight of the African coast when natural curiosity finally overcame Miraval and he approached Joseph,

'How the hell did you do that?'

Joseph rubbed his beard a little and pondered the question.

'Let us just say that I introduced the enemy to the Pillar of Severity.'

'What, my dear Joseph, is that supposed to mean?'

Joseph huffed. 'A little Qabalah. A little Magic.'

'You're a magician?'

'Not ... not really. Qabalah means the reception of an unwritten tradition. I was in Gerona some years ago. There is a wise Jew there. They call him Isaac the Blind. He had some ... philo-*sophical* skill. I simply invoked a world of confusion and disorder, that is: *Olam Ha-Tohu*. It seemed to work.'

'It did. But Joseph – '

'Yes?'

'How did the Berber understand you?'

'He didn't, of course. But he got the message, I think. It's all a question of *will*. The business with the sword simply provided the appropriate atmosphere. Since it worked, then we must infer that it was magical. It seems to me more and more, Miraval, that the greater part of life is like a play, such as you can see in a marketplace on Christian Saints' Days. If we want to – why, we can write our own parts and change the play.

'Let me put it another way. There are those who dream at night. Upon waking, their dream is forgotten. Then there are other men, and they are to be respected, who dream instead in the daytime and although they are invariably laughed at, they may yet come to shape the day for all men. The key to this process is an active Will. But of all wills, the most powerful is that of the Holy One – may His Name be praised! The universe is a dream of His. We can wake up within this dream and shape it – and, what is more, if our will is in accord with His, there is no limit to the Power at our disposal.

'In the case you have just seen, I was sure that the success of the pirates was not in accordance with His Will. Therefore I felt it right to exercise my own will in the matter. I have heard Christians say, "Not my will Lord, but thine," without really knowing the substance of this statement. The will of Him who made us is not misty or vague, but is always firm, clear and decisive. As, my dear friend, you have just observed, a true will is in every way perfect.'

'Surely, Joseph, this Power you speak of – it can be abused. The demons may use this power.'

'Quite so, Miraval. As above, so below. There is, you may say, War in Heaven as there is on Earth. But the will of man, divorced from the will of the Holy One, is a vain thing, and in the passage of time, the evil deeds of the wilful are either simply swallowed up by the sands or are remembered only as byewords for the folly of man. At the Last Day, even these will be forgotten. We live in a dream: a dream which every day is growing into Reality. What says the Preacher? "Though a sinner do evil an hundred times, and his days be prolonged, yet surely I know that it shall be well with them that fear God . . . "'

Miraval observed how Joseph's face had changed as he spoke. He had begun to glow, his moist eyes set upon some distant place.

'Will the deeds done in Love be remembered, Joseph – or are these vain too?'

'What kind of Love do you mean? The love of your Christ? That is remembered – though seldom practised. As for the *Fine Love* of the troubadour, most of such Love is surely vain. As the Preacher also writes: "I find more bitter than death the woman, whose heart is snares and nets, and her hands as bands: whoso pleaseth God shall escape from her; but the sinner shall be taken by her." A man should never be so foolish as to offer his soul before a woman. She has trampled upon more hearts than ever grapes were trodden for the vintage! But, alas, we are all burdened by our nature! Burdened, but not overcome. Think Miraval of the *Merkabah*, riding upon but never swallowed by the sea. There's much wisdom in it. Right! Now we must prepare to dock. We are nearly there.'

Tripoli

The crew of the *Merkabah* were all quite surprised by the eery quietness of Tripoli. Miraval sent Ahmed ashore to enquire of those few merchants on the dockside the reason for this unexpected peace. Joseph was visibly troubled by this anticlimax and rushed to the port side when Ahmed returned.

'My lord, captain Joseph, there was a riot here yesterday. Many women and children have been killed. The town is apparently split between different factions.'

'What factions, Ahmed? Please, this is very important.'

'It is very complicated, Joseph, but it seems there has been a rebellion in Tunis led by the caliph's viceroy, Abd al-Wahid. He has powerful friends in this city and they have risen against the emir. A tribe of Bedouin who had been encamped outside of the city for some months took advantage of the squabble in the palace and moved in to grab what they could – the palace guard having mutinied. There was an attack on the Jewish Quarter and many have been slaughtered – even though they had embraced Islam. The same is true of the Christians here. The streets are running with blood. Many ships left during the night. There is intense squabbling at the mosque. The *al-Murabitūn*, following the Malikite code, have taken the opportunity to oppose the *al-Muwahhidūn*.'

'The who?'

'We know them as Almohads. They say that they are the True believers in God's unity.'

'And the others?'

'As I recall, they believe the Koran to be literally true. They say the Almohads are corrupt. The point is. It's really too dangerous to stay.'

Joseph looked at Miraval. For the first time, Miraval noticed fear in Joseph's eyes. He scratched the back of his head. 'We cannot leave immediately. We must lay in supplies first. That will take a few hours.'

Miraval was suddenly faced with an alarming crisis. How could he reach Raghib now? He had expected a long search to find the Egyptian, but that was now out of the question. 'A few hours you say, Joseph?'

'Yes. I'm sorry but I simply cannot put the lives of my crew at risk. If the *al-Murabitūn* gain the upper hand, then some of my men could be slaughtered simply for working with non-Moslems – as for the rest of us, it's anyone's guess. The galleys at best, I should think.'

Miraval was thinking fast. 'Joseph, I need to confide some of my business to you.'

'It is a little late for that now, don't you think?'

'Maybe there's a chance. There is an Egyptian who works here. Runs a translating house. His name is – '

'Raghib abd-as-Ṣīna!'

'You know him?'

'Of course I know him. I have bought many books from this man. He is a Christian, you know. He is in the greatest danger. Perhaps he has left already. He's canny that way.'

'You know where he lives?'

'Yes. It is not far from here.'

Miraval thought for a moment. 'Ahmed, I want to beg a favour of you.'

'Yes, my lord. Whatever you wish. I can find this man. Don't worry about me.'

'You don't have to go.'

'You cannot go, my lord. Let me borrow some clothes from one of the crew. Joseph, how long will it take to get to Raghib?'

'I shall draw you a map. It should take no more than half an hour. You understand, Ahmed, that if you have not returned in two hours, I shall have to leave.'

Ahmed looked at Miraval. 'I shall be back.'

Ahmed set off running through the alleyways of Tripoli. The air was thick with smoke and the stench of burning and rotting flesh. Everywhere he looked there were mutilated bodies, covered in flies; bright red blood streamed down the mud-brick walls and overturned market stalls. Ahmed could hear distant shouting but could see no one. He reached the end of a street and was distressed to see it completely blocked by a pile of entangled corpses. He held his breath and tried to climb over it. His foot plunged into an exposed lung. He looked down and felt bile rise from his stomach to his throat. He felt dizzy and tried to reach the top of the putrid heap. His hand gripped a shock of hair. As he tried to pull himself up, he found he was holding on to the severed head of a young girl. Ahmed thought he would faint.

The next thing he knew he was on top of an adjacent flat roof, his long legs shaking and his mind trying to take in the terrible carnage about him. All about him he could see only smoke rising from almost every closely packed dwelling – a dense black fog which obscured the sun. About half a mile away he could see the flame of a torch, bobbing up and down as a column of men ran through the streets, chanting, chanting . . .

'What an evil sound!' thought Ahmed. He had hoped, when he had left Syria all those years ago, that he would never have to hear it again: the sound of the fanatic; of all that is most hateful in man; the blind horde that strikes at anything; the mob that mutilates because it is itself mutilated: bodies torn from minds, hearts sundered from sense, the self swimming in the multitude, declaring: 'We are right for we are many.'

Ahmed climbed back down into an alleyway and ran onwards. The chanting was getting louder. It began to ring in his ears. He could feel his heart pumping, pumping, pumping . . . And then he saw it: painted on a wall in red dye was an inscription, 'Street of the Books'. He walked down the empty alley until he found a door on which Raghib's name and business was written in Arabic and in Greek. Ahmed knocked on the door. There was no answer. He knocked again. Still no answer.

'Raghib abd-as-Ṣīna! Eugnostos! Miraval is here! Raimon de Miraval is here! Please open! Please!'

He heard a scuffling behind the door. 'Are you alone?'

'I am alone. Please open the door!'

'Where is the seigneur of Miraval?'

'He is at the dock. He needs to see you!'

Ahmed heard furniture being moved away from the door. Raghib's face poked from behind it, 'Who are you?'

'Ahmed. I am the seigneur's servant. I play drums!'

'Do you? No drums here.'

'May I come in?'

'Of course. You hear the mob?'

'Yes.'

'They're after me. Thank God I've sent the family back to Alexandria. The apprentices have gone, Ahmed. They're after me and my friend.'

'Can I come in? Really, Raghib, there isn't much time.'

'No. Not much time. You're right. What are we going to do? What are we going to do?' Raghib was clearly quite unnerved.

In front of Ahmed was a set of steps which led down to a long narrow room. On either side of a thin aisle were high tables upon which were scattered about loose leaves of parchments, books old and new, pens and inkwells. The apprentice translators had clearly left in a hurry.

'Well, young Ahmed, you can see the mess we're in. It all happened so quickly, you see. Quite terrible. Terrible!'

At the far end of the room, half in shadow, Ahmed saw an old man sitting down on a chair, his hands clasped on his knees, his head down and his eyes closed. He was wearing the white woollen robe which was the mark of an Islamic mystic, that is to say, the man was a *Sufi*. His beard matched the colour of his robe.

'Yes, yes, you have noticed my guest. He came from Marrakesh, Ahmed. All the way from Marrakesh to see Raghib. He came for books, you know. Books – and now look what has happened. Aristotle! He came for books on Aristotle and now all this has happened!'

'Please, Raghib! Please be calm.'

'He's meditating. Why aren't I meditating, Ahmed? Can you tell me that? I, Raghib abd-as-Ṣīna – I who have never been disturbed by anything. Merely a part of the great *Necessity*. Asking for nothing more. I – '

'Who is the man, Raghib?'

'Him! Him! Well, he is Ibn Rushd! Yes, Abū'l-Walīd Ibn Rushd. He is the greatest philosopher in the Empire!'

'What is he doing here?'

'Books. Poor man has been kicked out of the caliph's court. They said he denied the resurrection of the body! You see, Ahmed, he said that matter is the principle of individuation. Blame Aristotle, I say! And they will!'

'I don't understand, Raghib.'

'Of course. Who can? If the only thing dividing the unity of the eternal intellect is the body, then how can one imagine a multiplicity of disembodied souls? You see, Ahmed?'

'Not really, no.'

'No, well, let me put it to you directly. If the *al-Murabitūn* get hold of him, they will – '

'I see. You must rouse him, Raghib. At once. We have less than an hour to be aboard the *Merkabah*.'

'The *Merkabah*? Oh, if only I could have persuaded him to read Plato, this would never have happened! What do you mean "*Merkabah*"? It's a Jewish word.'

'The *Merkabah* is our ship. We shall take you away.'

'And leave my books?'

'Raghib, either come with me or die. You said it yourself. They're coming for you. If you want to save the philosopher, you had better move now!'

'Yes, you're quite right.'

'And there's another thing.'

'Can you hear that?'

'Yes, of course I can!'

'It's getting louder!'

'Raghib. The seigneur must have the book of the Cathars. He has come from Languedoc to bring it back.'

'Oh no, no, no. No, not that book. I was asked to take it out of the country. I was paid for my trouble. No, not that one. Look, wake him up, will you?'

Ahmed tried shaking the old philosopher. Ibn Rushd would not wake.

'The man must be in the second sphere by now. He's probably consorting with angels! Why should he want to be speaking with you?'

'He is going to have to come back down to earth pretty fast, then, is he not?'

'Well, I don't know. It might hurt him!'

'He'll get hurt if he doesn't!'

'But he might want to stay in the active intellect!'

'It's difficult to ask him, isn't it? – and anyway, you must bring the book of the Cathars. Come on, Raghib! If you don't bring it, then it will be destroyed!' Ahmed was desperately trying to awake Ibn Rushd. 'Surely the people who paid you did not want the book to be burnt by a mob?'

'Yes, Ahmed. Yes. You have a point there. Yesterday they burnt the holy shroud-making workshop and the relic-houses. The city made a fortune out of those things – the mob must be mad. Yes, Ahmed, now I think about it, I think I can glimpse the *Necessity* again. Yes, you are right. It is simply necessary to bring the book. Now, where did I put it?'

'Get me some water! Please, Raghib, we must wake him!'

'Water ... water. Yes, there's a jar at the back.'

'Then get it!'

'You get it, young man! I'm looking for the book!'

'Ah – he's coming round.'

The old man's eyes opened: 'Córdoba! Córdoba! I must go back to Córdoba!'

'He wants to go to Spain!'

'Why not? It's where he came from! Ah ... here it is.' Raghib pulled the lead box out from under one of the bookcases.'

'What of the copies and the translations?'

'All in the box, my boy. Oh, Abū, you have come back to us? I was missing you, old man.'

'There's trouble, is there not, Raghib?'

'Yes, Abū, old friend.'

'Are we leaving?'

'Can you make it to the dock?'

'Yes, yes. I feel strong now. Who's the boy?'

'It is Ahmed, he's going to take us to a ship. The mob is coming this way.'

'Nice boy. Come here, boy. What's your name?'

'Ahmed, sir.'

'Let me touch your face.'

'Later, sir, please, we have very little time.'

'No, boy. I have very little time. You have all your life. Let me get my papers.'

Ahmed opened the front door.

'No, Ahmed! We'll leave out the back.'

Ibn Rushd was on his feet now, staring at Ahmed as he made his way out of the back into a small courtyard. 'He's like an angel, Raghib. Here boy, take my arm. Good. That's better.'

By the time the group left the yard, they could hear the mob in the Street of Books.

'Please don't stop, Raghib. Times will change. Now do hurry.'

'What an absurd waste,' said Ibn Rushd. 'Men who cannot master the passions are soon mastered by them.'

'Are you ready to cast off, Yusuf?'

'Yes, master.'

'Please, Joseph. Just a few minutes more. I beg you.'

'Ahmed knew the deal.'

'A few minutes . . . '

'That noise is getting louder. That mob will burn the docks. One minute.'

Miraval was straining to see the dock in the darkness. 'I think . . . yes, it's Ahmed!'

'Joseph! Seigneur! Please, Ibn Rushd has fallen over!'

'Who's that?'

'It's Ahmed!'

'No, I can see that. Did he say Ibn Rushd?'

'Ahmed! My friend!'

'Please, seigneur. Ask Yusuf to come ashore. The old man has fallen over. He's unconscious.'

'Raghib?'

'No, seigneur. The old philosopher, Ibn Rushd.'

'He did say Ibn Rushd, Miraval! Yusuf! Go and help Ahmed!'

As Raghib climbed aboard the *Merkabah*, Miraval saw Yusuf carrying the old man along the dockside to the ship.

'Quickly! Quickly!' cried Ahmed.

'Cast off! Jump! Ahmed! Jump!'

'I can't!'

'For God's sake, Ahmed! Jump!'

The mob had reached the dockside, thrusting spears, torches and scimitars into the air. They came running towards Ahmed.

'Jump! Ahmed!' Ahmed jumped.

'Yusuf! Throw him the block!'

The mob started hurling their spears at the *Merkabah* and into the sea. The water was red with fire. Ahmed was swimming for his life. He caught hold of the block and Yusuf started to pull Ahmed aboard the ship.

'Give me your hand, Ahmed!' cried Miraval, leaning as far as he could over the side. 'Oh my God!'

A spear came hurtling at the *Merkabah*. 'No, it's fine, seigneur. They missed. I'm all right. I'm safe.'

The *Merkabah* sailed away from the madness of the mob. But they had to sail several miles before the torches disappeared from view.

'O Ahmed!' cried Miraval. 'I thought they would get you.'

'I said I would be back, seigneur.'

'Ahmed, you are a brave man. Were it not for your troubadour here, I should ask you to join my crew.'

'So long as the seigneur needs me, Joseph. I must stay with him.'

'Do you need him, Miraval?'

'Oh yes, Joseph. I need him.'

'Well, Ahmed, if you ever change your mind, seek me out! Now, about this philosopher you have brought aboard. What do you know of him?'

'Raghib said he was the greatest philosopher in the Empire.'

'Raghib! Of course, I'd forgotten! Raghib, where are you? It's your old friend Joseph!'

Raghib, who was tending Ibn Rushd at the prow shouted back, 'You still owe me money, you old – '

'Old! Old! Hah! Raghib, you're a wily old devil!'

'I have to be, Joseph. But I tell you, I'm going to let you off your debt if you take Abū'l-Walīd Ibn Rushd to Sicily for nothing.'

'Granted, Raghib. I take you both.' Joseph paused, inhaled deeply and turned to the happy troubadour. 'Well, Miraval, I can truthfully say that I have never in my life had a more distinguished crew aboard this ship. Now I know the *Merkabah* has real power! I must go and see to Ibn Rushd. His safety is most dear to me – he is a most extraordinary man. And now he is on my ship. Imagine it!'

Gérard was sitting glumly by the mast-head.

'Gérard, my friend, what's the matter?' asked Miraval.

'Nothing.'

'You can tell us.'

'It's just that – well, Ahmed here has proved himself a hero. You've got what you came for. Joseph Abulafia has found a kindred spirit. Raghib has found safety. Berteaux and Jacques are playing with Peire Vidal – and all I've done is gone on a shopping expedition to Cefalù! What can I tell the lads when I get home?'

'You can tell the lads, Gérard, that you sailed on the greatest ship on the ocean, with the greatest captain, the greatest troubadour, the greatest philosopher; that you have saved the ship by holding the tiller in the most appalling storm; that you stood face to face with the vilest pirates and did not flinch; and that you have faced the wrath of the maddest mob in history! Satisfied?'

'Well, now you put it that way, seigneur, I'm sure there's a tale to tell.'

'If *you* can't tell it, Gérard, no one can! So goodnight and I'll see you in the morning, bright and early!'

Ibn Rushd came round at noon the following day. It was a gorgeous day.

'Where's the boy? Where's my angel?'

'Ahmed!' called Joseph. 'I think he means you.'

Ahmed looked at Miraval and raised his eyebrows. 'You had better go.'

'Yes, old man, what's the matter?'

'Yesterday, my boy, I had a vision. I saw you flying in the second sphere. There was music; beautiful, beautiful music. But I was falling downwards, back to the *acquired intellect* and the demons of forgetfulness. And you, boy, *you* flew down and saved me. Allah is merciful! Allah is merciful! Come, let me hold you!'

'It was not I, old man, who carried you. It was Yusuf there. You should embrace him.'

'No, boy, be quiet. You do not understand me. There is another body – yes, another body. You did not carry me with your flesh. You carried me with your spirit. And your spirit had a shape like you.'

Ibn Rushd held Ahmed close to him, tears falling down his cheeks. 'Oh my boy, my boy . . . you have done more than you can ever imagine!'

Joseph was listening intently. He spoke up: 'Ibn Rushd. It is said that you teach that the oneness of the Creator is reflected in the unity of the universe – and yet that the Creator has made a plurality of intelligences.'

'Yes, of course – what is your name?'

'Joseph Abulafia.'

'Yes, Abulafia, Joseph. I have heard of your family. Toledo?'

'Yes!'

'Hmm. Yes, well, Joseph. You know it *is* possible. The unity is reflected in the interrelations of things. Everything touches everything else. Everything depends on everything else. Only the existence of matter makes it appear that we are separate.'

Miraval approached the little group at the prow. He had heard the word 'separate' and had thought of Azalaïs, and that perfect Love which always seemed so out of touch.

'*There is no reality besides Him*. But only a philosopher can penetrate the meaning of this. They did not like this at Marrakesh. They said the universe was created in *time*. But it is not. The universe is created *eternally*. Time is part of the world of matter. It is not absolute.'

'Yes!' said Joseph. 'The *Ain Soph*.'

'The *Ain Soph*: the Limitless, the unmanifest. You are a Qabalist, Joseph?'

'I have read some books.'

'Have you lived it?'

'I have.'

'Then you will understand what I am saying. In Marrakesh, they always believe in pictures – like the way we tell children. Like Ahmed here – what a picture he is! And yet he has shown me something. Something very important.'

'Tell me, Abū – '

'And who are you, sir?'

'Raimon de Miraval. I am a troubadour!'

'Oh! Joseph, you have a poet on your ship as well! This is

wonderful! Well, poet, you will know I am sure, that feeling of yearning for Truth and perfect beauty.'

'Yes, I know it. I know it well.'

'Yes, no doubt, being a troubadour, you are inclined to feel this most when close to your Lady – or shall I say, more correctly, when you are distant from her.'

'Yes!'

'And yet, when you are far from her body, you feel closer to her heart, yes?'

'That is so, yes.'

'Well, this is all I have tried to say in my books. If only *I* could sing!'

'What have you tried to say?' asked Joseph.

'The life of Allah is most clearly manifest in the spheres of intelligence which lie between the material earth and the perfection of heaven. But man, who is earthy in his bodily nature, turns away from the divine mind which is, in truth, all about him. Nevertheless, it has pleased Allah to reflect in the mind of man, a *potential* principle. If a man can learn to turn away from the obsession with his bodily needs, and give greater concentration to his *potential intellect*, he may acquire the immortality of mind. Thereby he may become a universal man! He may, if he be a Moslem take up the sūf, this simple garment of undyed wool which you see me wearing. This garment signifies that the needs of the body are simple – but the needs of the spirit are greater. When the individual mind begins to apprehend the eternal mind, then he rises – and his heart is filled with ecstasy and light! He begins to love! As I love this boy here.'

'It is said, Ibn Rushd,' said Joseph, 'that you deny life after death.'

'Yes, I am always being told this. But it depends on what you mean. *What* life? Of course, there is always life after death. The universe is all about appearance. Simply because a thing ceases to appear, it does not mean it ceases to exist! But what you refer to is the idea that the immortality which is open to what I have called the '*acquired intellect*' by virtue of its communion with the divine intellect, is not experienced as a particular mind – but as a moment in the never-ending, the timeless life of the *eternal intellect*. Perhaps this explains the feeling of ecstasy! We have lost the burden of our bodies! In this life, this is the aim of the Sūfi.'

'But do you live on as Ibn Rushd, philosopher?' asked Joseph.

'I sincerely hope not!' The Sūfi laughed. 'When you are as old as I am, you do not wish for more of this life!'

'But will you still be an individual?'

'That is what I am trying to say about my vision yesterday. I *saw* Ahmed not as a physical boy – though it is good to feel him close – but in another kind of body! And I remember that Allah is merciful; that He has made us for His delight – and I want to say something else, for I am getting tired and my eyes are growing dim. It is said that I am a great philosopher! People think I know everything. But I tell you, I know *nothing*. There is so much more than we can ever see in this life. So I say this to you: Death I welcome with open arms! But first I must make my philosophy clear – and for that, I must visit Córdoba where I am, if not understood, at least welcome. Now please leave me to sit with the boy and listen to the sea.'

Miraval and Joseph walked away from the old man together. Miraval looked at Joseph and said, 'Will anyone ever understand this man?'

'Miraval, I think that so long as people are content with the religion that offers them a chance to kill – so long as they are content with what they have got, I truly doubt it.'

'Do you understand what he means, Joseph?'

'A little. I shall need to live longer before I grasp it all.'

'Me too.'

9
Miraval-Cabardès

The little village of Miraval is shrouded in a fine autumn mist. The grass is wet and very green. Crows cry across the valley. Far from the world: the barking of a dog. Far, far away: Love is on fire! The sound of distant music: thump, thump! Clickety-click! The peace is broken. Tyres on gravel. Engine stops. Music stops.

'Ah ... listen to that!'

'What's that?'

'Listen! That's what *peace* sounds like. Good, isn't it?'

'Great! So is this it, then?'

'What d'ya mean? Isn't this *enough*?'

'It's so small.'

'*Small is beautiful*, my son!'

'This is where it all started?'

'This and a few places like it.'

'So what shall we do?'

'Do we have to *do* anything?'

'I suppose we could get out of the car.'

'OK. Let's go!'

The two men get out of the Mercedes. The soft slam of the doors echoes about the village. A middle-aged man looks over the fence of his garden. The garden leads down to the Orbiel, below the single wall that is all that is left of the castle. The man smiles sweetly. 'Bonjour!'

'Bonjour monsieur. Er ... nous venons pour voir le troubadour ... château.'

'Le troubadour n'est pas là, monsieur. Il est mort.'

'Did he say Amour?'

'No, *Mort* – Death. The troubadour is dead!'

The man by the fence looks closely at the taller of the two men. He is sure he has seen him before somewhere but cannot remember where. Was it in one of his wife's magazines? The other man he does not recognize. He returns to his garden.

'Who was that?'

'Oh, there's always a guardian over these places.'

'Like an angel?'

'Yeah, he's probably flown away now. You can never be sure with angels. You have to keep your eye on them.'

'I thought that was their job?'

'Angels aren't perfect you know. They slip up sometimes.'

The men look at the plaque set into the mound on which the ruin stands:

HERE LIVED RAIMON DE MIRAVAL
TROUBADOUR

'Amazing! That's all that's left. Lucky man.'

'Why lucky?'

'They didn't have TV and magazines then, and popular writing. I bet when he died, there was no benefit concert for his widow, no dredged-up old interviews, no shit thrown at him or absurd praise. Yeah, I guess that's what I'd like to leave. Just a plaque and me songs. I mean this place really proves it, doesn't it?'

'Proves what?'

'Well, here we are, nearly eight hundred years later and *we're* here and nobody knows we're here – and *he*'s here. This Raimon de Miraval. Still remembered, the spirit still alive. It shows you have to work in the spirit. That's the meaning of success, my boy. That's what it *really* means. Just think of where we've come from. Everyone chasing dreams, illusions about themselves – my illusions about myself; and here it's quiet. It's *real*. Maybe we should buy a house here. I could bring the family down once a year – or better still, come on my own. That would be great! Just one week a year to commune with fellow troubadours!'

'It would be, but look what happened when people got wind that Dalì was living down at Cadaquès. Dalì enjoys the attention. You don't.'

'Do you really think so? I doubt whether he *really* enjoys it. Anyway, we could keep it a secret – a really secret hideaway! I reckon this guy Miraval must have loved this place.'

The two men, both wearing drainpipe jeans and tee-shirts, begin to scramble up the mound to the ruins. The taller man is wearing a panama which he has cocked back, revealing a high forehead and large clear-rimmed spectacles with dark lenses. He is in his late thirties. His friend is a little younger. The mound is only about twenty feet high. They are looking over the parapet, feeling the wet ivy on the cool, crumbling stones and listening to the stream below them.

'I bet he used to bathe down there with his girl. I can just see them on the river bank there on a summer's day. I think these troubadours were really into sex, don't you think? I don't mean just fucking, but the whole erotic thing – the spiritual side of it ... What does the book say about this place?'

'Hang on. Let me find the page. Miraval. Canton of Mas-Cabardès. There's quite a lot on this.'

'We've got the time. I want to hear all of it.'

'Not a great poet, but an excellent writer.'

'Typical. *Where would they be without amplifiers*! Heard that before.'

'Lived from approximately 1165 to about 1229. A knight of the Carcassès whose family had been dispossessed of almost all their property in the Albigeois and the Rouergue by the viscounts of Carcassonne.'

'I bet that brought him closer to the working class! Sort of struggling gentry. Sounds like an old Saxon or Irishman after the Normans came. Before they took the only way out and became middle-class. Funny that he should have come from a dispossessed family, though. There's something familiar there.'

'Perhaps destined for the church, his literary culture more that of a clerk than a knight.'

'In other words, he could read! Destined for the church, huh? There's always God in a poet.'

'Friend of Raymonde VI, who became count of Toulouse in 1195.'

'I bet he was. That was the equivalent of a record contract. The courts of the region were like distribution outlets. I guess they had to keep the punters happy. Must have been better without records in a way, though. If you were into their music, you had to wait to hear it. Much more intense. *They cast their dreams across the seas*. The recording industry is like a cemetery of discarded plastic. We live in the age of the plastic spirit. Yeah, we've come a long way!'

'Did not play an important political role.'

'What the hell is that supposed to mean, I wonder? They'll say that about me too. "Should stick to music and keep out of Life!" Don't they think that making music is political? They always think music is peripheral.'

'Great love for Loba, wife of seigneur of Cabaretz – where we went yesterday. Her real name was Auda. She was called La Louve.'

'What's *Louve*?'

'Means she-wolf.'

'Amazing! Probably a twelth-century feminist!'

'Relationship grew into a sincere friendship. As great a love for the inconstant Azalaïs de Boissézon.'

'Beautiful name. *Azalaïs*. She sounds amazing, too. I bet she was a turn-on!'

'According to the Catalan lord, Uc de Mataplana, he repudiated his wife, Gaudairenca – '

'What did I tell you? I bet they never forgave him for that!'

' – And was about to marry Ermengarde de Castres, who married Olivier de Saissac on the same day on which she had promised to marry him.'

'Poor bastard! I bet that inspired some songs.'

'Attracted ladies with the elegant rigour of his moral *courtoisie*.'

'That sounds like one of those bad translations of a French text.'

'These guide-books are all the same!'

'Still, I accept it. If they listen to my songs in Russia, then, I ask meself, what is language? *Communication* – that's the point. I tell you something. When communication breaks down, then you'll get the politicians arguing about the place of grammar in schools! As if *that* was the problem!'

'It must be nearly lunchtime. Hungry?'

'Yeah. What was the name of that restaurant?'

'Le Table d'Hôte. At Labastide – '

'Labastard? Sounds perfect!'

'Labastide Esparbairenque.'

'I do love the French. They're so rude!'

The two men return to the car and drive the four miles up to the 'astonishing views provided by the simple terraced restaurant' at Labastide (as the guide-books puts it).

'Wow! It's like the Grand Canyon with trees!'

'I think the restaurant is closed. Maybe if they see it's you, they'll serve us. There's no one else here.'

'It's perfect!'

A young girl of about thirteen comes out of the dining room onto the terrace. She does not recognize him. 'Monsieur?'

'Er ... You ask her.'

'Mademoiselle, – '

'Madem*oiseau*!'

'Will you just hold it a second!'

'What? In front of the girl?'

'Excusez-moi, mademoiselle, pour mon ami.' The girl giggles.

'Mademoiselle, est-ce-qu'il ya le déjeuner ici pour nous?'

'Un moment, monsieur.' The girl steps back inside.

'Beautiful girl. Those lips – like Brigitte Bardot when she was hot!'

'Modest-looking, too. None of that foxy stuff.'

'Fit for a troubadour, my dear.'

The girl returns. 'Si vous voulez, messieurs. Crevettes à la mayonnaise, le potage, les crudités ...'

'She says they've got prawn cocktail and salad.'

'Perfect! I've been to some places, but this ... this is perfect. It's like ... whew! Inner Space! Say yes – she might change her mind!'

'Oui, mademoiselle. Ça sera très bien, merci.'

'Merci dotes and dozy votes!'

'Merci, monsieur. Si vous voulez, vous pouvez vous asseyez par là. La vue est très belle.'

The girl wipes the rain off the small trestle table overlooking the damp gorge and goes to fetch the bread, cutlery and table napkins.

'Wait till they hear about this in New York.'

'You breathe one word and the whole place will disappear! Don't you know magic when you feel it? You know, I've been thinking ... I can't ... the more I think about these Cathars and Gnostics or Cathar-Gnostics or mystic-Cathars or whatever you want to call these people. I mean nobody ever told us about these people at school. It was all Crusades and Robin Hood and Ivanhoe with Roger Moore and Basil Rathbone and bullshit.'

'But you *have* to search for it. It doesn't mean anything if you're just handed it all on a plate. It's like a jigsaw. You have to put the fragments together in your own mind. Like in *Citizen Kane.*'

'That's right! That's right! I remember saying to a friend once back in the Flower Power Era: "*Reality leaves a lot to the Imagination.*"'

'I bet you couldn't put that line into a song.'

'That *is* what a song is! But back to what I was trying to sing – say; all this Catharism and discovering God within and being suspicious of materialism, working on a spiritual level – and then these troubadours with their Love! Love! Love! and straining for the impossible – no, *not* the impossible. That's wrong. That's what "*they*" always say – *oh, you're a dreamer. Very nice. Now back to the office and reality*! Not "impossible" – the word is "*Unknown*". And they weren't afraid of it. They went for it – all the way. And now we're so afraid to look through the glass darkly. We want too much certainty. We think they were backward and crazy – but they're remembered. More than that – it's still here! I mean I haven't said or sung anything that these guys and these incredible women weren't saying all that time ago. It's the same message and you're right, you have to put it back together again for yourself. Ain't nobody gonna do it for you, kid!'

'Yeah, I see that. But you can understand why people are afraid of it. Look what happened to these Cathars.'

'What? Were they all burned?'

'Thousands of them. That's where we'll go next, if you like. There's all these ruined castles destroyed by the Crusaders.'

'Not the Crusaders again! Always the bloody Crusaders. Look at America now – still the bloody crusades! Crusade for good morals! Crusade for this, crusade for that! Always looking for *Other*. Something outside of their own guilty selves that they can go and hit. And if it fails, blame the president – after all "*we*" put him there! He's *Ours*! The Shit continues. So what is it? Albigensian Crusade Part 72 at your local party office at 3 o'clock. Bring your own blue rinse! We provide the face-lifts!'

His friend cracked up in laughter.

'It's funny on one level. I mean the people who defended the castles you're talking about, they must have sometimes looked down on all these guys with crosses on their chests and pissed themselves laughing.'

'They probably pissed on the Crusaders!'

'Right! Better than boiling oil! Who was that guy who led the Crusade against the Cathars.'

'Simon de Montfort.'

'Yeah, I can just see him praying before a battle: "Oh you wicked Cathars – if only you could see what a burden this Cross of Christ is. This is going to hurt me more than it hurts you!" Like the headmaster at school: "Don't think that I enjoy this!"'

'Ah! Here's the soup. Mademoiselle, une carafe de vin, s'il vous plaît.'

'Oui, monsieur.'

'I like it here. They don't bore you with a wine list that makes you feel poor or extravagant when all you want is to wet the whistle!'

'And it's always good. I haven't had a poor drink since we arrived.'

'Well, I've had enough to drink for a few years. Just a half glass for me ... Hmmm ... You know it bothers me – all these people who stand up for their own inner truth, the so-called heretics; why are they always burnt or kicked out, or shot? I don't understand it. Is truth suicidal or something? I mean, there were times when I was sure someone was going to pot me off 'cause of the stand we took on Peace and Love – and all the other so-called "irrelevant" or "harmless" causes we took on. Standing up from the crowd for what you believe in is one thing but I guess these Cathars just lived quietly – so maybe there's been some progress in the West. I suppose you can be a Gnostic on the quiet.'

'But there are no guarantees that that won't change. Humanity seems to go up and down. There's not a constant linear progress. I mean, going into people's homes and busting them for marijuana is a bit like the Inquisition. They never ask you in court: "Why do you want to smoke this demonic weed?" Guilty by association.'

'Yeah, Guilty by association with the Unknown. You're too close, boy! Come back to Daddy! But pot's only the tip of the iceberg. I suppose that now, we've come to *expect* the Spanish Inquisition!'

'There's a castle near here where it's said the Holy Grail was kept.'

'Oh that! That Holy Grail thing's been following me around for years. Well, there you are ... the Holy Grail. I mean it's ... that's a symbol of the Unknown. Something must have been going on at this place that couldn't be understood by those who came after. That's all that means. I mean, people look at me sometimes as if *I've* seen the fuckin' Grail. And all I'm doing is searching. The Quest is the important concept. The Grail's just an image. Anyhow, I'm more interested in this Raimon de Miraval guy. Was he burnt, too? What's the history? You've read the book.'

'Well, it seems that after many years of persuasion – political pressure on Raymonde of Toulouse and sending missionaries to convert the Cathars – the Pope finally got fed up with the intransigence of the count – hey, guess the name of the Pope?'

'Mick?'

'Nice try. Innocent. Innocent III.'

'Yeah, I remember reading about the massacre of the Innocent. Only Jesus survived!'

'I guess that sums it up. In 1208 there was a call to arms.'

'How old was Raimon de Miraval then?'

'Born in 1165 ... forty-three.'

'Oh great – there's still time!'

'The Crusade of Christian knights was led by Simon de Montfort and he swept down on the Languedoc and besieged any castle he could find. Sometimes killing indiscriminately – sometimes only burning the Cathars in great holocausts.'

'What did that prove? Don't tell me – it was for the sake of their immortal souls.'

'It says here that some of them actually chose to be burned. Didn't need to be pushed. "*Joyfully*", it says here.'

'Hmm. They must have known something we don't – or the Crusade had traumatized them. These Cathars, did they do the fighting?'

'No, they were defended by the local nobility.'

'I get it. "If anyone's going to deal with these people, it's not going to be you foreigners." Everybody needs a patron of some kind, I suppose. You're never alone with a Heretic!'

'What of our friend from the castle back there? Was he burned?'

'Well, there's no evidence that he was himself a Cathar – and since the Cathars were suspicious of sex and the beauty of the body ...'

'But imagine the effect of a beautiful, celibate Cathar woman on a guy like that. I mean if these troubadours are into uncharted waters of feeling and unreachable ladies, who would be more enticing than one of these spiritual women. Must have been overwhelming! These ladies were images of *Her* – the *Sophia* – the Wisdom that gets you out – back to Reality. Sorry, I interrupted you.'

'According to the book, it was in 1209 or maybe 1211 that Simon de Montfort took possession of Miraval's castle, while systematically setting up the machinery to destroy the independence and culture of the region. Seems that everything Miraval stood for was about to be completely destroyed. Must have been heartbreaking.'

'Heretics died but the heritage survives, huh? But I wonder if *he* was thinking it? Did *he* think it was all over? Finished. Wasted life – all that. You know, "Oh, isn't the world terrible and people are nasty so let's all give up and be nasty too!"'

'Says here that he wrote what was probably his last song, "*It pleases me to sing and to appear lovable*".'

'Rather ambiguous, that.'

'Oh, this is interesting. Remember Lastours and those castles on the mountain we saw there yesterday?'

'Le Château d'Amour?'

'Apparently de Montfort tried to take them by force but failed to do so – his only military failure of the campaign according to the book.'

'O Love Inviolate!'

'Interesting, that.'

'This Miraval must have been holing up with his mates there.'

'Apparently he went to Toulouse to see if Raymonde VI could get his castle back but Raymonde was too busy preparing for a reprisal in concert with Pere II – '

'Imagine it! Raymonde and Pere in concert. Madison Square Guardsman!'

' – The King of Aragon. In September 1213, Raymonde's army was completely routed by Simon de Montfort at the battle of Muret – and the king of Aragon was killed. Raymonde headed for Aragon to remuster support.'

'I must say I admire the spirit of these guys. They never stop. What about Miraval. Does it say what he did next?'

10
Love works in Silence

There is a work called the *Razon de amor*, a love poem, composed in the Catalan language in the early thirteenth century. The poet recounts how he has 'suffered' in France and Germany. He says that he has dwelt in Lombardy, a region of refuge for many heretics, where he has striven to learn the secret of the *Fine Love*. The anonymous poet tells how he finds himself in a paradisal garden. He is lying in an olive grove. He looks over to a nearby apple grove. Upon the uppermost branches of a tree in the grove he sees a silver vessel. The vessel contains clear red wine and has been placed there by the mistress of the garden for her lover. The wine possesses health-giving properties. It is good for the body. But there is another vessel on top of the apple tree. This vessel contains cool water. The poet is thirsty but is afraid to drink the water because he feels it may be enchanted.

He rests in a meadow by a cool fountain. He removes his clothes and drinks from the fountain. A lady – not the mistress of the garden – appears, singing a love song, and he recognizes her as his beloved because she is wearing the tokens which he has sent her. They converse in the language of Love but it happens that the lady must soon depart. The poet is left disconsolate. A dove appears, fluttering over the fountain and then over the apple grove. The dove tips the vessel of water into the vessel of wine. The poem ends.

'How do you like the poem, Raimon?'

'It's beautiful, Azalaïs.'

'How long will you stay here?'

'I leave for Lérida tomorrow.'

Raimon and Azalaïs looked into the fire and wrapped their capes closely to themselves. All about them on the hillside, below the castle of Montségur, were similar fires, glowing hotly outside a hundred little stone huts. From the deep blue air, streaked with crimson, the mountain of Montségur would resemble the embers of a friendly fire. But the real fire was burning within the inhabitants' hearts. Azalaïs had just returned from handing out loaves of bread to the visitors: knights and ladies who had come to visit their relatives, who had themselves come to Montségur for peace, meditation and reflection upon the terrible events which had befallen the country during the last four years.

'Did you ever imagine it would come to this, Azalaïs?'

'I think we have all known that it would come to this. But please don't think that this is the end. The tribulation will end. The gates of Hell will not prevail.'

'I still didn't think the count would lose the battle – not with the king of Aragon to help him ... You know that old Jacques was burnt at Termes? That was three years ago and I think of him often. I can still see him and hear him. I never realized how lucky we were all those years ago.'

'Don't dwell on the past, Raimon ... You know, I think a beard suits you now.'

'Thank you, my lady. It hides the lines but now my face is like the Pyrenees. Snow-topped!'

Azalaïs laughed. 'I'm sure it's coming to me, too.'

'Your hair is as lovely as ever, Azalaïs. It's amazing how you people seem to retain your looks longer.'

'Perhaps, Raimon, it is because we never give the matter any thought.'

Miraval looked about him. 'Funny. I never came here before. Something always held me back. But it's an extraordinary place. I never saw anything like it. You have your strange-looking castle, these odd huts and the villagers down there to help you.'

'It's growing, Raimon. This place is growing all the time. The more we are persecuted, the more people take an interest in us. The risk is enormous. But this attracts many people. People are still searching. Are you still searching, Raimon?'

'I don't know. So many things make sense to me now that didn't before. Things seem less intense. And that is doubly strange when you consider what has happened. I think when you're young, you think that because you have found something beautiful or true, then others will be happy to share it with you. Perhaps a little musical persuasion might be called for – but eventually you will win out. But later you come to see the stupidity of people. It's like a clot in the blood. If you think it has died out here, then it reappears there. But you learn of what you have been up against. And you value the fact that you have been called to *see*, and you know you are somehow right. When you are young – when I was young, I was always trying to convince myself of what was in my heart. I didn't really believe in it. I thought if others could see what I was doing – that it was *that* which would convince me. I know I'm not making very good sense – '

'You are, Raimon. I understand you.'

'Well, now the opinion of other people doesn't matter at all. Those who *see* will see.'

'We have come to feel this too, Raimon. We find that we need less preaching. The Holy Spirit seems to do the work for us. All we have to do is keep standing up!'

'Yes, this Holy Spirit. It's like it's always hanging over the earth and sometimes comes down like lightning – right to the earth and then things change. It needs a vessel, though.'

'Maybe that's why we think of the Spirit as a dove. It comes to earth to take us in its wings!'

'Montségur is like a beacon, then.'

'Yes.'

'Amazing!'

'I know you have lost Miraval. You could always come here and live with us.'

'That would be like escaping, Azalaïs. Miraval is more than just a home.'

'I understand.'

'Yes, you do. It's annoying sometimes – you always made the first move! You always seemed to see more clearly than I did.'

Azalaïs giggled. 'Hmm ... You flatterer! It was not always clear. I nearly left. Do you remember?'

'Of course I do. But I was sure you would not stay. And it has worked out for the better. Present or absent, I see better because of you. No other lady has matched you. My stupidity has always been to try and look for someone like you. And you were there all the time! I don't write any more. Not since I lost

Miraval, anyway. I did write something to be read to Aliénor, now that she's Raymonde's wife. But my heart wasn't in it. I hardly know if I dare send it now that her brother's dead. The song was quite optimistic. Maybe I'll rewrite it on the way. I don't know. My writing's gone right off these days. They used to be like olives – now they come out like shrivelled dates! It doesn't seem to matter any more.'

'Look at me, Raimon.'

They looked at each other. The smile which passed between them was the smile of wisdom – like old soldiers whose love was all in their hearts and did not need protestation or even poetry. Their Love had grown as True Love will. They waited for the sunrise.

'What has happened to the group?'

Miraval sighed. 'I thought we would be together forever, you know. Ahmed hung around at Miraval for two years before he told me he wanted to return to Syria. Last seen on board the *Merkabah*! He had been getting a lot of insults in the towns round about. Especially after the battle of Alarcos.'

'I remember that. Must be about sixteen years ago now. Everyone was convinced that the Almohads would overrun the whole of Christendom.'

'*I* never thought they would. Not after visiting Tripoli. It was clear that the caliph had as many enemies in his own territory as in Spain. And last year proved me right. That's another reason why I'm going to Catalonia. They say it's a growing place since the battle of Las Navas. I wish Berteaux had lived to see it. If only he could have held back for a few years. Since their defeat last year, the Almohads are finished there.'

'What happened to Berteaux?'

'Killed at Alarcos. He had been listening to Bertran de Born. It's typical, somehow. *There* was a troubadour who couldn't stop singing songs encouraging everyone to go to war – and *he* dies peacefully as a monk. And our Berteaux was killed. What a *waste*!'

'I'm very sorry, Raimon. I wish you'd told me all this years ago.'

'I didn't think it would interest you.'

'Oh Raimon! That's not true!'

Miraval bit his lip. 'Well . . . Gérard is still with us.'

'Where is he now?'

'I last saw him at Cabaretz. He's gone very glum. He used to be so funny – everything was a joke to him. Now he's filled with melancholy.'

'He's lost his best friends. He's lost his home. Poor man probably doesn't know where he is.'

'I told him that if things work out in Lérida – if I can get Raymonde to negotiate for my castle – then we can start again. And if we cannot get Miraval back, then he is to come and join me there anyhow. If I stay in Lérida, will you visit me there?'

'I'm sure that's possible. Many of us have gone to Catalonia and I believe some of us are in Lérida – and they will require our help. I shall speak to Guilhabert about it.'

'How is the old man?'

'He's doing very well. I don't know what we'd do without him. He is *so* popular. He helps out in the fields down there; gets to know the ordinary people, tells them stories; heals the sick. He will not take money for that. The children. They love him especially. He's not as arrogant as he used to be. In fact, he's quite a saint.'

'What of Raghib abd-as-Ṣīna?'

'Eugnostos?'

'Yes.'

'Comes and goes. Always brings back something interesting.'

'That man is pure mischief! But lovable all the same. Do you remember all that business about the secret book?'

'Of course I remember. But what happened between you and Raymonde when you got back. We never heard.'

'Looking back, it was quite hilarious. I took the translation and copy to Raymonde. He and his father studied the contents. They couldn't understand it at all. They showed it to the bishop of Toulouse. He was shocked, of course. Then a message came from the Papal Legate – Gregorio, I think his name was – saying that the caliph was no longer campaigning. He was dealing with his two brothers in Tunis and Majorca. And that even if Ya'qub should resume the attack on Castile, then it would be better for Raymonde to hold the border in case the defence broke down – which it did at Alarcos. But the Almohads never crossed the Pyrenees. Raymonde was off the hook, anyhow – so the whole point of pacifying the Pope was lost.

The way things turned out – it wouldn't have made any lasting difference anyway! Raymonde was *always* on a collision course with Rome. Anyhow, it was decided to keep the whole business of the Book under wraps. The Church did not want people enquiring as to the book's contents – even if it were burnt. It was a fiasco – the whole thing! Raghib gave me the original. I've brought it with me. I was hoping to present it back to him here before I left. I think it belongs here.'

'Do you think the whole voyage to Tripoli was a fiasco, too?'

'Greatest journey of my life. I met Joseph Abulafia, Ibn Rushd. It changed my life. Can't say how exactly. But the effects have been with me ever since. I don't know if you'll understand me but afterwards, I realized there was more to me than being a troubadour – either that or there was more to being a troubadour than I had ever imagined! Without that journey, I think I would have gone on chasing after you for the rest of my life.'

'I'm glad you didn't. It might have been flattering for me but it would have been terrible for you.'

'So you see there was something to that Book business which nobody saw.'

'It *was* a secret book then, Raimon!'

'I suppose it was. And now I've come to give it back. Is Raghib here?'

'*Always here*, Miraval.'

'Raghib!'

'Hello, old friend!'

Standing over the fire was the figure of Raghib, now very old indeed – but with a light in his eyes that had not dimmed but sparkled even brighter than before.

'O Raghib! I was so hoping you would be here!'

'Remember always, Raimon. The *Necessity*.'

'Yes, Raghib. The *Necessity*. At last I'm beginning to understand you! You simply *had* to be here, didn't you?'

'Yes, my friend.'

'Please sit with us. Have you any water, Azalaïs?'

'Don't trouble yourself, sister! I have brought some wine from the village. I'm sure Raimon de Miraval will join me, even if you don't.'

'Raghib. It's been twenty years!'

'What is this thing called *Time*? It is only a weak imitation of Eternity, that's what it is! Here we are, together for . . . for a moment. All our lives we worry about this and that – and the *Necessity* drags us through time to be where we must be. Your health, troubadour.'

'I raise this cup in memory of our friends. Some dead, some absent.'

'May the *Good God* bless us all!' said Azalaïs.

Miraval had tears in his eyes. They all did. Their vision began to blur with tiredness as the sun rose over the castle and they heard the singing of birds.

'I brought you the book, Raghib. I thought it should rest here.'

'No, no, no! No, this book is not for resting. No, this book is for moving. This is not a book for study. This is a book which makes men *move*! You must take it with you. It doesn't matter where you take it. It doesn't matter if you never think of it.'

'But I've had it for twenty years! I thought it was time to start again.'

'Time! *Time*! All you ever talk about is time! So you've had it for twenty years. So you might have it for another twenty years! Do you know how old this book is? This book has nothing to do with time. This castle. This is made of stone. It will fall. It is not the stones that matter. It is what the stones have *contained* that matters. Likewise your songs. People in the future will look at the words. But what did the words contain? Ask yourself *that* as you go now to Lérida! I do not want to bury your book in this castle. We have quite enough beautiful books already. Take the book away! Live, Miraval! Get away from here. Follow the *Necessity*. Go and *live*!'

Pink waves were gliding across the white sky above Montségur when Miraval awoke, his head resting in Azalaïs's lap, her soft hand stroking his frosty hair.

'Raghib! Where is Raghib? I must speak to him!' Miraval got up with a start.

'He's gone, Raimon. You remember what he's like. Hates conventional greetings, loathes goodbyes.'

'Have you been awake all night, Azalaïs?'

'Yes, Raimon. Very awake. I was indulging my memories. They seem sweeter and more intense in these times of war. How beautiful you were that night when you had ridden back from Cabaretz – when you thought I would not come.'

'*Beautiful*? I must have been as pale as this sky. It was Peire Vidal, victim of La Louve, whom I saw that night. Ah, *Loba* – she'll never change! It would take a battering ram to move her out of Lastours – indeed, Montfort tried it – but he was no match for the she-wolf of the Cabardès!'

Miraval began to pick himself up, shaking his legs to get his cold blood back into circulation and spreading his arms outwards and upwards. 'Look at this! I have put on weight! Didn't realize it till I saw you! Hmm ... Well,' he said abruptly, 'I suppose that's it, then. I must go to Lérida and hope that the count will see me.'

Azalaïs looked up to him with a look of barely suppressed anxiety – not for herself, but for him. Miraval, sensing her care, sighed: 'Oh Azalaïs, when will this damn war end?'

'Raimon, we don't know what we've started. But the war, my darling, is nothing new. It was going on before we were born and it will go on long after we have died. I was thinking about this while you were asleep. We had our springtime. We had our summer. We made Love together and we planted seeds. What more can anyone do?'

'I must get Miraval back! Can't let the Devil have it, can we?' Miraval tried hard to suppress his feelings as he mounted his horse. 'So, old Raimon de Miraval must keep the secret book of the Cathars yet.'

'Looks like it, Raimon. Oh, I almost forgot. I want you to take this.'

'What is it?'

'It's a stone from the castle. The castle defends us. I want it to defend you, too.'

'I shall keep it close. God bless you, Azalaïs de Boissézon! See you soon!'

'God-um ... Goodbye!'

So Miraval cantered down the great 'pog' of Montségur on a cool October morning and galloped eastwards out of the Ariège until he reached Perpignan where he took the crowded main route to Lérida and Santiago de Compostela. He wondered to himself, bearing in mind the appalling disaster of

Muret only a month before, whether he had any right to feel this good. But his visit to Montségur had renewed his flagging energies and he was looking forward to bringing cheer to his old friend, Raymonde.

To Lérida

Miraval passed by many merchants from Toulouse. He also observed many Cathars, walking, with small packs on their backs. He rode on: Prades; the walled town of Villerouge de Conflent; Serdinya. He tried not to be distracted by the emergent beauty of the road. Finally, at Olette, he stopped to rest himself and his horse. Olette was a most beautiful village, set in a valley and surrounded by high hills from which he began to feel the chill wind of the Pyrenees. For the moment, however, he simply admired the way the sun fell upon the firs, and thought of Miraval. The mountains on either side of the winding road were pocked with limestone caves. The terrain became wilder. The road became harder to follow until, having passed the Forêt de Campilles, it almost disappeared. Many a broken wagon lay forgotten by the track.

Fortunately, the road was still so busy that the fear of bandits was allayed. He rested again at Fontoedrouse. At this high point, he rested again. The night was drawing in as the dark sky began to envelop the red crags of the Roc de l'Aigle. He stopped the night at a crowded inn. The conversation was rich and warm. The Catalan merchants, who were travelling from Lérida and Barcelona to Toulouse, told endless stories of the defeat of the caliph Muḥammad at Las Navas de Tolosa – now a year ago, but its significance seemed to grow and grow as the merchants beheld the new commercial possibilities opening up in Castile as a result. On the other hand, the Toulousain merchants, seated on the other side of the tavern, were deeply depressed at the collapse of Raymonde's army and the consequent imposition of new levies by Simon de Montfort.

Miraval sat by himself, thinking about how he was going to make his approach to Raymonde. In his mind, he began rehearsing his lines – only instead of Raymonde, he had decided to direct his energies towards his wife, Aliénor, who had been such an encouragement to the troubadour for some years. But somehow, the words of his song were beginning to ring a bit hollow. The inn, meanwhile, had become extremely boisterous, and Miraval had to put his fingers in his ears as he read the words of his new *canso*:

> It pleases me to sing and appear lovable.

Well, that just about said it all, he thought. To appear lovable. This was no song of love. There was no real passion here. He read on:

> since the air is soft and the times gay,
> while in the orchards and the hedgerows
> I hear the chirping of the little birds
> who sit close together, mocking ...

Yes, 'mocking' was the right word ...

> amid the green, the white and the violet

He'd got the season wrong. Perhaps it would make her dream of spring as winter approached. Perhaps.

> It would be well that he should make up his mind –
> He who would desire that Love support him,
> Should take up the manners of a genuine lover!

Where was the old fire? He could not deny the reality of his feelings.

> A genuine lover, I am not he: I render what is expected!
> Therefore I have to fear neither pain nor heavy suffering;

What a relief! But would it work?

> I am not going to tremble for my conceit
> And yet, fear still renders me dumb:

There was truth in that!

> Before this beautiful lady of such high birth
> I dare neither show nor declare my feelings;
> And I shall hide them
> Until I have known her heart.

That was good. True and respectful. It might just work. It was a pity that war had so got in the way of his relationship with Raymonde. The count did not seem to have any time for him any more. Would he even consent to see him? These were the thoughts that made Miraval turn in his cold bed that windy night.

The next day's ride took him high up into the Pyrenees: their snow-covered peaks providing a perfect image for his nervous state, the more he thought of what might lay in wait for him in Lérida.

Great serrated rocks plunged into deep ravines, washed by gushing water which spewed out of crevices and crags, pushing all before it; felling trees and scraping scree, down, down to the cold river banks. Waterfalls and fountains; dizzy spaces where you thought you were falling as you were climbing – and it was so cold up there! But finally, after passing through the precarious village of Felges, the path began to wind down again. It was very tricky riding and Miraval's horse lost his footing a few times. At such a moment, Miraval would jump off and hold him firmly by the reins. Then he would walk him for a mile until the creature was more used to it. He missed Drummer.

Passing out of a veritable forest of dense bush, Miraval finally saw the village at the base of the Col de la Perxa: the gateway across the Pyrenees! How the Almohads had been expected to cross the Pyrenees with an army six hundred thousand strong defied all understanding. Miraval began to notice the appearance of strip farming. The fields, like shelves in the red earth, were full of peasants, or *labradores*, as they were known, who would occasionally wave to passers-by. Miraval noted the 'rustic capes' which they wore over their breeches, hose and shirts. They did look a charming sight, as the wind blew their capes into the air so that the fields seemed to be full of red and brown pennants. These were easy-going people, well embedded in a life which had not changed for as long as anyone could remember. Their only real enemy was the winter – and they were always well prepared for that. Miraval always waved back.

He liked to see the children on the road and wondered whether he had missed a great deal by not having any. He imagined himself as an old country priest, waddling along on unsturdy legs, showing the village children around all the wonders of nature, hoping to awaken in them that love of all things beautiful which had been his childhood discovery. For most of the people about him, Nature was a severe foe and love was a chilly coupling in a draughty hut. One day it would be different and those expectant faces would not sink into the expressionlessness that was cast over the peasantry in all the seasons save spring.

At Puigcerda, he observed a Contrapás: a little dance performed by the men of the town and watched with amusement by the townswomen. Round and round the men danced as a little boy beat a simple drum. Miraval hardly noticed that he was now riding across a plain of olive green. Still the same strip fields and the jolly capes – but the capes hung still and the air was warm again. In the distance behind him, the Pyrenees – ice-capped, like a set of teeth. If the mountains were teeth then Seo de Urgel lay happily upon the tongue, enclosed by the jaws of the Pyrenees.

Seo was the capital of the district of Urgellet and was ruled by a count-bishop. The bishop had ruled since the sixth century, until Seo had been taken by the Arabs. The Franks had retaken it three hundred years previously and in the last century the bishops had been granted rights over the whole of Andorra. Miraval marvelled, after the savagery of the mountains, at the Romanesque cathedral of Santa María. Built on an octagonal design by Lombard craftsmen, it had been consecrated in 1040 and completed thirty-eight years previously. To Miraval's eyes, it looked startlingly new – like a shaving of clear ice in the space of a cave.

Miraval would spend the night at Seo de Urgel, brushing up on his Catalan – a language not much different to his own. He was enjoying the tales of new building work and entertainments to be enjoyed in Lérida. He heard of a great high street, the Calle Mayor, lined with shops, on which there was a edifice: the Palacium Regis, next to some public baths built by the Arabs. This Arabic custom of frequenting public baths had been continued by the settlers who had arrived sixty-four years earlier when Lérida had been reconquered by Ramon Berenguer IV, count of Barcelona.

It was all such a different picture from that of the Languedoc he had left. There he had been forced to witness skies black with smoke, towns devastated, castles demolished, friends incarcerated, fields wasted, men and women incinerated. But this land seemed to be going through a rebirth. Surely a troubadour could find new *Joy* here. Miraval began to look again at his *canso* for the countess Aliénor:

> Although it is not a question here of entreaty
> nor of gaining recompense,
> Nevertheless I am plunged into confusion:
> I don't know how to make it look as if I'm not dissembling
> in making this picture of her great value.

'True enough. But perhaps a little too dour.'

> Because never a woman born of mortal mother
> has had, until now, as much Merit
> as could be compared to hers;

'That's much better! Irresistible!'

> Among all the ladies I know, so greatly esteemed
> that her Merit carries her to the heights.

'No! " ... carries her to the heights." It's too ... too distant.'

> Her Merit renders her to the company of the best.

'Not very poetic. But I can't think of anything else!'

Miraval moved to a theme in which he could move effortlessly. After all, this song was a matter of diplomacy. He did not expect to *win* the Lady!

> She accepts with good heart when one courts her gently.
> She loves entertainment and joy;

'That's a nice excuse! What lady does not?'

> But the uncouth type who butts in
> and who spreads only foolishness,
> would not be agreeable to her.
> Only the worthy are welcome to be close to her,
> and she shows them such a goodly face
> that each one of them sings her praises
> – and once they have been given leave
> they remain as if they were slaves.

'But I am no one's slave!' thought Miraval to himself as he fell to sleep. He dreamt of meeting new admirers in Lérida: ladies who would not be put off by his age, but who would see the youth of his heart and the beauty of his verses.

The road now joined on to the 'Via Francisca', which carried merchants and pilgrims to their various destinations. Much of the surface of the road was that laid by the Romans: the *Via Augusta* which had joined Rome to Cadiz. How did they do it? The road was again filled with legions. Not the orderly legions of Rome but legions of bedraggled Aragonese; unhappy survivors of the battle of Muret – and yet, now they had crossed the mountains, the soldiers were happy to be nearly home. Miraval knew that it was impossible to make friends with a retreating army and so kept his thoughts to himself as he rode on southwards.

It was getting hotter and his beard began to itch. He followed the road as it made its way by the banks of the river Segre. He passed by the *burgueses*, content in their capes, doublets, hose and satin-lined hats. The ladies were striking and Miraval was given much cause to smile at these black-haired maidens, wrapped tightly into their *gonellas* – one-piece dresses of silk and velvet, pleated at the waist and bound into embroidered halter-necks. He trotted across the green plains, beneath a clear blue sky through Organya, Peramola, Tiurana, La Serra, Artesa de Segre; until he rested again at Belaguer, less than forty miles from Lérida. He took a meal of menestra, a local rice dish, with a jar of Penellas, a warm red wine – dry, but not as earthy as he had been used to in the Languedoc. Before him rose the Castillo de los Condes de Urgel, another seat of the counts of Urgel; undergoing a renovation which was leaving the architects with serious doubts over what to do with the polychrome Arab wall designs, which all agreed to be outstanding but *unchristian*.

As Miraval looked again at his *canso*, he could hear workmen chipping half-heartedly at their predecessor's work. They sounded happy to finish the day's labour. Miraval was getting bored with the song. He gazed out across the Segre and, to the far distance, lost himself and his worries in the sandy brown hills that slid up from under the irregular plots of irrigated land. The publican came out to him – a young man of mixed Arab and Castilian descent and, Miraval guessed, a newcomer to the region, judging by the way he was rubbing his hands and his difficulty in finding the correct form of language and etiquette in addressing Miraval: 'Sir, your lordship. You are a new to our town. Great town, seigneur. Look at our new church. Rising like a sword. Belaguer beautiful place for us. Why you write?'

'I am a troubadour, sir.'

'Yes, sir. You write song of Love, yes?'

'For the sister of the King.'

'Oh poor King. Dead in Languedoc. Why he go to Languedoc? Lérida much better. Everything better in Lérida. Why fight the French when there are Arabs to fight? I don't understand it. Many of our boys taken away and dead. Yes, sir, you write song of Love. Much better.'

Miraval was amazed to find his Catalan superior to that of a local. But many of the inhabitants of Catalonia had come from Castile and Andalusia. This had led to new tensions among the populace but, for the time being, all were united in relief at the defeat of the caliph Muḥammad at Las Navas de Tolosa.

'Thanks to the Cid we are here. Thanks be to God. May the new King grow strong. He only a boy. God send him good advisor and friend. You, sir, friend of new king Jaime?'

'Yes, indeed.'

'You staying here for bed?'

'Yes.'

'Please come inside now. It is dark. Soldiers cause problem after it is dark.'

Inside the ragged hostelry, Miraval, by the light of a single candle, perused as much of his new song as his eyes could bear:

> I don't believe that next to hers
> The beauty of another lady could ever have more sparkle,
> The flower of a rose, when it opens
> Does not have her complexion;
> She is well formed and her proportions are charming:

How much longer could he go on with this?, he wondered. It was necessary. He must do it. *Miraval* mattered more than anything else.

> Her mouth delights the world and her eyes illumine it
> Never could Beauty add anything to her:
> For She has employed all the virtues

In such a way that nothing is left for the others
So my Lady will not get angry
If I am so eager in obtaining her good graces.
I have set my heart on abasing myself,

This line really stuck in Miraval's throat. It was not *him*. Not any more.

– Not to mislead myself in that which concerns Love

That was better.

I have always aspired to the highest object

True!

Whether away from home or in my own country;
And this is not to offer proof or to be presumptious in
respect of my lady;
Because of her, I have never expected anything more
Than a friendly welcome and her gentle greeting.

True again! The next verses seemed desperately inappropriate now – but he could think of nothing to replace them. In Lérida, he would.

Song, go speak on my behalf to the king
Let *Joy* guide it, dressed and nourished,
That there be nothing tortuous to him:
Provided that he recovers Montégut
and retakes his city of Carcassonne,
he will then be emperor of *Worthiness*
and the French and the Moslems
will dread his crown.

Some hope! That was enough for now. He would work through the rest at Lérida. Miraval slept peacefully, his old limbs weary and stiff.

Lérida

Miraval awoke quite late but set off for Lérida at speed. Time suddenly seemed very important to him. While vines and olives flourished in the surrounding countryside, he did not notice. His heart was filled with thoughts of seeing Raymonde again. It had been a long time. He would have his song ready. Aliénor would love it. He would regain Miraval for Love.

By late afternoon, he could see Lérida in the distance. Towering above it all was the castle of Zuda, high upon a hill and residence of the king of Aragon. Miraval's old heart began to leap. The castle was an Arabic structure, solid and austere, with curved sandy walls. Meanwhile, the rich burghers of the city were putting their money into the new cathedral, encouraged by the bishop, one Gombaldo de Camporells. The cathedral had still barely risen from its foundations, sunk some four years previously.

Miraval entered the city as some distant bells chimed 7 o'clock. The streets were still filled with the mixed population of Jews, Moors and Aragonese – each racial group hurrying to its respective quarter, the lines between them rigidly enforced. The Moslems lived outside the city and had their own market, the *Assoch* in the Calle de la Palma; the Jews were regarded less favourably and were installed in a small area of dark, narrow streets. There were many immigrants there too, and Miraval noticed the strange and nervous faces of Eastern Europeans who had moved there to take advantage of new laws which had freed the population from feudal servitude. Lights flashed from many buildings in its narrow streets. Many shops seemed unwilling to close. There were spice shops, knife shops, butchers, grocers, drapers, ironmongers. The last of the day's bread was being sold in the Plaça de San Joan; chickens in the Plaça dels Polls. Near the Arco del Puesta, an exquisite Arabic archway, Miraval passed through the Jewish Quarter with its many shops of silversmiths, parchment-makers, slaughterhouses, money changers, butchers, glovemakers, furriers and wine merchants. The city was still buzzing. Riding by the old Arab fortress of the Cuiraza with its delicate cusped arches, the final words for the new song began to take shape:

> My lady, you who have always supported me so well
> It is for you I have begun to sing again,
> And although I believed I should compose no more
> Before you had redeemed the fief
> Of Miraval, which I have lost.

That word, 'lost', always there ... But so was its necessary counterpart: finding and *being found*. There was a hidden hope in this loss. Miraval moved to the final verse in this double-spirit:

> But the king has promised me

Perhaps he had better change 'count' for 'king' in the present circumstances:

> But the count has promised me
> that, before long, he will render it,

Two more lines. That's all he would need – and the job would be done. So far, it was not brilliant – but it was a start.

It was now dark. Miraval found the high street, the Calle Mayor, and rode on past the public baths into Whore's Street. Several dusky women were hanging out of ivy-strewn balconies, spitting into the street. It had been a long day for them, too. Then it came:

> But the king has promised me
> that he will render it back to me
> So that, before long, we shall be able
> ladies and lovers
> to recover the *Joy* which we have lost!

At last! Miraval found himself again in sight of the castle of Zuda.

His attention was struck by the sight of the new main door to the cathedral. He got off his horse to take a closer look.

'What's that?' he asked a passer-by.

'*La Puerta dels Fillols.*'

'The Door of the Children! What a wonderful name for a door!' thought Miraval. He went up to take a closer look. A knife. A pain in the chest. Footsteps. Rattling of moneybags. Coins fall to the steps. Sick head and blood. Falling... Miraval reaches to his saddle. Books and papers fall to the stone, blood-spattered.

Two monks. They run to the body.

'Take him.'

'These papers?'

'Take the papers.'

'He is breathing! Hold him!'

The monks lay Miraval in a wagon. Over hard cobbles the wagon carries Miraval to the new Cistercian convent. Bright and new, it smells of lavender. Miraval is carried away. A new hospital. Young nuns.

'Who is he?'

'Stranger.'

'He is dead. Someone may come for him. His cloth is fine. Poor old man.'

'What shall I do with these?'

'Keep them. No, they are covered with blood. Evil humours. Take them outside.'

The young nun takes the book and the papers to the alley by the chapel. She is not used to being there in the dark. It might be dangerous. She can hear someone. She lifts the lid off a great pigskin bin and throws the book and the papers inside. She slams the lid down again and retreats inside, to the warmth and the familiar touch.

I can see a tramp.

THE MEMOIRS OF SHERLOCK HOLMES

ARTHUR CONAN DOYLE

A Wilco® Book
Outstanding works of universal interest

ISBN: 978-93-6312-690-9

THE MEMOIRS OF SHERLOCK HOLMES
By Arthur Conan Doyle
Complete and Unabridged

Cover design by Pia Alizé Hazarika
Cover illustration © Freepik

This edition printed & published in 2025 by
Wilco International LLP, Mumbai - India
Tel.: (91-22) 2204 1420 / 2284 2574
E-mail: wilco@wilcobooks.com
Website: wilcobooks.com
wilcopicturelibrary.com

Printed in India

ARTHUR CONAN DOYLE

(1859–1930)

Born in Edinburgh Scotland, Conan Doyle was educated in Jesuit schools, and later at Stonyhurst College, Lancashire, where he met and married Louise Hawkins in 1885.

Doyle qualified as a doctor in '85 and began his practice as an eye specialist, gradually taking to full-time writing. His first 'Sherlock Holmes' story, *A Study in Scarlet,* appeared in *Beeton's Christmas Annual* in 1887. 'Holmes' was serialised from 1891 onwards in the prestigious *Strand Magazine*. Coinciding with his father's institutionalization, the author devised the death of the detective in *Final Problem* in 1893.

Doyle subsequently wrote a full story, *The Hound of the Baskervilles,* five years later, reviving the popular sleuth, but the 'Holmes'-addicted readers demanded the full resurrection of their hero, which was done in *The Empty House* (1903), and appears as the first exciting Sherlock Holmes adventure in *The Return of Sherlock Holmes*.

Sixty stories and two pastiches of 'Sherlock Holmes' had appeared in various forms from 1887 to 1927, a lengthy run of four decades.

Knighted in 1902 for his work in connection with the Boer War,* Doyle served in the British Army as a doctor in the South African war. After his son's death in World War I, Conan Doyle dedicated himself to spiritual studies, by now fairly well-off with the earnings from his profession as a highly successful author.

Conan Doyle died in Crowborough in July 1930.

* (1899–1902). The Boer War was fought between Great Britain and the two Boer (Afrikaner) republics—the South African Republic (Transvaal) and the Orange Free State.

CONTENTS

Chapter 1

THE ADVENTURE OF SILVER BLAZE

"I am afraid, Watson, that I shall have to go," said Holmes as we sat down together to our breakfast one morning.

"Go! Where to?"

"To Dartmoor; to King's Pyland."

I was not surprised. Indeed, my only wonder was that he had not already been mixed up in this extraordinary case, which was the one topic of conversation through the length and breadth of England. For a whole day my companion had rambled about the room with his chin upon his chest and his brows knitted, charging and recharging his pipe with the strongest black tobacco, and absolutely deaf to any of my questions or remarks. Fresh editions of every paper had been sent up by our news agent, only to be glanced over and tossed down into a corner. Yet, silent as he was, I knew perfectly well what it was over which he was brooding. There was but one problem before the public which could challenge his powers of analysis, and that was the singular disappearance of the favourite for the Wessex Cup, and the tragic murder of its trainer. When, therefore, he suddenly announced his intention of setting out for the scene of the drama, it was only what I had both expected and hoped for.

"I should be most happy to go down with you if I should not be in the way," said I.

"My dear Watson, you would confer a great favour upon me by coming. And I think that your time will not be misspent, for there are points about the case which promise to make it an absolutely unique one. We have, I think, just time to catch our train at Paddington, and I will go further into the matter upon our journey. You would oblige me by bringing with you your very excellent field-glass."

And so it happened that an hour or so later I found myself in the corner of a first class carriage flying along en route for Exeter, while Sherlock Holmes, with his sharp, eager face framed in his ear-flapped travelling-cap, dipped rapidly into the bundle of fresh papers which he had procured at Paddington. We had left Reading far behind us before he thrust the last one of them under the seat and offered me his cigar-case.

"We are going well," said he, looking out of the window and glancing at his watch. "Our rate at present is fifty-three and a half miles an hour."

"I have not observed the quarter-mile posts," said I.

"Nor have I. But the telegraph posts upon this line are sixty yards apart, and the calculation is a simple one. I presume that you have looked into this matter of the murder of John Straker and the disappearance of Silver Blaze?"

"I've seen what the *Telegraph* and the *Chronicle* have to say."

"It is one of those cases where the art of the reasoner should be used rather for the sifting of details than for the acquiring of fresh evidence. The tragedy has been so uncommon, so complete, and of such personal importance to so many people that we are suffering from a plethora of surmise, conjecture, and hypothesis. The difficulty is to detach the framework of fact—of absolute undeniable fact—from the embellishment of theorists and reporters. Then, having established ourselves upon this sound basis, it is our duty to see what inferences may be drawn and what are the special points upon which the whole mystery turns. On Tuesday evening I received telegrams from both Colonel Ross, the owner of the horse, and from Inspector Gregory, who is looking after the case, inviting my cooperation."

"Tuesday evening!" I exclaimed. "And this is Thursday morning. Why didn't you go down yesterday?"

"Because I made a blunder, my dear Watson—which is, I am afraid, a more common occurrence than anyone would think who only knew me through your memoirs. The fact is that I could not believe it possible that the most remarkable horse in England could long remain concealed, especially in so sparsely inhabited a place as the north of Dartmoor. From hour to hour yesterday I expected to hear that he had been found, and that his abductor was the murderer of John Straker. When, however, another morning had come and I found that beyond the arrest of young Fitzroy Simpson nothing had been done, I felt that it was time for me to take action. Yet in some ways I feel that yesterday has not been wasted."

"You have formed a theory, then?"

"At least I have got a grip of the essential facts of the case. I shall enumerate them to you, for nothing clears up a case so much as stating it to another person, and I can hardly expect your cooperation if I do not show you the position from which we start."

I lay back against the cushions, puffing at my cigar, while Holmes, leaning forward, with his long, thin forefinger checking off the points upon the palm of his left hand, gave me a sketch of the events which had led to our journey.

"Silver Blaze," said he, "is from the Somomy stock and holds as brilliant a record as his famous ancestor. He is now in his fifth year and has brought in turn, each of the prizes of the turf to Colonel Ross, his fortunate owner. Up to the time of the catastrophe he was the first favourite for the Wessex Cup, the betting being three to one on him. He has always, however, been a prime favourite with the racing public and has never yet disappointed them, so that even at those odds enormous sums of money have been laid upon him. It is obvious, therefore, that there were many people who had the strongest interest in preventing Silver Blaze from being there at the fall of the flag next Tuesday.

"The fact was, of course, appreciated at King's Pyland, where the Colonel's training-stable is situated. Every precaution was taken to guard the favourite. The trainer, John Straker, is a retired jockey who rode in Colonel Ross's colours before he became too heavy for the weighing-chair. He has served the Colonel for five years as jockey and for seven as trainer, and has always shown himself to be a zealous and honest servant. Under him were three lads, for the establishment was a small one, containing only four horses in all. One of these lads sat up each night in the stable, while the others slept in the loft. All three bore excellent characters. John Straker, who is a married man, lived in a small villa about two hundred yards from the stables. He has no children, keeps one maidservant, and is comfortably off. The country round is very lonely, but about half a mile to the north there is a small cluster of villas which have been built by a Tavistock contractor for the use of invalids and others who may wish to enjoy the pure Dartmoor air. Tavistock itself lies two miles to the west, while across the moor, also about two miles distant, is the larger training establishment of Mapleton, which belongs to Lord Backwater and is managed by Silas Brown. In every other direction the moor is a complete wilderness, inhabited only by a few roaming gypsies. Such was the general situation last Monday night when the catastrophe occurred.

"On that evening the horses had been exercised and watered as usual, and the stables were locked up at nine o'clock. Two of the lads walked up to the trainer's house, where they had supper in the kitchen, while the third, Ned Hunter, remained on guard. At a few minutes after nine the maid, Edith Baxter, carried down to the stables his supper, which consisted of a dish of curried mutton. She took no liquid, as there was a water-tap in the stables, and it was the rule that the lad on duty should drink nothing else. The maid carried a lantern with her, as it was very dark and the path ran across the open moor."

"Edith Baxter was within thirty yards of the stables when a man appeared out of the darkness and called to her to stop. As she stepped into the circle of yellow light thrown by the lantern she saw that he was a person of gentlemanly bearing, dressed in a gray suit of tweeds, with a cloth cap. He wore gaiters and carried a heavy stick with a knob to it. She was most impressed, however, by the extreme pallor of his face and by the nervousness of his manner. His age, she thought, would be rather over thirty than under it.

"'Can you tell me where I am?' he asked. 'I had almost made up my mind to sleep on the moor when I saw the light of your lantern.'

"'You are quite close to the King's Pyland training stables,' said she.

"'Oh, indeed! What a stroke of luck!' he cried. 'I understand that a stable boy sleeps there alone every night. Perhaps that is his supper which you are carrying to him. Now I am sure that you would not be too proud to earn the price of a new dress, would you?' He took a piece of white paper folded up out of his waistcoat pocket. 'See that the boy has this tonight, and you shall have the prettiest frock that money can buy.'

"She was frightened by the earnestness of his manner and ran past him to the window through which she was accustomed to hand the meals. It was already opened, and Hunter was seated at the small table inside. She had begun to tell him of what had happened when the stranger came up again.

"'Good evening,' said he, looking through the window. 'I wanted to have a word with you.' The girl has sworn that as he spoke she noticed the corner of the little paper packet protruding from his closed hand.

"'What business have you here?' asked the lad.

"'It's business that may put something into your pocket,' said the other. 'You've two horses in for the Wessex Cup–Silver Blaze and Bayard. Let me have the straight tip and you won't be a loser. Is it a fact that at the weights Bayard could give the other a hundred yards in five furlongs, and that the stable have put their money on him?'

"'So, you're one of those damned touts!' cried the lad. 'I'll show you how we serve them in King's Pyland.' He sprang up and rushed across the stable to unloose the dog. The girl fled away to the house, but as she ran she looked back and saw that the stranger was leaning through the window. A minute later, however, when Hunter rushed out with the hound he was gone, and though he ran all round the buildings he failed to find any trace of him.'"

"One moment," I asked. "Did the stable boy, when he ran out with the dog, leave the door unlocked behind him?"

"Excellent, Watson, excellent!" murmured my companion. "The importance of the point struck me so forcibly that I sent a special wire to Dartmoor yesterday to clear the matter up. The boy locked the door before he left it. The window I may add, was not large enough for a man to get through.

"Hunter waited until his fellow-grooms had returned, when he sent a message to the trainer and told him what had occurred. Straker was excited at hearing the account, although he does not seem to have quite realized its true significance. It left him, however, vaguely uneasy, and Mrs. Straker, waking at one in the morning, found that he was dressing. In reply to her inquiries, he said that he could not sleep on account of his anxiety about the horses, and that he intended to walk down to the stables to see that all was well. She begged him to remain at home, as she could hear the rain pattering against the window, but in spite of her entreaties he pulled on his large mackintosh and left the house.

"Mrs. Straker awoke at seven in the morning to find that her husband had not yet returned. She dressed herself hastily, called the maid, and set off for the stables. The door was open; inside, huddled together upon a chair, Hunter was sunk in a state of absolute stupor, the favourite's stall was empty, and there were no signs of his trainer.

"The two lads who slept in the chaff-cutting loft above the harnessroom were quickly aroused. They had heard nothing during the night, for they are both sound sleepers. Hunter was obviously under the influence of some powerful drug, and as no sense could be got out of him, he was left to sleep it off while the two lads and the two women ran out in search of the absentees. They still had hopes that the trainer had for some reason taken out the horse for early exercise, but on ascending the knoll near the house, from which all the neighbouring moors were visible, they not only could see no signs of the missing favourite, but they perceived something which warned them that they were in the presence of a tragedy.

"About a quarter of a mile from the stables John Straker's overcoat was flapping from a furze-bush. Immediately beyond there was a bowl-shaped depression in the moor, and at the bottom of this was found the dead body of the unfortunate trainer. His head had been shattered by a savage blow from some heavy weapon, and he was wounded on the thigh, where there was a long, clean cut, inflicted evidently by some very sharp instrument. It was clear, however, that Straker had defended himself vigorously against his assailants, for in his right hand he held a small knife, which was clotted with blood up to the handle, while in his left he clasped a red and black silk cravat, which was recognized by the maid as having been worn on the preceding evening by the stranger who had visited the stables. Hunter, on recovering from his stupor, was also quite positive as to the ownership of the cravat. He was equally certain that the same stranger had, while standing at the window, drugged his curried mutton, and so deprived the stables of their watchman. As to the missing horse, there were abundant proofs in the mud which lay at the bottom of the fatal hollow that he had been there at the time of the struggle. But from that morning he has disappeared, and although a large reward has been offered, and all the gypsies of Dartmoor are on the alert, no news has come of him. Finally, an analysis has shown that the remains of his supper left by the stable-lad contained an appreciable quantity of powdered opium, while the people at the house partook of the same dish on the same night without any ill effect.

"Those are the main facts of the case, stripped of all surmise, and stated as baldly as possible. I shall now recapitulate what the police have done in the matter.

"Inspector Gregory, to whom the case has been committed, is an extremely competent officer. Were he but gifted with imagination he might rise to great heights in his profession. On his arrival he promptly found and arrested the man upon whom suspicion naturally rested. There was little difficulty in finding him, for he inhabited one of those villas which I have mentioned. His name, it appears, was Fitzroy Simpson. He was a man of excellent birth and education, who had squandered a fortune upon the turf, and who lived now by doing little quiet and genteel book-making in the sporting clubs of London. An examination of his betting-book shows that bets to the amount of five thousand pounds had been registered by him against the favourite. On being arrested he volunteered the statement that he had come down to Dartmoor in the hope of getting some information about the King's Pyland horses, and also about Desborough, the second favourite, which was in charge of Silas Brown at the Mapleton stables. He did not attempt to deny that he had acted as described upon the evening before, but declared that he had no sinister designs and had simply wished to obtain first-hand information. When confronted with his cravat he turned very pale and was utterly unable to account for its presence in the hand of the murdered man. His wet clothing showed that he had been out in the storm of the night before, and his stick, which was a Penang-lawyer weighted with lead, was just such a weapon as might, by repeated blows, have inflicted the terrible injuries to which the trainer had succumbed. On the other hand, there was no wound upon his person, while the state of Straker's knife would show that one at least of his assailants must bear his mark upon him. There you have it all in a nutshell, Watson, and if you can give me any light I shall be infinitely obliged to you."

I had listened with the greatest interest to the statement which Holmes, with characteristic clearness, had laid before me. Though most of the facts were familiar to me, I had not sufficiently appreciated their relative importance, nor their connection to each other.

"Is it not possible," I suggested, "that the incised wound upon Straker may have been caused by his own knife in the convulsive struggles which follow any brain injury?"

"It is more than possible; it is probable," said Holmes. "In that case one of the main points in favour of the accused disappears."

"And yet," said I, "even now I fail to understand what the theory of the police can be."

"I am afraid that whatever theory we state has very grave objections to it," returned my companion. "The police imagine, I take it, that this Fitzroy Simpson, having drugged the lad, and having in some way obtained a duplicate key, opened the stable door and took out the horse, with the intention, apparently, of kidnapping him altogether. His bridle is missing, so that Simpson must have put this on. Then, having left the door open behind him, he was leading the horse away over the moor when he was either met or overtaken by the trainer. A row naturally ensued. Simpson beat out the trainer's brains with his heavy stick without receiving any injury from the small knife which Straker used in self-defence, and then the thief either led the horse on to some secret hiding-place, or else it may have bolted during the struggle, and be now wandering out on the moors. That is the case, as it appears to the police, and improbable as it is, all other explanations are more improbable still. However, I shall very quickly test the matter when I am once upon the spot, and until then I cannot really see how we can get much further than our present position."

It was evening before we reached the little town of Tavistock, which lies, like the boss of a shield, in the middle of the huge circle of Dartmoor. Two gentlemen were awaiting us in the station—the one a tall, fair man with lion-like hair and beard and curiously penetrating light blue eyes; the other a small, alert person, very neat and dapper, in a frock coat and gaiters, with trim little side-whiskers and an eyeglass. The latter was Colonel Ross, the well-known sportsman; the other, Inspector Gregory; a man who was rapidly making his name in the English detective service.

"I am delighted that you have come down, Mr. Holmes," said the Colonel. "The inspector here has done all that could possibly be suggested, but I wish to leave no stone unturned in trying to avenge poor Straker and in recovering my horse."

"Have there been any fresh developments?" asked Holmes.

"I am sorry to say that we have made very little progress," said the inspector. "We have an open carriage outside, and as you would no doubt like to see the place before the light fails, we might talk it over as we drive."

A minute later we were all seated in a comfortable landau and were rattling through the quaint old Devonshire city. Inspector Gregory was full of his case and poured out a stream of remarks, while Holmes threw in an occasional question or interjection. Colonel Ross leaned back with his arms folded and his hat tilted over his eyes, while I listened with interest to the dialogue of the two detectives. Gregory was formulating his theory, which was almost exactly what Holmes had foretold in the train.

"The net is drawn pretty close round Fitzroy Simpson," he remarked, "and I believe myself that he is our man. At the same time I recognize that the evidence is purely circumstantial, and that some new development may upset it."

"How about Straker's knife?"

"We have quite come to the conclusion that he wounded himself in his fall."

"My friend Dr. Watson made that suggestion to me as we came down. If so, it would tell against this man Simpson."

"Undoubtedly. He has neither a knife nor any sign of a wound. The evidence against him is certainly very strong. He had a great interest in the disappearance of the favourite. He lies under suspicion of having poisoned the stable boy; he was undoubtedly out in the storm; he was armed with a heavy stick, and his cravat was found in the dead man's hand. I really think we have enough to go before a jury."

Holmes shook his head. "A clever counsel would tear it all to rags," said he. "Why should he take the horse out of the stable? If he wished to injure it, why could he not do it there? Has a duplicate key been found in his possession? What chemist sold him the powdered opium? Above all, where could he, a stranger to the district, hide a horse, and such a horse as this? What is his own explanation as to the paper which he wished the maid to give to the stable boy?"

"He says that it was a ten-pound note. One was found in his purse. But your other difficulties are not so formidable as they seem. He is not a stranger to the district. He has twice lodged at Tavistock in the summer. The opium was probably brought from London. The key, having served its purpose, would be hurled away. The horse may be at the bottom of one of the pits or old mines upon the moor."

"What does he say about the cravat?"

"He acknowledges that it is his and declares that he had

lost it. But a new element has been introduced into the case which may account for his leading the horse from the stable."

Holmes pricked up his ears.

"We have found traces which show that a party of gypsies encamped on Monday night within a mile of the spot where the murder took place. On Tuesday they were gone. Now, presuming that there was some understanding between Simpson and these gypsies, might he not have been leading the horse to them when he was overtaken, and may they not have him now?"

"It is certainly possible."

"The moor is being scoured for these gypsies. I have also examined every stable and outhouse in Tavistock, and for a radius of ten miles."

"There is another training-stable quite close, I understand?"

"Yes, and that is a factor which we must certainly not neglect. As Desborough, their horse, was second in the betting, they had an interest in the disappearance of the favourite. Silas Brown, the trainer, is known to have had large bets upon the event, and he was no friend to poor Straker. We have, however, examined the stables, and there is nothing to connect him with the affair."

"And nothing to connect this man Simpson with the interests of the Mapleton stables?"

"Nothing at all."

Holmes leaned back in the carriage, and the conversation ceased. A few minutes later our driver pulled up at a neat little red-brick villa with overhanging eaves which stood by the road. Some distance off, across a paddock, lay a long gray-tiled outbuilding. In every other direction the low curves of the moor, bronze-coloured from the fading ferns, stretched away to the skyline, broken only by the steeples of Tavistock, and by a cluster of houses away to the westward which marked the Mapleton stables. We all sprang out with the exception of Holmes, who continued to lean back with his eyes fixed upon the sky in front of him, entirely absorbed in his own thoughts. It was only when I touched his arm that he roused himself with a violent start and stepped out of the carriage.

"Excuse me," said he, turning to Colonel Ross, who had looked at him in some surprise. "I was day-dreaming." There was a gleam in his eyes and a suppressed excitement in his manner which convinced me, used as I was to his ways, that his hand was upon a clue, though I could not imagine where he had found it.

"Perhaps you would prefer at once to go on to the scene of the crime, Mr. Holmes?" said Gregory.

"I think that I should prefer to stay here a little and go into one or two questions of detail. Straker was brought back here, I presume?"

"Yes, he lies upstairs. The inquest is tomorrow."

"He has been in your service some years, Colonel Ross?"

"I have always found him an excellent servant."

"I presume that you made an inventory of what he had in his pockets at the time of his death, Inspector?"

"I have the things themselves in the sitting room if you would care to see them."

"I should be very glad." We all filed into the front room and sat round the central table while the inspector unlocked a square tin box and laid a small heap of things before us. There was a box of vestas, two inches of tallow candle, an ADP brier-root pipe, a pouch of sealskin with half an ounce of long-cut

Cavendish, a silver watch with a gold chain, five sovereigns in gold, an aluminium pencil-case, a few papers, and an ivory-handled knife with a very delicate, inflexible blade marked Weiss & Co., London.

"This is a very singular knife," said Holmes, lifting it up and examining it minutely. "I presume, as I see bloodstains upon it, that it is the one which was found in the dead man's grasp. Watson, this knife is surely in your line?"

"It is what we call a cataract knife," said I.

"I thought so. A very delicate blade devised for very delicate work. A strange thing for a man to carry with him upon a rough expedition, especially as it would not shut in his pocket."

"The tip was guarded by a disc of cork which we found beside his body," said the inspector. "His wife tells us that the knife had lain upon the dressing table, and that he had picked it up as he left the room. It was a poor weapon, but perhaps the best that he could lay his hands on at the moment."

"Very possibly. How about these papers?"

"Three of them are receipted hay-dealers' accounts. One of them is a letter of instructions from Colonel Ross. This other is a milliner's account for thirty-seven pounds fifteen made out by Madame Lesurier, of Bond Street, to William Derbyshire. Mrs. Straker tells us that Derbyshire was a friend of her husband's, and that occasionally his letters were addressed here."

"Madame Derbyshire had somewhat expensive tastes," remarked Holmes, glancing down the account. "Twenty-two guineas is rather heavy for a single costume. However, there appears to be nothing more to learn, and we may now go down to the scene of the crime."

As we emerged from the sitting room a woman, who had been waiting in the passage, took a step forward and laid her hand upon the inspector's sleeve. Her face was haggard and thin and eager, stamped with the print of a recent horror.

"Have you got them? Have you found them?" she panted.

"No, Mrs. Straker. But Mr. Holmes here has come from London to help us, and we shall do all that is possible."

"Surely I met you in Plymouth at a garden-party some little time ago, Mrs. Straker?" said Holmes.

"No, sir; you are mistaken."

"Dear me! Why, I could have sworn to it. You wore a costume of dove-coloured silk with ostrich-feather trimming."

"I never had such a dress, sir," answered the lady.

"Ah, that quite settles it," said Holmes. And with an apology he followed the inspector outside. A short walk across the moor took us to the hollow in which the body had been found. At the brink of it was the furze-bush upon which the coat had been hung.

"There was no wind that night, I understand," said Holmes.

"None, but very heavy rain."

"In that case the overcoat was not blown against the furze-bushes, but placed there."

"Yes, it was laid across the bush."

"You fill me with interest. I perceive that the ground has been trampled up a good deal. No doubt many feet have been here since Monday night."

"A piece of matting has been laid here at the side, and we have all stood upon that."

"Excellent."

"In this bag I have one of the boots which Straker wore, one of Fitzroy Simpson's shoes, and a cast horseshoe of Silver Blaze."

"My dear Inspector, you surpass yourself!" Holmes took the bag, and, descending into the hollow, he pushed the matting into a more central position. Then stretching himself upon his face and leaning his chin upon his hands, he made a careful study of the trampled mud in front of him. "Hullo!" said he suddenly. "What's this?" It was a wax vesta, half burned, which was so coated with mud that it looked at first like a little chip of wood.

"I cannot think how I came to overlook it," said the inspector with an expression of annoyance.

"It was invisible, buried in the mud. I only saw it because I was looking for it."

"What! You expected to find it?"

"I thought it not unlikely."

He then took the boots from the bag and compared the impressions of each of them with marks upon the ground. Then he clambered up to the rim of the hollow and crawled about among the ferns and bushes.

"I am afraid that there are no more tracks," said the inspector. "I have examined the ground very carefully for a hundred yards in each direction."

"Indeed!" said Holmes, rising. "I should not have the impertinence to do it again after what you say. But I should like to take a little walk over the moor before it grows dark that I may know my ground tomorrow, and I think that I shall put this horseshoe into my pocket for luck."

Colonel Ross, who had shown some signs of impatience at my companion's quiet and systematic method of work, glanced at his watch.

"I wish you would come back with me, Inspector," said he. "There are several points on which I should like your advice, and especially as to whether we do not owe it to the public to remove our horse's name from the entries for the cup."

"Certainly not," cried Holmes with decision. "I should let the name stand."

The Colonel bowed. "I am very glad to have had your opinion, sir," said he. "You will find us at poor Straker's house when you have finished your walk, and we can drive together into Tavistock."

He turned back with the inspector, while Holmes and I walked slowly across the moor. The sun was beginning to sink behind the stable of Mapleton, and the long, sloping plain in front of us was tinged with gold, deepening into rich, ruddy browns where the faded ferns and brambles caught the evening light. But the glories of the landscape were all wasted upon my companion, who was sunk in the deepest thought.

"It's this way, Watson," said he at last. "We may leave the question of who killed John Straker for the instant and confine ourselves to finding out what has become of the horse. Now, supposing that he broke away during or after the tragedy, where could he have gone to? The horse is a very gregarious creature. If left to himself his instincts would have been either to return to King's Pyland or go over to Mapleton. Why should he run wild upon the moor? He would surely have been seen by now. And why should gypsies kidnap him? These people always clear out when they hear of trouble, for they do not wish to be pestered by the police. They could not hope to sell such a horse. They would run a great risk and gain nothing by taking him. Surely that is clear."

"Where is he, then?"

"I have already said that he must have gone to King's Pyland or to Mapleton. He is not at King's Pyland. Therefore he is at Mapleton. Let us take that as a working hypothesis and see what it leads us to. This part of the moor, as the inspector remarked, is very hard and dry. But it falls away towards Mapleton, and you can see from here that there is a long hollow over yonder, which must have been very wet on Monday night. If our supposition is correct, then the horse must have crossed that, and there is the point where we should look for his tracks."

We had been walking briskly during this conversation, and a few more minutes brought us to the hollow in question. At Holmes's request I walked down the bank to the right, and he to the left, but I had not taken fifty paces before I heard him give a shout and saw him waving his hand to me. The track of a horse was plainly outlined in the soft earth in front of him, and the shoe which he took from his pocket exactly fitted the impression.

"See the value of imagination," said Holmes. "It is the one quality which Gregory lacks. We imagined what might have happened, acted upon the supposition, and find ourselves justified. Let us proceed."

We crossed the marshy bottom and passed over a quarter of a mile of dry, hard turf. Again the ground sloped, and again we came on the tracks. Then we lost them for half a mile, but only to pick them up once more quite close to Mapleton. It was Holmes who saw them first and he stood pointing with a look of triumph upon his face. A man's track was visible beside the horse's.

"The horse was alone before," I cried.

"Quite so. It was alone before. Hullo, what is this?"

The double track turned sharp off and took the direction of King's Pyland. Holmes whistled, and we both followed along after it. His eyes were on the trail, but I happened to look a little to one side and saw to my surprise the same tracks coming back again in the opposite direction.

"One for you, Watson," said Holmes when I pointed it out. "You have saved us a long walk, which would have brought us back on our own traces. Let us follow the return track."

We had not to go far. It ended at the paving of asphalt which led up to the gates of the Mapleton stables. As we approached, a groom ran out from them.

"We don't want any loiterers about here," said he.

"I only wished to ask a question," said Holmes, with his finger and thumb in his waistcoat pocket. "Should I be too early to see your master, Mr. Silas Brown, if I were to call at five o'clock tomorrow morning?"

"Bless you, sir, if anyone is about he will be, for he is always the first stirring. But here he is, sir, to answer your questions for himself. No, sir, no, it is as much as my place is worth to let him see me touch your money. Afterwards, if you like."

As Sherlock Holmes replaced the half-crown which he had drawn from his pocket, a fierce-looking elderly man strode out from the gate with a hunting-crop swinging in his hand.

"What's this, Dawson!" he cried. "No gossiping! Go about your business! And you, what the devil do you want here?"

"Ten minutes' talk with you, my good sir," said Holmes in the sweetest of voices.

"I've no time to talk to every gadabout. We want no strangers here. Be off, or you may find a dog at your heels."

Holmes leaned forward and whispered something in the trainer's ear. He started violently and flushed to the temples.

"It's a lie!" he shouted. "An infernal lie!"

"Very good. Shall we argue about it here in public or talk it over in your parlour?"

"Oh, come in if you wish to."

Holmes smiled. "I shall not keep you more than a few minutes, Watson," said he. "Now, Mr. Brown, I am quite at your disposal."

It was twenty minutes, and the reds had all faded into grays before Holmes and the trainer reappeared. Never have I seen such a change as had been brought about in Silas Brown in that short time. His face was ashy pale, beads of perspiration shone upon his brow, and his hands shook until the hunting-crop wagged like a branch in the wind. His bullying, overbearing manner was all gone too, and he cringed along at my companion's side like a dog with its master.

"Your instructions will be done. It shall all be done," said he.

"There must be no mistake," said Holmes, looking round at him.

The other winced as he read the menace in his eyes.

"Oh, no, there shall be no mistake. It shall be there. Should I change it first or not?"

Sherlock Holmes thought a little and then burst out laughing. "No, don't," said he, "I shall write to you about it. No tricks, now, or—"

"Oh, you can trust me, you can trust me!"

"Yes, I think I can. Well, you'll hear from me tomorrow."

He turned upon his heel, disregarding the trembling hand which the other held out to him, and thereafter we set off for King's Pyland.

"A more perfect compound of the bully, coward, and sneak than Master Silas Brown I have seldom met with," remarked Holmes as we trudged along together.

"He has the horse, then?"

"He tried to bluster out of it, but I described to him so exactly what his actions had been upon that morning that he is convinced that I was watching him. Of course you observed the peculiarly square toes in the impressions, and that his own boots exactly corresponded to them. Again, of course no subordinate would have dared to do such a thing. I described to him how, when according to his custom he was the first down, he perceived a strange horse wandering over the moor. How he went out to it, and his astonishment at recognizing, from the white forehead which has given the favourite its name, that chance had put in his power the only horse which could beat the one upon which he had put his money. Then I described how his first impulse had been to lead him back to King's Pyland, and how the devil had shown him how he could hide the horse until the race was over, and how he had led it back and concealed it at Mapleton. When I told him every detail he gave it up and thought only of saving his own skin."

"But his stables had been searched?"

"Oh, an old horse-faker like him has many a dodge."

"But are you not afraid to leave the horse in his power now, since he has every interest in injuring it?"

"My dear fellow, he will guard it as the apple of his eye. He knows that his only hope of mercy is to produce it safe."

"Colonel Ross did not impress me as a man who would be likely to show much mercy in any case."

"The matter does not rest with Colonel Ross. I follow my own methods and tell as much or as little as I choose. That is the advantage of being unofficial. I don't know whether you observed it, Watson, but the Colonel's manner has been just a trifle cavalier to me. I am inclined now to have a little amusement at his expense. Say nothing to him about the horse."

"Certainly not without your permission."

"And of course this is all quite a minor point compared to the question of who killed John Straker."

"And you will devote yourself to that?"

"On the contrary, we both go back to London by the night train."

I was thunderstruck by my friend's words. We had only been a few hours in Devonshire, and that he should give up an investigation which he had begun so brilliantly was quite incomprehensible to me. Not a word more could I draw from him until we were back at the trainer's house. The Colonel and the inspector were awaiting us in the parlour.

"My friend and I return to town by the night express," said Holmes. "We have had a charming little breath of your beautiful Dartmoor air."

The inspector opened his eyes, and the Colonel's lip curled in a sneer.

"So you despair of arresting the murderer of poor Straker," said he.

Holmes shrugged his shoulders. "There are certainly grave difficulties in the way," said he. "I have every hope, however, that your horse will start upon Tuesday, and I beg that you will have your jockey in readiness. Might I ask for a photograph of Mr. John Straker?"

The inspector took one from an envelope and promptly handed it to him.

"My dear Gregory, you anticipate all my wants. If I might ask you to wait here for an instant, I have a question which I should like to put to the maid."

"I must say that I am rather disappointed in our London consultant," said Colonel Ross bluntly as my friend left the room. "I do not see that we are any further than when he came."

"At least you have his assurance that your horse will run," said I.

"Yes, I have his assurance," said the Colonel with a shrug of his shoulders. "I should prefer to have the horse."

I was about to make some reply in defence of my friend when he entered the room again.

"Now, gentlemen," said he, "I am quite ready for Tavistock."

As we stepped into the carriage one of the stable-lads held the door open for us. A sudden idea seemed to occur to Holmes, for he leaned forward and touched the lad upon the sleeve.

"You have a few sheep in the paddock," he said. "Who attends to them?"

"I do, sir."

"Have you noticed anything amiss with them of late?"

"Well, sir, not of much account, but three of them have gone lame, sir."

I could see that Holmes was extremely pleased, for he chuckled and rubbed his hands together.

"A long shot, Watson, a very long shot," said he, pinching my arm. "Gregory, let me recommend to your attention this singular epidemic among the sheep. Drive on, coachman!"

Colonel Ross still wore an expression which showed the poor opinion which he had formed of my companion's ability, but I saw by the inspector's face that his attention had been keenly aroused.

"You consider that to be important?" he asked.

"Exceedingly so."

"Is there any particular point to which you would wish to draw my attention?"

"To the curious incident of the dog in the night-time."

"The dog did nothing in the night-time."

"That was the curious incident," remarked Sherlock Holmes. Four days later Holmes and I were again in the train, bound for Winchester to see the race for the Wessex Cup. Colonel Ross met us by appointment outside the station, and we drove in his drag to the course beyond the town. His face was grave, and his manner was cold in the extreme.

"I have seen nothing of my horse," said he.

"I suppose that you would know him when you saw him?" asked Holmes.

The Colonel was very angry. "I have been on the turf for twenty years and never was asked such a question as that before," said he.

"A child would know Silver Blaze with his white forehead and his mottled off-foreleg."

"How is the betting?"

"Well, that is the curious part of it. You could have got fifteen to one yesterday, but the price has become shorter and shorter, until you can hardly get three to one now."

"Hum!" said Holmes. "Somebody knows something, that is clear."

As the drag drew up in the enclosure near the grandstand I glanced at the card to see the entries.

Wessex Plate [it ran] *50 sovs. each h ft with 1000 sovs. added, for four and five year olds. Second, £300. Third. £200. New course* (*one mile and five furlongs*).

1. Mr. Heath Newton's The Negro. Red cap. Cinnamon jacket.
2. Colonel Wardlaw's Pugilist. Pink cap. Blue and black Jacket.
3. Lord Backwater's Desborough. Yellow cap and sleeves.
4. Colonel Ross's Silver Blaze. Black cap. Red jacket.
5. Duke of Balmoral's Iris. Yellow and black stripes.
6. Lord Singleford's Rasper. Purple cap. Black sleeves.

"We scratched our other one and put all hopes on your word," said the Colonel. "Why, what is that? Silver Blaze favourite?"

"Five to four against Silver Blaze!" roared the ring. "Five to four against Silver Blaze! Five to fifteen against Desborough! Five to four on the field!"

"There are the numbers up," I cried. "They are all six very much there."

"All six there? Then my horse is running," cried the Colonel in great agitation. "But I don't see him. My colours have not passed."

"Only five have passed. This must be he."

As I spoke a powerful bay horse swept out from the weighing enclosure and cantered past us, bearing on its back the well-known black and red of the Colonel.

"That's not my horse," cried the owner. "That beast has not a white hair upon its body. What is this that you have done, Mr. Holmes?"

"Well, well, let us see how he gets on," said my friend imperturbably. For a few minutes he gazed through my field-glass. "Capital! An excellent start!" he cried suddenly. "There they are, coming round the curve!"

From our drag we had a superb view as they came up the straight. The six horses were so close together that a carpet could have covered them, but halfway up the yellow of the Mapleton stable showed to the front. Before they reached us, however, Desborough's bolt was shot, and the Colonel's horse, coming away with a rush, passed the post a good six lengths before its rival, the Duke of Balmoral's Iris making a bad third.

"It's my race, anyhow," gasped the Colonel, passing his hand over his eyes. "I confess that I can make neither head nor tail of it. Don't you think that you have kept up your mystery long enough, Mr. Holmes?"

"Certainly, Colonel, you shall know everything. Let us all go round and have a look at the horse together. Here he is," he continued as we made our way into the weighing enclosure, where only owners and their friends find admittance. "You have only to wash his face and his leg in spirits of wine, and you will find that he is the same old Silver Blaze as ever."

"You take my breath away!"

"I found him in the hands of a faker and took the liberty of running him just as he was sent over."

"My dear sir, you have done wonders. The horse looks very fit and well. It never went better in its life. I owe you a thousand apologies for having doubted your ability. You have done me a great service by recovering my horse. You would do me a greater still if you could lay your hands on the murderer of John Straker."

"I have done so," said Holmes quietly.

The Colonel and I stared at him in amazement. "You have got him! Where is he, then?"

"He is here."

"Here! Where?"

"In my company at the present moment."

The Colonel flushed angrily. "I quite recognize that I am under obligations to you, Mr. Holmes," said he, "but I must regard what you have just said as either a very bad joke or an insult."

Sherlock Holmes laughed. "I assure you that I have not associated you with the crime, Colonel," said he. "The real murderer is standing immediately behind you." He stepped past and laid his hand upon the glossy neck of the thoroughbred.

"The horse!" cried both the Colonel and myself.

"Yes, the horse. And it may lessen his guilt if I say that it was done in self-defence, and that John Straker was a man who was entirely unworthy of your confidence. But there goes the bell, and as I stand to win a little on this next race, I shall defer a lengthy explanation until a more fitting time."

We had the corner of a Pullman car to ourselves that evening as we whirled back to London, and I fancy that the journey was a short one to Colonel Ross as well as to myself as we listened to our companion's narrative of the events which had occurred at the Dartmoor training-stables upon that Monday night, and the means by which he had unravelled them.

"I confess," said he, "that any theories which I had formed from the newspaper reports were entirely erroneous. And yet there were indications there, had they not been overlaid by other details which concealed their true import. I went to Devonshire with the conviction that Fitzroy Simpson was the true culprit, although, of course, I saw that the evidence against him was by no means complete. It was while I was in the carriage, just as we reached the trainer's house, that the immense significance of the curried mutton occurred to me. You may remember that I was distrait and remained sitting after you had all alighted. I was marvelling in my own mind how I could possibly have overlooked so obvious a clue."

"I confess," said the Colonel, "that even now I cannot see how it helps us."

"It was the first link in my chain of reasoning. Powdered opium is by no means tasteless. The flavour is not disagreeable, but it is perceptible. Were it mixed with any ordinary dish the eater would undoubtedly detect it and would probably eat no more. A curry was exactly the medium which would disguise this taste. By no possible supposition could this stranger, Fitzroy Simpson, have caused curry to be served in the trainer's family that night, and it is surely too monstrous a coincidence to suppose that he happened to come along with powdered opium upon the very night when a dish happened to be served which would disguise the flavour. That is unthinkable. Therefore Simpson becomes eliminated from the case, and our attention centres upon Straker and his wife, the only two people who could have chosen curried mutton for supper that night. The opium was added after the dish was set aside for the stable boy, for the others had the same for supper with no ill effects. Which of them, then, had access to that dish without the maid seeing them?

"Before deciding that question I had grasped the significance of the silence of the dog, for one true inference invariably suggests others. The Simpson incident had shown me that a dog was kept in the stables, and yet, though someone had been in and had fetched out a horse, he had not barked enough to arouse the two lads in the loft. Obviously the midnight visitor was someone whom the dog knew well.

"I was already convinced, or almost convinced, that John Straker went down to the stables in the dead of the night and took out Silver Blaze. For what purpose? For a dishonest one, obviously, or why should he drug his own stable boy? And yet I was at a loss to know why. There have been cases before now where trainers have made sure of great sums of money by laying against their own horses through agents and then preventing them from winning by fraud. Sometimes it is a pulling jockey. Sometimes it is some surer and subtler means. What was it here? I hoped that the contents of his pockets might help me to form a conclusion. And they did so. You cannot have forgotten the singular knife which was found in the dead man's hand, a knife which certainly no sane man would choose for a weapon. It was, as Dr. Watson told us, a form of knife which is used for the most delicate operations known in surgery. And it was to be used for a delicate operation that night. You must know, with your wide experience of turf matters, Colonel Ross, that it is possible to make a slight nick upon the tendons of a horse's ham, and to do it subcutaneously, so as to leave absolutely no trace. A horse so treated would develop a slight lameness, which would be put down to a strain in exercise or a touch of rheumatism, but never to foul play."

"Villain! Scoundrel!" cried the Colonel.

"We have here the explanation of why John Straker wished to take the horse out on to the moor. So spirited a creature would have certainly roused the soundest of sleepers when it felt the prick of the knife. It was absolutely necessary to do it in the open air."

"I have been blind!" cried the Colonel. "Of course that was why he needed the candle and struck the match."

"Undoubtedly. But in examining his belongings I was fortunate enough to discover not only the method of the crime but even its motives. As a man of the world, Colonel, you know that men do not carry other people's bills about in their pockets. We have most of us quite enough to do to settle our own. I at once concluded that Straker was leading a double life and keeping a second establishment. The nature of the bill showed that there was a lady in the case, and one who had expensive tastes. Liberal as you are with your servants, one can hardly expect that they can buy twenty-guinea walking dresses for their ladies. I questioned Mrs. Straker as to the dress without her knowing it, and, having satisfied myself that it had never reached her, I made a note of the milliner's address and felt that by calling there with Straker's photograph I could easily dispose of the mythical Derbyshire.

"From that time on all was plain. Straker had led out the horse to a hollow where his light would be invisible. Simpson in his flight had dropped his cravat, and Straker had picked it up with some idea, perhaps, that he might use it in securing the horse's leg. Once in the hollow, he had got behind the horse and had struck a light; but the creature, frightened at the sudden glare, and with the strange instinct of animals feeling that some mischief was intended, had lashed out, and the steel shoe had struck Straker full on the forehead. He had already, in spite of the rain, taken off his overcoat in order to do his delicate task, and so, as he fell, his knife gashed his thigh. Do I make it clear?"

"Wonderful!" cried the Colonel. "Wonderful! You might have been there!"

"My final shot was, I confess, a very long one. It struck me that so astute a man as Straker would not undertake this delicate tendon-nicking without a little practise. What could he practise on? My eyes fell upon the sheep, and I asked a question which, rather to my surprise, showed that my surmise was correct.

"When I returned to London I called upon the milliner, who had recognized Straker as an excellent customer of the name of Derbyshire, who had a very dashing wife, with a strong partiality for expensive dresses. I have no doubt that this woman had plunged him over head and ears in debt, and so led him into this miserable plot."

"You have explained all but one thing," cried the Colonel. "Where was the horse?"

"Ah, it bolted, and was cared for by one of your neighbours. We must have an amnesty in that direction, I think. This is Clapham Junction, if I am not mistaken, and we shall be in Victoria in less than ten minutes. If you care to smoke a cigar in our rooms, Colonel, I shall be happy to give you any other details which might interest you."

Chapter 2

THE ADVENTURE OF THE YELLOW FACE

[*In publishing these short sketches based upon the numerous cases in which my companion's singular gifts have made us the listeners to, and eventually the actors in, some strange drama, it is only natural that I should dwell rather upon his successes than upon his failures. And this not so much for the sake of his reputation—for, indeed, it was when he was at his wits' end that his energy and his versatility were most admirable—but because where he failed it happened too often that no one else succeeded, and that the tale was left forever without a conclusion. Now and again, however, it chanced that even when he erred the truth was still discovered. I have noted of some half-dozen cases of the kind; the adventure of the Musgrave Ritual and that which I am about to recount are the two which present the strongest features of interest.*]

SHERLOCK Holmes was a man who seldom took exercise for exercise's sake. Few men were capable of greater muscular effort, and he was undoubtedly one of the finest boxers of his weight that I have ever seen; but he looked upon aimless bodily exertion as a waste of energy, and he seldom bestirred himself save where there was some professional object to be served. Then he was absolutely untiring and indefatigable. That he should have kept himself in training under such circumstances is remarkable, but his diet was usually of the sparest, and his habits were simple to the verge of austerity. Save for the occasional use of cocaine, he had no vices, and he only turned to the drug as a protest against the monotony of existence when cases were scanty and the papers uninteresting.

One day in early spring he had so far relaxed as to go for a walk with me in the Park, where the first faint shoots of green were breaking out upon the elms, and the sticky spear-heads of the chestnut were just beginning to burst into their five-fold leaves. For two hours we rambled about together, in silence for the most part, as befits two men who know each other intimately. It was nearly five before we were back in Baker Street once more.

"Beg pardon, sir," said our page-boy as he opened the door "There's been a gentleman here asking for you, sir."

"Holmes glanced reproachfully at me. "So much for afternoon walks!" said he. "Has this gentleman gone, then?"

"Yes, sir."

"Didn't you ask him in?"

"Yes, sir, he came in."

"How long did he wait?"

"Half an hour, sir. He was a very restless gentleman, sir, a-walkin' and a-stampin' all the time he was here. I was waitin' outside the door, sir, and I could hear him. At last he's out into the passage, and he cries, 'Is that man *never* goin' to come?' Those were his very words, sir. 'You'll only need to wait a little longer,' says I. "Then I'll wait in the open air, for I feel half choked,' says he. 'I'll be back before long.' And with that he ups and he outs, and all I could say wouldn't hold him back."

"Well, well, you did your best," said Holmes as we walked into our room. "It's very annoying, though, Watson. I was badly in need of a case, and this looks, from the man's impatience, as if it were of importance. Hullo! That's not your pipe on the table. He must have left his behind him. A nice old brier with a good long stem of what the tobacconists call amber. I wonder how many real amber mouthpieces there are in London? Some people think that a fly in it is a sign. Well, he must have been disturbed in his mind to leave a pipe behind him which he evidently values highly."

"How do you know that he values it highly?" I asked.

"Well, I should put the original cost of the pipe at seven and sixpence. Now it has, you see, been twice mended, once in the wooden stem and once in the amber. Each of these mends, done, as you observe, with silver bands, must have cost more than the pipe did originally. The man must value the pipe highly when he prefers to patch it up rather than buy a new one with the same money."

"Anything else?" I asked, for Holmes was turning the pipe about in his hand and staring at it in his peculiar pensive way. He held it up and tapped on it with his long, thin forefinger, as a professor might who was lecturing on a bone.

"Pipes are occasionally of extraordinary interest," said he. "Nothing has more individuality, save perhaps watches and bootlaces. The indications here, however, are neither very marked nor very important. The owner is obviously a muscular man, left-handed, with an excellent set of teeth, careless in his habits, and with no need to practise economy."

My friend threw out the information in a very offhand way, but I saw that he cocked his eye at me to see if I had followed his reasoning.

"You think a man must be well-to-do if he smokes a seven-shiling pipe?" said I.

"This is Grosvenor mixture at eightpence an ounce," Holmes answered, knocking a little out on his palm. "As he might get an excellent smoke for half the price, he has no need to practise economy."

"And the other points?"

"He has been in the habit of lighting his pipe at lamps and gas-jets. You can see that it is quite charred all down one side. Of course a match could not have done that. Why should a man hold a match to the side of his pipe? But you cannot light it at a lamp without getting the bowl charred. And it is all on the right side of the pipe. From that I gather that he is a left-handed man. You hold your own pipe to the lamp and see how naturally you, being right-handed, hold the left side to the flame. You might do it once the other way, but not as a constancy. This has always been held so. Then he has bitten through his amber. It takes a muscular, energetic fellow, and one with a good set of teeth, to do that. But if I am not mistaken I hear him upon the stair, so we shall have something more interesting than his pipe to study."

An instant later our door opened, and a tall young man entered the room. He was well but quietly dressed in a dark gray suit, and carried a brown wideawake in his hand. I should have put him at about thirty, though he was really some years older.

"I beg your pardon," said he with some embarrassment, "I suppose I should have knocked. Yes, of course I should have knocked. The fact is that I am a little upset, and you must put it all down to that." He passed his hand over his forehead like a man who is half dazed, and then fell rather than sat down upon a chair.

"I can see that you have not slept for a night or two," said Holmes in his easy, genial way. "That tries a man's nerves more than work, and more even than pleasure. May I ask how I can help you?"

"I wanted your advice, sir. I don't know what to do, and my whole life seems to have gone to pieces."

"You wish to employ me as a consulting detective?"

"Not that only. I want your opinion as a judicious man as a man of the world. I want to know what I ought to do next. I hope to God you'll be able to tell me."

He spoke in little, sharp, jerky outbursts, and it seemed to me that to speak at all was very painful to him, and that his will all through was overriding his inclinations.

"It's a very delicate thing," said he. "One does not like to speak of one's domestic affairs to strangers. It seems dreadful to discuss the conduct of one's wife with two men whom I have never seen before. It's horrible to have to do it. But I've got to the end of my tether, and I must have advice."

"My dear Mr. Grant Munro," began Holmes.

Our visitor sprang from his chair. "What!" he cried, "you know my name?"

"If you wish to preserve your incognito," said Holmes, smiling, "I would suggest that you cease to write your name upon the lining of your hat, or else that you turn the crown towards the person whom you are addressing. I was about to say that my friend and I have listened to a good many strange secrets in this room, and that we have had the good fortune to bring peace to many troubled souls. I trust that we may do as much for you. Might I beg you, as time may prove to be of importance, to furnish me with the facts of your case without further delay?"

Our visitor again passed his hand over his forehead, as if he found it bitterly hard. From every gesture and expression I could see that he was a reserved, self-contained man, with a dash of pride in his nature; he seemed more likely to hide his wounds than to expose them. Then suddenly, with a fierce gesture of his closed hand, like one who throws reserve to the winds, he began:

"The facts are these, Mr. Holmes," said he. "I am a married man and have been so for three years. During that time my wife and I have loved each other as fondly and lived as happily as any two that ever were joined. We have not had a difference, not one, in thought or word or deed. And now, since last Monday, there has suddenly sprung up a barrier between us, and I find that there is something in her life and in her thoughts of which I know as little as if she were the woman who brushes by me in the street. We are estranged, and I want to know why."

"Now there is one thing that I want to impress upon you before I go any further, Mr. Holmes. Effie loves me. Don't let there be any mistake about that. She loves me with her whole heart and soul, and never more than now. I know it. I feel it. I don't want to argue about that. A man can tell easily enough when a woman loves him. But there's this secret between us, and we can never be the same until it is cleared."

"Kindly let me have the facts, Mr. Munro," said Holmes with some impatience.

"I'll tell you what I know about Effie's history. She was a widow when I met her first, though quite young—only twenty-five. Her name then was Mrs. Hebron. She went out to America when she was young and lived in the town of Atlanta, where she married this Hebron, who was a lawyer with a good practice. They had one child, but the yellow fever broke out badly in the place, and both husband and child died of it. I have seen his death certificate. This sickened her of America, and she came back to live with a maiden aunt at Pinner, in Middlesex. I may mention that her husband had left her comfortably off, and that she had a capital of about four thousand five hundred pounds, which had been so well invested by him that it returned an average of seven per cent. She had only been six months at Pinner when I met her; we fell in love with each other, and we married a few weeks afterwards."

"I am a hop merchant myself, and as I have an income of seven or eight hundred, we found ourselves comfortably off and took a nice eighty-pound-a-year villa at Norbury. Our little place was very countrified, considering that it is so close to town. We had an inn and two houses a little above us, and a single cottage at the other side of the field which faces us, and except those there were no houses until you got halfway to the station. My business took me into town at certain seasons, but in summer I had less to do, and then in our country home my wife and I were just as happy as could be wished. I tell you that there never was a shadow between us until this accursed affair began.

"There's one thing I ought to tell you before I go further. When we married, my wife made over all her property to me rather against my will, for I saw how awkward it would be if my business affairs went wrong. However, she would have it so, and it was done.

"Well, about six weeks ago she came to me.

"'Jack,' said she, 'when you took my money you said that if ever I wanted any I was to ask you for it.'

"'Certainly' said I. 'It's all your own.'

"'Well,' said she, 'I want a hundred pounds.'

"I was a bit staggered at this, for I had imagined it was simply a new dress or something of the kind that she was after.

"'What on earth for?' I asked.

"'Oh,' said she in her playful way, 'you said that you were only my banker, and bankers never ask questions, you know.'

"'If you really mean it, of course you shall have the money,' said I.

"'Oh, yes, I really mean it.'

"'And you won't tell me what you want it for?'

"'Some day, perhaps, but not just at present, Jack.'

"So I had to be content with that, though it was the first time that there had ever been any secret between us. I gave her a check, and I never thought anymore of the matter. It may have nothing to do with what came afterwards, but I thought it only right to mention it.

"Well, I told you just now that there is a cottage not far from our house. There is just a field between us, but to reach it you have to go along the road and then turn down a lane. Just beyond it is a nice little grove of Scotch firs, and I used to be very fond of strolling down there, for trees are always a neighbourly kind of thing. The cottage had been standing empty this eight months, and it was a pity, for it was a pretty two-storied place, with an old-fashioned porch and a honey-suckle about it. I have stood many a time and thought what a neat little homestead it would make.

"Well, last Monday evening I was taking a stroll down that way when I met an empty van coming up the lane and saw a pile of carpets and things lying about on the grass-plot beside the porch. It was clear that the cottage had at last been let. I walked past it, and then stopping, as an idle man might, I ran my eye over it and wondered what sort of folk they were who had come to live so near us. And as I looked I suddenly became aware that a face was watching me out of one of the upper windows.

"I don't know what there was about that face, Mr. Holmes, but it seemed to send a chill right down my back. I was some little way off, so that I could not make out the features, but there was something unnatural and inhuman about the face. That was the impression that I had, and I moved quickly forward to get a nearer view of the person who was watching me. But as I did so the face suddenly disappeared, so suddenly that it seemed to have been plucked away into the darkness of the room. I stood for five minutes thinking the business over and trying to analyze my impressions. I could not tell if the face was that of a man or a woman. It had been too far from me for that. But its colour was what had impressed me most. It was of a livid chalky white, and with something set and rigid about it which was shockingly unnatural. So disturbed was I that I determined to see a little more of the new inmates of the cottage. I approached and knocked at the door, which was instantly opened by a tall, gaunt woman with a harsh, forbidding face.

"'What may you be wantin'?' she asked in a distinct Northern accent.

"'I am your neighbour over yonder' said I, nodding towards my house. 'I see that you have only just moved in, so I thought that if I could be of any help to you in any—'

"'Ay, we'll just ask ye when we want ye,' said she, and shut the door in my face. Annoyed at the churlish rebuff, I turned my back and walked home. All evening, though I tried to think of other things, my mind would still turn to the apparition at the window and the rudeness of the woman. I determined to say nothing about the former to my wife, for she is a nervous, highly strung woman, and I had no wish that she should share the unpleasant impression which had been produced upon myself. I remarked to her, however, before I fell asleep, that the cottage was now occupied, to which she returned no reply.

"I am usually an extremely sound sleeper. It has been a standing jest in the family that nothing could ever wake me during the night. And yet somehow on that particular night, whether it may have been the slight excitement produced by my little adventure or not I know not, but I slept much more lightly than usual. Half in my dreams I was dimly conscious that something was going on in the room, and gradually became aware that my wife had dressed herself and was slipping on her mantle and her bonnet. My lips were parted to murmur out some sleepy words of surprise or remonstrance at this untimely preparation, when suddenly my half-opened eyes fell upon her face, illuminated by the candle-light, and astonishment held me dumb. She wore an expression such as I had never seen before such as I should have thought her incapable of assuming. She was deadly pale and breathing fast, glancing furtively towards the bed as she fastened her mantle to see if she had disturbed me. Then, thinking that I was still asleep, she slipped noiselessly from the room, and an instant later I heard a sharp creaking which could only come from the hinges of the front door. I sat up in bed and rapped my knuckles against the rail to make certain that I was truly awake. Then I took my watch from under the pillow. It was three in the morning. What on this earth could my wife be doing out on the country road at three in the morning?

"I had sat for about twenty minutes turning the thing over in my mind and trying to find some possible explanation. The more I thought, the more extraordinary and inexplicable did it appear. I was still puzzling over it when I heard the door gently close again, and her footsteps coming up the stairs.

"'Where in the world have you been, Effie?' I asked as she entered."

"She gave a violent start and a kind of gasping cry when I spoke, and that cry and start troubled me more than all the rest, for there was something indescribably guilty about them. My wife had always been a woman of a frank, open nature, and it gave me a chill to see her slinking into her own room and crying out and wincing when her own husband spoke to her.

"'You awake, Jack!' she cried with a nervous laugh. 'Why, I thought that nothing could awake you.'

"'Where have you been?' I asked, more sternly.

"'I don't wonder that you are surprised,' said she, and I could see that her fingers were trembling as she undid the fastenings of her mantle. 'Why, I never remember having done such a thing in my life before. The fact is that I felt as though I were choking and had a perfect longing for a breath of fresh air. I really think that I should have fainted if I had not gone out. I stood at the door for a few minutes, and now I am quite myself again.'

"All the time that she was telling me this story she never once looked in my direction, and her voice was quite unlike her usual tones. It was evident to me that she was saying what was false. I said nothing in reply, but turned my face to the wall, sick at heart, with my mind filled with a thousand venomous doubts and suspicions. What was it that my wife was concealing from me? Where had she been during that strange expedition? I felt that I should have no peace until I knew, and yet I shrank from asking her again after once she had told me what was false. All the rest of the night I tossed and tumbled, framing theory after theory, each more unlikely than the last.

"I should have gone to the City that day, but I was too disturbed in my mind to be able to pay attention to business matters. My wife seemed to be as upset as myself, and I could see from the little questioning glances which she kept shooting at me that she understood that I disbelieved her statement, and that she was at her wits' end what to do. We hardly exchanged a word during breakfast, and immediately afterwards I went out for a walk that I might think the matter out in the fresh morning air.

"I went as far as the Crystal Palace, spent an hour in the grounds, and was back in Norbury by one o'clock. It happened that my way took me past the cottage, and I stopped for an instant to look at the windows and to see if I could catch a glimpse of the strange face which had looked out at me on the day before. As I stood there, imagine my surprise, Mr. Holmes, when the door suddenly opened and my wife walked out.

"I was struck dumb with astonishment at the sight of her, but my emotions were nothing to those which showed themselves upon her face when our eyes met. She seemed for an instant to wish to shrink back inside the house again; and then, seeing how useless all concealment must be, she came forward, with a very white face and frightened eyes which belied the smile upon her lips.

"'Ah, Jack,' she said, 'I have just been in to see if I can be of any assistance to our new neighbours. Why do you look at me like that, Jack? You are not angry with me?'

"'So,' said I, 'this is where you went during the night.'

"'What do you mean?' she cried.

"'You came here. I am sure of it. Who are these people that you should visit them at such an hour?'

"'I have not been here before.'

"'How can you tell me what you know is false?' I cried. 'Your very voice changes as you speak. When have I ever had a secret from you? I shall enter that cottage, and I shall probe the matter to the bottom.'

"'No, Jack, for God's sake!' she gasped in uncontrollable emotion. Then, as I approached the door, she seized my sleeve and pulled me back with convulsive strength.

"'I implore you not to do this, Jack,' she cried. 'I swear that I will tell you everything some day, but nothing but misery can come of it if you enter that cottage.' Then, as I tried to shake her off, she clung to me in a frenzy of entreaty.

"'Trust me, Jack!' she cried. 'Trust me only this once. You will never have cause to regret it. You know that I would not have a secret from you if it were not for your own sake. Our whole lives are at stake in this. If you come home with me all will be well. If you force your way into that cottage all is over between us.'

"There was such earnestness, such despair, in her manner that her words arrested me, and I stood irresolute before the door.

"'I will trust you on one condition, and on one condition only,' said I at last. 'It is that this mystery comes to an end from now. You are at liberty to preserve your secret, but you must promise me that there shall be no more nightly visits, no more doings which are kept from my knowledge. I am willing to forget those which are past if you will promise that there shall be no more in the future.'

"'I was sure that you would trust me,' she cried with a great sigh of relief. 'It shall be just as you wish. Come away—oh, come away up to the house.'

"Still pulling at my sleeve, she led me away from the cottage. As we went I glanced back, and there was that yellow livid face watching us out of the upper window. What link could there be between that creature and my wife? Or how could the coarse, rough woman whom I had seen the day before be connected with her? It was a strange puzzle, and yet I knew that my mind could never know ease again until I had solved it.

"For two days after this I stayed at home, and my wife appeared to abide loyally by our engagement, for, as far as I know, she never stirred out of the house. On the third day, however, I had ample evidence that her solemn promise was not enough to hold her back from this secret influence which drew her away from her husband and her duty.

"I had gone into town on that day, but I returned by the 2:40 instead of the 3:36, which is my usual train. As I entered the house the maid ran into the hall with a startled face.

"'Where is your mistress?' I asked.

"'I think that she has gone out for a walk,' she answered.

"My mind was instantly filled with suspicion. I rushed upstairs to make sure that she was not in the house. As I did so I happened to glance out of one of the upper windows and saw the maid with whom I had just been speaking running across the field in the direction of the cottage. Then of course I saw exactly what it all meant. My wife had gone over there and had asked the servant to call her if I should return. Tingling with anger, I rushed down and hurried across, determined to end the matter once and forever. I saw my wife and the maid hurrying back along the lane, but I did not stop to speak with them. In the cottage lay the secret which was casting a shadow over my life. I vowed that, come what might, it should be a secret no longer. I did not even knock when I reached it, but turned the handle and rushed into the passage.

"It was all still and quiet upon the ground floor. In the kitchen a kettle was singing on the fire, and a large black cat lay coiled up in the basket; but there was no sign of the woman whom I had seen before. I ran into the other room, but it was equally deserted. Then I rushed up the stairs only to find two other rooms empty and deserted at the top. There was no one at all in the whole house. The furniture and pictures were of the most common and vulgar description, save in the one chamber at the window of which I had seen the strange face. That was comfortable and elegant, and all my suspicions rose into a fierce, bitter flame when I saw that on the mantelpiece stood a copy of a full-length photograph of my wife, which had been taken at my request only three months ago.

"I stayed long enough to make certain that the house was absolutely empty. Then I left it, feeling a weight at my heart such as I had never had before. My wife came out into the hall as I entered my house; but I was too hurt and angry to speak with her, and, pushing past her, I made my way into my study. She followed me, however, before I could close the door.

"'I am sorry that I broke my promise, Jack,' said she, 'but if you knew all the circumstances I am sure that you would forgive me.'

"'Tell me everything, then,' said I.

"'I cannot, Jack, I cannot,' she cried.

"'Until you tell me who it is that has been living in that cottage, and who it is to whom you have given that photograph, there can never be any confidence between us,' said I, and breaking away from her I left the house. That was yesterday, Mr. Holmes, and I have not seen her since, nor do I know anything more about this strange business. It is the first shadow that has come between us, and it has so shaken me that I do not know what I should do for the best. Suddenly this morning it occurred to me that you were the man to advise me, so I have hurried to you now, and I place myself unreservedly in your hands. If there is any point which I have not made clear, pray question me about it. But, above all, tell me quickly what I am to do, for this misery is more than I can bear."

Holmes and I had listened with the utmost interest to this extraordinary statement, which had been delivered in the jerky, broken fashion of a man who is under the influence of extreme emotion. My companion sat silent now for some time, with his chin upon his hand, lost in thought.

"Tell me," said he at last, "could you swear that this was a man's face which you saw at the window?"

"Each time that I saw it I was some distance away from it, so that it is impossible for me to say."

"You appear, however, to have been disagreeably impressed by it."

"It seemed to be of an unusual colour and to have a strange rigidity about the features. When I approached it vanished with a jerk."

"How long is it since your wife asked you for a hundred pounds?"

"Nearly two months."

"Have you ever seen a photograph of her first husband?"

"No, there was a great fire at Atlanta very shortly after his death, and all her papers were destroyed."

"And yet she had a certificate of death. You say that you saw it."

"Yes, she got a duplicate after the fire."

"Did you ever meet anyone who knew her in America?"

"No."

"Did she ever talk of revisiting the place?"

"No."

"Or get letters from it?"

"No."

"Thank you. I should like to think over the matter a little now. If the cottage is now permanently deserted we may have some difficulty. If, on the other hand, as I fancy is more likely, the inmates were warned of your coming and left before you entered yesterday, then they may be back now, and we should clear it all up easily. Let me advise you, then, to return to Norbury and to examine the windows of the cottage again. If you have reason to believe that it is inhabited, do not force your way in, but send a wire to my friend and me. We shall be with you within an hour of receiving it, and we shall then very soon get to the bottom of the business."

"And if it is still empty?"

"In that case I shall come out tomorrow and talk it over with you. Goodbye, and, above all, do not fret until you know that you really have a cause for it."

"I am afraid that this is a bad business, Watson," said my companion as he returned after accompanying Mr. Grant Munro to the door. "What do you make of it?"

"It had an ugly sound," I answered.

"Yes. There's blackmail in it, or I am much mistaken."

"And who is the blackmailer?"

"Well, it must be the creature who lives in the only comfortable room in the place and has her photograph above his fireplace. Upon my word, Watson, there is something very attractive about that livid face at the window, and I would not have missed the case for worlds."

"You have a theory?"

"Yes, a provisional one. But I shall be surprised if it does not turn out to be correct. This woman's first husband is in that cottage."

"Why do you think so?"

"How else can we explain her frenzied anxiety that her second one should not enter it? The facts, as I read them, are something like this: This woman was married in America. Her husband developed some hateful qualities, or shall we say he contracted some loathsome disease and became a leper or an imbecile? She flies from him at last, returns to England, changes her name, and starts her life, as she thinks, afresh. She has been married three years and believes that her position is quite secure, having shown her husband the death certificate of some man whose name she has assumed, when suddenly her whereabouts is discovered by her first husband, or, we may suppose, by some unscrupulous woman who has attached herself to the invalid. They write to the wife and threaten to come and expose her. She asks for a hundred pounds and endeavours to buy them off. They come in spite of it, and when the husband mentions casually to the wife that there are newcomers in the cottage, she knows in some way that they are her pursuers. She waits until her husband is asleep, and then she rushes down to endeavour to persuade them to leave her in peace. Having no success, she goes again next morning, and her husband meets her, as he has told us, as she comes out. She promises him then not to go there again, but two days afterwards the hope of getting rid of those dreadful neighbours was too strong for her, and she made another attempt, taking down with her the photograph which had probably been demanded from her. In the midst of this interview the maid rushed in to say that the master had come home, on which the wife, knowing that he would come straight down to the cottage, hurried the inmates out at the back door, into the grove of fir-trees, probably, which was mentioned as standing near. In this way he found the place deserted. I shall be very much surprised, however, if it is still so when he reconnoitres it this evening. What do you think of my theory?"

"It is all surmise."

"But at least it covers all the facts. When new facts come to our knowledge which cannot be covered by it, it will be time enough to reconsider it. We can do nothing more until we have a message from our friend at Norbury."

But we had not a very long time to wait for that. It came just as we had finished our tea.

> 'The cottage is still tenanted,' it said. 'Have seen the face again at the window. Will meet the seven o'clock train and will take no steps until you arrive.'

He was waiting on the platform when we stepped out, and we could see in the light of the station lamps that he was very pale, and quivering with agitation.

"They are still there, Mr. Holmes," said he, laying his hand hard upon my friend's sleeve. "I saw lights in the cottage as I came down. We shall settle it now once and for all."

"What is your plan, then?" asked Holmes as he walked down the dark tree-lined road.

"I am going to force my way in and see for myself who is in the house. I wish you both to be there as witnesses."

"You are quite determined to do this in spite of your wife's warning that it is better that you should not solve the mystery?"

"Yes, I am determined."

"Well, I think that you are in the right. Any truth is better than indefinite doubt. We had better go up at once. Of course, legally, we are putting ourselves hopelessly in the wrong; but I think that it is worth it."

It was a very dark night, and a thin rain began to fall as we turned from the highroad into a narrow lane, deeply rutted, with hedges on either side. Mr. Grant Munro pushed impatiently forward, however, and we stumbled after him as best we could.

"There are the lights of my house," he murmured, pointing to a glimmer among the trees. "And here is the cottage which I am going to enter."

We turned a corner in the lane as he spoke, and there was the building close beside us. A yellow bar falling across the black foreground showed that the door was not quite closed, and one window in the upper story was brightly illuminated. As we looked, we saw a dark blur moving across the blind.

"There is that creature!" cried Grant Munro. "You can see for yourselves that someone is there. Now follow me, and we shall soon know all."

We approached the door, but suddenly a woman appeared out of the shadow and stood in the golden track of the lamplight. I could not see her face in the darkness, but her arms were thrown out in an attitude of entreaty.

"For God's sake, don't, Jack!" she cried. "I had a presentiment that you would come this evening. Think better of it, dear! Trust me again, and you will never have cause to regret it."

"I have trusted you too long, Effie," he cried sternly. "Leave go of me! I must pass you. My friends and I are going to settle this matter once and forever!" He pushed her to one side, and we followed closely after him. As he threw the door open an old woman ran out in front of him and tried to bar his passage, but he thrust her back, and an instant afterwards we were all upon the stairs. Grant Munro rushed into the lighted room at the top, and we entered at his heels.

It was a cosy, well-furnished apartment, with two candles burning upon the table and two upon the mantelpiece. In the corner, stooping over a desk, there sat what appeared to be a little girl. Her face was turned away as we entered, but we could see that she was dressed in a red frock, and that she had long white gloves on. As she whisked round to us, I gave a cry of surprise and horror. The face which she turned towards us was of the strangest livid tint, and the features were absolutely devoid of any expression. An instant later the mystery was explained. Holmes, with a laugh, passed his hand behind the child's ear, a mask peeled off from her countenance, and there was a little coal-black negress, with all her white teeth flashing in amusement at our amazed faces. I burst out laughing, out of sympathy with her merriment; but Grant Munro stood staring, with his hand clutching his throat.

"My God!" he cried. "What can be the meaning of this?"

"I will tell you the meaning of it," cried the lady, sweeping into the room with a proud, set face. "You have forced me, against my own judgment, to tell you, and now we must both make the best of it. My husband died at Atlanta. My child survived."

"Your child?"

She drew a large silver locket from her bosom. "You have never seen this open."

"I understood that it did not open."

She touched a spring, and the front hinged back. There was a portrait within of a man strikingly handsome and intelligent-looking, but bearing unmistakable signs upon his features of his African descent.

"That is John Hebron, of Atlanta," said the lady, "and a nobler man never walked the earth. I cut myself off from my race in order to wed him, but never once while he lived did I for an instant regret it. It was our misfortune that our only child took after his people rather than mine. It is often so in such matches, and little Lucy is darker far than ever her father was. But dark or fair, she is my own dear little girlie, and her mother's pet."

The little creature ran across at the words and nestled up against the lady's dress.

"When I left her in America," she continued, "it was only because her health was weak, and the change might have done her harm. She was given to the care of a faithful Scotch woman who had once been our servant. Never for an instant did I dream of disowning her as my child. But when chance threw you in my way, Jack, and I learned to love you, I feared to tell you about my child. God forgive me, I feared that I should lose you, and I had not the courage to tell you. I had to choose between you, and in my weakness I turned away from my own little girl. For three years I have kept her existence a secret from you, but I heard from the nurse, and I knew that all was well with her. At last, however, there came an overwhelming desire to see the child once more. I struggled against it, but in vain. Though I knew the danger, I determined to have the child over, if it were but for a few weeks. I sent a hundred pounds to the nurse, and I gave her instructions about this cottage, so that she might come as a neighbour, without my appearing to be in any way connected with her. I pushed my precautions so far as to order her to keep the child in the house during the daytime, and to cover up her little face and hands so that even those who might see her at the window should not gossip about there being a black child in the neighbourhood. If I had been less cautious I might have been more wise, but I was half crazy with fear that you should learn the truth.

"It was you who told me first that the cottage was occupied. I should have waited for the morning, but I could not sleep for excitement, and so at last I slipped out, knowing how difficult it is to awake you. But you saw me go, and that was the beginning of my troubles. Next day you had my secret at your mercy, but you nobly refrained from pursuing your advantage. Three days later, however, the nurse and child only just escaped from the back door as you rushed in at the front one. And now tonight you at last know all, and I ask you what is to become of us, my child and me?" She clasped her hands and waited for an answer.

It was a long ten minutes before Grant Munro broke the silence, and when his answer came it was one of which I love to think. He lifted the little child, kissed her, and then, still carrying her, he held his other hand out to his wife and turned towards the door.

"We can talk it over more comfortably at home," said he. "I am not a very good man, Effie, but I think that I am a better one than you have given me credit for being."

Holmes and I followed them down the lane, and my friend plucked at my sleeve as we came out.

"I think," said he, "that we shall be of more use in London than in Norbury."

Not another word did he say of the case until late that night, when he was turning away, with his lighted candle, for his bedroom.

"Watson," said he, "if it should ever strike you that I am getting a little over-confident in my powers, or giving less pains to a case than it deserves, kindly whisper 'Norbury' in my ear, and I shall be infinitely obliged to you."

Chapter 3

THE ADVENTURE OF THE STOCKBROKER'S CLERK

SHORTLY after my marriage I had bought a connection in the Paddington district. Old Mr. Farquhar, from whom I purchased it, had at one time an excellent general practice; but his age, and an affliction of the nature of St. Vitus's dance from which he suffered, had very much thinned it. The public not unnaturally goes on the principle that he who would heal others must himself be whole, and looks askance at the curative powers of the man whose own case is beyond the reach of his drugs. Thus as my predecessor weakened his practice declined, until when I purchased it from him it had sunk from twelve hundred to little more than three hundred a year. I had confidence, however, in my own youth and energy and was convinced that in a very few years the concern would be as flourishing as ever.

For three months after taking over the practice I was kept very closely at work and saw little of my friend Sherlock Holmes, for I was too busy to visit Baker Street, and he seldom went anywhere himself save upon professional business. I was surprised, therefore, when, one morning in June, as I sat reading the *British Medical Journal* after breakfast, I heard a ring at the bell, followed by the high, somewhat strident tones of my old companion's voice.

"Ah, my dear Watson," said he, striding into the room, "I am very delighted to see you! I trust that Mrs. Watson has entirely recovered from all the little excitements connected with our adventure of the *Sign of Four*."

"Thank you, we are both very well," said I, shaking him warmly by the hand.

"And I hope, also," he continued, sitting down in the rocking-chair, "that the cares of medical practice have not entirely obliterated the interest which you used to take in our little deductive problems."

"On the contrary," I answered, "it was only last night that I was looking over my old notes, and classifying some of our past results."

"I trust that you don't consider your collection closed."

"Not at all. I should wish nothing better than to have some more of such experiences."

"Today, for example?"

"Yes, today, if you like."

"And as far off as Birmingham?"

"Certainly, if you wish it."

"And the practice?"

"I do my neighbour's when he goes. He is always ready to work off the debt."

"Ha! Nothing could be better," said Holmes, leaning back in his chair and looking keenly at me from under his half-closed lids. "I perceive that you have been unwell lately. Summer colds are always a little trying."

"I was confined to the house by a severe chill for three days last week. I thought, however, that I had cast off every trace of it."

"So you have. You look remarkably robust."

"How, then, did you know of it?"

"My dear fellow, you know my methods."

"You deduced it, then?"

"Certainly."

"And from what?"

"From your slippers."

I instinctively glanced down at the new patent-leathers which I was wearing.

"How on earth—" I began, but Holmes answered my question before it was asked.

"Your slippers are new," he said. "You could not have had them more than a few weeks. The soles which you are at this moment presenting to me are slightly scorched. For a moment I thought they might have got wet and been burned in the drying. But near the in-step there is a small circular wafer of paper with the shopman's hieroglyphics upon it. Damp would of course have removed this. You had, then, been sitting with your feet outstretched to the fire, which a man would hardly do even in so wet a June as this if he were in his full health."

Like all Holmes' reasoning the thing seemed simplicity itself when it was once explained. He read the thought upon my features, and his smile had a tinge of bitterness.

"I am afraid that I rather give myself away when I explain," said he. "Results without causes are much more impressive. You are ready to come to Birmingham, then?"

"Certainly. What is the case?"

"You shall hear it all in the train. My client is outside in a four-wheeler. Can you come at once?"

"In an instant." I scribbled a note to my neighbour, rushed upstairs to explain the matter to my wife, and joined Holmes upon the doorstep.

"Your neighbour is a doctor," said Holmes, nodding at the brass plate.

"Yes, he bought a practice as I did."

"An old-established one?"

"Just the same as mine. Both have been ever since the houses were built."

"Ah! Then you got hold of the best of the two."

" I think I did. But how do you know?"

"By the steps, my boy. Yours are worn three inches deeper than his. But this gentleman in the cab is my client, Mr. Hall Pycroft. Allow me to introduce you to him. Whip your horse up, cabby, for we have only just time to catch our train."

The man whom I found myself facing was a well-built, fresh-complexioned young fellow, with a frank, honest face and a slight, crisp, yellow moustache. He wore a very shiny top hat and a neat suit of sober black, which made him look what he was—a smart young City man, of the class who have been labelled cockneys, but who give us our crack volunteer regiments, and who turn out more fine athletes and sportsmen than any body of men in these islands. His round, ruddy face was naturally full of cheeriness, but the corners of his mouth seemed to me to be pulled down in a half-comical distress. It was not, however, until we were in a first class carriage and well started upon our journey to Birmingham that I was able to learn what the trouble was which had driven him to Sherlock Holmes.

"We have a clear run here of seventy minutes," Holmes remarked.

"I want you, Mr. Hall Pycroft, to tell my friend your very interesting experience exactly as you have told it to me, or with more detail if possible. It will be of use to me to hear the succession of events again. It is a case, Watson, which may prove to have something in it, or may prove to have nothing, but which, at least, presents those unusual and *outre* features which are as dear to you as they are to me. Now, Mr. Pycroft, I shall not interrupt you again."

Our young companion looked at me with a twinkle in his eye.

"The worst of the story is," said he, "that I show myself up as such a confounded fool. Of course it may work out all right, and I don't see that I could have done otherwise; but if I have lost my crib and get nothing in exchange I shall feel what a soft Johnny I have been. I'm not very good at telling a story, Dr. Watson, but it is like this with me."

"I used to have a billet at Coxon & Woodhouse's, of Draper Gardens, but they were let in early in the spring through the Venezuelan loan, as no doubt you remember, and came a nasty cropper. I have been with them five years, and old Coxon gave me a ripping good testimonial when the smash came, but of course we clerks were all turned adrift, the twenty-seven of us. I tried here and tried there, but there were lots of other chaps on the same lay as myself, and it was a perfect frost for a long time. I had been taking three pounds a week at Coxon's, and I had saved about seventy of them, but I soon worked my way through that and out at the other end. I was fairly at the end of my tether at last, and could hardly find the stamps to answer the advertisements or the envelopes to stick them to. I had worn out my boots paddling up office stairs, and I seemed just as far from getting a billet as ever.

"At last I saw a vacancy at Mawson & Williams's, the great stock-broking firm in Lombard Street. I dare say E.C. is not much in your line, but I can tell you that this is about the richest house in London. The advertisement was to be answered by letter only. I sent in my testimonial and application, but without the least hope of getting it. Back came an answer by return, saying that if I would appear next Monday I might take over my new duties at once, provided that my appearance was satisfactory. No one knows how these things are worked. Some people say that the manager just plunges his hand into the heap and takes the first that comes. Anyhow it was my innings that time, and I don't ever wish to feel better pleased. The screw was a pound a week rise, and the duties just about the same as at Coxon's.

"And now I come to the queer part of the business. I was in diggings out Hampstead way—17 Potter's Terrace. Well, I was sitting doing a smoke that very evening after I had been promised the appointment, when up came my landlady with a card which had 'Arthur Pinner, Financial Agent,' printed upon it. I had never heard the name before and could not imagine what he wanted with me, but of course I asked her to show him up. In he walked, a middle-sized, dark-haired, dark-eyed, black-bearded man, with a touch of the sheeny about his nose. He had a brisk kind of way with him and spoke sharply, like a man who knew the value of time.

"'Mr. Hall Pycroft, I believe?' said he.

"'Yes, sir,' I answered, pushing a chair towards him.

"'Lately engaged at Coxon & Woodhouse's?'

"'Yes, sir.'

"'And now on the staff of Mawson's.'

"'Quite so.'

"'Well,' said he, 'the fact is that I have heard some really extraordinary stories about your financial ability. You remember

Parker, who used to be Coxon's manager. He can never say enough about it.'

"Of course I was pleased to hear this. I had always been pretty sharp in the office, but I had never dreamed that I was talked about in the city in this fashion.

"'You have a good memory?' said he.

"'Pretty fair,' I answered modestly.

"'Have you kept in touch with the market while you have been out of work?' he asked.

"'Yes. I read the stock-exchange list every morning.'

"'Now that shows real application!' he cried. 'That is the way to prosper! You won't mind my testing you, will you? Let me see. How are Ayrshires?'

"'A hundred and six and a quarter to a hundred and five and seven-eighths.'

"'And New Zealand consolidated?'

"'A hundred and four.'

"'And British Broken Hills?'

"'Seven to seven-and-six.'

"'Wonderful!' he cried with his hands up. 'This quite fits in with all that I had heard. My boy, my boy, you are very much too good to be a clerk at Mawson's!'

"This outburst rather astonished me, as you can think. 'Well,' said I, 'other people don't think quite so much of me as you seem to do, Mr. Pinner. I had a hard enough fight to get this berth, and I am very glad to have it.'

"'Pooh, man; you should soar above it. You are not in your true sphere. Now, I'll tell you how it stands with me. What I have to offer is little enough when measured by your ability, but when compared with Mawson's it's light to dark. Let me see. When do you go to Mawson's?'

"'On Monday.'

"'Ha, ha! I think I would risk a little sporting flutter that you don't go there at all.'

"'Not go to Mawson's?'

"'No, sir. By that day you will be the business manager of the Franco-Midland Hardware Company, Limited, with a hundred and thirty-four branches in the towns and villages of France, not counting one in Brussels and one in San Remo.'

"This took my breath away. 'I never heard of it,' said I.

"'Very likely not. It has been kept very quiet, for the capital was all privately subscribed, and it's too good a thing to let the public into. My Brother, Harry Pinner, is promoter, and joins the board after allotment as managing director. He knew I was in the swim down here and asked me to pick up a good man cheap. A young, pushing man with plenty of snap about him. Parker spoke of you, and that brought me here tonight. We can only offer you a beggarly five hundred to start with.'

"'Five hundred a year!' I shouted.

"'Only that at the beginning; but you are to have an overriding commission of one per cent on all business done by your agents, and you may take my word for it that this will come to more than your salary.'

"'But I know nothing about hardware.'

"'Tut, my boy, you know about figures.'

"My head buzzed, and I could hardly sit still in my chair. But suddenly a little chill of doubt came upon me.

"'I must be frank with you,' said I. 'Mawson only gives me two hundred, but Mawson is safe. Now, really, I know so little about your company that—'

"'Ah, smart, smart!' he cried in a kind of ecstasy of delight. 'You are the very man for us. You are not to be talked over, and quite right too. Now, here's a note for a hundred pounds, and if you think that we can do business you may just slip it into your pocket as an advance upon your salary.'

"'That is very handsome,' said I. 'When should I take over my new duties?'

"'Be in Birmingham tomorrow at one,' said he. 'I have a note in my pocket here which you will take to my brother. You will find him at 126B Corporation Street, where the temporary offices of the company are situated. Of course he must confirm your engagement, but between ourselves it will be all right.'

"Really, I hardly know how to express my gratitude, Mr. Pinner said I.

"'Not at all, my boy. You have only got your deserts. There are one or two small things—mere formalities—which I must arrange with you. You have a bit of paper beside you there. Kindly write upon it.'

"I am perfectly willing to act as business manager to the Franco Midland Hardware Company, Limited, at a minimum salary of £500.

"I did as he asked, and he put the paper in his pocket.

"'There is one other detail,' said he. 'What do you intend to do about Mawson's?'

"I had forgotten all about Mawson's in my joy. 'I'll write and resign,' said I.

"'Precisely what I don't want you to do. I had a row over you with Mawson's manager. I had gone up to ask him about you, and he was very offensive; accused me of coaxing you away from the service of the firm, and that sort of thing. At last I fairly lost my temper. If you want good men you should pay them a good price,' said I.

"'He would rather have our small price than your big one,' said he.

"I'll lay you a fiver," said I, "that when he has my offer you'll never so much as hear from him again.

"'Done!' said he. 'We picked him out of the gutter, and he won't leave us so easily.' Those were his very words.'

"'The impudent scoundrel!' I cried. 'I've never so much as seen him in my life. Why should I consider him in any way? I shall certainly not write if you would rather I didn't.'

"'Good! That's a promise,' said he, rising from his chair. 'Well, I'm delighted to have got so good a man for my brother. Here's your advance of a hundred pounds, and here is the letter. Make a note of the address, 126B Corporation Street, and remember that one o'clock tomorrow is your appointment. Goodnight, and may you have all the fortune that you deserve!'

"That's just about all that passed between us, as near as I can remember. You can imagine, Dr. Watson, how pleased I was at such an extraordinary bit of good fortune. I sat up half the night hugging myself over it, and next day I was off to Birmingham in a train that would take me in plenty time for my appointment. I took my things to a hotel in New Street, and then I made my way to the address which had been given me.

"It was a quarter of an hour before my time, but I thought that would make no difference. 126B was a passage between two large shops, which led to a winding stone stair, from which there were many flats, let as offices to companies or professional men. The names of the occupants were painted at the bottom on the wall, but there was no such name as the Franco-Midland Hardware Company, Limited. I stood for a few minutes with my heart in my boots, wondering whether the whole thing was an elaborate hoax or not, when up came a man and addressed me. He was very like the chap I had seen the night before, the same figure and voice, but he was clean-shaven and his hair was lighter.

"'Are you Mr. Hall Pycroft?' he asked.

"'Yes,' said I.

"'Oh! I was expecting you, but you are a trifle before your time. I had a note from my brother this morning in which he sang your praises very loudly.'

"'I was just looking for the offices when you came.'

"'We have not got our name up yet, for we only secured these temporary premises last week. Come up with me, and we will talk the matter over.'

"I followed him to the top of a very lofty stair, and there, right under the slates, were a couple of empty, dusty little rooms, uncarpeted and uncurtained, into which he led me. I had thought of a great office with shining tables and rows of clerks, such as I was used to, and I daresay I stared rather straight at the two deal chairs and one little table, which with a ledger and a wastepaper basket, made up the whole furniture.

"'Don't be disheartened, Mr. Pycroft,' said my new acquaintance, seeing the length of my face. 'Rome was not built in a day, and we have lots of money at our backs, though we don't cut much dash yet in offices. Pray sit down, and let me have your letter.'

"I gave it to him, and he read it over very carefully.

"'You seem to have made a vast impression upon my brother Arthur,' said he, 'and I know that he is a pretty shrewd judge. He swears by London, you know; and I by Birmingham; but this time I shall follow his advice. Pray consider yourself definitely engaged.'

"'What are my duties?' I asked.

"'You will eventually manage the great depot in Paris, which will pour a flood of English crockery into the shops of a hundred and thirty-four agents in France. The purchase will be completed in a week, and meanwhile you will remain in Birmingham and make yourself useful.'

"'How?'

"For answer, he took a big red book out of a drawer.

"'This is a directory of Paris,' said he, 'with the trades after the names of the people. I want you to take it home with you, and to mark off all the hardware-sellers, with their addresses. It would be of the greatest use to me to have them.'

"'Surely, there are classified lists?' I suggested.

"'Not reliable ones. Their system is different from ours. Stick at it, and let me have the lists by Monday, at twelve. Good day, Mr. Pycroft. If you continue to show zeal and intelligence you will find the company a good master.'

"I went back to the hotel with the big book under my arm, and with very conflicting feelings in my breast. On the one hand, I was definitely engaged and had a hundred pounds in my pocket; on the other, the look of the offices, the absence of name on the wall, and other of the points which would strike a businessman had left a bad impression as to the position of my employers. However, come what might, I had my money, so I settled down to my task. All Sunday I was kept hard at work, and yet by Monday I had only got as far as H. I went round to my employer, found him in the same dismantled kind of room, and was told to keep at it until Wednesday, and then come again. On Wednesday it was still unfinished, so I hammered away until Friday—that is, yesterday. Then I brought it round to Mr. Harry Pinner.

"'Thank you very much,' said he, 'I fear that I underrated the difficulty of the task. This list will be of very material assistance to me.'

"'It took some time,' said I.

"'And now,' said he, 'I want you to make a list to the furniture shops, for they all sell crockery.'

"'Very good.'

"'And you can come up tomorrow evening at seven and let me know how you are getting on. Don't overwork yourself. A couple of hours at Day's Music Hall in the evening would do you no harm after your labours.' He laughed as he spoke, and I saw with a thrill that his second tooth upon the left-hand side had been very badly stuffed with gold.

Sherlock Holmes rubbed his hands with delight, and I stared with astonishment at our client.

"You may well look surprised, Dr. Watson, but it is this way," said he: "When I was speaking to the other chap in London, at the time that he laughed at my not going to Mawson's, I happened to notice that his tooth was stuffed in this very identical fashion. The glint of the gold in each case caught my eye, you see. When I put that with the voice and figure being the same, and only those things altered which might be changed by a razor or a wig, I could not doubt that it was the same man. Of course you expect two brothers to be alike, but not that they should have the same tooth stuffed in the same way. He bowed me out, and I found myself in the street, hardly knowing whether I was on my head or my heels. Back I went to my hotel, put my head in a basin of cold water, and tried to think it out. Why had he sent me from London to Birmingham? Why had he got there before me? And why had he written a letter from himself to himself? It was altogether too much for me, and I could make no sense of it. And then suddenly it struck me that what was dark to me might be very light to Mr. Sherlock Holmes. I had just time to get up to town by the night train to see him this morning, and to bring you both back with me to Birmingham."

There was a pause after the stockbroker's clerk had concluded his surprising experience. Then Sherlock Holmes cocked his eye at me, leaning back on the cushions with a pleased and yet critical face, like a connoisseur who has just taken his first sip of a comet vintage.

"Rather fine, Watson, is it not?" said he. "There are points in it which please me. I think that you will agree with me that an interview with Mr. Arthur Harry Pinner in the temporary offices of the Franco-Midland Hardware Company, Limited, would be a rather interesting experience for both of us."

"But how can we do it?" I asked.

"Oh, easily enough," said Hall Pycroft cheerily. "You are two friends of mine who are in want of a billet, and what could be more natural than that I should bring you both round to the managing director?"

"Quite so, of course," said Holmes. "I should like to have a look at the gentleman and see if I can make anything of his little game. What qualities have you, my friend, which would make your services so valuable? Or is it possible that—" He began biting his nails and staring blankly out of the window, and we hardly drew another word from him until we were in New Street.

At seven o'clock that evening we were walking, the three of us, down Corporation Street to the company's offices.

"It is no use our being at all before our time," said our client. "He only comes there to see me, apparently, for the place is deserted up to the very hour he names."

"That is suggestive," remarked Holmes.

"By Jove, I told you so!" cried the clerk. "That's he walking ahead of us there."

He pointed to a smallish, dark, well-dressed man who was bustling along the other side of the road. As we watched him he looked across at a boy who was bawling out the latest edition of the evening paper, and, running over among the cabs and busses, he bought one from him. Then, clutching it in his hand, he vanished through a doorway.

"There he goes!" cried Hall Pycroft. "These are the company's offices into which he has gone. Come with me, and I'll fix it up as easily as possible."

Following his lead, we ascended five stories, until we found ourselves outside a half-opened door, at which our client tapped. A voice within bade us enter, and we entered a bare, unfurnished room such as Hall Pycroft had described. At the single table sat the man whom we had seen in the street, with his evening paper spread out in front of him, and as he looked up at us it seemed to me that I had never looked upon a face which bore such marks of grief, and of something beyond grief of a horror such as comes to few men in a lifetime. His brow glistened with perspiration, his cheeks were of the dull, dead white of a fish's belly, and his eyes were wild and staring. He looked at his clerk as though he failed to recognize him, and I could see by the astonishment depicted upon our conductor's face that this was by no means the usual appearance of his employer.

"You look ill, Mr. Pinner!" he exclaimed.

"Yes, I am not very well," answered the other, making obvious efforts to pull himself together and licking his dry lips before he spoke. "Who are these gentlemen whom you have brought with you?"

"One is Mr. Harris, of Bermondsey, and the other is Mr. Price, of this town," said our clerk glibly. "They are friends of mine and gentlemen of experience, but they have been out of a place for some little time, and they hoped that perhaps you might find an opening for them in the company's employment."

"Very possibly! very possibly!" cried Mr. Pinner with a ghastly smile. "Yes, I have no doubt that we shall be able to do something for you. What is your particular line, Mr. Harris?"

"I am an accountant," said Holmes.

"Ah, yes, we shall want something of the sort. And you, Mr. Price?"

"A clerk," said I.

"I have every hope that the company may accommodate you. I will let you know about it as soon as we come to any conclusion. And now I beg that you will go. For God's sake leave me to myself!"

These last words were shot out of him, as though the constraint which he was evidently setting upon himself had suddenly and utterly burst asunder. Holmes and I glanced at each other, and Hall Pycroft took a step towards the table.

"You forget, Mr. Pinner, that I am here by appointment to receive some directions from you," said he.

"Certainly, Mr. Pycroft, certainly," the other resumed in a calmer tone. "You may wait here a moment and there is no reason why your friends should not wait with you. I will be entirely at your service in three minutes, if I might trespass upon your patience so far." He rose with a very courteous air, and, bowing to us, he passed out through a door at the farther end of the room, which he closed behind him.

"What now?" whispered Holmes. "Is he giving us the slip?"

"Impossible," answered Pycroft.

"Why so?"

"That door leads into an inner room."

"There is no exit?"

"None."

"Is it furnished?"

"It was empty yesterday."

"Then what on earth can he be doing? There is something which I don't understand in this matter. If ever a man was three parts mad with terror, that man's name is Pinner. What can have put the shivers on him?"

"He suspects that we are detectives," I suggested.

"That's it," cried Pycroft.

Holmes shook his head. "He did not turn pale. He *was* pale when we entered the room," said he. "It is just possible that—"

His words were interrupted by a sharp rat-tat from the direction of the inner door.

"What the deuce is he knocking at his own door for?" cried the clerk.

Again and much louder came the rat-tat-tat. We all gazed expectantly at the closed door. Glancing at Holmes, I saw his face turn rigid, and he leaned forward in intense excitement. Then suddenly came a low guggling, gargling sound, and a brisk drumming upon woodwork. Holmes sprang frantically across the room and pushed at the door. It was fastened on the inner side. Following his example, we threw ourselves upon it with all our weight. One hinge snapped, then the other, and down came the door with a crash. Rushing over it, we found ourselves in the inner room. It was empty.

But it was only for a moment that we were at fault. At one corner, the corner nearest the room which we had left, there was a second door. Holmes sprang to it and pulled it open. A coat and waistcoat were lying on the floor, and from a hook behind the door, with his own braces round his neck, was hanging the managing director of the Franco-Midland Hardware Company. His knees were drawn up, his head hung at a dreadful angle to his body, and the clatter of his heels against the door made the noise which had broken in upon our conversation. In an instant I had caught him round the waist, and held him up while Holmes and Pycroft untied the elastic bands which had disappeared between the livid creases of skin. Then we carried him into the other room, where he lay with a clay-coloured face, puffing his purple lips in and out with every breath—a dreadful wreck of all that he had been but five minutes before.

"What do you think of him, Watson?" asked Holmes.

I stooped over him and examined him. His pulse was feeble and intermittent, but his breathing grew longer, and there was a little shivering of his eyelids, which showed a thin white slit of ball beneath.

"It has been touch and go with him," said I, "but he'll live now. Just open that window, and hand me the water carafe." I undid his collar, poured the cold water over his face, and raised and sank his arms until he drew a long, natural breath. "It's only a question of time now," said I as I turned away from him.

Holmes stood by the table, with his hands deep in his trousers' pockets and his chin upon his breast.

"I suppose we ought to call the police in now," said he. "And yet I confess that I'd like to give them a complete case when they come."

"It's a blessed mystery to me," cried Pycroft, scratching his head.

"Whatever they wanted to bring me all the way up here for, and then—"

"Pooh! All that is clear enough," said Holmes impatiently. "It is this last sudden move."

"You understand the rest, then?"

"I think that it is fairly obvious. What do you say, Watson?"

I shrugged my shoulders. "I must confess that I am out of my depths," said I.

"Oh, surely if you consider the events at first they can only point to one conclusion."

"What do you make of them?"

"Well, the whole thing hinges upon two points. The first is the making of Pycroft write a declaration by which he entered the service of this preposterous company. Do you not see how very suggestive that is?"

"I am afraid I miss the point."

"Well, why did they want him to do it? Not as a business matter, for these arrangements are usually verbal, and there was no earthly business reason why this should be an exception. Don't you see, my young friend, that they were very anxious to obtain a specimen of your handwriting, and had no other way of doing it?"

"And why?"

"Quite so. Why? When we answer that we have made some progress with our little problem. Why? There can be only one adequate reason. Someone wanted to learn to imitate your writing and had to procure a specimen of it first. And now if we pass on to the second point we find that each throws light upon the other. That point is the request made by Pinner that you should not resign your place, but should leave the manager of this important business in the full expectation that a Mr. Hall Pycroft, whom he had never seen, was about to enter the office upon the Monday morning."

"My God!" cried our client, "What a blind beetle I have been!"

"Now you see the point about the handwriting. Suppose that someone turned up in your place who wrote a completely different hand from that in which you had applied for the vacancy, of course the game would have been up. But in the interval the rogue had learned to imitate you, and his position was therefore secure, as I presume that nobody in the office had ever set eyes upon you."

"Not a soul," groaned Hall Pycroft.

"Very good. Of course it was of the utmost importance to prevent you from thinking better of it, and also to keep you from coming into contact with anyone who might tell you that your double was at work in Mawson's office. Therefore they gave you a handsome advance on your salary, and ran you off to the Midlands, where they gave you enough work to do to prevent your going to London, where you might have burst their little game up. That is all plain enough."

"But why should this man pretend to be his own brother?"

"Well, that is pretty clear also. There are evidently only two of them in it. The other is impersonating you at the office. This one acted as your engager, and then found that he could not find you an employer without admitting a third person into his plot. That he was most unwilling to do. He changed his appearance as far as he could, and trusted that the likeness, which you could not fail to observe, would be put down to a family resemblance. But for the happy chance of the gold stuffing, your suspicions would probably never have been aroused."

Hall Pycroft shook his clenched hands in the air. "Good Lord!" he cried, "while I have been fooled in this way, what has this other Hall Pycroft been doing at Mawson's? What should we do, Mr. Holmes? Tell me what to do."

"We must wire to Mawson's."

"They shut at twelve on Saturdays."

"Never mind. There may be some doorkeeper or attendant."

"Ah, yes, they keep a permanent guard there on account of the value of the securities that they hold. I remember hearing it talked of in the City."

"Very good, we shall wire to him and see if all is well, and if a clerk of your name is working there. That is clear enough, but what is not so clear is why at sight of us one of the rogues should instantly walk out of the room and hang himself."

"The paper!" croaked a voice behind us. The man was sitting up, blanched and ghastly, with returning reason in his eyes, and hands which rubbed nervously at the broad red band which still encircled his throat.

"The paper! Of course!" yelled Holmes in a paroxysm of excitement. "Idiot that I was! I thought so much of our visit that the paper never entered my head for an instant. To be sure, the secret must lie there." He flattened it out upon the table, and a cry of triumph burst from his lips. "Look at this, Watson," He cried. "It is a London paper an early edition of the Evening Standard. Here is what we want. Look at the headlines: 'Crime in the City. Murder at Mawson & Williams's. Gigantic attempted Robbery. Capture of the Criminal.' Here, Watson, we are all equally anxious to hear it, so kindly read it aloud to us."

It appeared from its position in the paper to have been the one event of importance in town, and the account of it ran in this way:

A desperate attempt at robbery, culminating in the death of one man and the capture of the criminal, occurred this afternoon in the City. For some time back Mawson &

Williams, the famous financial house, have been the guardians of securities which amount in the aggregate to a sum of considerably over a million sterling. So conscious was the manager of the responsibility which devolved upon him in consequence of the great interests at stake that safes of the very latest construction have been employed, and an armed watchman has been left day and night in the building. It appears that last week a new clerk named Hall Pycroft was engaged by the firm. This person appears to have been none other than Beddington, the famous forger and cracksman, who, with his brother, has only recently emerged from a five years' spell of penal servitude. By some means, which are not yet clear, he succeeded in winning, under a false name, this official position in the office, which he utilized in order to obtain mouldings of various locks, and a thorough knowledge of the position of the strongroom and the safes.

It is customary at Mawson's for the clerks to leave at midday on Saturday. Sergeant Tuson, of the City police, was somewhat surprised, therefore, to see a gentleman with a carpet-bag come down the steps at twenty minutes past one. His suspicions being aroused, the sergeant followed the man, and with the aid of Constable Pollock succeeded, after a most desperate resistance, in arresting him. It was at once clear that a daring and gigantic robbery had been committed. Nearly a hundred thousand pounds' worth of American railway bonds, with a large amount of scrip in mines and other companies, was discovered in the bag. On examining the premises the body of the unfortunate watchman was found doubled up and thrust into the largest of the safes, where it would not have been discovered until Monday morning had it not been for the prompt action of Sergeant Tuson. The man's skull had been shattered by a blow from a poker delivered from behind. There could be no doubt that Beddington had obtained entrance by pretending that he had left something behind him, and having murdered the watchman, rapidly rifled the large safe, and then made off with his booty. His brother, who usually works with him, has not appeared in this job as far as can at present be ascertained, although the police are making energetic inquiries as to his whereabouts.

"Well, we may save the police some little trouble in that direction," said Holmes, glancing at the haggard figure huddled up by the window. "Human nature is a strange mixture, Watson. You see that even a villain and murderer can inspire such affection that his brother turns to suicide when he learns that his neck is forfeited. However, we have no choice as to our action. The doctor and I will remain on guard, Mr. Pycroft, if you will have the kindness to step out for the police."

Chapter 4

THE ADVENTURE OF THE '*GLORIA SCOTT*'

"I have some papers here," said my friend Sherlock Holmes as we sat one winter's night on either side of the fire, "which I really think, Watson, that it would be worth your while to glance over. These are the documents in the extraordinary case of the *Gloria Scott,* and this is the message which struck Justice of the Peace Trevor dead with horror when he read it."

He had picked from a drawer a little tarnished cylinder, and, undoing the tape, he handed me a short note scrawled upon a half-sheet of slate-gray paper.

The supply of game for London is going steadily up,' it ran. 'Headkeeper Hudson, we believe, has been now told to receive all orders for fly-paper and for preservation of your hen-pheasant's life.

As I glanced up from reading this enigmatical message, I saw Holmes chuckling at the expression upon my face.

"You look a little bewildered," said he.

"I cannot see how such a message as this could inspire horror. It seems to me to be rather grotesque than otherwise."

"Very likely. Yet the fact remains that the reader, who was a fine robust old man, was knocked clean down by it as if it had been the butt end of a pistol."

"You arouse my curiosity," said I. "But why did you say just now that there were very particular reasons why I should study this case?"

"Because it was the first in which I was ever engaged."

I had often endeavoured to elicit from my companion what had first turned his mind in the direction of criminal research, but had never caught him before in a communicative humour. Now he sat forward in his armchair and spread out the documents upon his knees. Then he lit his pipe and sat for some time smoking and turning them over.

"You never heard me talk of Victor Trevor?" he asked. "He was the only friend I made during the two years I was at college. I was never a very sociable fellow, Watson, always rather fond of moping in my rooms and working out my own little methods of thought, so that I never mixed much with the men of my year. Bar fencing and boxing I had few athletic tastes, and then my line of study was quite distinct from that of the other fellows, so that we had no points of contact at all. Trevor was the only man I knew, and that only through the accident of his bull terrier freezing on to my ankle one morning as I went down to chapel.

"It was a prosaic way of forming a friendship, but it was effective. I was laid by the heels for ten days, and Trevor used to come in to inquire after me. At first it was only a minute's chat, but soon his visits lengthened, and before the end of the term we were close friends. He was a hearty, full-blooded fellow, full of spirits and energy, the very opposite to me in most respects, but we had some subjects in common, and it was a bond of union when I found that he was as friendless as I. Finally he invited me down to his father's place at Donnithorpe, in Norfolk, and I accepted his hospitality for a month of the long vacation.

"Old Trevor was evidently a man of some wealth and consideration, a J.P., and a landed proprietor. Donnithorpe is a little hamlet just to the north of Langmere, in the country of the Broads. The house was an old-fashioned, widespread, oak-beamed brick building, with a fine lime-lined avenue leading up to it. There was excellent wild-duck shooting in the fens, remarkably good fishing, a small but select library, taken over, as I understood, from a former occupant, and a tolerable cook, so that he would be a fastidious man who could not put in a pleasant month there.

"Trevor senior was a widower, and my friend his only son.

"There had been a daughter, I heard, but she had died of diphtheria while on a visit to Birmingham. The father interested me extremely. He was a man of little culture, but with a considerable amount of rude strength, both physically and mentally. He knew hardly any books, but he had travelled far, had seen much of the world, and had remembered all that he had learned. In person he was a thick-set, burly man with a shock of grizzled hair, a brown, weather-beaten face, and blue eyes which were keen to the verge of fierceness. Yet he had a reputation for kindness and charity on the countryside, and was noted for the leniency of his sentences from the bench.

"One evening, shortly after my arrival, we were sitting over a glass of port after dinner, when young Trevor began to talk about those habits of observation and inference which I had already formed into a system, although I had not yet appreciated the part which they were to play in my life. The old man evidently thought that his son was exaggerating in his description of one or two trivial feats which I had performed.

"'Come, now, Mr. Holmes,' said he, laughing good-humouredly. 'I'm an excellent subject, If you can deduce anything from me.'

"'I fear there is not very much,' I answered. 'I might suggest that you have gone about in fear of some personal attack within the last twelve months.'

"The laugh faded from his lips, and he stared at me in great surprise.

"'Well, that's true enough,' said he. 'You know, Victor,' turning to his son, 'when we broke up that poaching gang they swore to knife us, and Sir Edward Holly has actually been attacked. I've always been on my guard since then, though I have no idea how you know it.'

"'You have a very handsome stick,' I answered. 'By the inscription I observed that you had not had it more than a year. But you have taken some pains to bore the head of it and pour melted lead into the hole so as to make it a formidable weapon. I argued that you would not take such precautions unless you had some danger to fear.'

"'Anything else?' he asked, smiling.

"'You have boxed a good deal in your youth.'

"'Right again. How did you know it? Is my nose knocked a little out of the straight?'

"'No,' said I. 'It is your ears. They have the peculiar flattening and chickening which marks the boxing man.'

"'Anything else?'"

"'You have done a good deal of digging by your callosities.'

"'Made all my money at the gold fields.'

"'You have been in New Zealand.'

"'Right again.'

"'You have visited Japan.'

"'Quite true.'

"'And you have been most intimately associated with someone whose initials were J.A., and whom you afterwards were eager to entirely forget.'

"Mr. Trevor stood slowly up, fixed his large blue eyes upon me with a strange wild stare, and then pitched forward, with his face among the nutshells which strewed the cloth, in a dead faint.

"You can imagine, Watson, how shocked both his son and I were. His attack did not last long, however, for when we undid his collar and sprinkled the water from one of the finger-glasses over his face, he gave a gasp or two and sat up.

"'Ah, boys,' said he, forcing a smile, 'I hope I haven't frightened you. Strong as I look, there is a weak place in my heart, and it does not take much to knock me over. I don't know how you manage this, Mr. Holmes, but it seems to me that all the detectives of fact and of fancy would be children in your hands. That's your line of life, sir, and you may take the word of a man who has seen something of the world.'

"And that recommendation, with the exaggerated estimate of my ability with which he prefaced it, was, if you will believe me, Watson, the very first thing which ever made me feel that a profession might be made out of what had up to that time been the merest hobby. At the moment, however, I was too much concerned at the sudden illness of my host to think of anything else.

"'I hope that I have said nothing to pain you?' said I.

"'Well, you certainly touched upon rather a tender point. Might I ask how you know, and how much you know?' He spoke now in a half jesting fashion, but a look of terror still lurked at the back of his eyes.

"'It is simplicity itself,' said I. 'When you bared your arm to draw that fish into the boat I saw that J. A. had been tattooed in the bend of the elbow. The letters were still legible, but it was perfectly clear from their blurred appearance, and from the staining of the skin round them, that efforts had been made to obliterate them. It was obvious, then, that those initials had once been very familiar to you, and that you had afterwards wished to forget them.'

"'What an eye you have!' he cried with a sigh of relief. 'It is just as you say. But we won't talk of it. Of all ghosts the ghosts of our old loves are the worst. Come into the billiard room and have a quiet cigar.'

"From that day, amid all his cordiality, there was always a touch of suspicion in Mr. Trevor's manner towards me. Even his son remarked it. 'You've given the governor such a turn,' said he, 'that he'll never be sure again of what you know and what you don't know.' He did not mean to show it, I am sure, but it was so strongly in his mind that it peeped out at every action. At last I became so convinced that I was causing him uneasiness that I drew my visit to a close. On the very day, however, before I left, an incident occurred which proved in the sequel to be of importance.

"We were sitting out upon the lawn on garden chairs, the three of us, basking in the sun and admiring the view across the Broads, when a maid came out to say that there was a man at the door who wanted to see Mr. Trevor.

"'What is his name?' asked my host.

"'He would not give any.'

"'What does he want, then?'

"'He says that you know him, and that he only wants a moment's conversation.'

"'Show him round here.' An instant afterwards there appeared a little wizened fellow with a cringing manner and a shambling style of walking. He wore an open jacket, with a splotch of tar on the sleeve, a red-and-black check shirt, dungaree trousers, and heavy boots badly worn. His face was thin and brown and crafty, with a perpetual smile upon it, which showed an irregular line of yellow teeth, and his crinkled hands were half closed in a way that is distinctive of sailors. As he came slouching across the lawn I heard Mr. Trevor make a sort of hiccoughing noise in his throat, and, jumping out of his chair, he ran into the house. He was back in a moment, and I smelt a strong reek of brandy as he passed me.

"'Well, my man,' said he. 'What can I do for you?'

"The sailor stood looking at him with puckered eyes, and with the same loose-lipped smile upon his face.

"'You don't know me?' he asked.

"'Why, dear me, it is surely Hudson,' said Mr. Trevor in a tone of surprise.

"'Hudson it is, sir,' said the seaman. 'Why, it's thirty year and more since I saw you last. Here you are in your house, and me still picking my salt meat out of the harness cask.'

"'Tut, you will find that I have not forgotten old times,' cried Mr. Trevor, and, walking towards the sailor, he said something in a low voice. 'Go into the kitchen,' he continued out loud, 'and you will get food and drink. I have no doubt that I shall find you a situation.'

"'Thank you, sir' said the seaman, touching his forelock. 'I'm just off a two-yearer in an eight-knot tramp, short-handed at that, and I wants a rest. I thought I'd get it either with Mr. Beddoes or with you.'

"'Ah!' cried Mr. Trevor. 'You know where Mr. Beddoes is?'

"'Bless you, sir, I know where all my old friends are,' said the fellow with a sinister smile, and he slouched off after the maid to the kitchen. Mr. Trevor mumbled something to us about having been shipmate with the man when he was going back to the diggings, and then, leaving us on the lawn, he went indoors. An hour later, when we entered the house, we found him stretched dead drunk upon the dining room sofa. The whole incident left a most ugly impression upon my mind, and I was not sorry next day to leave Donnithorpe behind me, for I felt that my presence must be a source of embarrassment to my friend.

"All this occurred during the first month of the long vacation. I went up to my London rooms, where I spent seven weeks working out a few experiments in organic chemistry. One day, however, when the autumn was far advanced and the vacation drawing to a close, I received a telegram from my friend imploring me to return to Donnithorpe, and saying that he was in great need of my advice and assistance. Of course I dropped everything and set out for the North once more.

"He met me with the dog-cart at the station, and I saw at a glance that the last two months had been very trying ones for him. He had grown thin and careworn, and had lost the loud, cheery manner for which he had been remarkable.

"'The governor is dying,' were the first words he said.

"'Impossible!' I cried. 'What is the matter?'

"'Apoplexy. Nervous shock. He's been on the verge all day. I doubt if we shall find him alive.'

"I was, as you may think, Watson, horrified at this unexpected news.

"'What has caused it?' I asked.

"'Ah, that is the point. Jump in and we can talk it over while we drive. You remember that fellow who came upon the evening before you left us?'

"'Perfectly.'

"'Do you know who it was that we let into the house that day?'

"'I have no idea.'

"'It was the devil, Holmes,' he cried.

"I stared at him in astonishment.

"'Yes, it was the devil himself. We have not had a peaceful hour since—not one. The governor has never held up his head from that evening, and now the life has been crushed out of him and his heart broken, all through this accursed Hudson.'

"'What power had he, then?'

"'Ah, that is what I would give so much to know. The kindly, charitable good old governor—how could he have fallen into the clutches of such a ruffian! But I am so glad that you have come, Holmes. I trust very much to your judgment and discretion, and I know that you will advise me for the best.'

"We were dashing along the smooth white country road, with the long stretch of the Broads in front of us glimmering in the red light of the setting sun. From a grove upon our left I could already see the high chimneys and the flagstaff which marked the squire's dwelling.

"'My father made the fellow gardener,' said my companion, 'and then, as that did not satisfy him, he was promoted to be butler. The house seemed to be at his mercy, and he wandered about and did what he chose in it. The maids complained of his drunken habits and his vile language. The dad raised their wages all round to recompense them for the annoyance. The fellow would take the boat and my father's best gun and treat himself to little shooting trips. And all this with such a sneering, leering, insolent face that I would have knocked him down twenty times over if he had been a man of my own age. I tell you, Holmes, I have had to keep a tight hold upon myself all this time; and now I am asking myself whether, if I had let myself go a little more, I might not have been a wiser man.

"'Well, matters went from bad to worse with us, and this animal Hudson became more and more intrusive, until at last, on his making some insolent reply to my father in my presence one day, I took him by the shoulders and turned him out of the room. He slunk away with a livid face and two venomous eyes which uttered more threats than his tongue could do. I don't know what passed between the poor dad and him after that, but the dad came to me next day and asked me whether I would mind apologizing to Hudson. I refused, as you can imagine, and asked my father how he could allow such a wretch to take such liberties with himself and his household.'

"'Ah, my boy,' said he, 'it is all very well to talk, but you don't know how I am placed. But you shall know, Victor. I'll see that you shall know, come what may. You wouldn't believe harm of your poor old father, would you, lad?' He was very much moved and shut himself up in the study all day, where I could see through the window that he was writing busily.

"'That evening there came what seemed to me to be a grand release, for Hudson told us that he was going to leave us. He walked into the dining room as we sat after dinner and announced his intention in the thick voice of a half-drunken man.'

"'I've had enough of Norfolk,' said he. 'I'll run down to Mr. Beddoes in Hampshire. He'll be as glad to see me as you were, I daresay'

"'You're not going away in an unkind spirit, Hudson, I hope,' said my father with a tameness which made my blood boil.

"'I've not had my 'pology,' said he sulkily, glancing in my direction.

"'Victor, you will acknowledge that you have used this worthy fellow rather roughly,' said the dad, turning to me.

"'On the contrary, I think that we have both shown extraordinary patience towards him,' I answered.

"'Oh, you do, do you?' he snarled. 'Very good, mate. We'll see about that!'

"'He slouched out of the room and half an hour afterwards left the house, leaving my father in a state of pitiable nervousness. Night after night I heard him pacing his room, and it was just as he was recovering his confidence that the blow did at last fall.'

"'And how?' I asked eagerly.

"'In a most extraordinary fashion. A letter arrived for my father yesterday evening, bearing the Fordingham postmark. My father read it, clapped both his hands to his head, and began running round the room in little circles like a man who has been driven out of his senses. When I at last drew him down on to the sofa, his mouth and eyelids were all puckered on one side, and I saw that he had a stroke. Dr. Fordham came over at once. We put him to bed, but the paralysis has spread, he has shown no sign of returning consciousness, and I think that we shall hardly find him alive.'

"'You horrify me, Trevor!' I cried. 'What then could have been in this letter to cause so dreadful a result?'

"'Nothing. There lies the inexplicable part of it. The message was absurd and trivial. Ah, my God, it is as I feared!'

"As he spoke we came round the curve of the avenue and saw in the fading light that every blind in the house had been drawn down. As we dashed up to the door, my friend's face convulsed with grief, a gentleman in black emerged from it.

"'When did it happen, doctor?' asked Trevor.

"'Almost immediately after you left.'

"'Did he recover consciousness?'

"'For an instant before the end.'

"'Any message for me?'

"'Only that the papers were in the back drawer of the Japanese cabinet.'

"My friend ascended with the doctor to the chamber of death, while I remained in the study, turning the whole matter over and over in my head, and feeling as sombre as ever I had done in my life. What was the past of this Trevor, pugilist, traveller, and gold-digger, and how had he placed himself in the power of this acid-faced seaman? Why, too, should he faint at an allusion to the half-effaced initials upon his arm and die of fright when he had a letter from Fordingham? Then I remembered that Fordingham was in Hampshire, and that this Mr. Beddoes, whom the seaman had gone to visit and presumably to blackmail, had also been mentioned as living in Hampshire. The letter, then, might either come from Hudson, the seaman, saying that he had betrayed the guilty secret which appeared to exist, or it might come from Beddoes, warning an old confederate that such a betrayal was imminent. So far it seemed clear enough. But then how could this letter be trivial and grotesque, as described by the son? He must have misread it. If so, it must have been one of those ingenious secret codes which mean one thing while they seem to mean another. I must see this letter. If there was a hidden meaning in it, I was confident that I could pluck it forth. For an hour I sat pondering over it in the gloom, until at last a weeping maid brought in a lamp, and close at her heels came my friend Trevor, pale but composed, with these very papers which lie upon my knee held in his grasp. He sat down opposite to me, drew the lamp to the edge of the table, and handed me a short note scribbled, as you see, upon a single sheet of gray paper.

> *'The supply of game for London is going steadily up,' it ran. 'Head-keeper Hudson, we believe, has been now told to receive all orders for fly-paper and for preservation of your hen-pheasant's life.'*

"I daresay my face looked as bewildered as yours did just now when first I read this message. Then I reread it very carefully. It was evidently as I had thought, and some secret meaning must lie buried in this strange combination of words. Or could it be that there was a prearranged significance to such phrases as 'fly-paper' and 'hen-pheasant'? Such a meaning would be arbitrary and could not be deduced in any way. And yet I was loath to believe that this was the case, and the presence of the word Hudson seemed to show that the subject of the message was as I had guessed, and that it was from Beddoes rather than the sailor. I tried it backward, but the combination 'life pheasant's hen' was not encouraging. Then I tried alternate words, but neither 'the of for' nor 'supply game London' promised to throw any light upon it.

"And then in an instant the key of the riddle was in my hands, and I saw that every third word, beginning with the first, would give a message which might well drive old Trevor to despair."

"It was short and terse, the warning, as I now read it to my companion:

The game is up. Hudson has told all. Fly for your life.

"Victor Trevor sank his face into his shaking hands. 'It must be that, I suppose,' said he. 'This is worse than death, for it means disgrace as well. But what is the meaning of these 'head-keepers' and 'hen-pheasants'?'

"'It means nothing to the message, but it might mean a good deal to us if we had no other means of discovering the sender. You see that he has begun by writing 'The. . . game. . . is,' and so on. Afterwards he had, to fulfil the prearranged cipher, to fill in any two words in each space. He would naturally use the first words which came to his mind, and if there were so many which referred to sport among them, you may be tolerably sure that he is either an ardent shot or interested in breeding. Do you know anything of this Beddoes?'

"'Why, now that you mention it,' said he, 'I remember that my poor father used to have an invitation from him to shoot over his preserves every autumn.'

"'Then it is undoubtedly from him that the note comes,' said I. 'It only remains for us to find out what this secret was which the sailor Hudson seems to have held over the heads of these two wealthy and respected men.'

"'Alas, Holmes, I fear that it is one of sin and shame!' cried my friend. 'But from you I shall have no secrets. Here is the statement which was drawn up by my father when he knew that the danger from Hudson had become imminent. I found it in the Japanese cabinet, as he told the doctor. Take it and read it to me, for I have neither the strength nor the courage to do it myself.'

"These are the very papers, Watson, which he handed to me, and I will read them to you, as I read them in the old study that night to him. They are endorsed outside, as you see, 'Some particulars of the voyage of the bark *Gloria Scott*, from her leaving Falmouth on the 8th October, 1855, to her destruction in N. Lat. 15° 20', W. Long. 25° 14', on Nov. 6th.' It is in the form of a letter, and runs in this way:

My dear, dear son, now that approaching disgrace begins to darken the closing years of my life, I can write with all truth and honesty that it is not the terror of the law, it is not the loss of my position in the county, nor is it my fall in the eyes of all who have known me, which cuts me to the heart; but it is the thought that you should come to blush for me—you who love me and who have seldom, I hope, had reason to do other than respect me. But if the blow falls which is forever hanging over me, then I should wish you to read this, that you may know straight from me how far I have been to blame. On the other hand, if all should go well (which may kind God Almighty grant!), then, if by any chance this paper should be still undestroyed and should fall into your hands, I conjure you, by all you hold sacred, by the memory of your dear mother, and by the love which has been between us, to hurl it into the fire and to never give one thought to it again.

If then your eye goes on to read this line, I know that I shall already have been exposed and dragged from my home, or, as is more likely, for you know that my heart is weak, be lying with my tongue sealed forever in death. In either case the time for suppression is past, and every word which I tell you is the naked truth, and this I swear as I hope for mercy.

My name, dear lad, is not Trevor. I was James Armitage in my younger days, and you can understand now the shock that it was to me a few weeks ago when your college friend addressed me in words which seemed to imply that he had surprised my secret. As Armitage it was that I entered a London banking-house, and as Armitage I was convicted of breaking my country's laws, and was sentenced to transportation. Do not think very harshly of me, laddie. It was a debt of honour, so called, which I had to pay, and I used money which was not my own to do it, in the certainty that I could replace it before there could be any possibility of its being missed. But the most dreadful ill-luck pursued me. The money which I had reckoned upon never came to hand, and a premature examination of accounts exposed my deficit. The case might have been dealt leniently with, but the laws were more harshly administered thirty years ago than now, and on my twenty-third birthday I found myself chained as a felon with thirty-seven other convicts in the 'tween-decks of the bark Gloria Scott bound for Australia.

It was the year '55, when the Crimean War was at its height, and the old convict ships had been largely used as transports in the Black Sea. The government was compelled, therefore, to use smaller and less suitable vessels for sending out their prisoners. The Gloria Scott had been in the Chinese tea-trade, but she was an old-fashioned, heavy-bowed, broad-beamed craft, and the new clippers had cut her out. She was a five-hundred-ton boat; and besides her thirty-eight jailbirds, she carried twenty-six of a crew, eighteen soldiers, a captain, three mates, a doctor, a chaplain, and four warders. Nearly a hundred souls were in her, all told, when we set sail from Falmouth.

The partitions between the cells of the convicts instead of being of thick oak, as is usual in convict-ships, were quite thin and frail. The man next to me, upon the aft side, was one whom I had particularly noticed when we were led down the quay. He was a young man with a clear, hairless face, a long, thin nose, and rather nut-cracker jaws. He carried his head very jauntily in the air, had a swaggering style of walking, and was, above all else, remarkable for his extraordinary height. I don't think any of our heads would have come up to his shoulder, and I am sure that he could not have measured less than six and a half feet. It was strange among so many sad and weary faces to see one which was full of energy and resolution. The sight of it was to me like a fire in a snowstorm. I was glad, then, to find that he was my neighbour, and gladder still when, in the dead of the night, I heard a whisper close to my ear and found that he had managed to cut an opening in the board which separated us.

"Hullo, chummy!" said he, "what's your name, and what are you here for?"

I answered him, and asked in turn who I was talking with.

"I'm Jack Prendergast," said he, "and by God! You'll learn to bless my name before you've done with me."

I remembered hearing of his case, for it was one which had made an immense sensation throughout the country some time before my own arrest. He was a man of good family and of great ability, but of incurably vicious habits, who had by an ingenious system of fraud obtained huge sums of money from the leading London merchants.

"Ha, ha! You remember my case," said he proudly.

"Very well, indeed."

"Then maybe you remember something queer about it?"

"What was that, then?"

"I'd had nearly a quarter of a million, hadn't I?"

"So it was said."

"But none was recovered, eh?"

"No."

"Well, where d'ye suppose the balance is?" he asked.

"I have no idea," said I.

"Right between my finger and thumb," he cried. "By God! I've got more pounds to my name than you've hairs on your head. And if you've money, my son, and know how to handle it and spread it, you can do *anything*. Now, you don't think it likely that a man who could do anything is going to wear his breeches out sitting in the stinking hold of a rat-gutted, beetle-ridden, mouldy old coffin of a Chin China coaster. No, sir, such a man will look after himself and will look after his chums. You may lay to that! You hold on to him, and you may kiss the book that he'll haul you through."

That was his style of talk, and at first I thought it meant nothing; but after a while, when he had tested me and sworn me in with all possible solemnity, he let me understand that there really was a plot to gain command of the vessel. A dozen of the prisoners had hatched it before they came aboard, Prendergast was the leader, and his money was the motive power.

"I'd a partner," said he, "a rare good man, as true as a stock to a barrel. He's got the dibbs, he has, and where do you think he is at this moment? Why, he's the chaplain of this ship—the chaplain, no less! he came aboard with a black coat, and his papers right, and money enough in his box to buy the thing right up from keel to main-truck. The crew are his, body and soul. He could buy 'em at so much a gross with a cash discount, and he did it before ever they signed on. He's got two of the warders and Mereer, the second mate, and he'd get the captain himself, if he thought him worth it."

"What are we to do, then?" I asked.

"What do you think?" said he. "We'll make the coats of some of these soldiers redder than ever the tailor did."

"But they are armed," said I.

"And so shall we be, my boy. There's a brace of pistols for every mother's son of us; and if we can't carry this ship, with the crew at our back, it's time we were all sent to a young misses' boarding-school. You speak to your mate upon the left tonight, and see if he is to be trusted."

I did so and found my other neighbour to be a young fellow in much the same position as myself, whose crime had been forgery. His name was Evans, but he afterwards changed it, like myself, and he is now a rich and prosperous man in the south of England. He was ready enough to join the conspiracy, as the only means of saving ourselves, and before we had crossed the bay there were only two of the prisoners who were not in the secret. One of these was of weak mind, and we did not dare to trust him, and the other was suffering from jaundice and could not be of any use to us.

From the beginning there was really nothing to prevent us from taking possession of the ship. The crew were a set of ruffians, specially picked for the job. The sham chaplain came into our cells to exhort us, carrying a black bag, supposed to be full of tracts, and so often did he come that by the third day we had each stowed away at the foot of our beds a file, a brace of pistols, a pound of powder, and twenty slugs. Two of the warders were agents of Prendergast, and the second mate was his right-hand man. The captain, the two mates, two warders, Lieutenant Martin, his eighteen soldiers, and the doctor were all that we had against us. Yet, safe as it was, we determined to neglect no precaution, and to make our attack suddenly by night. It came, however, more quickly than we expected, and in this way.

One evening, about the third week after our start, the doctor had come down to see one of the prisoners who was ill, and, putting his hand down on the bottom of his bunk, he felt the outline of the pistols. If he had been silent he might have blown the whole thing, but he was a nervous little chap, so he gave a cry of surprise and turned so pale that the man knew what was up in an instant and seized him. He was gagged before he could give the alarm and tied down upon the bed. He had unlocked the door that led to the deck, and we were through it in a rush. The two sentries were shot down, and so was a corporal who came running to see what was the matter. There were two more soldiers at the door of the stateroom, and their muskets seemed not to be loaded, for they never fired upon us, and they were shot while trying to fix their bayonets. Then we rushed on into the captain's cabin, but as we pushed open the door there was an explosion from within, and there he lay with his brains smeared over the chart of the Atlantic which was pinned upon the table, while the chaplain stood with a smoking pistol in his hand at his elbow. The two mates had both been seized by the crew, and the whole business seemed to be settled.

The stateroom was next the cabin, and we flocked in there and flopped down on the settees, all speaking together, for we were just mad with the feeling that we were free once more. There were lockers all round, and Wilson, the sham chaplain, knocked one of them in, and pulled out a dozen of brown sherry. We cracked off the necks of the bottles, poured the stuff out into tumblers, and were just tossing them off when in an instant without warning there came the roar of muskets in our ears, and the saloon was so full of smoke that we could not see across the table. When it cleared again the place was a shambles. Wilson and eight others were wriggling on the top of each other on the floor, and the blood and the brown sherry on that table turn me sick now when I think of it. We were so cowed by the sight that I think we should have given the job up if it had not been for Prendergast. He bellowed like a bull and rushed for the door with all that were left alive at his heels. Out we ran, and there on the poop were the lieutenant and ten of his men. The swing skylights above the saloon table had been a bit open, and they had fired on us through the slit. We got on them before they could load, and they stood to it like men; but we had the upper hand of them, and in five minutes it was all over. My God! Was there ever a slaughter-house like that ship! Prendergast was like a raging devil, and he picked the soldiers up as if they had been children and threw them overboard alive or dead. There was one sergeant that was horribly wounded and yet kept on swimming for a surprising time until someone in mercy blew out his brains. When the fighting was over there was no one left of our enemies except just the warders, the mates, and the doctor.

It was over them that the great quarrel arose. There were many of us who were glad enough to win back our freedom, and yet who had no wish to have murder on our souls. It was one thing to knock the soldiers over with their muskets in their hands, and it was another to stand by while men were being killed in cold blood. Eight of us, five convicts and three sailors, said that we would not see it done. But there was no moving Prendergast and those who were with him. Our only chance of safety lay in making a clean job of it, said he, and he would not leave a tongue with power to wag in a witness-box. It nearly came to our sharing the fate of the prisoners, but at last he said that if we wished we might take a boat and go. We jumped at the offer, for we were already sick of these bloodthirsty doings, and we saw that there would be worse before it was done. We were given a suit of sailor togs each, a barrel of water, two casks, one of junk and one of biscuits, and a compass. Prendergast threw us over a chart, told us that we were shipwrecked mariners whose ship had foundered in Lat. 15° North and Long. 25° West, and then cut the painter and let us go.

And now I come to the most surprising part of my story, my dear son. The seamen had hauled the fore-yard aback during the rising, but now as we left them they brought it square again, and as there was a light wind from the north and east the bark began to draw slowly away from us. Our boat lay, rising and falling, upon the long, smooth rollers, and Evans and I, who were the most educated of the party, were sitting in the sheets working out our position and planning what coast we should make for. It was a nice question, for the Cape Verdes were about five hundred miles to the north of us, and the African coast about seven hundred to the east. On the whole, as the wind was coming round to the north, we thought that Sierra Leone might be best and turned our head in that direction, the bark being at that time nearly hull down on our starboard quarter. Suddenly as we looked at her we saw a dense black cloud of smoke shoot up from her, which hung like a monstrous tree upon the sky line. A few seconds later a roar like thunder burst upon our ears, and as the smoke thinned away there was no sign left of the *Gloria Scott*. In an instant we swept the boat's head round again and pulled with all our strength for the place where the haze still trailing over the water marked the scene of this catastrophe.

It was a long hour before we reached it, and at first we feared that we had come too late to save anyone. A splintered boat and a number of crates and fragments of spars rising and falling on the waves showed us where the vessel had foundered; but there was no sign of life, and we had turned away in despair, when we heard a cry for help and saw at some distance a piece of wreckage with a man lying stretched across it. When we pulled him aboard the boat he proved to be a young seaman of the name of Hudson, who was so burned and exhausted that he could give us no account of what had happened until the following morning.

It seemed that after we had left, Prendergast and his gang had proceeded to put to death the five remaining prisoners. The two warders had been shot and thrown overboard, and so also had the third mate. Prendergast then descended into the 'tween-decks and with his own hands cut the throat of the unfortunate surgeon. There only remained the first mate, who was a bold and active man. When he saw the convict approaching him with the bloody knife in his hand he kicked off his bonds, which he had somehow contrived to loosen, and rushing down the deck he plunged into the after-hold. A dozen convicts, who descended with their pistols in search of him, found him with a matchbox in his hand seated beside an open powder-barrel, which was one of a hundred carried on board, and swearing that he would blow all hands up if he were in any way molested. An instant later the explosion occurred, though Hudson thought it was caused by the misdirected bullet of one of the convicts rather than the mate's match. Be the cause what it may, it was the end of the *Gloria Scott* and of the rabble who held command of her.

Such, in a few words, my dear boy, is the history of this terrible business in which I was involved. Next day we were picked up by the brig *Hotspur*, bound for Australia, whose captain found no difficulty in believing that we were the survivors of a passenger ship which had foundered. The transport ship *Gloria Scott* was set down by the Admiralty as being lost at sea, and no word has ever leaked out as to her true fate. After an excellent voyage the *Hotspur* landed us at Sydney, where Evans and I changed our names and made our way to the diggings, where, among the crowds who were gathered from all nations, we had no difficulty in losing our former identities. The rest I need not relate. We prospered, we travelled, we came back as rich colonials to England, and we bought country estates. For more than twenty years we have led peaceful and useful lives, and we hoped that our past was forever buried. Imagine, then, my feelings when in the seaman who came to us I recognized instantly the man who had been picked off the wreck. He had tracked us down somehow and had set himself to live upon our fears. You will understand now how it was that I strove to keep the peace with him, and you will in some measure sympathize with me in the fears which fill me, now that he has gone from me to his other victim with threats upon his tongue.'

"Underneath is written in a hand so shaky as to be hardly legible:"

Beddoes writes in cipher to say H. has told all. Sweet Lord, have mercy on our souls!

"That was the narrative which I read that night to young Trevor, and I think, Watson, that under the circumstances it was a dramatic one. The good fellow was heart-broken at it, and went out to the Terai tea planting, where I hear that he is doing well. As to the sailor and Beddoes, neither of them was ever heard of again after that day on which the letter of warning was written. They both disappeared utterly and completely. No complaint had been lodged with the police, so that Beddoes had mistaken a threat for a deed. Hudson had been seen lurking about, and it was believed by the police that he had done away with Beddoes and had fled. For myself I believe that the truth was exactly the opposite. I think that it is most probable that Beddoes, pushed to desperation and believing himself to have been already betrayed, had revenged himself upon Hudson, and had fled from the country with as much money as he could lay his hands on. Those are the facts of the case, Doctor, and if they are of any use to your collection, I am sure that they are very heartily at your service."

Chapter 5

THE ADVENTURE OF THE MUSGRAVE RITUAL

An anomaly which often struck me in the character of my friend Sherlock Holmes was that, although in his methods of thought he was the neatest and most methodical of mankind, and although also he affected a certain quiet primness of dress, he was nonetheless in his personal habits one of the most untidy men that ever drove a fellow-lodger to distraction. Not that I am in the least conventional in that respect myself. The rough-and-tumble work in Afghanistan, coming on the top of natural Bohemianism of disposition, has made me rather more lax than befits a medical man. But with me there is a limit, and when I find a man who keeps his cigars in the coal-scuttle, his tobacco in the toe end of a Persian slipper, and his unanswered correspondence transfixed by a jack-knife into the very centre of his wooden mantelpiece, then I begin to give myself virtuous airs. I have always held, too, that pistol practice should be distinctly an open-air pastime; and when Holmes, in one of his queer humours, would sit in an armchair with his hair-trigger and a hundred Boxer cartridges and proceed to adorn the opposite wall with a patriotic V. R. done in bullet-pocks, I felt strongly that neither the atmosphere nor the appearance of our room was improved by it.

Our chambers were always full of chemicals and of criminal relics which had a way of wandering into unlikely positions, and of turning up in the butter-dish or in even less desirable places. But his papers were my great crux. He had a horror of destroying documents, especially those which were connected with his past cases, and yet it was only once in every year or two that he would muster energy to docket and arrange them; for, as I have mentioned somewhere in these incoherent memoirs, the outbursts of passionate energy when he performed the remarkable feats with which his name is associated were followed by reactions of lethargy during which he would lie about with his violin and his books, hardly moving save from the sofa to the table. Thus month after month his papers accumulated until every corner of the room was stacked with bundles of manuscript which were on no account to be burned, and which could not be put away save by their owner. One winter's night, as we sat together by the fire, I ventured to suggest to him that, as he had finished pasting extracts into his commonplace book, he might employ the next two hours in making our room a little more habitable. He could not deny the justice of my request, so with a rather rueful face he went off to his bedroom, from which he returned presently pulling a large tin box behind him. This he placed in the middle of the floor, and, squatting down upon a stool in front of it, he threw back the lid. I could see that it was already a third full of bundles of paper tied up with red tape into separate packages.

"There are cases enough here, Watson," said he, looking at me with mischievous eyes. "I think that if you knew all that I had in this box you would ask me to pull some out instead of putting others in."

"These are the records of your early work, then?" I asked. "I have often wished that I had notes of those cases."

"Yes, my boy, these were all done prematurely before my biographer had come to glorify me." He lifted bundle after bundle in a tender, caressing sort of way. "They are not all successes, Watson," said he. "But there are some pretty little problems among them. Here's the record of the Tarleton murders, and the case of Vamberry, the wine merchant, and the adventure of the old Russian woman, and the singular affair of the aluminum crutch, as well as a full account of Ricoletti of the club-foot, and his abominable wife. And here—ah, now, this really is something a little *recherche*."

He dived his arm down to the bottom of the chest and brought up a small wooden box with a sliding lid such as children's toys are kept in. From within he produced a crumpled piece of paper, an old-fashioned brass key, a peg of wood with a ball of string attached to it, and three rusty old discs of metal.

"Well, my boy, what do you make of this lot?" he asked, smiling at my expression.

"It is a curious collection."

"Very curious, and the story that hangs round it will strike you as being more curious still."

"These relics have a history, then?"

"So much so that they *are* history."

"What do you mean by that?"

Sherlock Holmes picked them up one by one and laid them along the edge of the table. Then he reseated himself in his chair and looked them over with a gleam of satisfaction in his eyes.

"These," said he, "are all that I have left to remind me of the adventure of the Musgrave Ritual."

I had heard him mention the case more than once, though I had never been able to gather the details.

"I should be so glad," said I. "If you would give me an account of it."

"And leave the litter as it is?" he cried mischievously. "Your tidiness won't bear much strain, after all, Watson. But I should be glad that you should add this case to your annals, for there are points in it which make it quite unique in the criminal records of this or, I believe, of any other country. A collection of my trifling achievements would certainly be incomplete which contained no account of this very singular business.

"You may remember how the affair of the *Gloria Scott*, and my conversation with the unhappy man whose fate I told you of, first turned my attention in the direction of the profession which has become my life's work. You see me now when my name has become known far and wide, and when I am generally recognized both by the public and by the official force as being a final court of appeal in doubtful cases. Even when you knew me first, at the time of the affair which you have commemorated in *A Study in Scarlet,* I had already established a considerable, though not a very lucrative, connection. You can hardly realize, then, how difficult I found it at first, and how long I had to wait before I succeeded in making any headway.

"When I first came up to London I had rooms in Montague Street, just round the corner from the British Museum, and there I waited, filling in my too abundant leisure time by studying all those branches of science which might make me more efficient. Now and again cases came in my way, principally through the introduction of old fellow-students, for during my last years at the university there was a good deal of talk there about myself and my methods. The third of these cases was that of the Musgrave Ritual, and it is to the interest which was aroused by that singular chain of events, and the large issues which proved to be at stake, that I trace my first stride towards the position which I now hold.

"Reginald Musgrave had been in the same college as myself, and I had some slight acquaintance with him. He was not generally popular among the undergraduates, though it always seemed to me that what was set down as pride was really an attempt to cover extreme natural diffidence. In appearance he was a man of an exceedingly aristocratic type, thin, high-nosed, and large-eyed, with languid and yet courtly manners. He was indeed a scion of one of the very oldest families in the kingdom, though his branch was a cadet one which had separated from the northern Musgraves some time in the sixteenth century and had established itself in western Sussex, where the Manor House of Hurlstone is perhaps the oldest inhabited building in the county. Something of his birth-place seemed to cling to the man, and I never looked at his pale, keen face or the poise of his head without associating him with gray archways and mullioned windows and all the venerable wreckage of a feudal keep. Once or twice we drifted into talk, and I can remember that more than once he expressed a keen interest in my methods of observation and inference.

"For four years I had seen nothing of him until on a morning he walked into my room in Montague Street. He had changed little, was dressed like a young man of fashion—he was always a bit of a dandy—and preserved the same quiet, suave manner which had formerly distinguished him.

"'How has all gone with you, Musgrave?' I asked after we had cordially shaken hands.

"'You probably heard of my poor father's death,' said he; 'he was carried off about two years ago. Since then I have of course had the Hurlstone estate to manage, and as I am member for my district as well, my life has been a busy one. But I understand, Holmes, that you are turning to practical ends those powers with which you used to amaze us?'

"'Yes,' said I, 'I have taken to living by my wits.'

"'I am delighted to hear it, for your advice at present would be exceedingly valuable to me. We have had some very strange doings at Hurlstone, and the police have been able to throw no light upon the matter. It is really the most extraordinary and inexplicable business.'

"You can imagine with what eagerness I listened to him, Watson, for the very chance for which I had been panting during all those months of inaction seemed to have come within my reach. In my inmost heart I believed that I could succeed where others failed, and now I had the opportunity to test myself."

"'Pray let me have the details,' I cried."

"Reginald Musgrave sat down opposite to me and lit the cigarette which I had pushed towards him."

"'You must know,' said he, 'that though I am a bachelor, I have to keep up a considerable staff of servants at Hurlstone, for it is a rambling old place and takes a good deal of looking after. I preserve, too, and in the pheasant months I usually have a house-party, so that it would not do to be short-handed. Altogether there are eight maids, the cook, the butler, two footmen, and a boy. The garden and the stables of course have a separate staff.'

'Of these servants the one who had been longest in our service was Brunton, the butler. He was a young schoolmaster out of place when he was first taken up by my father, but he was a man of great energy and character, and he soon became quite invaluable in the household. He was a well-grown, handsome man, with a splendid forehead, and though he has been with us for twenty years he cannot be more than forty now. With his personal advantages and his extraordinary gifts—for he can speak several languages and play nearly every musical instrument—it is wonderful that he should have been satisfied so long in such a position, but I suppose that he was comfortable and lacked energy to make any change. The butler of Hurlstone is always a thing that is remembered by all who visit us.

'But this paragon has one fault. He is a bit of a Don Juan, and you can imagine that for a man like him it is not a very difficult part to play in a quiet country district. When he was married it was all right, but since he has been a widower we have had no end of trouble with him. A few months ago we were in hopes that he was about to settle down again, for he became engaged to Rachel Howells, our second housemaid; but he has thrown her over since then and taken up with Janet Tregellis, the daughter of the head gamekeeper. Rachel—who is a very good girl, but of an excitable Welsh temperament—had a sharp touch of brain-fever and goes about the house now—or did until yesterday—like a black-eyed shadow of her former self. That was our first drama at Hurlstone; but a second one came to drive it from our minds, and it was prefaced by the disgrace and dismissal of butler Brunton.

'This was how it came about. I have said that the man was intelligent, and this very intelligence has caused his ruin, for it seems to have led to an insatiable curiosity about things which did not in the least concern him. I had no idea of the lengths to which this would carry him until the merest accident opened my eyes to it.

'I have said that the house is a rambling one. One day last week—on Thursday night, to be more exact—I found that I could not sleep, having foolishly taken a cup of strong *café noir* after my dinner. After struggling against it until two in the morning, I felt that it was quite hopeless, so I rose and lit the candle with the intention of continuing a novel which I was reading. The book, however, had been left in the billiard room, so I pulled on my dressing gown and started off to get it.

'In order to reach the billiard room I had to descend a flight of stairs and then to cross the head of a passage which led to the library and the gun room. You can imagine my surprise when, as I looked down this corridor, I saw a glimmer of light coming from the open door of the library. I had myself extinguished the lamp and closed the door before coming to bed. Naturally my first thought was of burglars. The corridors at Hurlstone have their walls largely decorated with trophies of old weapons. From one of these I picked a battle-axe, and then, leaving my candle behind me, I crept on tiptoe down the passage and peeped in at the open door.

'Brunton, the butler, was in the library. He was sitting, fully dressed, in an easy-chair, with a slip of paper which looked like a map upon his knee, and his forehead sunk forward upon his hand in deep thought. I stood dumb with astonishment, watching him from the darkness. A small taper on the edge of the table shed a feeble light which sufficed to show me that he was fully dressed. Suddenly, as I looked, he rose from his chair, and, walking over to a bureau at the side, he unlocked it and drew out one of the drawers. From this he took a paper, and, returning to his seat, he flattened it out beside the taper on the edge of the table and began to study it with minute attention. My indignation at this calm examination of our family documents overcame me so far that I took a step forward, and Brunton, looking up, saw me standing in the doorway. He sprang to his feet, his face turned livid with fear, and he thrust into his breast the chart-like paper which he had been originally studying.

'"'So!' said I. 'This is how you repay the trust which we have reposed in you. You will leave my service tomorrow.'

'He bowed with the look of a man who is utterly crushed and slunk past me without a word. The taper was still on the table, and by its light I glanced to see what the paper was which Brunton had taken from the bureau. To my surprise it was nothing of any importance at all, but simply a copy of the questions and answers in the singular old observance called the Musgrave Ritual. It is a sort of ceremony peculiar to our family, which each Musgrave for centuries past has gone through on his coming of age—a thing of private interest, and perhaps of some little importance to the archraeologist, like our own blazonings and charges, but of no practical use whatever.'

"'We had better come back to the paper afterwards,' said I.

"'If you think it really necessary,' he answered with some hesitation. 'To continue my statement, however: I relocked the bureau, using the key which Brunton had left, and I had turned to go when I was surprised to find that the butler had returned, and was standing before me.

"'Mr. Musgrave, sir,' he cried in a voice which was hoarse with emotion, 'I can't bear disgrace, sir. I've always been proud above my station in life, and disgrace would kill me. My blood will be on your head, sir—it will, indeed—if you drive me to despair. If you cannot keep me after what has passed, then for God's sake let me give you notice and leave in a month, as if of my own free will. I could stand that, Mr. Musgrave, but not to be cast out before all the folk that I know so well.'

"'You don't deserve much consideration, Brunton,' I answered.

"'Your conduct has been most infamous. However, as you have been a long time in the family, I have no wish to bring public disgrace upon you. A month, however, is too long. Take yourself away in a week, and give what reason you like for going.'

"'Only a week, sir?' he cried in a despairing voice. 'A fortnight—say at least a fortnight!'

"'A week,' I repeated, 'and you may consider yourself to have been very leniently dealt with.'

'He crept away, his face sunk upon his breast, like a broken man, while I put out the light and returned to my room.'

'For two days after this Brunton was most assiduous in his attention to his duties. I made no allusion to what had passed and waited with some curiosity to see how he would cover his disgrace. On the third morning, however, he did not appear, as was his custom, after breakfast to receive my instructions for the day. As I left the dining room I happened to meet Rachel Howells, the maid. I have told you that she had only recently recovered from an illness and was looking so wretchedly pale and wan that I remonstrated with her for being at work.'

"'You should be in bed,' I said. 'Come back to your duties when you are stronger.'

'She looked at me with so strange an expression that I began to suspect that her brain was affected.'

"'I am strong enough, Mr. Musgrave,' said she.

"'We will see what the doctor says,' I answered. 'You must stop work now, and when you go downstairs just say that I wish to see Brunton.'

"'The butler is gone,' said she.

"'Gone! Gone where?'

"'He is gone. No one has seen him. He is not in his room. Oh, yes, he is gone, he is gone!' She fell back against the wall with shriek after shriek of laughter, while I, horrified at this sudden hysterical attack, rushed to the bell to summon help. The girl was taken to her room, still screaming and sobbing, while I made inquiries about Brunton. There was no doubt about it that he had disappeared. His bed had not been slept in, he had been seen by no one since he had retired to his room the night before, and yet it was difficult to see how he could have left the house, as both windows and doors were found to be fastened in the morning. His clothes, his watch, and even his money were in his room, but the black suit which he usually wore was missing. His slippers, too, were gone, but his boots were left behind. Where then could butler Brunton have gone in the night, and what could have become of him now?'

'Of course we searched the house from cellar to garret, but there was no trace of him. It is, as I have said, a labyrinth of an old house, especially the original wing, which is now practically uninhabited; but we ransacked every room and cellar without discovering the least sign of the missing man. It was incredible to me that he could have gone away leaving all his property behind him, and yet where could he be? I called in the local police, but without success. Rain had fallen on the night before, and we examined the lawn and the paths all round the house, but in vain. Matters were in this state, when a new development quite drew our attention away from the original mystery.

'For two days Rachel Howells had been so ill, sometimes delirious, sometimes hysterical, that a nurse had been employed to sit up with her at night. On the third night after Brunton's disappearance, the nurse, finding her patient sleeping nicely, had dropped into a nap in the armchair, when she woke in the early morning to find the bed empty, the window open, and no signs of the invalid. I was instantly aroused, and, with the two footmen, started off at once in search of the missing girl. It was not difficult to tell the direction which she had taken, for, starting from under her window, we could follow her footmarks easily across the lawn to the edge of the mere, where they vanished close to the gravel path which leads out of the grounds. The lake there is eight feet deep, and you can imagine our feelings when we saw that the trail of the poor demented girl came to an end at the edge of it.

'Of course, we had the drags at once and set to work to recover the remains, but no trace of the body could we find. On the other hand, we brought to the surface an object of a most unexpected kind. It was a linen bag which contained within it a mass of old rusted and discoloured metal and several dull-coloured pieces of pebble or glass. This strange find was all that we could get from the mere, and, although we made every possible search and inquiry yesterday, we know nothing of the fate either of Rachel Howells or of Richard Brunton. The county police are at their wit's end, and I have come up to you as a last resource.'

"You can imagine, Watson, with what eagerness I listened to this extraordinary sequence of events, and endeavoured to piece them together, and to devise some common thread upon which they might all hang. The butler was gone. The maid was gone. The maid had loved the butler, but had afterwards had cause to hate him. She was of Welsh blood, fiery and passionate. She had been terribly excited immediately after his disappearance. She had flung into the lake a bag containing some curious contents. These were all factors which had to be taken into consideration, and yet none of them got quite to the heart of the matter. What was the starting-point of this chain of events? There lay the end of this tangled line.

"'I must see that paper, Musgrave,' said I, 'which this butler of yours thought it worth his while to consult, even at the risk of the loss of his place.'

"'It is rather an absurd business, this ritual of ours,' he answered. 'But it has at least the saving grace of antiquity to excuse it. I have a copy of the questions and answers here if you care to run your eye over them.'

"He handed me the very paper which I have here, Watson, and this is the strange catechism to which each Musgrave had to submit when he came to man's estate. I will read you the questions and answers as they stand."

"Whose was it?"

"His who is gone."

"Who shall have it?"

"He who will come."

"Where was the sun?"

"Over the oak."

"Where was the shadow?"

"Under the elm."

"How was it stepped?"

"North by ten and by ten, east by five and by five, south by two and by two, west by one and by one, and so under."

"What shall we give for it?"

"All that is ours."

"Why should we give it?"

"For the sake of the trust."

"'The original has no date, but is in the spelling of the middle of the seventeenth century,' remarked Musgrave. 'I am afraid, however, that it can be of little help to you in solving this mystery.'

"'At least,' said I, 'it gives us another mystery, and one which is even more interesting than the first. It may be that the solution of the one may prove to be the solution of the other. You will excuse me, Musgrave, if I say that your butler appears to me to have been a very clever man, and to have had a clearer insight than ten generations of his masters.'

"'I hardly follow you,' said Musgrave. 'The paper seems to me to be of no practical importance.'

"'But to me it seems immensely practical, and I fancy that Brunton took the same view. He had probably seen it before that night on which you caught him.'

"'It is very possible. We took no pains to hide it.'

"'He simply wished, I should imagine, to refresh his memory upon that last occasion. He had, as I understand, some sort of map or chart which he was comparing with the manuscript, and which he thrust into his pocket when you appeared.'

"'That is true. But what could he have to do with this old family custom of ours, and what does this rigmarole mean?'

"'I don't think that we should have much difficulty in determining that,' said I; 'with your permission we will take the first train down to Sussex and go a little more deeply into the matter upon the spot.'

"The same afternoon saw us both at Hurlstone. Possibly you have seen pictures and read descriptions of the famous old building, so I will confine my account of it to saying that it is built in the shape of an L, the long arm being the more modern portion, and the shorter the ancient nucleus from which the other has developed. Over the low, heavily-lintelled door, in the centre of this old part, is chiselled the date, 1607, but experts are agreed that the beams and stonework are really much older than this. The enormously thick walls and tiny windows of this part had in the last century driven the family into building the new wing, and the old one was used now as a storehouse and a cellar, when it was used at all. A splendid park with fine old timber surrounds the house, and the lake, to which my client had referred, lay close to the avenue, about two hundred yards from the building."

"I was already firmly convinced, Watson, that there were not three separate mysteries here, but one only, and that if I could read the Musgrave Ritual alright I should hold in my hand the clue which would lead me to the truth concerning both the butler Brunton and the maid Howells. To that then I turned all my energies. Why should this servant be so anxious to master this old formula? Evidently because he saw something in it which had escaped all those generations of country squires, and from which he expected some personal advantage. What was it then, and how had it affected his fate?

"It was perfectly obvious to me, on reading the Ritual, that the measurements must refer to some spot to which the rest of the document alluded, and that if we could find that spot we should be in a fair way towards finding what the secret was which the old Musgraves had thought it necessary to embalm in so curious a fashion. There were two guides given us to start with, an oak and an elm. As to the oak there could be no question at all. Right in front of the house, upon the left-hand side of the drive, there stood a patriarch among oaks, one of the most magnificent trees that I have ever seen.

"'That was there when your ritual was drawn up,' said I as we drove past it."

"'It was there at the Norman Conquest in all probability,' he answered. 'It has a girth of twenty-three feet.'

"Here was one of my fixed points secured.

"'Have you any old elms?' I asked.

"'There used to be a very old one over yonder, but it was struck by lightning ten years ago, and we cut down the stump.'

"'You can see where it used to be?'

"'Oh, yes.'

"'There are no other elms?'

"'No old ones, but plenty of beeches.'

"'I should like to see where it grew.'

"We had driven up in a dog-cart, and my client led me away at once, without our entering the house, to the scar on the lawn where the elm had stood. It was nearly midway between the oak and the house. My investigation seemed to be progressing.

"'I suppose it is impossible to find out how high the elm was?' I asked.

"'I can give you it at once. It was sixty-four feet.'

"'How do you come to know it?' I asked in surprise.

"'When my old tutor used to give me an exercise in trigonometry, it always took the shape of measuring heights. When I was a lad I worked out the heights of every tree and building in the estate.'

"This was an unexpected piece of luck. My data were coming more quickly than I could have reasonably hoped.

"'Tell me,' I asked, 'did your butler ever ask you such a question?'

"Reginald Musgrave looked at me in astonishment. 'Now that you call it to my mind,' he answered, 'Brunton *did* ask me about the height of the tree some months ago in connection with some little argument with the groom.'

"This was excellent news, Watson, for it showed me that I was on the right road. I looked up at the sun. It was low in the heavens, and I calculated that in less than an hour it would lie just above the top-most branches of the old oak. One condition mentioned in the Ritual would then be fulfilled. And the shadow of the elm must mean the farther end of the shadow, otherwise the trunk would have been chosen as the guide. I had, then, to find where the far end of the shadow would fall when the sun was just clear of the oak.

"That must have been difficult, when the elm was no longer there."

"Well, at least I knew that if Brunton could do it, I could also. Besides, there was no real difficulty. I went with Musgrave to his study and whittled myself this peg, to which I tied this long string with a knot at each yard. Then I took two lengths of a fishing-rod, which came to just six feet, and I went back with my client to where the elm had been. The sun was just grazing the top of the oak. I fastened the rod on end, marked out the direction of the shadow, and measured it. It was nine feet in length.

"Of course the calculation now was a simple one. If a rod of six feet threw a shadow of nine, a tree of sixty-four feet would throw one of ninety-six, and the line of the one would of course be the line of the other. I measured out the distance, which brought me almost to the wall of the house, and I thrust a peg into the spot. You can imagine my exultation, Watson, when within two inches of my peg I saw a conical depression in the ground. I knew that it was the mark made by Brunton in his measurements, and that I was still upon his trail.

"From this starting-point I proceeded to step, having first taken the cardinal points by my pocket-compass. Ten steps with each foot took me along parallel with the wall of the house, and again I marked my spot with a peg. Then I carefully paced off five to the east and two to the south. It brought me to the very threshold of the old door. Two steps to the west meant now that I was to go two paces down the stone-flagged passage, and this was the place indicated by the Ritual."

"Never have I felt such a cold chill of disappointment, Watson. For a moment it seemed to me that there must be some radical mistake in my calculations. The setting sun shone full upon the passage floor, and I could see that the old, foot-worn gray stones with which it was paved were firmly cemented together, and had certainly not been moved for many a long year. Brunton had not been at work here. I tapped upon the floor, but it sounded the same all over, and there was no sign of any crack or crevice. But, fortunately, Musgrave, who had begun to appreciate the meaning of my proceedings, and who was now as excited as myself, took out his manuscript to check my calculations.

"'And under,' he cried. 'You have omitted the 'and under.'"

"I had thought that it meant that we were to dig, but now, of course, I saw at once that I was wrong. 'There is a cellar under this then?' I cried.

"'Yes, and as old as the house. Down here, through this door.'

"We went down a winding stone stair, and my companion, striking a match, lit a large lantern which stood on a barrel in the corner. In an instant it was obvious that we had at last come upon the true place, and that we had not been the only people to visit the spot recently.

"It had been used for the storage of wood, but the billets, which had evidently been littered over the floor, were now piled at the sides, so as to leave a clear space in the middle. In this space lay a large and heavy flagstone with a rusted iron ring in the centre to which a thick shepherd's-check muffler was attached.

"'By Jove!' cried my client. 'That's Brunton's muffler. I have seen it on him and could swear to it. What has the villain been doing here?'

"At my suggestion a couple of the county police were summoned to be present, and I then endeavoured to raise the stone by pulling on the cravat. I could only move it slightly, and it was with the aid of one of the constables that I succeeded at last in carrying it to one side. A black hole yawned beneath into which we all peered, while Musgrave, kneeling at the side, pushed down the lantern.

"A small chamber about seven feet deep and four feet square lay open to us. At one side of this was a squat, brass-bound wooden box, the lid of which was hinged upward, with this curious old-fashioned key projecting from the lock. It was furred outside by a thick layer of dust, and damp and worms had eaten through the wood, so that a crop of livid fungi was growing on the inside of it. Several discs of metal, old coins apparently, such as I hold here, were scattered over the bottom of the box, but it contained nothing else.

"At the moment, however, we had no thought for the old chest, for our eyes were riveted upon that which crouched beside it. It was the figure of a man, clad in a suit of black, who squatted down upon his hams with his forehead sunk upon the edge of the box and his two arms thrown out on each side of it. The attitude had drawn all the stagnant blood to the face, and no man could have recognized that distorted liver-coloured countenance; but his height, his dress, and his hair were all sufficient to show my client, when we had drawn the body up, that it was indeed his missing butler. He had been dead some days, but there was no wound or bruise upon his person to show how he had met his dreadful end. When his body had been carried from the cellar we found ourselves still confronted with a problem which was almost as formidable as that with which we had started.

"I confess that so far, Watson, I had been disappointed in my investigation. I had reckoned upon solving the matter when once I had found the place referred to in the Ritual; but now I was there, and was apparently as far as ever from knowing what it was which the family had concealed with such elaborate precautions. It is true that I had thrown a light upon the fate of Brunton, but now I had to ascertain how that fate had come upon him, and what part had been played in the matter by the woman who had disappeared. I sat down upon a keg in the corner and thought the whole matter carefully over.

"You know my methods in such cases, Watson. I put myself in the man's place, and, having first gauged his intelligence, I try to imagine how I should myself have proceeded under the same circumstances. In this case the matter was simplified by Brunton's intelligence being quite first-rate, so that it was unnecessary to make any allowance for the personal equation, as the astronomers have dubbed it. He knew that something valuable was concealed. He had spotted the place. He found that the stone which covered it was just too heavy for a man to move unaided. What would he do next? He could not get help from outside, even if he had someone whom he could trust, without the unbarring of doors and considerable risk of detection. It was better, if he could, to have his helpmate inside the house. But whom could he ask? This girl had been devoted to him. A man always finds it hard to realize that he may have finally lost a woman's love, however badly he may have treated her. He would try by a few attentions to make his peace with the girl Howells, and then would engage her as his accomplice. Together they would come at night to the cellar, and their united force would suffice to raise the stone. So far I could follow their actions as if I had actually seen them.

"But for two of them, and one a woman, it must have been heavy work, the raising of that stone. A burly Sussex policeman and I had found it no light job. What would they do to assist them? Probably what I should have done myself. I rose and examined carefully the different billets of wood which were scattered round the floor. Almost at once I came upon what I expected. One piece, about three feet in length, had a very marked indentation at one end, while several were flattened at the sides as if they had been compressed by some considerable weight. Evidently, as they had dragged the stone up, they had thrust the chunks of wood into the chink until at last when the opening was large enough to crawl through, they would hold it open by; a billet placed lengthwise, which might very well become indented at the lower end, since the whole weight of the stone would press it down on to the edge of this other slab. So far I was still on safe ground.

"And now how was I to proceed to reconstruct this midnight drama? Clearly, only one could fit into the hole, and that one was Brunton. The girl must have waited above. Brunton then unlocked the box, handed up the contents presumably—since they were not to be found—and then—and then what happened?

"What smouldering fire of vengeance had suddenly sprung into flame in this passionate Celtic woman's soul when she saw the man who had wronged her—wronged her, perhaps, far more than we suspected—in her power? Was it a chance that the wood had slipped and that the stone had shut Brunton into what had become his sepulchre? Had she only been guilty of silence as to his fate? Or had some sudden blow from her hand dashed the support away and sent the slab crashing down into its place? Be that as it might, I seemed to see that woman's figure still clutching at her treasure trove and flying wildly up the winding stair, with her ears ringing perhaps with the muffled screams from behind her and with the drumming of frenzied hands against the slab of stone which was choking her faithless lover's life out.

"Here was the secret of her blanched face, her shaken nerves, her peals of hysterical laughter on the next morning. But what had been in the box? What had she done with that? Of course, it must have been the old metal and pebbles which my client had dragged from the mere. She had thrown them in there at the first opportunity to remove the last trace of her crime.

"For twenty minutes I had sat motionless, thinking the matter out. Musgrave still stood with a very pale face, swinging his lantern and peering down into the hole.

"'These are coins of Charles the First,' said he, holding out the few which had been in the box; 'you see we were right in fixing our date for the Ritual.'

"'We may find something else of Charles the First,' I cried, as the probable meaning of the first two questions of the Ritual broke suddenly upon me. 'Let me see the contents of the bag which you fished from the mere.'

"We ascended to his study, and he laid the debris before me. I could understand his regarding it as of small importance when I looked at it, for the metal was almost black and the stones lusterless and dull. I rubbed one of them on my sleeve, however, and it glowed afterwards like a spark in the dark hollow of my hand. The metal work was in the form of a double ring, but it had been bent and twisted out of its original shape.

"'You must bear in mind,' said I, 'that the royal party made head in England even after the death of the king, and that when they at last fled they probably left many of their most precious possessions buried behind them, with the intention of returning for them in more peaceful times.'

"'My ancestor, Sir Ralph Musgrave, was a prominent cavalier and the right-hand man of Charles the Second in his wanderings,' said my friend.

"'Ah, indeed!' I answered. 'Well now, I think that really should give us the last link that we wanted. I must congratulate you on coming into the possession, though in rather a tragic manner, of a relic which is of great intrinsic value, but of even greater importance as a historical curiosity.'

"'What is it, then?' he gasped in astonishment.

"'It is nothing less than the ancient crown of the kings of England.'

"'The crown!'

"'Precisely. Consider what the Ritual says. "How does it run?" "Who was it?" "His who is gone." That was after the execution of Charles then, "Who shall have it?" "He who will come." That was Charles the Second, whose advent was already foreseen. There can, I think, be no doubt that this battered and shapeless diadem once encircled the brows of the royal Stuarts.'

"'And how came it in the pond?'

"'Ah, that is a question that will take some time to answer.' And with that I sketched out to him the whole long chain of surmise and of proof which I had constructed. The twilight had closed in and the moon was shining brightly in the sky before my narrative was finished.

"'And how was it then that Charles did not get his crown when he returned?' asked Musgrave, pushing back the relic into its linen bag.

"Ah, there you lay your finger upon the one point which we shall probably never be able to clear up. It is likely that the Musgrave who held the secret died in the interval, and by some oversight left this guide to his descendant without explaining the meaning of it. From that day to this it has been handed down from father to son. Until at last it came within reach of a man who tore its secret out of it and lost his life in the venture.'

"And that's the story of the Musgrave Ritual, Watson. They have the crown down at Hurlstone—though they had some legal bother and a considerable sum to pay before they were allowed to retain it. I am sure that if you mentioned my name they would be happy to show it to you. Of the woman nothing was ever heard, and the probability is that she got away out of England and carried herself and the memory of her crime to some land beyond the seas.

Chapter 6

THE ADVENTURE OF THE REIGATE PUZZLE

It was some time before the health of my friend Mr. Sherlock Holmes recovered from the strain caused by his immense exertions in the spring of '87. The whole question of the Netherland-Sumatra Company and of the colossal schemes of Baron Maupertuis are too recent in the minds of the public, and are too intimately concerned with politics and finance to be fitting subjects for this series of sketches. They led, however, in an indirect fashion to a singular and complex problem which gave my friend an opportunity of demonstrating the value of a fresh weapon among the many with which he waged his lifelong battle against crime.

On referring to my notes I see that it was upon the fourteenth of April that I received a telegram from Lyons which informed me that Holmes was lying ill in the Hotel Dulong. Within twenty-four hours I was in his sickroom and was relieved to find that there was nothing formidable in his symptoms. Even his iron constitution, however, had broken down under the strain of an investigation which had extended over two months, during which period he had never worked less than fifteen hours a day and had more than once, as he assured me, kept to his task for five days at a stretch. Even the triumphant issue of his labours could not save him from reaction after so terrible an exertion, and at a time when Europe was ringing with his name and when his room was literally ankle-deep with congratulatory telegrams I found him a prey to the blackest depression. Even the knowledge that he had succeeded where the police of three countries had failed, and that he had outmanoeuvred at every point the most accomplished swindler in Europe, was insufficient to rouse him from his nervous prostration.

Three days later we were back in Baker Street together; but it was evident that my friend would be much the better for a change, and the thought of a week of spring time in the country was full of attractions to me also. My old friend, Colonel Hayter, who had come under my professional care in Afghanistan, had now taken a house near Reigate in Surrey and had frequently asked me to come down to him upon a visit. On the last occasion he had remarked that if my friend would only come with me he would be glad to extend his hospitality to him also. A little diplomacy was needed, but when Holmes understood that the establishment was a bachelor one, and that he would be allowed the fullest freedom, he fell in with my plans and a week after our return from Lyons we were under the Colonel's roof. Hayter was a fine old soldier who had seen much of the world, and he soon found, as I had expected, that Holmes and he had much in common.

On the evening of our arrival we were sitting in the Colonel's gun room after dinner, Holmes stretched upon the sofa, while Hayter and I looked over his little armory of Eastern weapons.

"By the way," said he suddenly, "I think I'll take one of these pistols upstairs with me in case we have an alarm."

"An alarm!" said I.

"Yes, we've had a scare in this part lately. Old Acton, who is one of our county magnates, had his house broken into last Monday. No great damage done, but the fellows are still at large."

"No clue?" asked Holmes, cocking his eye at the Colonel.

"None as yet. But the affair is a petty one, one of our little country crimes, which must seem too small for your attention, Mr. Holmes, after this great international affair."

Holmes waved away the compliment, though his smile showed that it had pleased him.

"Was there any feature of interest?"

"I fancy not. The thieves ransacked the library and got very little for their pains. The whole place was turned upside down, drawers burst open, and presses ransacked, with the result that an odd volume of Pope's *Homer,* two plated candlesticks, an ivory letter-weight, a small oak barometer, and a ball of twine are all that have vanished."

"What an extraordinary assortment!" I exclaimed.

"Oh, the fellows evidently grabbed hold of everything they could get."

Holmes grunted from the sofa.

"The county police ought to make something of that," said he.

"Why, it is surely obvious that—"

But I held up a warning finger.

"You are here for a rest, my dear fellow. For heaven's sake don't get started on a new problem when your nerves are all in shreds."

Holmes shrugged his shoulders with a glance of comic resignation towards the Colonel, and the talk drifted away into less dangerous channels.

It was destined, however, that all my professional caution should be wasted, for next morning the problem obtruded itself upon us in such a way that it was impossible to ignore it, and our country visit took a turn which neither of us could have anticipated. We were at breakfast when the colonel's butler rushed in with all his propriety shaken out of him.

"Have you heard the news, sir?" He gasped. "At the Cunningham's, sir!"

"Burglary!" cried the Colonel, with his coffee-cup in mid-air.

"Murder!"

The Colonel whistled. "By Jove!" said he. "Who's killed, then? The J. P. or his son?"

"Neither, sir. It was William the coachman. Shot through the heart, sir, and never spoke again."

"Who shot him, then?"

"The burglar, sir. He was off like a shot and got clean away. He'd just broke in at the pantry window when William came on him and met his end in saving his master's property."

"What time?"

"It was last night, sir, somewhere about twelve."

"Ah, then, we'll step over afterwards," said the Colonel, coolly settling down to his breakfast again. "It's a baddish business," he added when the butler had gone; "he's our leading man about here, is old Cunningham, and a very decent fellow too. He'll be cut up over this, for the man has been in his service for years and was a good servant. It's evidently the same villains who broke into Acton's."

"And stole that very singular collection," said Holmes thoughtfully.

"Precisely."

"Hum! It may prove the simplest matter in the world, but all the same at first glance this is just a little curious, is it not? A gang of burglars acting in the country might be expected to vary the scene of their operations, and not to crack two cribs in the same district within a few days. When you spoke last night of taking precautions I remember that it passed through my mind that this was probably the last parish in England to which the thief or thieves would be likely to turn their attention—which shows that I have still much to learn."

"I fancy it's some local practitioner," said the Colonel. "In that case, of course, Acton's and Cunningham's are just the places he would go for, since they are far the largest about here."

"And richest?"

"Well, they ought to be, but they've had a lawsuit for some years which has sucked the blood out of both of them, I fancy. Old Acton has some claim on half Cunningham's estate, and the lawyers have been at it with both hands."

"If it's a local villain there should not be much difficulty in running him down," said Holmes with a yawn. "All right, Watson, I don't intend to meddle."

"Inspector Forrester, sir," said the butler, throwing open the door. The official, a smart, keen-faced young fellow, stepped into the room. "Good morning, Colonel," said he. "I hope I don't intrude, but we hear that Mr. Holmes of Baker Street is here."

The Colonel waved his hand towards my friend, and the inspector bowed.

"We thought that perhaps you would care to step across, Mr. Holmes."

"The fates are against you, Watson," said he, laughing. "We were chatting about the matter when you came in,

Inspector. Perhaps you can let us have a few details." As he leaned back in his chair in the familiar attitude I knew that the case was hopeless.

"We had no clue in the Acton affair. But here we have plenty to go on, and there's no doubt it is the same party in each case. The man was seen."

"Ah!"

"Yes, sir. But he was off like a deer after the shot that killed poor William Kirwan was fired. Mr. Cunningham saw him from the bedroom window, and Mr. Alec Cunningham saw him from the back passage. It was quarter to twelve when the alarm broke out. Mr. Cunningham had just got into bed, and Mr. Alec was smoking a pipe in his dressing gown. They both heard William, the coachman, calling for help, and Mr. Alec ran down to see what was the matter. The back door was open, and as he came to the foot of the stairs he saw two men wrestling together outside. One of them fired a shot, the other dropped, and the murderer rushed across the garden and over the hedge. Mr. Cunningham, looking out of his bedroom, saw the fellow as he gained the road, but lost sight of him at once. Mr. Alec stopped to see if he could help the dying man, and so the villain got clean away. Beyond the fact that he was a middle-sized man and dressed in some dark stuff, we have no personal clue; but we are making energetic inquiries, and if he is a stranger we shall soon find him out."

"What was this William doing there? Did he say anything before he died?"

"Not a word. He lives at the lodge with his mother, and as he was a very faithful fellow we imagine that he walked up to the house with the intention of seeing that all was right there.

Of course this Acton business has put everyone on their guard. The robber must have just burst open the door—the lock has been forced—when William came upon him."

"Did William say anything to his mother before going out?"

"She is very old and deaf, and we can get no information from her. 'The shock has made her half-witted, but I understand that she was never very bright. There is one very important circumstance, however. Look at this!"

He took a small piece of torn paper from a notebook and spread it out upon his knee.

"This was found between the finger and thumb of the dead man. It appears to be a fragment torn from a larger sheet. You will observe that the hour mentioned upon it is the very time at which the poor fellow met his fate. You see that his murderer might have torn the rest of the sheet from him or he might have taken this fragment from the murderer. It reads almost as though it were an appointment."

Holmes took up the scrap of paper, a facsimile of which is here reproduced.

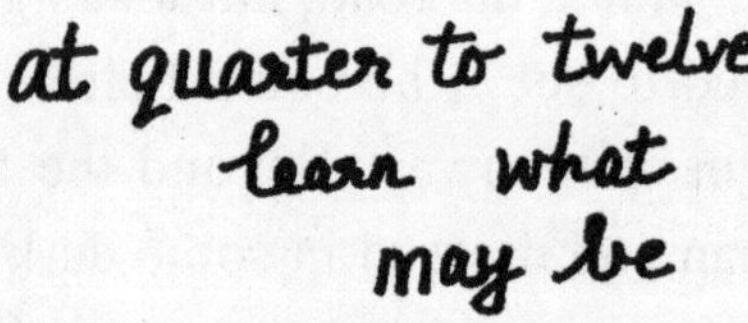
at quarter to twelve
learn what
may be

"Presuming that it is an appointment," continued the inspector, "it is of course a conceivable theory that this William Kirwan, though he had the reputation of being an honest man, may have been in league with the thief. He may have met him there, may even have helped him to break in the door, and then they may have fallen out, between themselves."

"This writing is of extraordinary interest," said Holmes, who had been examining it with intense concentration. "These are much deeper waters than I had thought." He sank his head upon his hands, while the inspector smiled at the effect which his case had had upon the famous London specialist.

"Your last remark," said Holmes presently, "as to the possibility of there being an understanding between the burglar and the servant, and this being a note of appointment from one to the other, is an ingenious and not entirely impossible supposition. But this writing opens up—" He sank his head into his hands again and remained for some minutes in the deepest thought. When he raised his face again I was surprised to see that his cheek was tinged with colour, and his eyes as bright as before his illness. He sprang to his feet with all his old energy.

"I'll tell you what," said he, "I should like to have a quiet little glance into the details of this case. There is something in it which fascinates me extremely. If you will permit me, Colonel, I will leave my friend Watson and you, and I will step round with the inspector to test the truth of one or two little fancies of mine. I will be with you again in half an hour."

An hour and a half had elapsed before the inspector returned alone.

"Mr. Holmes is walking up and down in the field outside," said he.

"He wants us all four to go up to the house together."

"To Mr. Cunningham's?"

"Yes, sir."

"What for?"

The inspector shrugged his shoulders. "I don't quite know, sir. Between ourselves, I think Mr. Holmes has not quite got over his illness yet. He's been behaving very queerly, and he is very much excited."

"I don't think you need alarm yourself," said I. "I have usually found that there was method in his madness."

"Some folk might say there was madness in his method," muttered the inspector. "But he's all on fire to start, Colonel, so we had best go out if you are ready."

We found Holmes pacing up and down in the field, his chin sunk upon his breast, and his hands thrust into his trousers pockets.

"The matter grows in interest," said he. "Watson, your country trip has been a distinct success. I have had a charming morning."

"You have been up to the scene of the crime, I understand," said the Colonel.

"Yes, the inspector and I have made quite a little reconnaissance together."

"Any success?"

"Well, we have seen some very interesting things. I'll tell you what we did as we walk. First of all, we saw the body of this unfortunate man. He certainly died from a revolver wound as reported."

"Had you doubted it, then?"

"Oh, it is as well to test everything. Our inspection was not wasted. We then had an interview with Mr. Cunningham and his son, who were able to point out the exact spot where the murderer had broken through the garden-hedge in his flight. That was of great interest."

"Naturally."

"Then we had a look at this poor fellow's mother. We could get no information from her, however, as she is very old and feeble."

"And what is the result of your investigations?"

"The conviction that the crime is a very peculiar one. Perhaps our visit now may do something to make it less obscure. I think that we are both agreed, Inspector, that the fragment of paper in the dead man's hand, bearing, as it does, the very hour of his death written upon it, is of extreme importance."

"It should give a clue, Mr. Holmes."

"It *does* give a clue. Whoever wrote that note was the man who brought William Kirwan out of his bed at that hour. But where is the rest of that sheet of paper?"

"I examined the ground carefully in the hope of finding it," said the inspector.

"It was torn out of the dead man's hand. Why was someone so anxious to get possession of it? Because it incriminated him. And what would he do with it? Thrust it into his pocket, most likely, never noticing that a corner of it had been left in the grip of the corpse. If we could get the rest of that sheet it is obvious that we should have gone a long way towards solving the mystery."

"Yes, but how can we get at the criminal's pocket before we catch the criminal?"

"Well, well, it was worth thinking over. Then there is another obvious point. The note was sent to William. The man who wrote it could not have taken it; otherwise, of course, he might have delivered his own message by word of mouth. Who brought the note, then? Or did it come through the post?"

"I have made inquiries," said the inspector. "William received a letter by the afternoon post yesterday. The envelope was destroyed by him."

"Excellent!" cried Holmes, clapping the inspector on the back.

"You've seen the postman. It is a pleasure to work with you. Well, here is the lodge, and if you will come up, Colonel, I will show you the scene of the crime."

We passed the pretty cottage where the murdered man had lived and walked up an oak-lined avenue to the fine old Queen Anne house, which bears the date of Malplaquet upon the lintel of the door. Holmes and the inspector led us round it until we came to the side gate, which is separated by a stretch of garden from the hedge which lines the road. A constable was standing at the kitchen door.

"Throw the door open, officer," said Holmes. "Now, it was on those stairs that young Mr. Cunningham stood and saw the two men struggling just where we are. Old Mr. Cunningham was at that window—the second on the left—and he saw the fellow get away just to the left of that bush. So did the son. They are both sure of it on account of the bush. Then Mr. Alec ran out and knelt beside the wounded man. The ground is very hard, you see, and there are no marks to guide us." As he spoke two men came down the garden path, from round the angle of the house. The one was an elderly man, with a strong, deep-lined, heavy-eyed face; the other a dashing young fellow, whose bright, smiling expression and showy dress were in strange contrast with the business which had brought us there.

"Still at it, then?" said he to Holmes. "I thought you Londoners were never at fault. You don't seem to be so very quick, after all."

"Ah, you must give us a little time," said Holmes good-humouredly.

"You'll want it," said young Alec Cunningham. "Why, I don't see that we have any clue at all."

"There's only one," answered the inspector. "We thought that if we could only find—Good heavens, Mr. Holmes! what is the matter?"

My poor friend's face had suddenly assumed the most dreadful expression. His eyes rolled upward, his features writhed in agony, and with a suppressed groan he dropped on his face upon the ground. Horrified at the suddenness and severity of the attack, we carried him into the kitchen, where he lay back in a large chair and breathed heavily for some minutes. Finally, with a shamefaced apology for his weakness, he rose once more.

"Watson would tell you that I have only just recovered from a severe illness," he explained. "I am liable to these sudden nervous attacks."

"Shall I send you home in my trap?" asked old Cunningham.

"Well, since I am here, there is one point on which I should like to feel sure. We can very easily verify it."

"What was it?"

"Well, it seems to me that it is just possible that the arrival of this poor fellow William was not before, but after, the entrance of the burglar into the house. You appear to take it for granted that although the door was forced the robber never got in."

"I fancy that is quite obvious," said Mr. Cunningham gravely.

"Why, my son Alec had not yet gone to bed, and he would certainly have heard anyone moving about."

"Where was he sitting?"

"I was smoking in my dressing room."

"Which window is that?"

"The last on the left, next my father's."

"Both of your lamps were lit, of course?"

"Undoubtedly."

"There are some very singular points here," said Holmes, smiling. "Is it not extraordinary that a burglar—and a burglar who had some previous experience—should deliberately break into a house at a time when he could see from the lights that two of the family were still afoot?"

"He must have been a cool hand."

"Well, of course, if the case were not an odd one we should not have been driven to ask you for an explanation," said young Mr. Alec. "But as to your ideas that the man had robbed the house before William tackled him, I think it a most absurd notion. Wouldn't we have found the place disarranged and missed the things which he had taken?"

"It depends on what the things were," said Holmes. "You must remember that we are dealing with a burglar who is a very peculiar fellow, and who appears to work on lines of his own. Look, for example, at the queer lot of things which he took from Acton's—what was it?—a ball of string, a letter-weight, and I don't know what other odds and ends."

"Well, we are quite in your hands, Mr. Holmes," said old Cunningham. "Anything which you or the inspector may suggest will most certainly be done."

"In the first place," said Holmes, "I should like you to offer a reward—coming from yourself, for the officials may take a little time before they would agree upon the sum, and these things cannot be done too promptly. I have jotted down the form here, if you would not mind signing it. Fifty pounds was quite enough, I thought."

"I would willingly give five hundred," said the J.P., taking the slip of paper and the pencil which Holmes handed to him. "This is not quite correct, however," he added, glancing over the document.

"I wrote it rather hurriedly."

"You see you begin, 'Whereas, at about a quarter to one on Tuesday morning an attempt was made,' and so on. It was at a quarter to twelve, as a matter of fact."

I was pained at the mistake, for I knew how keenly Holmes would feel any slip of the kind. It was his specialty to be accurate as to fact, but his recent illness had shaken him, and this one little incident was enough to show me that he was still far from being himself. He was obviously embarrassed for an instant, while the inspector raised his eyebrows, and Alec Cunningham burst into a laugh. The old gentleman corrected the mistake, however, and handed the paper back to Holmes.

"Get it printed as soon as possible," he said; "I think your idea is an excellent one."

Holmes put the slip of paper carefully away into his pocketbook.

"And now," said he, "it really would be a good thing that we should all go over the house together and make certain that this rather erratic burglar did not, after all, carry anything away with him."

Before entering, Holmes made an examination of the door which had been forced. It was evident that a chisel or strong knife had been thrust in, and the lock forced back with it. We could see the marks in the wood where it had been pushed in.

"You don't use bars, then?" he asked.

"We have never found it necessary."

"You don't keep a dog?"

"Yes, but he is chained on the other side of the house."

"When do the servants go to bed?"

"About ten."

"I understand that William was usually in bed also at that hour?"

"Yes."

"It is singular that on this particular night he should have been up. Now, I should be very glad if you would have the kindness to show us over the house, Mr. Cunningham."

A stone-flagged passage, with the kitchens branching away from it, led by a wooden staircase directly to the first floor of the house. It came out upon the landing opposite to a second more ornamental stair which came up from the front hall. Out of this landing opened the drawing room and several bedrooms, including those of Mr. Cunningham and his son. Holmes walked slowly, taking keen note of the architecture of the house. I could tell from his expression that he was on a hot scent, and yet I could not in the least imagine in what direction his inferences were leading him.

"My good sir," said Mr. Cunningham, with some impatience, "this is surely very unnecessary. That is my room at the end of the stairs and my son's is the one beyond it. I leave it to your judgment whether it was possible for the thief to have come up here without disturbing us."

"You must try round and get on a fresh scent, I fancy," said the son with a rather malicious smile.

"Still, I must ask you to humour me a little further. I should like, for example, to see how far the windows of the bedrooms command the front. This, I understand, is your son's room"—he pushed open the door—"And that, I presume is the dressing room in which he sat smoking when the alarm was given. Where does the window of that look out to?" He stepped across the bedroom, pushed open the door, and glanced round the other chamber.

"I hope that you are satisfied now?" said Mr. Cunningham somewhat tartly.

"Thank you, I think I have seen all that I wished."

"Then if it is really necessary we can go into my room."

"If it is not too much trouble."

The J.P. shrugged his shoulders and led the way into his own chamber, which was a plainly furnished and commonplace room. As we moved across it in the direction of the window, Holmes fell back until he and I were the last of the group. Near the foot of the bed stood a dish of oranges and a carafe of water. As we passed it, Holmes to my unutterable astonishment, leaned over in front of me and deliberately knocked the whole thing over. The glass smashed into a thousand pieces and the fruit rolled about into every corner of the room.

"You've done it now, Watson," said he coolly. "A pretty mess you've made of the carpet."

I stooped in some confusion and began to pick up the fruit, understanding for some reason my companion desired me to take the blame upon myself. The others did the same and set the table on its legs again.

"Hullo!" cried the inspector, "where's he got to?"

Holmes had disappeared.

"Wait here an instant," said young Alec Cunningham. "The fellow is off his head, in my opinion. Come with me, father, and see where he has got to!"

They rushed out of the room, leaving the inspector, the Colonel, and me staring at each other.

"Upon my word, I am inclined to agree with Master Alec," said the official. "It may be the effect of this illness, but it seems to me that—"

His words were cut short by a sudden scream of "Help! Help! Murder!" with a thrill I recognized the voice as that of my friend. I rushed madly from the room on to the landing. The cries, which had sunk down into a hoarse, inarticulate shouting, came from the room which we had first visited. I dashed in, and on into the dressing room beyond. The two Cunninghams were bending over the prostrate figure of Sherlock Holmes, the younger clutching his throat with both hands, while the elder seemed to be twisting one of his wrists. In an instant the three of us had torn them away from him, and Holmes staggered to his feet, very pale and evidently greatly exhausted.

"Arrest these men, Inspector," he gasped.

"On what charge?"

"That of murdering their coachman, William Kirwan."

The inspector stared about him in bewilderment. "Oh, come now, Mr. Holmes," said he at last, "I'm sure you don't really mean to—"

"Tut, man, look at their faces!" cried Holmes curtly.

Never certainly have I seen a plainer confession of guilt upon human countenances. The older man seemed numbed and dazed, with a heavy, sullen expression upon his strongly marked face. The son, on the other hand, had dropped all that jaunty, dashing style which had characterized him, and the ferocity of a dangerous wild beast gleamed in his dark eyes and distorted his handsome features. The inspector said nothing, but, stepping to the door, he blew his whistle. Two of his constables came at the call.

"I have no alternative, Mr. Cunningham," said he. "I trust that this may all prove to be an absurd mistake, but you can see that—Ah, would you? Drop it!" He struck out with his hand, and a revolver which the younger man was in the act of cocking clattered down upon the floor.

"Keep that," said Holmes, quietly putting his foot upon it; "you will find it useful at the trial. But this is what we really wanted." He held up a little crumpled piece of paper.

"The remainder of the sheet!" cried the inspector.

"Precisely."

"And where was it?"

"Where I was sure it must be. I'll make the whole matter clear to you presently. I think, Colonel, that you and Watson might return now, and I will be with you again in an hour at the furthest. The inspector and I must have a word with the prisoners, but you will certainly see me back at luncheon time."

Sherlock Holmes was as good as his word, for about one o'clock he rejoined us in the colonel's smoking-room. He was accompanied by a little elderly gentleman, who was introduced to me as the Mr. Acton whose house had been the scene of the original burglary.

"I wished Mr. Acton to be present while I demonstrated this small matter to you," said Holmes, "for it is natural that he should take a keen interest in the details. I am afraid, my dear Colonel, that you must regret the hour that you took in such a stormy petrel as I am."

"On the contrary," answered the Colonel warmly, "I consider it the greatest privilege to have been permitted to study your methods of working. I confess that they quite surpass my expectations, and that I am utterly unable to account for your result. I have not yet seen the vestige of a clue."

"I am afraid that my explanation may disillusion you, but it has always been my habit to hide none of my methods, either from my friend Watson or from anyone who might take an intelligent interest in them. But, first, as I am rather shaken by the knocking about which I had in the dressing room, I think that I shall help myself to a dash of your brandy, Colonel. My strength has been rather tried of late."

"I trust you had no more of those nervous attacks."

Sherlock Holmes laughed heartily. "We will come to that in its turn," said he. "I will lay an account of the case before you in its due order, showing you the various points which guided me in my decision. Pray interrupt me if there is any inference which is not perfectly clear to you."

"It is of the highest importance in the art of detection to be able to recognize, out of a number of facts, which are incidental and which vital. Otherwise your energy and attention must be dissipated instead of being concentrated. Now, in this case there was not the slightest doubt in my mind from the first that the key of the whole matter must be looked for in the scrap of paper in the dead man's hand."

"Before going into this, I would draw your attention to the fact that, if Alec Cunningham's narrative was correct, and if the assailant, after shooting William Kirwan, had *instantly* fled, then it obviously could not be he who tore the paper from the dead man's hand. But if it was not he, it must have been Alec Cunningham himself, for by the time that the old man had descended several servants were upon the scene. The point is a simple one, but the inspector had overlooked it because he had started with the supposition that these county magnates had had nothing to do with the matter. Now, I make a point of never having any prejudices, and of following docilely wherever fact may lead me, and so, in the very first stage of the investigation, I found myself looking a little askance at the part which had been played by Mr. Alec Cunningham."

"And now I made a very careful examination of the corner of paper which the inspector had submitted to us. It was at once clear to me that it formed part of a very remarkable document. Here it is. Do you not now observe something very suggestive about it?"

"It has a very irregular look," said the Colonel.

"My dear sir," cried Holmes, "there cannot be the least doubt in the world that It has been written by two persons doing alternate words. When I draw your attention to the strong t's of 'at' and 'to,' and ask you to compare them with the weak ones of 'quarter' and 'twelve,' you will instantly recognize the fact. A very brief analysis of these four words would enable you to say with the utmost confidence that the 'learn' and the 'maybe' are written in the stronger hand, and the 'what' in the weaker."

"By jove, it's as clear as day!' cried the colonel. "Why on earth should two men write a letter in such a fashion?"

"Obviously the business was a bad one, and one of the men who distrusted the other was determined that, whatever was done, each should have an equal hand in it. Now, of the two men, it is clear that the one who wrote the 'at' and 'to' was the ringleader."

"How do you get at that?"

"We might deduce it from the mere character of the one hand as compared with the other. But we have more assured reasons than that for supposing it. If you examine this scrap with attention you will come to the conclusion that the man with the stronger hand wrote all his words first, leaving blanks for the other to fill up. These blanks were not always sufficient, and you can see that the second man had a squeeze to fit his 'quarter' in between the 'at' and the 'to', showing that the latter were already written. The man who wrote all his words first is undoubtedly the man who planned the affair."

"Excellent!" cried Mr. Acton.

"But very superficial," said Holmes. "We come now, however, to a point which is of importance. You may not be aware that the deduction of a man's age from his writing is one which has been brought to considerable accuracy by experts. In normal cases one can place a man in his true decade with tolerable confidence. I say normal cases because ill-health and physical weakness reproduce the signs of old age, even when the invalid is a youth. In this case, looking at the bold, strong hand of the one, and the rather broken-backed appearance of the other, which still retains its legibility although the *t's* have begun to lose their crossing, we can say that the one was a young man and the other was advanced in years without being positively decrepit."

"Excellent!" cried Mr. Acton again.

"There is a further point, however, which is subtler and of greater interest. There is something in common between these hands. They belong to men who are blood relatives. It may be most obvious to you in the Greek *e's,* but to me there are many small points which indicate the same thing. I have no doubt at all that a family mannerism can be traced in these two specimens of writing. I am only, of course, giving you the leading results now of my examination of the paper. There were twenty-three other deductions which would be of more interest to experts than to you. They all tend to deepen the impression upon my mind that the Cunninghams, father and son, had written this letter.

"Having got so far, my next step was, of course, to examine into the details of the crime, and to see how far they would help us. I went up to the house with the inspector and saw all that was to be seen. The wound upon the dead man was, as I was able to determine with absolute confidence, fired from a revolver at the distance of something over four yards. There was no powder-blackening on the clothes. Evidently, therefore, Alec Cunningham had lied when he said that the two men were struggling when the shot was fired. Again, both father and son agreed as to the place where the man escaped into the road. At that point, however, as it happens, there is a broadish ditch, moist at the bottom. As there were no indications of boot-marks about this ditch, I was absolutely sure not only that the Cunninghams had again lied but that there had never been any unknown man upon the scene at all.

"And now I have to consider the motive of this singular crime. To get at this, I endeavoured first of all to solve the reason of the original burglary at Mr. Acton's. I understood, from something which the Colonel told us, that a lawsuit had been going on between you, Mr. Acton, and the Cunninghams. Of course, it instantly occurred to me that they had broken into your library with the intention of getting at some document which might be of importance in the case."

"Precisely so," said Mr. Acton. "There can be no possible doubt as to their intentions. I have the clearest claim upon half of their present estate, and if they could have found a single paper—which, fortunately, was in the strongbox of my solicitors—they would undoubtedly have crippled our case."

"There you are," said Holmes, smiling. "It was a dangerous, reckless attempt in which I seem to trace the influence of young Alec. Having found nothing, they tried to divert suspicion by making it appear to be an ordinary burglary, to which end they carried off whatever they could lay their hands upon. That is all clear enough, but there was much that was still obscure. What I wanted, above all, was to get the missing part of that note. I was certain that Alec had torn it out of the dead man's hand, and almost certain that he must have thrust it into the pocket of his dressing gown. Where else could he have put it? The only question was whether it was still there. It was worth an effort to find out, and for that object we all went up to the house."

"The Cunninghams joined us, as you doubtless remember, outside the kitchen door. It was, of course, of the very first importance that they should not be reminded of the existence of this paper, otherwise they would naturally destroy it without delay. The inspector was about to tell them the importance which we attached to it when, by the luckiest chance in the world, I tumbled down in a sort of fit and so changed the conversation."

"Good heavens!" cried the Colonel, laughing, "do you mean to say all our sympathy was wasted and your fit an imposture?"

"Speaking professionally, it was admirably done," cried I, looking in amazement at this man who was forever confounding me with some new phase of his astuteness.

"It is an art which is often useful," said he. "When I recovered I managed, by a device which had perhaps some little merit of ingenuity, to get old Cunningham to write the word 'twelve,' so that I might compare it with the 'twelve' upon the paper."

"Oh, what an ass I have been!" I exclaimed.

"I could see that you were commiserating me over my weakness," said Holmes, laughing. "I was sorry to cause you the sympathetic pain which I know that you felt. We then went upstairs together, and, having entered the room and seen the dressing gown hanging up behind the door, I contrived, by upsetting a table, to engage their attention for the moment and slipped back to examine the pockets. I had hardly got the paper, however—which was, as I had expected, in one of them—when the two Cunninghams were on me, and would, I verily believe, have murdered me then and there but for your prompt and friendly aid. As it is, I feel that young man's grip on my throat now, and the father has twisted my wrist round in the effort to get the paper out of my hand. They saw that I must know all about it, you see, and the sudden change from absolute security to complete despair made them perfectly desperate.

"I had a little talk with old Cunningham afterwards as to the motive of the crime. He was tractable enough, though his son was a perfect demon, ready to blow out his own or anybody else's brains if he could have got to his revolver. When Cunningham saw that the case against him was so strong he lost all heart and made a clean breast of everything. It seems that William had secretly followed his two masters on the night when they made their raid upon Mr. Acton's and, having thus got them into his power, proceeded, under threats of exposure, to levy blackmail upon them. Mr Alec, however, was a dangerous man to play games of that sort with. It was a stroke of positive genius on his part to see in the burglary scare which was convulsing the countryside an opportunity of plausibly getting rid of the man whom he feared. William was decoyed up and shot, and had they only got the whole of the note and paid a little more attention to detail in their accessories, it is very possible that suspicion might never have been aroused."

"And the note?" I asked.

Sherlock Holmes placed the subjoined paper before us.

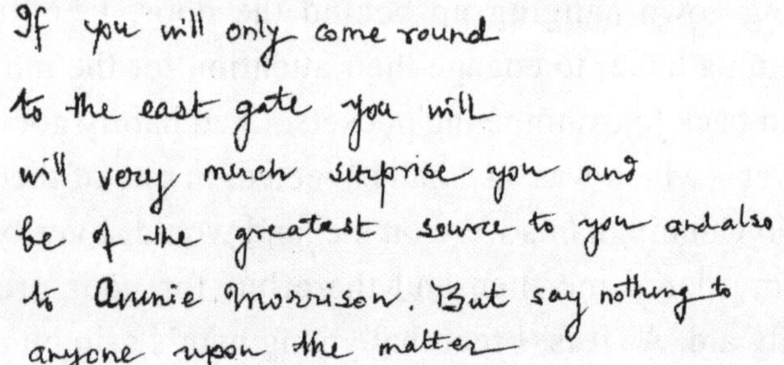

If you will only come round
to the east gate you will
will very much surprise you and
be of the greatest source to you and also
to Annie Morrison. But say nothing to
anyone upon the matter

"It is very much the sort of thing that I expected," said he. "Of course, we do not yet know what the relations may have been between Alec Cunningham, William Kirwan, and Annie Morrison. The result shows that the trap was skilfully baited. I am sure that you cannot fail to be delighted with the traces of heredity shown in the *p*'s and in the tails of the *g*'s. The absence of the *i*-dots in the old man's writing is also most characteristic. Watson, I think our quiet rest in the country has been a distinct success, and I shall certainly return much invigorated to Baker Street tomorrow."

Chapter 7

THE ADVENTURE OF THE CROOKED MAN

ONE summer night, a few months after my marriage, I was seated by my own hearth smoking a last pipe and nodding over a novel, for my day's work had been an exhausting one. My wife had already gone upstairs, and the sound of the locking of the hall door some time before told me that the servants had also retired. I had risen from my seat and was knocking out the ashes of my pipe when I suddenly heard the clang of the bell.

I looked at the clock. It was a quarter to twelve. This could not be a visitor at so late an hour. A patient evidently, and possibly an all-night sitting. With a wry face I went out into the hall and opened the door. To my astonishment it was Sherlock Holmes who stood upon my step.

" Ah, Watson," said he, "I hoped that I might not be too late to catch you."

"My dear fellow, pray come in."

"You look surprised, and no wonder! Relieved, too, I fancy! Hum! You still smoke the Arcadia mixture of your bachelor days, then! There's no mistaking that fluffy ash upon your coat. It's easy to tell that you have been accustomed to wear a uniform, Watson. You'll never pass as a pure-bred civilian as long as you keep that habit of carrying your handkerchief in your sleeve. Could you put me up tonight?"

"With pleasure."

"You told me that you had bachelor quarters for one, and I see that you have no gentleman visitor at present. Your hat-stand proclaims as much."

"I shall be delighted if you will stay."

"Thank you. I'll fill the vacant peg then. Sorry to see that you've had the British workman in the house. He's a token of evil. Not the drains, I hope?"

"No, the gas."

"Ah! He has left two nail-marks from his boot upon your linoleum just where the light strikes it. No, thank you, I had some supper at Waterloo, but I'll smoke a pipe with you with pleasure."

I handed him my pouch, and he seated himself opposite to me and smoked for some time in silence. I was well aware that nothing but business of importance would have brought him to me at such an hour, so I waited patiently until he should come round to it.

"I see that you are professionally rather busy just now," said he, glancing very keenly across at me.

"Yes, I've had a busy day," I answered. "It may seem very foolish in your eyes," I added, "but really I don't know how you deduced it."

Holmes chuckled to himself.

"I have the advantage of knowing your habits, my dear Watson," said he. "When your round is a short one you walk, and when it is a long one you use a hansom. As I perceive that your boots, although used, are by no means dirty, I cannot doubt that you are at present busy enough to justify the hansom."

"Excellent!" I cried.

"Elementary," said he. "It is one of those instances where the reasoner can produce an effect which seems remarkable to his neighbour, because the latter has missed the one little point which is the basis of the deduction. The same may be said, my dear fellow, for the effect of some of these little sketches of yours, which is entirely meretricious, depending as it does upon your retaining in your own hands some factors in the problem which are never imparted to the reader. Now, at present I am in the position of these same readers, for I hold in this hand several threads of one of the strangest cases which ever perplexed a man's brain, and yet I lack the one or two which are needful to complete my theory. But I'll have them, Watson, I'll have them!" His eyes kindled and a slight flush sprang into his thin cheeks. For an instant the veil had lifted upon his keen, intense nature, but for an instant only. When I glanced again his face had resumed that red-Indian composure which had made so many regard him as a machine rather than a man.

"The problem presents features of interest," said he. "I may even say exceptional features of interest. I have already looked into the matter, and have come, as I think, within sight of my solution. If you could accompany me in that last step you might be of considerable service to me."

"I should be delighted."

"Could you go as far as Aldershot tomorrow?"

"I have no doubt Jackson would take my practice."

"Very good. I want to start by the 11:10 from Waterloo."

"That would give me time."

"Then, if you are not too sleepy, I will give you a sketch of what has happened, and of what remains to be done."

"I was sleepy before you came. I am quite wakeful now."

"I will compress the story as far as may be done without omitting anything vital to the case. It is conceivable that you may even have read some account of the matter. It is the supposed murder of Colonel Barclay, of the Royal Munsters, at Aldershot, which I am investigating."

"I have heard nothing of it."

"It has not excited much attention yet, except locally. The facts are only two days old. Briefly they are these:

The Royal Munsters is, as you know, one of the most famous Irish regiments in the British Army. It did wonders both in the Crimea and the Mutiny, and has since that time distinguished itself upon every possible occasion. It was commanded up to Monday night by James Barclay, a gallant veteran, who started as a full private, was raised to commissioned rank for his bravery at the time of the Mutiny, and so lived to command the regiment in which he had once carried a musket."

"Colonel Barclay had married at the time when he was a sergeant, and his wife, whose maiden name was Miss Nancy Devoy, was the daughter of a former colour-sergeant in the same corps. There was, therefore, as can be imagined, some little social friction when the young couple (for they were still young) found themselves in their new surroundings. They appear, however, to have quickly adapted themselves, and Mrs. Barclay has always, I understand, been as popular with the ladies of the regiment as her husband was with his brother officers. I may add that she was a woman of great beauty, and that even now, when she has been married for upward of thirty years, she is still of a striking and queenly appearance.

"Colonel Barclay's family life appears to have been a uniformly happy one. Major Murphy, to whom I owe most of my facts, assures me that he has never heard of any misunderstanding between the pair. On the whole, he thinks that Barclay's devotion to his wife was greater than his wife's to Barclay. He was acutely uneasy if he were absent from her for a day. She, on the other hand, though devoted and faithful, was less obtrusively affectionate. But they were regarded in the regiment as the very model of a middle-aged couple. There was absolutely nothing in their mutual relations to prepare people for the tragedy which was to follow.

"Colonel Barclay himself seems to have had some singular traits in his character. He was a dashing, jovial old soldier in his usual mood, but there were occasions on which he seemed to show himself capable of considerable violence and vindictiveness. This side of his nature, however, appears never to have been turned towards his wife. Another fact which had struck Major Murphy and three out of five of the other officers with whom I conversed was the singular sort of depression which came upon him at times. As the major expressed it, the smile had often been struck from his mouth, as if by some invisible hand, when he has been joining in the gaieties and chaff of the mess-table. For days on end, when the mood was on him, he has been sunk in the deepest gloom. This and a certain tinge of superstition were the only unusual traits in his character which his brother officers had observed. The latter peculiarity took the form of a dislike to being left alone, especially after dark. This puerile feature in a nature which was conspicuously manly had often given rise to comment and conjecture.

"The first battalion of the Royal Munsters (which is the old One Hundred and Seventeenth) has been stationed at Aldershot for some years. The married officers live out of barracks, and the Colonel has during all this time occupied a villa called 'Lachine', about half a mile from the north camp. The house stands in its own grounds, but the west side of it is not more than thirty yards from the highroad. A coachman and two maids form the staff of servants. These working people with their master and mistress were the sole occupants of Lachine, for the Barclays had no children, nor was it usual for them to have resident visitors.

"Now for the events at Lachine between nine and ten on the evening of last Monday.

"Mrs. Barclay was, it appears, a member of the Roman Catholic Church and had interested herself very much in the establishment of the Guild of St. George, which was formed in connection with the Watt Street Chapel for the purpose of supplying the poor with cast-off clothing. A meeting of the Guild had been held that evening at eight, and Mrs. Barclay had hurried over her dinner in order to be present at it. When leaving the house she was heard by the coachman to make some commonplace remark to her husband, and to assure him that she would be back before very long. She then called for Miss Morrison, a young lady who lives in the next villa, and the two went off together to their meeting. It lasted forty minutes, and at a quarter-past nine Mrs. Barclay returned home, having left Miss Morrison at her door as she passed.

"There is a room which is used as a morning room at Lachine. This faces the road and opens by a large glass folding-door on to the lawn. The lawn is thirty yards across and is only divided from the highway by a low wall with an iron rail above it. It was into this room that Mrs. Barclay went upon her return. The blinds were not down, for the room was seldom used in the evening, but Mrs. Barclay herself lit the lamp and then rang the bell, asking Jane Stewart, the housemaid, to bring her a cup of tea, which was quite contrary to her usual habits. The Colonel had been sitting in the dining room, but, hearing that his wife had returned, he joined her in the morning room. The coachman saw him cross the hall and enter it. He was never seen again alive.

"The tea which had been ordered was brought up at the end of ten minutes; but the maid, as she approached the door, was surprised to hear the voices of her master and mistress in furious altercation. She knocked without receiving any answer, and even turned the handle, but only to find that the door was locked upon the inside. Naturally enough she ran down to tell the cook, and the two women with the coachman came up into the hall and listened to the dispute which was still raging. They all agreed that only two voices were to be heard, those of Barclay and of his wife. Barclay's remarks were subdued and abrupt so that none of them were audible to the listeners. The lady's, on the other hand, were most bitter, and when she raised her voice could be plainly heard. 'You coward!' she repeated over and over again. 'What can be done now? What can be done now? Give me back my life. I will never so much as breathe the same air with you again! You coward! You coward!' Those were scraps of her conversation, ending in a sudden dreadful cry in the man's voice, with a crash, and a piercing scream from the woman. Convinced that some tragedy had occurred, the coachman rushed to the door and strove to force it, while scream after scream issued from within. He was unable, however, to make his way in, and the maids were too distracted with fear to be of any assistance to him. A sudden thought struck him, however, and he ran through the hall door and round to the lawn upon which the long French windows open. One side of the window was open, which I understand was quite usual in the summertime, and he passed without difficulty into the room. His mistress had ceased to scream and was stretched insensible upon a couch, while with his feet tilted over the side of an armchair, and his head upon the ground near the corner of the fender, was lying the unfortunate soldier stone dead in a pool of his own blood.

"Naturally, the coachman's first thought, on finding that he could do nothing for his master, was to open the door. But here an unexpected and singular difficulty presented itself. The key was not in the inner side of the door, nor could he find it anywhere in the room. He went out again, therefore, through the window, and, having obtained the help of a policeman and of a medical man, he returned. The lady, against whom naturally the strongest suspicion rested, was removed to her room, still in a state of insensibility. The colonel's body was then placed upon the sofa and a careful examination made of the scene of the tragedy.

"The injury from which the unfortunate veteran was suffering was found to be a jagged cut some two inches long at the back part of his head, which had evidently been caused by a violent blow from a blunt weapon. Nor was it difficult to guess what that weapon may have been. Upon the floor, close to the body, was lying a singular club of hard carved wood with a bone handle. The Colonel possessed a varied collection of weapons brought from the different countries in which he had fought, and it is conjectured by the police that this club was among his trophies. The servants deny having seen it before, but among the numerous curiosities in the house it is possible that it may have been overlooked. Nothing else of importance was discovered in the room by the police, save the inexplicable fact that neither upon Mrs. Barclay's person nor upon that of the victim nor in any part of the room was the missing key to be found. The door had eventually to be opened by a locksmith from Aldershot.

"That was the state of things, Watson, when upon the Tuesday morning I, at the request of Major Murphy, went down to Aldershot to supplement the efforts of the police. I think that you will acknowledge that the problem was already one of interest, but my observations soon made me realize that it was in truth much more extraordinary than would at first sight appear.

"Before examining the room I cross-questioned the servants, but only succeeded in eliciting the facts which I have already stated. One other detail of interest was remembered by Jane Stewart, the housemaid. You will remember that on hearing the sound of the quarrel she descended and returned with the other servants. On that first occasion, when she was alone, she says that the voices of her master and mistress were sunk so low that she could hardly hear anything, and judged by their tones rather than their words that they had fallen out. On my pressing her however, she remembered that she heard the word David uttered twice by the lady. The point is of the utmost importance as guiding us towards the reason of the sudden quarrel. The Colonel's name, you remember, was James.

"There was one thing in the case which had made the deepest impression both upon the servants and the police. This was the contortion of the Colonel's face. It had set, according to their account, into the most dreadful expression of fear and horror which a human countenance is capable of assuming. More than one person fainted at the mere sight of him, so terrible was the effect. It was quite certain that he had foreseen his fate, and that it had caused him the utmost horror. This, of course, fitted in well enough with the police theory, if the Colonel could have seen his wife making a murderous attack upon him. Nor was the fact of the wound being on the back of his head a fatal objection to this, as he might have turned to avoid the blow. No information could be got from the lady herself, who was temporarily insane from an acute attack of brain-fever.

"From the police I learned that Miss Morrison, who you remember went out that evening with Mrs. Barclay, denied having any knowledge of what it was which had caused the ill-humour in which her companion had returned.

"Having gathered these facts, Watson, I smoked several pipes over them, trying to separate those which were crucial from others which were merely incidental. There could be no question that the most distinctive and suggestive point in the case was the singular disappearance of the door-key. A most careful search had failed to discover it in the room. Therefore it must have been taken from it. But neither the Colonel nor the colonel's wife could have taken it. That was perfectly clear. Therefore a third person must have entered the room. And that third person could only have come in through the window. It seemed to me that a careful examination of the room and the lawn might possibly reveal some traces of this mysterious individual. You know my methods, Watson. There was not one of them which I did not apply to the inquiry. And it ended by my discovering traces, but very different ones from those which I had expected. There had been a man in the room, and he had crossed the lawn coming from the road. I was able to obtain five very clear impressions of his footmarks: one in the roadway itself, at the point where he had climbed the low wall, two on the lawn, and two very faint ones upon the stained boards near the window where he had entered. He had apparently rushed across the lawn, for his toe marks were much deeper than his heels. But it was not the man who surprised me. It was his companion."

"His companion!"

Holmes pulled a large sheet of tissue-paper out of his pocket and carefully unfolded it upon his knee.

"What do you make of that?" he asked.

The paper was covered with the tracings of the footmarks of some small animal. It had five well-marked footpads, an indication of long nails, and the whole print might be nearly as large as a dessert-spoon.

"It's a dog," said I.

"Did you ever hear of a dog running up a curtain? I found distinct traces that this creature had done so."

"A monkey, then?"

"But it is not the print of a monkey."

"What can it be, then?"

"Neither dog nor cat nor monkey nor any creature that we are familiar with. I have tried to reconstruct it from the measurements. Here are four prints where the beast has been standing motionless. You see that it is no less than fifteen inches from fore-foot to hind. Add to that the length of neck and head, and you get a creature not much less than two feet long—probably more if there is any tail. But now observe this other measurement. The animal has been moving, and we have the length of its stride. In each case it is only about three inches. You have an indication, you see, of a long body with very short legs attached to it. It has not been considerate enough to leave any of its hair behind it. But its general shape must be what I have indicated, and it can run up a curtain, and it is carnivorous."

"How do you deduce that?"

"Because it ran up the curtain. A canary's cage was hanging in the window, and its aim seems to have been to get at the bird."

"Then what was the beast?"

"Ah, if I could give it a name it might go a long way towards solving the case. On the whole, it was probably some creature of the weasel and stoat tribe—and yet it is larger than any of these that I have seen."

"But what had it to do with the crime?"

"That, also, is still obscure. But we have learned a good deal, you perceive. We know that a man stood in the road looking at the quarrel between the Barclays—the blinds were up and the room lighted. We know, also, that he ran across the lawn, entered the room, accompanied by a strange animal, and that he either struck the Colonel or, as is equally possible, that the Colonel fell down from sheer fright at the sight of him, and cut his head on the corner of the fender. Finally we have the curious fact that the intruder carried away the key with him when he left."

"Your discoveries seem to have left the business more obscure than it was before," said I.

"Quite so. They undoubtedly showed that the affair was much deeper than was at first conjectured. I thought the matter over, and I came to the conclusion that I must approach the case from another aspect. But really, Watson, I am keeping you up, and I might just as well tell you all this on our way to Aldershot tomorrow."

"Thank you, you have gone rather too far to stop."

"It is quite certain that when Mrs. Barclay left the house at half past seven she was on good terms with her husband. She was never, as I think I have said, ostentatiously affectionate, but she was heard by the coachman chatting with the Colonel in a friendly fashion. Now, it was equally certain that, immediately on her return, she had gone to the room in which she was least likely to see her husband, had flown to tea as an agitated woman will, and finally, on his coming in to her, had broken into violent recriminations. Therefore something had occurred between seven-thirty and nine o'clock which had completely altered her feelings towards him. But Miss Morrison had been with her during the whole of that hour and a half. It was absolutely certain, therefore, in spite of her denial, that she must know something of the matter."

"My first conjecture was that possibly there had been some passages between this young lady and the old soldier, which the former had now confessed to the wife. That would account for the angry return, and also for the girl's denial that anything had occurred. Nor would it be entirely incompatible with most of the words overheard. But there was the reference to David, and there was the known affection of the Colonel for his wife to weigh against it, to say nothing of the tragic intrusion of this other man, which might, of course, be entirely disconnected with what had gone before. It was not easy to pick one's steps, but, on the whole, I was inclined to dismiss the idea that there had been anything between the Colonel and Miss Morrison, but more than ever convinced that the young lady held the clue as to what it was which had turned Mrs. Barclay to hatred of her husband. I took the obvious course, therefore, of calling upon Miss M., of explaining to her that I was perfectly certain that she held the facts in her possession, and of assuring her that her friend, Mrs. Barclay, might find herself in the dock upon a capital charge unless the matter were cleared up."

"Miss Morrison is a little ethereal slip of a girl, with timid eyes and blond hair, but I found her by no means wanting in shrewdness and common sense. She sat thinking for some time after I had spoken, and then, turning to me with a brisk air of resolution, she broke into a remarkable statement which I will condense for your benefit.

"'I promised my friend that I would say nothing of the matter, and a promise is a promise,' said she; 'but if I can really help her when so serious a charge is laid against her, and when her own mouth, poor darling, is closed by illness, then I think I am absolved from my promise. I will tell you exactly what happened upon Monday evening.'

"'We were returning from the Watt Street Mission about a quarter to nine o'clock. On our way we had to pass through Hudson Street, which is a very quiet thoroughfare. There is only one lamp in it, upon the left-hand side, and as we approached this lamp I saw a man coming towards us with his back very bent, and something like a box slung over one of his shoulders. He appeared to be deformed, for he carried his head low and walked with his knees bent. We were passing him when he raised his face to look at us in the circle of light thrown by the lamp, and as he did so he stopped and screamed out in a dreadful voice, "My God, it's Nancy!" Mrs. Barclay turned as white as death and would have fallen down had the dreadful-looking creature not caught hold of her. I was going to call for the police, but she, to my surprise, spoke quite civilly to the fellow.

"'I thought you had been dead this thirty years, Henry,' said she in a shaking voice.

"'So I have,' said he, and it was awful to hear the tones that he said it in. He had a very dark, fearsome face, and a gleam in his eyes that comes back to me in my dreams. His hair and whiskers were shot with gray, and his face was all crinkled and puckered like a withered apple.

"'Just walk on a little way, dear,' said Mrs. Barclay; 'I want to have a word with this man. There is nothing to be afraid of.' She tried to speak boldly, but she was still deadly pale and could hardly get her words out for the trembling of her lips.

"I did as she asked me, and they talked together for a few minutes. Then she came down the street with her eyes blazing, and I saw the crippled wretch standing by the lamp-post and shaking his clenched fists in the air as if he were mad with rage. She never said a word until we were at the door here, when she took me by the hand and begged me to tell no one what had happened.

"'It's an old acquaintance of mine who has come down in the world," said she. When I promised her I would say nothing she kissed me, and I have never seen her since. I have told you now the whole truth, and if I withheld it from the police it is because I did not realize then the danger in which my dear friend stood. I know that it can only be to her advantage that everything should be known.

"There was her statement, Watson, and to me, as you can imagine, it was like a light on a dark night. Everything which had been disconnected before began at once to assume its true place, and I had a shadowy presentiment of the whole sequence of events. My next step obviously was to find the man who had produced such a remarkable impression upon Mrs. Barclay. If he were still in Aldershot it should not be a very difficult matter. There are not such a very great number of civilians, and a deformed man was sure to have attracted attention. I spent a day in the search, and by evening—this very evening, Watson—I had run him down. The man's name is Henry Wood, and he lives in lodgings in this same street in which the ladies met him. He has only been five days in the place. In the character of a registration-agent I had a most interesting gossip with his landlady. The man is by trade a conjurer and performer, going round the canteens after night-fall, and giving a little entertainment at each. He carries some creature about with him in that box, about which the landlady seemed to be in considerable trepidation, for she had never seen an animal like it. He uses it in some of his tricks according to her account. So much the woman was able to tell me, and also that it was a wonder the man lived, seeing how twisted he was, and that he spoke in a strange tongue sometimes, and that for the last two nights she had heard him groaning and weeping in his bedroom. He was all right, as far as money went, but in his deposit he had given her what looked like a bad florin. She showed it to me, Watson, and it was an Indian rupee.

"So now, my dear fellow, you see exactly how we stand and why it is I want you. It is perfectly plain that after the ladies parted from this man he followed them at a distance, that he saw the quarrel between husband and wife through the window, that he rushed in, and that the creature which he carried in his box got loose. That is all very certain. But he is the only person in this world who can tell us exactly what happened in that room."

" And you intend to ask him?"

"Most certainly—but in the presence of a witness."

"And I am the witness?"

"If you will be so good. If he can clear the matter up, well and good. If he refuses, we have no alternative but to apply for a warrant."

"But how do you know he'll be there when we return?"

"You may be sure that I took some precautions. I have one of my Baker Street boys mounting guard over him who would stick to him like a burr, go where he might. We shall find him in Hudson Street tomorrow, Watson, and meanwhile I should be the criminal myself if kept you out of bed any longer."

It was midday when we found ourselves at the scene of the tragedy, and, under my companion's guidance, we made our way at once to Hudson Street. In spite of his capacity for concealing his emotions, I could easily see that Holmes was in a state of suppressed excitement, while I was myself tingling with that half-sporting, half-intellectual pleasure which I invariably experienced when I associated myself with him in his investigations.

"This is the street," said he as we turned into a short thoroughfare lined with plain two-storied brick houses. "Ah, here is Simpson to report."

"He's in all right, Mr. Holmes," cried a small street Arab, running up to us.

"Good, Simpson " said Holmes, patting him on the head. "Come along, Watson. This is the house." He sent in his card with a message that he had come on important business, and a moment later we were face to face with the man whom we had come to see. In spite of the warm weather he was crouching over a fire, and the little room was like an oven. The man sat all twisted and huddled in his chair in a way which gave an indescribable impression of deformity; but the face which he turned towards us, though worn and swarthy, must at some time have been remarkable for its beauty. He looked suspiciously at us now out of yellow-shot, bilious eyes, and, without speaking or rising, he waved towards two chairs.

"Mr. Henry Wood, late of India, I believe," said Sherlock Holmes affably.

"I've come over this little matter of Colonel Barclay's death."

"What should I know about that?"

"That's what I want to ascertain. You know, I suppose, that unless the matter is cleared up, Mrs. Barclay, who is an old friend of yours, will in all probability be tried for murder."

The man gave a violent start.

"I don't know who you are," he cried, "nor how you come to know what you do know, but will you swear that this is true that you tell me?"

"Why, they are only waiting for her to come to her senses to arrest her."

"My God! Are you in the police yourself?"

"No"

"What business is it of yours, then?"

"It's every man's business to see justice done."

"You can take my word that she is innocent."

"Then you are guilty."

"No, I am not."

"Who killed Colonel James Barclay, then?"

"It was a just Providence that killed him. But, mind you this, that if I had knocked his brains out, as it was in my heart to do, he would have had no more than his due from my hands. If his own guilty conscience had not struck him down it is likely enough that I might have had his blood upon my soul. You want me to tell the story. Well, I don't know why I shouldn't, for there's no cause for me to be ashamed of it.

"It was in this way, sir. You see me now with my back like a camel and my ribs all awry, but there was a time when Corporal Henry Wood was the smartest man in the One Hundred and Seventeenth foot. We were in India, then, in cantonments, at a place we'll call Bhurtee. Barclay, who died the other day, was sergeant in the same company as myself, and the belle of the regiment, ay, and the finest girl that ever had the breath of life between her lips, was Nancy Devoy, the daughter of the colour-sergeant. There were two men that loved her, and one that she loved, and you'll smile when you look at this poor thing huddled before the fire and hear me say that it was for my good looks that she loved me.

"Well, though I had her heart, her father was set upon her marrying Barclay. I was a harum-scarum, reckless lad, and he had had an education and was already marked for the sword-belt. But the girl held true to me, and it seemed that I would have had her when the Mutiny broke out, and all hell was loose in the country.

"We were shut up in Bhurtee, the regiment of us with half a battery of artillery, a company of Sikhs, and a lot of civilians and women-folk. There were ten thousand rebels round us, and they were as keen as a set of terriers round a rat-cage. About the second week of it our water gave out, and it was a question whether we could communicate with General Neill's column, which was moving up-country. It was our only chance, for we could not hope to fight our way out with all the women and children, so I volunteered to go out and to warn General Neill of our danger. My offer was accepted, and I talked it over with Sergeant Barclay, who was supposed to know the ground better than any other man, and who drew up a route by which I might get through the rebel lines. At ten o'clock the same night I started off upon my journey. There were a thousand lives to save, but it was of only one that I was thinking when I dropped over the wall that night.

"My way ran down a dried-up watercourse, which we hoped would screen me from the enemy's sentries; but as I crept round the corner of it I walked right into six of them, who were crouching down in the dark waiting for me. In an instant I was stunned with a blow and bound hand and foot. But the real blow was to my heart and not to my head, for as I came to and listened to as much as I could understand of their talk, I heard enough to tell me that my comrade, the very man who had arranged the way I was to take, had betrayed me by means of a native servant into the hands of the enemy.

"Well, there's no need for me to dwell on that part of it. You know now what James Barclay was capable of. Bhurtee was relieved by Neill next day, but the rebels took me away with them in their retreat, and it was many a long year before ever I saw a white face again. I was tortured and tried to get away, and was captured and tortured again. You can see for yourselves the state in which I was left. Some of them that fled into Nepaul took me with them, and then afterwards I was up past Darjeeling. The hill-folk up there murdered the rebels who had me, and I became their slave for a time until I escaped; but instead of going south I had to go north, until I found myself among the Afghans. There I wandered about for many a year, and at last came back to the Punjab, where I lived mostly among the natives and picked up a living by the conjuring tricks that I had learned. What use was it for me, a wretched cripple, to go back to England or to make myself known to my old comrades? Even my wish for revenge would not make me do that. I had rather that Nancy and my old pals should think of Harry Wood as having died with a straight back, than see him living and crawling with a stick like a chimpanzee. They never doubted that I was dead, and I meant that they never should. I heard that Barclay had married Nancy, and that he was rising rapidly in the regiment, but even that did not make me speak.

"But when one gets old one has a longing for home. For years I've been dreaming of the bright green fields and the hedges of England. At last I determined to see them before I died. I saved enough to bring me across, and then I came here where the soldiers are, for I know their ways and how to amuse them and so earn enough to keep me."

"Your narrative is most interesting," said Sherlock Holmes. "I have already heard of your meeting with Mrs. Barclay, and your mutual recognition. You then, as I understand, followed her home and saw through the window an altercation between her husband and her, in which she doubtless cast his conduct to you in his teeth. Your own feelings overcame you, and you ran across the lawn and broke in upon them."

"I did, sir, and at the sight of me he looked as I have never seen a man look before, and over he went with his head on the fender. But he was dead before he fell. I read death on his face as plain as I can read that text over the fire. The bare sight of me was like a bullet through his guilty heart."

" And then?"

"Then Nancy fainted, and I caught up the key of the door from her hand, intending to unlock it and get help. But as I was doing it, it seemed to me better to leave it alone and get away, for the thing might look black against me, and anyway my secret would be out if I were taken. In my haste I thrust the key into my pocket, and dropped my stick while I was chasing Teddy, who had run up the curtain. When I got him into his box, from which he had slipped, I was off as fast as I could run."

"Who's Teddy?" asked Holmes.

The man leaned over and pulled up the front of a kind of hutch in the corner. In an instant out there slipped a beautiful reddish-brown creature, thin and lithe, with the legs of a stoat, a long, thin nose, and a pair of the finest red eyes that ever I saw in an animal's head.

"It's a mongoose," I cried.

"Well, some call them that, and some call them ichneumon," said the man. "Snake-catcher is what I call them, and Teddy is amazing quick on cobras. I have one here without the fangs, and Teddy catches it every night to please the folk in the canteen."

"Any other point, sir?"

"Well, we may have to apply to you again if Mrs. Barclay should prove to be in serious trouble."

"In that case, of course, I'd come forward."

"But if not, there is no object in raking up this scandal against a dead man, foully as he has acted. You have at least the satisfaction of knowing that for thirty years of his life his conscience bitterly reproached him for his wicked deed. Ah, there goes Major Murphy on the other side of the street. Goodbye, Wood. I want to learn if anything has happened since yesterday."

We were in time to overtake the major before he reached the corner.

"Ah, Holmes," he said, "I suppose you have heard that all this fuss has come to nothing?"

"What then?"

"The inquest is just over. The medical evidence showed conclusively that death was due to apoplexy. You see it was quite a simple case, after all."

"Oh, remarkably superficial," said Holmes, smiling. "Come, Watson, I don't think we shall be wanted in Aldershot anymore."

"There's one thing," said I as we walked down to the station. "If the husband's name was James, and the other was Henry, what was this talk about David?"

"That one word, my dear Watson, should have told me the whole story had I been the ideal reasoner which you are so fond of depicting. It was evidently a term of reproach."

"Of reproach?"

"Yes; David strayed a little occasionally, you know, and on one occasion in the same direction as Sergeant James Barclay. You remember the small affair of Uriah and Bathsheba? My biblical knowledge is a trifle rusty, I fear, but you will find the story in the first or second of Samuel."

Chapter 8

THE ADVENTURE OF THE RESIDENT PATIENT

In glancing over the somewhat incoherent series of memoirs with which I have endeavoured to illustrate a few of the mental peculiarities of my friend Mr. Sherlock Holmes, I have been struck by the difficulty—which I have experienced in picking out examples which shall in every way answer my purpose. For in those cases in which Holmes has performed some *tour de force* of analytical reasoning, and has demonstrated the value of his peculiar methods of investigation, the facts themselves have often been so slight or so commonplace that I could not feel justified in laying them before the public. On the other hand, it has frequently happened that he has been concerned in some research where the facts have been of the most remarkable and dramatic character, but where the share which he has himself taken in determining their causes has been less pronounced than I, as his biographer, could wish. The small matter which I have chronicled under the heading of *A Study in Scarlet*, and that other later one connected with the loss of the *Gloria Scott*, may serve as examples of this Scylla and Charybdis which are forever threatening the historian. It may be that in the business of which I am now about to write, the part which my friend played is not sufficiently accentuated; and yet the whole train of circumstances is so remarkable that I cannot bring myself to omit it entirely from this series.

I cannot be sure of the exact date, for some of my memoranda upon the matter have been mislaid, but it must have been towards the end of the first year during which Holmes and I shared chambers in Baker Street. It was boisterous October weather, and we had both remained indoors all day, I because I feared with my shaken health to face the keen autumn wind, while he was deep in some of those abstruse chemical investigations which absorbed him utterly as long as he was engaged upon them. Towards evening, however, the breaking of a test-tube brought his research to a premature ending, and he sprang up from his chair with an exclamation of impatience and a clouded brow.

"A day's work ruined, Watson," said he, striding across to the window. "Ha! the stars are out and the wind has fallen. What do you say to a ramble through London?"

I was weary of our little sitting room and gladly acquiesced. For three hours we strolled about together, watching the ever-changing kaleidoscope of life as it ebbs and flows through Fleet Street and the Strand. Holmes had shaken off his temporary ill-humour, and his characteristic talk, with its keen observance of detail and subtle power of inference, held me amused and enthralled. It was ten o'clock before we reached Baker Street again. A brougham was waiting at our door.

"Hum! A doctor's—general practitioner, I perceive," said Holmes. "Not been long in practice, but has a good deal to do. Come to consult us, I fancy! Lucky we came back!"

I was sufficiently conversant with Holmes's methods to be able to follow his reasoning, and to see that the nature and state of the various medical instruments in the wicker basket which hung in the lamplight inside the brougham had given him the data for his swift deduction. The light in our window above showed that this late visit was indeed intended for us. With some curiosity as to what could have sent a brother medico to us at such an hour, I followed Holmes into our sanctum.

A pale, taper-faced man with sandy whiskers rose up from a chair by the fire as we entered. His age may not have been more than three or four and thirty, but his haggard expression and unhealthy hue told of a life which had sapped his strength and robbed him of his youth. His manner was nervous and shy, like that of a sensitive gentleman, and the thin white hand which he laid on the mantelpiece as he rose was that of an artist rather than of a surgeon. His dress was quiet and sombre—a black frock coat, dark trousers, and a touch of colour about his necktie.

"Good evening, Doctor," said Holmes cheerily. "I am glad to see that you have only been waiting a very few minutes."

"You spoke to my coachman, then?"

"No, it was the candle on the side table that told me. Pray resume your seat and let me know how I can serve you."

"My name is Dr. Percy Trevelyan," said our visitor, "and I live at 403, Brook Street."

"Are you not the author of a monograph upon obscure nervous lesions?" I asked.

His pale cheeks flushed with pleasure at hearing that his work was known to me.

"I so seldom hear of the work that I thought it was quite dead," said he. "My publishers gave me a most discouraging account of its sale. You are yourself, I presume, a medical man?"

"A retired army surgeon."

"My own hobby has always been nervous disease. I should wish to make it an absolute specialty, but of course a man must take what he can get at first. This, however, is beside the question, Mr. Sherlock Holmes, and I quite appreciate how valuable your time is. The fact is that a very singular train of events has occurred recently at my house in Brook Street, and tonight they came to such a head that I felt it was quite impossible for me to wait another hour before asking for your advice and assistance."

Sherlock Holmes sat down and lit his pipe. "You are very welcome to both," said he. "Pray let me have a detailed account of what the circumstances are which have disturbed you."

"One or two of them are so trivial," said Dr. Trevelyan, "that really I am almost ashamed to mention them. But the matter is so inexplicable, and the recent turn which it has taken is so elaborate, that I shall lay it all before you, and you shall judge what is essential and what is not.

"I am compelled, to begin with, to say something of my own college career. I am a London University man, you know, and I am sure that you will not think that I am unduly singing my own praises if I say that my student career was considered by my professors to be a very promising one. After I had graduated I continued to devote myself to research, occupying a minor position in King's College Hospital, and I was fortunate enough to excite considerable interest by my research into the pathology of catalepsy, and finally to win the Bruce Pinkerton prize and medal by the monograph on nervous lesions to which your friend has just alluded. I should not go too far if I were to say that there was a general impression at that time that a distinguished career lay before me.

"But the one great stumbling-block lay in my want of capital. As you will readily understand, a specialist who aims high is compelled to start in one of a dozen streets in the Cavendish Square quarter, all of which entail enormous rents and furnishing expenses. Besides this preliminary outlay, he must be prepared to keep himself for some years, and to hire a presentable carriage and horse. To do this was quite beyond my power, and I could only hope that by economy I might in ten years' time save enough to enable me to put up my plate. Suddenly, however, an unexpected incident opened up quite a new prospect to me.

"This was a visit from a gentleman of the name of Blessington, who was a complete stranger to me. He came up into my room one morning, and plunged into business in an instant.

"'You are the same Percy Trevelyan who has had so distinguished a career and won a great prize lately?' said he.

"I bowed.

"'Answer me frankly,' he continued, 'for you will find it to your interest to do so. You have all the cleverness which makes a successful man. Have you the tact?'

"I could not help smiling at the abruptness of the question.

"'I trust that I have my share,' I said.

"'Any bad habits? Not drawn towards drink, eh?'

"'Really, sir!' I cried.

"'Quite right! That's all right! But I was bound to ask. With all these qualities, why are you not in practice?'

"I shrugged my shoulders.

"'Come, come!' said he in his bustling way. 'It's the old story. More in your brains than in your pocket, eh? What would you say if I were to start you in Brook Street?'

"I stared at him in astonishment.

"'Oh, it's for my sake, not for yours,' he cried. 'I'll be perfectly frank with you, and if it suits you it will suit me very well. I have a few thousands to invest, d'ye see, and I think I'll sink them in you.'

"'But why?' I gasped.

"'Well, it's just like any other speculation, and safer than most.'

"'What am I to do, then?'

"'I'll tell you. I'll take the house, furnish it, pay the maids, and run the whole place. All you have to do is just to wear out your chair in the consulting room. I'll let you have pocket-money and everything. Then you hand over to me three quarters of what you earn, and you keep the other quarter for yourself.'

"This was the strange proposal, Mr. Holmes, with which the man Blessington approached me. I won't weary you with the account of how we bargained and negotiated. It ended in my moving into the house next Lady Day, and starting in practice on very much the same conditions as he had suggested. He came himself to live with me in the character of a resident patient. His heart was weak, it appears, and he needed constant medical supervision. He turned the two best rooms of the first floor into a sitting room and bedroom for himself. He was a man of singular habits, shunning company and very seldom going out. His life was irregular, but in one respect he was regularity itself. Every evening, at the same hour, he walked into the consulting room, examined the books, put down five and three-pence for every guinea that I had earned, and carried the rest off to the strongbox in his own room.

"I may say with confidence that he never had occasion to regret his speculation. From the first it was a success. A few good cases and the reputation which I had won in the hospital brought me rapidly to the front, and during the last few years I have made him a rich man.

"So much, Mr. Holmes, for my past history and my relations with Mr. Blessington. It only remains for me now to tell you what has occurred to bring me here tonight.

"Some weeks ago Mr. Blessington came down to me in, as it seemed to me, a state of considerable agitation. He spoke of some burglary which, he said, had been committed in the West End, and he appeared, I remember, to be quite unnecessarily excited about it, declaring that a day should not pass before we should add stronger bolts to our windows and doors. For a week he continued to be in a peculiar state of restlessness, peering continually out of the windows, and ceasing to take the short walk which had usually been the prelude to his dinner. From his manner it struck me that he was in mortal dread of something or somebody, but when I questioned him upon the point he became so offensive that I was compelled to drop the subject. Gradually, as time passed, his fears appeared to die away, and he renewed his former habits, when a fresh event reduced him to the pitiable state of prostration in which he now lies.

"What happened was this. Two days ago I received the letter which I now read to you. Neither address nor date is attached to it:

> *'A Russian nobleman who is now resident in England,' it runs, 'would be glad to avail himself of the professional assistance of Dr. Percy Trevelyan. He has been for some years a victim to cataleptic attacks, on which, as is well known, Dr. Percy Trevelyan is an authority. He proposes to call at about a quarter-past six tomorrow evening, if Dr. Trevelyan will make it convenient to be at home.'*

"This letter interested me deeply, because the chief difficulty in the study of catalepsy is the rareness of the disease. You may believe, then, that I was in my consulting room when, at the appointed hour, the page showed in the patient.

"He was an elderly man, thin, demure, and commonplace—by no means the conception one forms of a Russian nobleman. I was much more struck by the appearance of his companion. This was a tall young man, surprisingly handsome, with a dark, fierce face, and the limbs and chest of a Hercules. He had his hand under the other's arm as they entered, and helped him to a chair with a tenderness which one would hardly have expected from his appearance.

"'You will excuse my coming in, Doctor,' said he to me, speaking English with a slight lisp. 'This is my father, and his health is a matter of the most overwhelming importance to me.'

"I was touched by this filial anxiety. 'You would, perhaps, care to remain during the consultation?' said I.

"'Not for the world,' he cried with a gesture of horror. 'It is more painful to me than I can express. If I were to see my father in one of these dreadful seizures I am convinced that I should never survive it. My own nervous system is an exceptionally sensitive one. With your permission, I will remain in the waiting room while you go into my father's case.'

"To this, of course, I assented, and the young man withdrew. The patient and I then plunged into a discussion of his case, of which I took exhaustive notes. He was not remarkable for intelligence, and his answers were frequently obscure, which I attributed to his limited acquaintance with our language. Suddenly, however, as I sat writing, he ceased to give any answer at all to my inquiries, and on my turning towards him I was shocked to see that he was sitting bolt upright in his chair, staring at me with a perfectly blank and rigid face. He was again in the grip of his mysterious malady.

"My first feeling, as I have just said, was one of pity and horror. My second, I fear, was rather one of professional satisfaction. I made notes of my patient's pulse and temperature, tested the rigidity of his muscles, and examined his reflexes. There was nothing markedly abnormal in any of these conditions, which harmonized with my former experiences. I had obtained good results in such cases by the inhalation of nitrite of amyl, and the present seemed an admirable opportunity of testing its virtues. The bottle was downstairs in my laboratory, so, leaving my patient seated in his chair, I ran down to get it. There was some little delay in finding it—five minutes, let us say—and then I returned. Imagine my amazement to find the room empty and the patient gone.

"Of course, my first act was to run into the waiting room. The son had gone also. The hall door had been closed, but not shut. My page who admits patients is a new boy and by no means quick. He waits downstairs and runs up to show patients out when I ring the consulting room bell. He had heard nothing, and the affair remained a complete mystery. Mr. Blessington came in from his walk shortly afterwards, but I did not say anything to him upon the subject, for, to tell the truth, I have got in the way of late of holding as little communication with him as possible.

"Well, I never thought that I should see anything more of the Russian and his son, so you can imagine my amazement when, at the very same hour this evening, they both came marching into my consulting room, just as they had done before.

"'I feel that I owe you a great many apologies for my abrupt departure yesterday, Doctor,' said my patient.

"'I confess that I was very much surprised at it,' said I.

"'Well, the fact is,' he remarked, 'that when I recover from these attacks my mind is always very clouded as to all that has gone before. I woke up in a strange room, as it seemed to me, and made my way out into the street in a sort of dazed way when you were absent.'

"'And I,' said the son, 'seeing my father pass the door of the waiting room, naturally thought that the consultation had come to an end. It was not until we had reached home that I began to realize the true state of affairs.'

"'Well,' said I, laughing, 'there is no harm done except that you puzzled me terribly; so if you, sir, would kindly step into the waiting room I shall be happy to continue our consultation which was brought to so abrupt an ending.'

"For half an hour or so I discussed the old gentleman's symptom with him, and then, having prescribed for him, I saw him go off upon the arm of his son.

"I have told you that Mr. Blessington generally chose this hour of the day for his exercise. He came in shortly afterwards and passed upstairs. An instant later I heard him running down, and he burst into my consulting room like a man who is mad with panic.

"'Who has been in my room?' he cried.

"'No one,' said I.

"'It's a lie!' he yelled. 'Come up and look!'

"I passed over the grossness of his language, as he seemed half out of his mind with fear. When I went upstairs with him he pointed to several footprints upon the light carpet.

"'Do you mean to say those are mine?' he cried.

"They were certainly very much larger than any which he could have made, and were evidently quite fresh. It rained hard this afternoon, as you know, and my patients were the only people who called. It must have been the case, then, that the man in the waiting room had, for some unknown reason, while I was busy with the other, ascended to the room of my resident patient. Nothing had been touched or taken, but there were the footprints to prove that the intrusion was an undoubted fact.

"Mr. Blessington seemed more excited over the matter than I should have thought possible, though of course it was enough to disturb anybody's peace of mind. He actually sat crying in an armchair, and I could hardly get him to speak coherently. It was his suggestion that I should come round to you, and of course I at once saw the propriety of it, for certainly the incident is a very singular one, though he appears to completely overrate its importance. If you would only come back with me in my brougham, you would at least be able to soothe him, though I can hardly hope that you will be able to explain this remarkable occurrence.

Sherlock Holmes had listened to this long narrative with an intentness which showed me that his interest was keenly aroused. His face was as impassive as ever, but his lids had drooped more heavily over his eyes, and his smoke had curled up more thickly from his pipe to emphasize each curious episode in the doctor's tale. As our visitor concluded, Holmes sprang up without a word, handed me my hat, picked his own from the table, and followed Dr. Trevelyan to the door. Within a quarter of an hour we had been dropped at the door of the physician's residence in Brook Street, one of those sombre, flat-faced houses which one associates with a West End practice. A small page admitted us, and we began at once to ascend the broad, well-carpeted stair.

But a singular interruption brought us to a standstill. The light at the top was suddenly whisked out, and from the darkness came a reedy, quavering voice.

"I have a pistol," it cried. "I give you my word that I'll fire if you come any nearer."

"This really grows outrageous, Mr. Blessington," cried Dr. Trevelyan.

"Oh, then it is you, Doctor," said the voice with a great heave of relief. "But those other gentlemen, are they what they pretend to be?"

We were conscious of a long scrutiny out of the darkness.

"Yes, yes, it's all right," said the voice at last. "You can come up, and I am sorry if my precautions have annoyed you."

He relit the stair gas as he spoke, and we saw before us a singular-looking man, whose appearance, as well as his voice, testified to his jangled nerves. He was very fat, but had apparently at some time been much fatter, so that the skin hung about his face in loose pouches, like the cheeks of a bloodhound. He was of a sickly colour, and his thin, sandy hair seemed to bristle up with the intensity of his emotion. In his hand he held a pistol, but he thrust it into his pocket as we advanced.

"Good evening, Mr. Holmes," said he. "I am sure I am very much obliged to you for coming round. No one ever needed your advice more than I do. I suppose that Dr. Trevelyan has told you of this most unwarrantable intrusion into my rooms."

"Quite so," said Holmes. "Who are these two men, Mr. Blessington, and why do they wish to molest you?"

"Well, well," said the resident patient in a nervous fashion, "of course it is hard to say that. You can hardly expect me to answer that, Mr. Holmes."

"Do you mean that you don't know?"

"Come in here, if you please. Just have the kindness to step in here."

He led the way into his bedroom, which was large and comfortably furnished.

"'You see that,' said he, pointing to a big black box at the end of his bed. 'I have never been a very rich man, Mr. Holmes—never made but one investment in my life, as Dr. Trevelyan would tell you. But I don't believe in bankers. I would never trust a banker, Mr. Holmes. Between ourselves, what little I have is in that box, so you can understand what it means to me when unknown people force themselves into my rooms."

Holmes looked at Blessington in his questioning way and shook his head.

"I cannot possibly advise you if you try to deceive me," said he.

"But I have told you everything."

Holmes turned on his heel with a gesture of disgust. "Goodnight, Dr. Trevelyan," said he.

" And no advice for me?" cried Blessington in a breaking voice.

"My advice to you, sir, is to speak the truth."

A minute later we were in the street and walking for home. We had crossed Oxford Street and were halfway down Harley Street before I could get a word from my companion.

"Sorry to bring you out on such a fool's errand, Watson," he said at last. "It is an interesting case, too, at the bottom of it."

"I can make little of it," I confessed.

"Well, it is quite evident that there are two men—more, perhaps, but at least two—who are determined for some reason to get at this fellow Blessington. I have no doubt in my mind that both on the first and on the second occasion that young man penetrated to Blessington's room, while his confederate, by an ingenious device, kept the doctor from interfering."

"And the catalepsy?"

"A fraudulent imitation, Watson, though I should hardly dare to hint as much to our specialist. It is a very easy complaint to imitate. I have done it myself."

"And then?"

"By the purest chance Blessington was out on each occasion. Their reason for choosing so unusual an hour for a consultation was obviously to insure that there should be no other patient in the waiting room. It just happened, however, that this hour coincided with Blessington's constitutional, which seems to show that they were not very well acquainted with his daily routine. Of course, if they had been merely after plunder they would at least have made some attempt to search for it. Besides, I can read in a man's eye when it is his own skin that he is frightened for. It is inconceivable that this fellow could have made two such vindictive enemies as these appear to be without knowing of it. I hold it, therefore, to be certain that he does know who these men are, and that for reasons of his own he suppresses it. It is just possible that tomorrow may find him in a more communicative mood."

"Is there not one alternative," I suggested, "grotesquely improbable, no doubt, but still just conceivable? Might the whole story of the cataleptic Russian and his son be a concoction of Dr. Trevelyan's, who has, for his own purposes, been in Blessington's rooms?"

I saw in the gaslight that Holmes wore an amused smile at this brilliant departure of mine.

"My dear fellow," said he, "it was one of the first solutions which occurred to me, but I was soon able to corroborate the doctor's tale. This young man has left prints upon the stair-carpet which made it quite superfluous for me to ask to see those which he had made in the room. When I tell you that his shoes were square-toed instead of being pointed like Blessington's, and were quite an inch and a third longer than the doctor's, you will acknowledge that there can be no doubt as to his individuality. But we may sleep on it now, for I shall be surprised if we do not hear something further from Brook Street in the morning."

Sherlock Holmes's prophecy was soon fulfilled, and in a dramatic fashion. At half-past seven next morning, in the first dim glimmer of daylight, I found him standing by my bedside in his dressing gown.

"There's a brougham waiting for us, Watson," said he.

"What's the matter, then?"

"The Brook Street business."

"Any fresh news?"

"Tragic, but ambiguous," said he, pulling up the blind. "Look at this—a sheet from a notebook, with 'For God's sake come at once. P.T.', scrawled upon it in pencil. Our friend, the doctor, was hard put to it when he wrote this. Come along, my dear fellow, for it's an urgent call."

In a quarter of an hour or so, we were back at the physician's house. He came running out to meet us with a face of horror.

"Oh, such a business!" he cried with his hands to his temples.

"What then?"

"Blessington has committed suicide!"

Holmes whistled.

"Yes, he hanged himself during the night."

We had entered, and the doctor had preceded us into what was evidently his waiting room.

"I really hardly know what I am doing," he cried. "The police are already upstairs. It has shaken me most dreadfully."

"When did you find it out?"

"He has a cup of tea taken in to him early every morning. When the maid entered, about seven, there the unfortunate fellow was hanging in the middle of the room. He had tied his cord to the hook on which the heavy lamp used to hang, and he had jumped off from the top of the very box that he showed us yesterday."

Holmes stood for a moment in deep thought.

"With your permission," said he at last, "I should like to go upstairs and look into the matter."

We both ascended, followed by the doctor.

It was a dreadful sight which met us as we entered the bedroom door. I have spoken of the impression of flabbiness which this man Blessington conveyed. As he dangled from the hook it was exaggerated and intensified until he was scarce human in his appearance. The neck was drawn out like a plucked chicken's, making the rest of him seem the more obese and unnatural by the contrast. He was clad only in his long nightdress, and his swollen ankles and ungainly feet protruded starkly from beneath it. Beside him stood a smart-looking police-inspector, who was taking notes in a pocketbook.

"Ah, Mr. Holmes," said he heartily as my friend entered, "I am delighted to see you."

"Good morning, Lanner," answered Holmes; "you won't think me an intruder, I am sure. Have you heard of the events which led up to this affair?"

"Yes, I heard something of them."

"Have you formed any opinion?"

"As far as I can see, the man has been driven out of his senses by fright. The bed has been well slept in, you see. There's his impression, deep enough. It's about five in the morning, you know, that suicides are most common. That would be about his time for hanging himself. It seems to have been a very deliberate affair."

"I should say that he has been dead about three hours, judging by the rigidity of the muscles," said I.

"Noticed anything peculiar about the room?" asked Sherlock Holmes.

"Found a screw-driver and some screws on the wash-hand stand. Seems to have smoked heavily during the night, too. Here are four cigar-ends that I picked out of the fireplace."

"Hum!" said Holmes, "have you got his cigar-holder?"

"No, I have seen none."

"His cigar-case, then?"

"Yes, it was in his coat-pocket."

Holmes opened it and smelled the single cigar which it contained.

"Oh, this is a Havana, and these others are cigars of the peculiar sort which are imported by the Dutch from their East Indian colonies. They are usually wrapped in straw, you know, and are thinner for their length than any other brand." He picked up the four ends and examined them with his pocket-lens.

"Two of these have been smoked from a holder and two without," said he. "Two have been cut by a not very sharp knife, and two have had the ends bitten off by a set of excellent teeth. This is no suicide, Mr. Lanner. It is a very deeply planned and cold-blooded murder."

"Impossible!" cried the inspector.

"And why?"

"Why should anyone murder a man in so clumsy a fashion as by hanging him?"

"That is what we have to find out."

"How could they get in?"

"Through the front door."

"It was barred in the morning."

"Then it was barred after them."

"How do you know?"

"I saw their traces. Excuse me a moment, and I may be able to give you some further information about it."

He went over to the door, and turning the lock he examined it in his methodical way. Then he took out the key, which was on the inside, and inspected that also. The bed, the carpet, the chairs, the mantelpiece, the dead body, and the rope were each in turn examined, until at last he professed himself satisfied, and with my aid and that of the inspector cut down the wretched object and laid it reverently under a sheet.

"How about this rope?" he asked.

"It is cut off this," said Dr. Trevelyan, drawing a large coil from under the bed. "He was morbidly nervous of fire, and always kept this beside him, so that he might escape by the window in case the stairs were burning."

"That must have saved them trouble," said Sherlock Holmes thoughtfully.

"Yes, the actual facts are very plain, and I shall be surprised if by the afternoon I cannot give you the reasons for them as well. I will take this photograph of Blessington, which I see upon the mantelpiece, as it may help me in my inquiries."

"But you have told us nothing!" cried the doctor.

"Oh, there can be no doubt as to the sequence of events," said Holmes. "There were three of them in it: the young man, the old man, and a third, to whose identity I have no clue. The first two, I need hardly remark, are the same who masqueraded as the Russian count and his son, so we can give a very full description of them. They were admitted by a confederate inside the house. If I might offer you a word of advice, Inspector, it would be to arrest the page, who, as I understand, has only recently come into your service, Doctor."

"The young imp cannot be found," said Dr. Trevelyan; "the maid and the cook have just been searching for him."

Holmes shrugged his shoulders.

"He has played a not unimportant part in this drama," said he.

"The three men having ascended the stairs, which they did on tiptoe, the elder man first, the younger man second, and the unknown man in the rear—"

"My dear Holmes!" I ejaculated.

"Oh, there could be no question as to the superimposing of the footmarks. I had the advantage of learning which was which last night. They ascended, then, to Mr. Blessington's room, the door of which they found to be locked. With the help of a wire, however, they forced round the key. Even without the lens you will perceive, by the scratches on this ward, where the pressure was applied."

"On entering the room their first proceeding must have been to gag Mr. Blessington. He may have been asleep, or he may have been so paralyzed with terror as to have been unable to cry out. These walls are thick, and it is conceivable that his shriek, if he had time to utter one, was unheard."

"Having secured him, it is evident to me that a consultation of some sort was held. Probably it was something in the nature of a judicial proceeding. It must have lasted for some time, for it was then that these cigars were smoked. The older man sat in that wicker chair; it was he who used the cigar-holder. The younger man sat over yonder; he knocked his ash off against the chest of drawers. The third fellow paced up and down. Blessington, I think, sat upright in the bed, but of that I cannot be absolutely certain.

"Well, it ended by their taking Blessington and hanging him. The matter was so prearranged that it is my belief that they brought with them some sort of block or pulley which might serve as a gallows. That screw-driver and those screws were, as I conceive, for fixing it up. Seeing the hook, however, they naturally saved themselves the trouble. Having finished their work they made off, and the door was barred behind them by their confederate."

We had all listened with the deepest interest to this sketch of the night's doings, which Holmes had deduced from signs so subtle and minute that, even when he had pointed them out to us, we could scarcely follow him in his reasonings. The inspector hurried away on the instant to make inquiries about the page, while Holmes and I returned to Baker Street for breakfast.

"I'll be back by three," said he when we had finished our meal. "Both the inspector and the doctor will meet me here at that hour, and I hope by that time to have cleared up any little obscurity which the case may still present."

Our visitors arrived at the appointed time, but it was a quarter to four before my friend put in an appearance. From his expression as he entered, however, I could see that all had gone well with him.

"Any news, Inspector?"

"We have got the boy, sir."

"Excellent, and I have got the men."

"You have got them!" we cried, all three.

"Well, at least I have got their identity. This so-called Blessington is as I expected, well known at headquarters, and so are his assailants. Their names are Biddle, Hayward, and Moffat."

"The Worthingdon bank gang," cried the inspector.

"Precisely," said Holmes.

"Then Blessington must have been Sutton."

"Exactly," said Holmes.

"Why, that makes it as clear as crystal," said the inspector. But Trevelyan and I looked at each other in bewilderment.

"You must surely remember the great Worthingdon bank business," said Holmes. "Five men were in it—these four and a fifth called Cartwright. Tobin, the caretaker, was murdered, and the thieves got away with seven thousand pounds. This was in 1875. They were all five arrested, but the evidence against them was by no means conclusive. This Blessington or Sutton, who was the worst of the gang, turned informer. On his evidence Cartwright was hanged and the other three got fifteen years apiece. When they got out the other day, which was some years before their full term, they set themselves, as you perceive, to hunt down the traitor and to avenge the death of their comrade upon him. Twice they tried to get at him and failed; a third time, you see, it came off. Is there anything further which I can explain, Dr. Trevelyan?"

"I think you have made it all remarkably clear," said the doctor.

"No doubt the day on which he was so perturbed was the day when he had seen of their release in the newspapers."

"Quite so. His talk about a burglary was the merest blind."

"But why could he not tell you this?"

"Well, my dear sir, knowing the vindictive character of his old associates, he was trying to hide his own identity from everybody as long as he could. His secret was a shameful one, and he could not bring himself to divulge it. However, wretch as he was, he was still living under the shield of British law, and I have no doubt, Inspector, that you will see that, though that shield may fail to guard, the sword of justice is still there to avenge."

Such were the singular circumstances in connection with the Resident Patient and the Brook Street Doctor. From that night nothing has been seen of the three murderers by the police, and it is surmised at Scotland Yard that they were among the passengers of the ill-fated steamer *Norah Creina,* which was lost some years ago with all hands upon the Portuguese coast, some leagues to the north of Oporto. The proceedings against the page broke down for want of evidence, and the Brook Street Mystery, as it was called, has never until now been fully dealt with in any public print.

Chapter 9

THE ADVENTURE OF THE GREEK INTERPRETER

DURING my long and intimate acquaintance with Mr. Sherlock Holmes I had never heard him refer to his relations, and hardly ever to his own early life. This reticence upon his part had increased the somewhat inhuman effect which he produced upon me, until sometimes I found myself regarding him as an isolated phenomenon, a brain without a heart, as deficient in human sympathy as he was pre-eminent in intelligence. His aversion to women and his disinclination to form new friendships were both typical of his unemotional character, but not more so than his complete suppression of every reference to his own people. I had come to believe that he was an orphan with no relatives living; but one day, to my very great surprise, he began to talk to me about his brother.

It was after tea on a summer evening, and the conversation, which had roamed in a desultory, spasmodic fashion from golf clubs to the causes of the change in the obliquity of the ecliptic, came round at last to the question of atavism and hereditary aptitudes. The point under discussion was, how far any singular gift in an individual was due to his ancestry and how far to his own early training.

"In your own case," said I, "from all that you have told me, it seems obvious that your faculty of observation and your peculiar facility for deduction are due to your own systematic training."

"To some extent," he answered thoughtfully. "My ancestors were country squires, who appear to have led much the same life as is natural to their class. But, nonetheless, my turn that way is in my veins, and may have come with my grandmother, who was the sister of Vernet, the French artist. Art in the blood is liable to take the strangest forms."

"But how do you know that it is hereditary?"

"Because my brother Mycroft possesses it in a larger degree than I do."

This was news to me indeed. If there were another man with such singular powers in England, how was it that neither police nor public had heard of him? I put the question, with a hint that it was my companion's modesty which made him acknowledge his brother as his superior. Holmes laughed at my suggestion.

"My dear Watson," said he, "I cannot agree with those who rank modesty among the virtues. To the logician all things should be seen exactly as they are, and to underestimate one's self is as much a departure from truth as to exaggerate one's own powers. When I say, therefore, that Mycroft has better powers of observation than I, you may take it that I am speaking the exact and literal truth."

"Is he your junior?"

"Seven years my senior."

"How comes it that he is unknown?"

"Oh, he is very well known in his own circle."

"Where, then?"

"Well, in the Diogenes Club, for example."

I had never heard of the institution, and my face must have proclaimed as much, for Sherlock Holmes pulled out his watch.

"The Diogenes Club is the queerest club in London, and Mycroft one of the queerest men. He's always there from quarter to five to twenty to eight. It's six now, so if you care for a stroll this beautiful evening, I shall be very happy to introduce you to two curiosities."

Five minutes later we were in the street, walking towards Regent's Circus.

"You wonder," said my companion, "why it is that Mycroft does not use his powers for detective work. He is incapable of it."

"But I thought you said—"

"I said that he was my superior in observation and deduction. If the art of the detective began and ended in reasoning from an armchair, my brother would be the greatest criminal agent that ever lived. But he has no ambition and no energy. He will not even go out of his way to verify his own solutions, and would rather be considered wrong than take the trouble to prove himself right. Again and again I have taken a problem to him, and have received an explanation which has afterwards proved to be the correct one. And yet he was absolutely incapable of working out the practical points which must be gone into before a case could be laid before a judge or jury."

"It is not his profession, then?"

"By no means. What is to me a means of livelihood is to him the merest hobby of a dilettante. He has an extraordinary faculty for figures, and audits the books in some of the government departments. Mycroft lodges in Pall Mall, and he walks round the corner into Whitehall every morning and back every evening. From year's end to year's end he takes no other exercise, and is seen nowhere else, except only in the Diogenes Club, which is just opposite his rooms."

"I cannot recall the name."

"Very likely not. There are many men in London, you know, who, some from shyness, some from misanthropy, have no wish for the company of their fellows. Yet they are not averse to comfortable chairs and the latest periodicals. It is for the convenience of these that the Diogenes Club was started, and it now contains the most unsociable and unclubable men in town. No member is permitted to take the least notice of any other one. Save in the Stranger's Room, no talking is, under any circumstances, allowed, and three offences, if brought to the notice of the committee, render the talker liable to expulsion. My brother was one of the founders, and I have myself found it a very soothing atmosphere."

We had reached Pall Mall as we talked, and were walking down it from the St. James's end. Sherlock Holmes stopped at a door some little distance from the Carlton, and, cautioning me not to speak, he led the way into the hall. Through the glass panelling I caught a glimpse of a large and luxurious room, in which a considerable number of men were sitting about and reading papers, each in his own little nook. Holmes showed me into a small chamber which looked out into Pall Mall, and then, leaving me for a minute, he came back with a companion whom I knew could only be his brother.

Mycroft Holmes was a much larger and stouter man than Sherlock. His body was absolutely corpulent, but his face, though massive, had preserved something of the sharpness of expression which was so remarkable in that of his brother. His eyes, which were of a peculiarly light, watery gray, seemed to always retain that faraway, introspective look which I had only observed in Sherlock's when he was exerting his full powers.

"I am glad to meet you, sir," said he, putting out a broad, fat hand like the flipper of a seal. "I hear of Sherlock everywhere since you became his chronicler. By the way, Sherlock, I expected to see you round last week to consult me over that Manor House case. I thought you might be a little out of your depth."

"No, I solved it," said my friend, smiling.

"It was Adams, of course."

"Yes, it was Adams."

"I was sure of it from the first." The two sat down together in the bow-window of the club. "To anyone who wishes to study mankind this is the spot," said Mycroft. "Look at the magnificent types! Look at these two men who are coming towards us, for example."

"The billiard-marker and the other?"

"Precisely. What do you make of the other?"

The two men had stopped opposite the window. Some chalk marks over the waistcoat pocket were the only signs of billiards which I could see in one of them. The other was a very small, dark fellow, with his hat pushed back and several packages under his arm.

"An old soldier, I perceive," said Sherlock.

"And very recently discharged," remarked the brother.

"Served in India, I see."

"And a non-commissioned officer."

"Royal Artillery, I fancy," said Sherlock.

"And a widower."

"But with a child."

"Children, my dear boy, children."

"Come," said I, laughing, "this is a little too much."

"Surely," answered Holmes, "it is not hard to say that a man with that bearing, expression of authority, and sun-baked skin, is a soldier, is more than a private, and is not long from India."

"That he has not left the service long is shown by his still wearing his ammunition boots, as they are called," observed Mycroft.

"He had not the cavalry stride, yet he wore his hat on one side, as is shown by the lighter skin on that side of his brow. His weight is against his being a sapper. He is in the artillery."

"Then, of course, his complete mourning shows that he has lost someone very dear. The fact that he is doing his own shopping looks as though it were his wife. He has been buying things for children, you perceive. There is a rattle, which shows that one of them is very young. The wife probably died in childbed. The fact that he has a picture-book under his arm shows that there is another child to be thought of."

I began to understand what my friend meant when he said that his brother possessed even keener faculties than he did himself. He glanced across at me and smiled. Mycroft took snuff from a tortoise-shell box and brushed away the wandering grains from his coat front with a large, red silk handkerchief.

"By the way, Sherlock," said he, "I have had something quite after your own heart—a most singular problem—submitted to my judgment. I really had not the energy to follow it up save in a very incomplete fashion, but it gave me a basis for some pleasing speculations. If you would care to hear the facts—"

"My dear Mycroft, I should be delighted."

The brother scribbled a note upon a leaf of his pocket-book, and, ringing the bell, he handed it to the waiter.

"I have asked Mr. Melas to step across," said he. "He lodges on the floor above me, and I have some slight acquaintance with him, which led him to come to me in his perplexity. Mr. Melas is a Greek by extraction, as I understand, and he is a remarkable linguist. He earns his living partly as interpreter in the law courts and partly by acting as guide to any wealthy Orientals who may visit the Northumberland Avenue hotels. I think I will leave him to tell his very remarkable experience in his own fashion."

A few minutes later we were joined by a short, stout man whose olive face and coal-black hair proclaimed his Southern origin, though his speech was that of an educated Englishman. He shook hands eagerly with Sherlock Holmes, and his dark eyes sparkled with pleasure when he understood that the specialist was anxious to hear his story.

"I do not believe that the police credit me—on my word, I do not," said he in a wailing voice. "Just because they have never heard of it before, they think that such a thing cannot be. But I know that I shall never be easy in my mind until I know what has become of my poor man with the sticking-plaster upon his face."

"I am all attention," said Sherlock Holmes.

"This is Wednesday evening," said Mr. Melas. "Well, then, it was Monday night—only two days ago, you understand—that all this happened. I am an interpreter, as perhaps my neighbour there has told you. I interpret all languages—or nearly all—but as I am a Greek by birth and with a Grecian name, it is with that particular tongue that I am principally associated. For many years I have been the chief Greek interpreter in London, and my name is very well known in the hotels.

"It happens not unfrequently that I am sent for at strange hours by foreigners who get into difficulties, or by travellers who arrive late and wish my services. I was not surprised, therefore, on Monday night when a Mr. Latimer, a very fashionably dressed young man, came up to my rooms and asked me to accompany him in a cab which was waiting at the door. A Greek friend had come to see him upon business, he said, and as he could speak nothing but his own tongue, the services of an interpreter were indispensable. He gave me to understand that his house was some little distance off, in Kensington, and he seemed to be in a great hurry, bustling me rapidly into the cab when we had descended to the street.

"I say into the cab, but I soon became doubtful as to whether it was not a carriage in which I found myself. It was certainly more roomy than the ordinary four-wheeled disgrace to London, and the fittings, though frayed, were of rich quality. Mr. Latimer seated himself opposite to me and we started off through Charing Cross and up the Shaftesbury Avenue. We had come out upon Oxford Street and I had ventured some remark as to this being a roundabout way to Kensington, when my words were arrested by the extraordinary conduct of my companion.

"He began by drawing a most formidable-looking bludgeon loaded with lead from his pocket, and switching it backward and forward several times, as if it to test its weight and strength. Then he placed it without a word upon the seat beside him. Having done this, he drew up the windows on each side, and I found to my astonishment that they were covered with paper so as to prevent my seeing through them.

"'I am sorry to cut off your view, Mr. Melas,' said he. 'The fact is that I have no intention that you should see what the place is to which we are driving. It might possibly be inconvenient to me if you could find your way there again.'

"As you can imagine, I was utterly taken aback by such an address. My companion was a powerful, broad-shouldered young fellow, and, apart from the weapon, I should not have had the slightest chance in a struggle with him.

"'This is very extraordinary conduct, Mr. Latimer' I stammered. 'You must be aware that what you are doing is quite illegal.'

"'It is somewhat of a liberty, no doubt,' said he, 'but we'll make it up to you. I must warn you, however, Mr. Melas, that if at any time tonight you attempt to raise an alarm or do anything which is against my interests, you will find it a very serious thing. I beg you to remember that no one knows where you are, and that, whether you are in this carriage or in my house, you are equally in my power.'

"His words were quiet, but he had a rasping way of saying them, which was very menacing. I sat in silence wondering what on earth could be his reason for kidnapping me in this extraordinary fashion.

"Whatever it might be, it was perfectly clear that there was no possible use in my resisting, and that I could only wait to see what might befall.

"For nearly two hours we drove without my having the least clue as to where we were going. Sometimes the rattle of the stones told of a paved causeway, and at others our smooth, silent course suggested asphalt; but, save by this variation in sound, there was nothing at all which could in the remotest way help me to form a guess as to where we were. The paper over each window was impenetrable to light, and a blue curtain was drawn across the glasswork in front. It was a quarter-past seven when we left Pall Mall, and my watch showed me that it was ten minutes to nine when we at last came to a standstill. My companion let down the window, and I caught a glimpse of a low, arched doorway with a lamp burning above it. As I was hurried from the carriage it swung open, and I found myself inside the house, with a vague impression of a lawn and trees on each side of me as I entered. Whether these were private grounds, however, or *bona-fide* country was more than I could possibly venture to say.

"There was a coloured gas lamp inside which was turned so low that I could see little save that the hall was of some size and hung with pictures. In the dim light I could make out that the person who had opened the door was a small, mean-looking, middle-aged man with rounded shoulders. As he turned towards us the glint of the light showed me that he was wearing glasses.

"'Is this Mr. Melas, Harold?' said he.

"'Yes.'

"'Well done, well done! No ill-will, Mr. Melas, I hope, but we could not get on without you. If you deal fair with us you'll not regret it, but if you try any tricks, God help you!' He spoke in a nervous, jerky fashion, and with little giggling laughs in between, but somehow he impressed me with fear more than the other.

"'What do you want with me?' I asked.

"'Only to ask a few questions of a Greek gentleman who is visiting us, and to let us have the answers. But say no more than you are told to say, or—' here came the nervous giggle again—'you had better never have been born.'

"As he spoke he opened a door and showed the way into a room which appeared to be very richly furnished, but again the only light was afforded by a single lamp half-turned down. The chamber was certainly large, and the way in which my feet sank into the carpet as I stepped across it told me of its richness. I caught glimpses of velvet chairs, a high white marble mantelpiece, and what seemed to be a suit of Japanese armour at one side of it. There was a chair just under the lamp, and the elderly man motioned that I should sit in it. The younger had left us, but he suddenly returned through another door, leading with him a gentleman clad in some sort of loose dressing gown who moved slowly towards us. As he came into the circle of dim light which enabled me to see him more clearly I was thrilled with horror at his appearance. He was deadly pale and terribly emaciated, with the protruding, brilliant eyes of a man whose spirit was greater than his strength. But what shocked me more than any signs of physical weakness was that his face was grotesquely criss-crossed with sticking-plaster, and that one large pad of it was fastened over his mouth.

"'Have you the slate, Harold?' cried the older man, as this strange being fell rather than sat down into a chair. 'Are his hands loose? Now, then, give him the pencil. You are to ask the questions, Mr. Melas, and he will write the answers. Ask him first of all whether he is prepared to sign the papers?'

"The man's eyes flashed fire.

"'Never!' he wrote in Greek upon the slate.

"'On no conditions?' I asked at the bidding of our tyrant.

"'Only if I see her married in my presence by a Greek priest whom I know.'

"The man giggled in his venomous way.

"'You know what awaits you, then?'

"'I care nothing for myself.'

"These are samples of the questions and answers which made up our strange half-spoken, half-written conversation. Again and again I had to ask him whether he would give in and sign the documents. Again and again I had the same indignant reply. But soon a happy thought came to me. I took to adding on little sentences of my own to each question, innocent ones at first, to test whether either of our companions knew anything of the matter, and then, as I found that they showed no sign I played a more dangerous game. Our conversation ran something like this:

"'You can do no good by this obstinacy. *Who are you*!'

"'I care not. *I am a stranger in London*.'

"'Your fate will be on your own head. *How long have you been here*?'

"'Let it be so. *Three weeks*.'

"'The property can never be yours. *What ails you*?'

"'It shall not go to villains. *They are starving me*.'

"'You shall go free if you sign. *What house is this*?'

"'I will never sign. *I do not know*.'

"'You are not doing her any service. *What is your name*?'

"'Let me hear her say so. *Kratides*.'

"'You shall see her if you sign. *Where are you from*?'

"'Then I shall never see her. *Athens*.'

"Another five minutes, Mr. Holmes, and I should have wormed out the whole story under their very noses. My very next question might have cleared the matter up, but at that instant the door opened and a woman stepped into the room. I could not see her clearly enough to know more than that she was tall and graceful, with black hair, and clad in some sort of loose white gown.

"'Harold,' said she, speaking English with a broken accent. 'I could not stay away longer. It is so lonely up there with only—Oh, my God, it is Paul!'

"These last words were in Greek, and at the same instant the man with a convulsive effort tore the plaster from his lips, and screaming out 'Sophy! Sophy!' rushed into the woman's arms. Their embrace was but for an instant, however, for the younger man seized the woman and pushed her out of the room, while the elder easily overpowered his emaciated victim and dragged him away through the other door. For a moment I was left alone in the room, and I sprang to my feet with some vague idea that I might in some way get a clue to what this house was in which I found myself. Fortunately, however, I took no steps, for looking up I saw that the older man was standing in the doorway, with his eyes fixed upon me.

"'That will do, Mr. Melas,' said he. 'You perceive that we have taken you into our confidence over some very private business. We should not have troubled you, only that our friend who speaks Greek and who began these negotiations has been forced to return to the East. It was quite necessary for us to find someone to take his place, and we were fortunate in hearing of your powers.'

"I bowed.

"'There are five sovereigns here,' said he, walking up to me, 'which will, I hope, be a sufficient fee. But remember,' he added, tapping me lightly on the chest and giggling, 'if you speak to a human soul about this—one human soul, mind-well, may God have mercy upon your soul!'

"I cannot tell you the loathing and horror with which this insignificant-looking man inspired me. I could see him better now as the lamplight shone upon him. His features were peaky and sallow, and his little pointed beard was thready and ill-nourished. He pushed his face forward as he spoke and his lips and eyelids were continually twitching like a man with St. Vitus's dance. I could not help thinking that his strange, catchy little laugh was also a symptom of some nervous malady. The terror of his face lay in his eyes, however, steel gray, and glistening coldly with a malignant, inexorable cruelty in their depths.

"'We shall know if you speak of this,' said he. 'We have our own means of information. Now you will find the carriage waiting, and my friend will see you on your way.'

"I was hurried through the hall and into the vehicle, again obtaining that momentary glimpse of trees and a garden. Mr. Latimer followed closely at my heels and took his place opposite to me without a word. In silence we again drove for an interminable distance with the windows raised, until at last, just after midnight, the carriage pulled up.

"'You will get down here, Mr. Melas,' said my companion. 'I am sorry to leave you so far from your house, but there is no alternative. Any attempt upon your part to follow the carriage can only end in injury to yourself.'

"He opened the door as he spoke, and I had hardly time to spring out when the coachman lashed the horse and the carriage rattled away. I looked around me in astonishment. I was on some sort of a healthy common mottled over with dark clumps of furze-bushes. Far away stretched a line of houses, with a light here and there in the upper windows. On the other side I saw the red signal-lamps of a railway.

"The carriage which had brought me was already out of sight. I stood gazing round and wondering where on earth I might be, when I saw someone coming towards me in the darkness. As he came up to me I made out that he was a railway porter.

"'Can you tell me what place this is?' I asked.

"'Wandsworth Common,' said he.

"'Can I get a train into town?'

"'If you walk on a mile or so to Clapham Junction,' said he, 'you'll just be in time for the last to Victoria.'

"So that was the end of my adventure, Mr. Holmes. I do not know where I was, nor whom I spoke with, nor anything, save what I have told you. But I know that there is foul play going on, and I want to help that unhappy man if I can. I told the whole story to Mr. Mycroft Holmes next morning, and subsequently to the police."

We all sat in silence for some little time after listening to this extraordinary narrative. Then Sherlock looked across at his brother.

"Any steps?" he asked.

Mycroft picked up the *Daily News*, which was lying on the side table.

He began reading:

"'Anybody supplying any information as to the whereabouts of a Greek gentleman named Paul Kratides, from Athens, who is unable to speak English, will be rewarded. A similar reward paid to anyone giving information about a Greek lady whose first name is Sophy. —X 2473.' That was in all the dailies. No answer."

"How about the Greek legation?"

"I have inquired. They know nothing."

"A wire to the head of the Athens police, then?"

"Sherlock has all the energy of the family," said Mycroft,

turning to me. “Well, you take the case up by all means and let me know if you do any good.”

“Certainly,” answered my friend, rising from his chair. “I’ll let you know, and Mr. Melas also. In the meantime, Mr. Melas, I should certainly be on my guard if I were you, for of course they must know through these advertisements that you have betrayed them.”

As we walked home together, Holmes stopped at a telegraph office and sent off several wires.

“You see, Watson,” he remarked, “our evening has been by no means wasted. Some of my most interesting cases have come to me in this way through Mycroft. The problem which we have just listened to, although it can admit of but one explanation, has still some distinguishing features.”

“You have hopes of solving it?”

“Well, knowing as much as we do, it will be singular indeed if we fail to discover the rest. You must yourself have formed some theory which will explain the facts to which we have listened.”

“In a vague way, yes.”

“What was your idea, then?”

“It seemed to me to be obvious that this Greek girl had been carried off by the young Englishman named Harold Latimer.”

“Carried off from where?”

“Athens, perhaps.”

Sherlock Holmes shook his head. “This young man could not talk a word of Greek. The lady could talk English fairly well. Inference—that she had been in England some little time, but he had not been in Greece.”

"Well, then, we will presume that she had once come on a visit to England, and that this Harold had persuaded her to fly with him."

"That is more probable."

"Then the brother—for that, I fancy, must be the relationship—comes over from Greece to interfere. He imprudently puts himself into the power of the young man and his older associate. They seize him and use violence towards him in order to make him sign some papers to make over the girl's fortune—of which he may be trustee—to them. This he refuses to do. In order to negotiate with him they have to get an interpreter, and they pitch upon this Mr. Melas, having used some other one before. The girl is not told of the arrival of her brother and finds it out by the merest accident."

"Excellent, Watson!" cried Holmes. "I really fancy that you are not far from the truth. You see that we hold all the cards, and we have only to fear some sudden act of violence on their part. If they give us time we must have them."

"But how can we find where this house lies?"

"Well, if our conjecture is correct and the girl's name is or was Sophy Kratides, we should have no difficulty in tracing her. That must be our main hope, for the brother is, of course, a complete stranger. It is clear that some time has elapsed since this Harold established these relations with the girl—some weeks, at any rate—since the brother in Greece has had time to hear of it and come across. If they have been living in the same place during this time, it is probable that we shall have some answer to Mycroft's advertisement."

We had reached our house in Baker Street while we had been talking. Holmes ascended the stair first, and as he opened the door of our room he gave a start of surprise. Looking over his shoulder, I was equally astonished. His brother Mycroft was sitting smoking in the armchair.

"Come in, Sherlock! Come in, sir," said he blandly, smiling at our surprised faces. "You don't expect such energy from me, do you, Sherlock? But somehow this case attracts me."

"How did you get here?"

"I passed you in a hansom."

"There has been some new development?"

"I had an answer to my advertisement."

"Ah!"

"Yes, it came within a few minutes of your leaving."

"And to what effect?"

Mycroft Holmes took out a sheet of paper.

"Here it is," said he, "written with a J pen on royal cream paper by a middle-aged man with a weak constitution.

Sir [he says]:

In answer to your advertisement of today's date, I beg to inform you that I know the young lady in question very well. If you should care to call upon me I could give you some particulars as to her painful history. She is living at present at The Myrtles, Beckenham.

Yours faithfully,

J. Davenport.

"He writes from Lower Brixton," said Mycroft Holmes. "Do you not think that we might drive to him now, Sherlock, and learn these particulars?"

"My dear Mycroft, the brother's life is more valuable than the sister's story. I think we should call at Scotland Yard for Inspector Gregson and go straight out to Beckenham. We know that a man is being done to death, and every hour may be vital."

"Better pick up Mr. Melas on our way," I suggested. "We may need an interpreter."

"Excellent," said Sherlock Holmes. "Send the boy for a four-wheeler, and we shall be off at once." He opened the table-drawer as he spoke, and I noticed that he slipped his revolver into his pocket.

"Yes," said he in answer to my glance, "I should say, from what we have heard, that we are dealing with a particularly dangerous gang."

It was almost dark before we found ourselves in Pall Mall, at the rooms of Mr. Melas. A gentleman had just called for him, and he was gone.

"Can you tell me where?" asked Mycroft Holmes.

"I don't know, sir," answered the woman who had opened the door; "I only know that he drove away with the gentleman in a carriage."

"Did the gentleman give a name?"

"No, sir."

"He wasn't a tall, handsome, dark young man?"

"Oh, no, sir. He was a little gentleman, with glasses, thin in the face, but very pleasant in his ways, for he was laughing all the time that he was talking."

"Come along!" cried Sherlock Holmes abruptly. "This grows serious," he observed as we drove to Scotland Yard. "These men have got hold of Melas again. He is a man of no physical courage, as they are well aware from their experience the other night. This villain was able to terrorize him the instant that he got into his presence. No doubt they want his professional services, but, having used him, they may be inclined to punish him for what they will regard as his treachery."

Our hope was that, by taking train, we might get to Beckenham as soon as or sooner than the carriage. On reaching Scotland Yard, however, it was more than an hour before we could get Inspector Gregson and comply with the legal formalities which would enable us to enter the house. It was a quarter to ten before we reached London Bridge, and half past before the four of us alighted on the Beckenham platform. A drive of half a mile brought us to The Myrtles—a large, dark house standing back from the road in its own grounds. Here we dismissed our cab and made our way up the drive together.

"The windows are all dark," remarked the inspector. "The house seems deserted."

"Our birds are flown and the nest empty," said Holmes.

"Why do you say so?"

"A carriage heavily loaded with luggage has passed out during the last hour."

The inspector laughed. "I saw the wheel-tracks in the light of the gate-lamp, but where does the luggage come in?"

"You may have observed the same wheel-tracks going the other way. But the outward-bound ones were very much deeper—so much so that we can say for a certainty that there was a very considerable weight on the carriage."

"You get a trifle beyond me there," said the inspector, shrugging his shoulders. "It will not be an easy door to force, but we will try if we cannot make someone hear us."

He hammered loudly at the knocker and pulled at the bell, but without any success. Holmes had slipped away, but he came back in a few minutes.

"I have a window open," said he.

"It is a mercy that you are on the side of the force, and not against it, Mr. Holmes," remarked the inspector as he noted the clever way in which my friend had forced back the catch. "Well, I think that under the circumstances we may enter without an invitation."

One after the other we made our way into a large apartment, which was evidently that in which Mr. Melas had found himself. The inspector had lit his lantern, and by its light we could see the two doors, the curtain, the lamp, and the suit of Japanese mail as he had described them. On the table lay two glasses, an empty brandy-bottle, and the remains of a meal.

"What is that?" asked Holmes suddenly.

We all stood still and listened. A low moaning sound was coming from somewhere over our heads. Holmes rushed to the door and out into the hall. The dismal noise came from upstairs. He dashed up, the inspector and I at his heels, while his brother Mycroft followed as quickly as his great bulk would permit.

Three doors faced us upon the second floor, and it was from the centre of these that the sinister sounds were issuing, sinking sometimes into a dull mumble and rising again into a shrill whine. It was locked, but the key had been left on the outside. Holmes flung open the door and rushed in, but he was out again in an instant, with his hand to his throat.

"It's charcoal," he cried. "Give it time. It will clear."

Peering in, we could see that the only light in the room came from a dull blue flame which flickered from a small brass tripod in the centre. It threw a livid, unnatural circle upon the floor, while in the shadows beyond we saw the vague loom of two figures which crouched against the wall. From the open door there reeked a horrible poisonous exhalation which set us gasping and coughing. Holmes rushed to the top of the stairs to draw in the fresh air, and then, dashing into the room, he threw up the window and hurled the brazen tripod out into the garden.

"We can enter in a minute," he gasped, darting out again. "Where is a candle? I doubt if we could strike a match in that atmosphere. Hold the light at the door and we shall get them out, Mycroft, now!"

With a rush we got to the poisoned men and dragged them out into the well-lit hall. Both of them were blue-lipped and insensible, with swollen, congested faces and protruding eyes. Indeed, so distorted were their features that, save for his black beard and stout figure, we might have failed to recognize in one of them the Greek interpreter who had parted from us only a few hours before at the Diogenes Club. His hands and feet were securely strapped together, and he bore over one eye the marks of a violent blow. The other, who was secured in a similar fashion, was a tall man in the last stage of emaciation, with several strips of sticking-plaster arranged in a grotesque pattern over his face. He had ceased to moan as we laid him down, and a glance showed me that for him at least our aid had come too late. Mr. Melas, however, still lived, and in less than an hour, with the aid of ammonia and brandy, I had the satisfaction of seeing him open his eyes, and of knowing that my hand had drawn him back from that dark valley in which all paths meet.

It was a simple story which he had to tell, and one which did but confirm our own deductions. His visitor, on entering his rooms, had drawn a life-preserver from his sleeve, and had so impressed him with the fear of instant and inevitable death that he had kidnapped him for the second time. Indeed, it was almost mesmeric, the effect which this giggling ruffian had produced upon the unfortunate linguist, for he could not speak of him save with trembling hands and a blanched cheek. He had been taken swiftly to Beckenham, and had acted as interpreter in a second interview, even more dramatic than the first, in which the two Englishmen had menaced their prisoner with instant death if he did not comply with their demands. Finally, finding him proof against every threat, they had hurled him back into his prison, and after reproaching Melas with his treachery, which appeared from the newspaper advertisement, they had stunned him with a blow from a stick, and he remembered nothing more until he found us bending over him.

And this was the singular case of the Grecian Interpreter, the explanation of which is still involved in some mystery. We were able to find out, by communicating with the gentleman who had answered the advertisement, that the unfortunate young lady came of a wealthy Grecian family, and that she had been on a visit to some friends in England. While there she had met a young man named Harold Latimer, who had acquired an ascendency over her and had eventually persuaded her to fly with him. Her friends, shocked at the event, had contented themselves with informing her brother at Athens, and had then washed their hands of the matter. The brother, on his arrival in England, had imprudently placed himself in the power of Latimer and of his associate, whose name was Wilson Kemp—a man of the foulest antecedents. These two, finding that through his ignorance of the language he was helpless in their hands, had kept him a prisoner, and had endeavoured by cruelty and starvation to make him sign away his own and his sister's property. They had kept him in the house without the girl's knowledge, and the plaster over the face had been for the purpose of making recognition difficult in case she should ever catch a glimpse of him. Her feminine perceptions, however, had instantly seen through the disguise when, on the occasion of the interpreter's visit, she had seen him for the first time. The poor girl, however, was herself a prisoner, for there was no one about the house except the man who acted as coachman, and his wife, both of whom were tools of the conspirators. Finding that their secret was out, and that their prisoner was not to be coerced, the two villains with the girl had fled away at a few hours' notice from the furnished house which they had hired, having first, as they thought, taken vengeance both upon the man who had defied and the one who had betrayed them.

Months afterwards a curious newspaper cutting reached us from Buda-Pesth. It told how two Englishmen who had been travelling with a woman had met with a tragic end. They had each been stabbed, it seems, and the Hungarian police were of opinion that they had quarrelled and had inflicted mortal injuries upon each other. Holmes, however, is, I fancy, of a different way of thinking, and he holds to this day that, if one could find the Grecian girl, one might learn how the wrongs of herself and her brother came to be avenged.

Chapter 10

THE ADVENTURE OF THE NAVAL TREATY

THE July which immediately succeeded my marriage was made memorable by three cases of interest, in which I had the privilege of being associated with Sherlock Holmes and of studying his methods. I find them recorded in my notes under the headings of 'The Adventure of the Second Stain', 'The Adventure of the Naval Treaty', and 'The Adventure of the Tired Captain'. The first of these, however, deals with interests of such importance and implicates so many of the first families in the kingdom that for many years it will be impossible to make it public. No case, however, in which Holmes was engaged has ever illustrated the value of his analytical methods so clearly or has impressed those who were associated with him so deeply. I still retain an almost *verbatim* report of the interview in which he demonstrated the true facts of the case to Monsieur Dubugue of the Paris police, and Fritz von Waldbaum, the well-known specialist of Dantzig, both of whom had wasted their energies upon what proved to be side issues. The new century will have come, however, before the story can be safely told. Meanwhile I pass on to the second on my list, which promised also at one time to be of national importance and was marked by several incidents which give it a quite unique character.

During my school days I had been intimately associated with a lad named Percy Phelps, who was of much the same age as myself, though he was two classes ahead of me. He was a very brilliant boy and carried away every prize which the school had to offer, finishing his exploits by winning a scholarship which sent him on to continue his triumphant career at Cambridge. He was, I remember, extremely well connected, and even when we were all little boys together we knew that his mother's brother was Lord Holdhurst, the great conservative politician. This gaudy relationship did him little good at school. On the contrary, it seemed rather a piquant thing to us to chevy him about the playground and hit him over the shins with a wicket. But it was another thing when he came out into the world. I heard vaguely that his abilities and the influences which he commanded had won him a good position at the Foreign Office, and then he passed completely out of my mind until the following letter recalled his existence:

Briarbrae, Woking.

My Dear Watson,

I have no doubt that you can remember "Tadpole" Phelps, who was in the fifth form when you were in the third. It is possible even that you may have heard that through my uncle's influence I obtained a good appointment at the Foreign Office, and that I was in a situation of trust and honour until a horrible misfortune came suddenly to blast my career.

There is no use writing the details of that dreadful event. In the event of your acceding to my request it is probable that I shall have to narrate them to you. I have only just recovered from nine weeks of brain-fever and am still exceedingly weak. Do you think that you could bring your friend Mr. Holmes down to see me? I should like to have his opinion of the case, though the authorities assure me that nothing more can be done. Do try to bring him down, and as soon as possible. Every minute seems an hour while I live in this state of horrible suspense. Assure him that if I have not asked his advice sooner it was not because I did not appreciate his talents, but because I have been off my head ever since the blow fell. Now I am clear again, though I dare not think of it too much for fear of a relapse. I am still so weak that I have to write, as you see, by dictating. Do try to bring him.

Your old schoolfellow,

Percy Phelps.

There was something that touched me as I read this letter, something pitiable in the reiterated appeals to bring Holmes. So moved was I that even had it been a difficult matter I should have tried it, but of course I knew well that Holmes loved his art, so that he was ever as ready to bring his aid as his client could be to receive it. My wife agreed with me that not a moment should be lost in laying the matter before him, and so within an hour of breakfast-time I found myself back once more in the old rooms in Baker Street.

Holmes was seated at his side table clad in his dressing gown and working hard over a chemical investigation. A large curved retort was boiling furiously in the bluish flame of a Bunsen burner, and the distilled drops were condensing into a two-litre measure. My friend hardly glanced up as I entered, and I, seeing that his investigation must be of importance, seated myself in an armchair and waited. He dipped into this bottle or that, drawing out a few drops of each with his glass pipette, and finally brought a test-tube containing a solution over to the table. In his right hand he held a slip of litmus-paper.

"You come at a crisis, Watson," said he. "If this paper remains blue, all is well. If it turns red, it means a man's life." He dipped it into the test-tube and it flushed at once into a dull, dirty crimson. "Hum! I thought as much!" he cried. "I will be at your service in an instant, Watson. You will find tobacco in the Persian slipper." He turned to his desk and scribbled off several telegrams, which were handed over to the page-boy. Then he threw himself down into the chair opposite and drew up his knees until his fingers clasped round his long, thin shins.

"A very commonplace little murder," said he. "You've got something better, I fancy. You are the stormy petrel of crime, Watson. What is it?"

I handed him the letter, which he read with the most concentrated attention.

"It does not tell us very much, does it?" he remarked as he handed it back to me.

"Hardly anything."

"And yet the writing is of interest."

"But the writing is not his own."

"Precisely. It is a woman's."

"A man's surely," I cried.

"No, a woman's, and a woman of rare character. You see, at the commencement of an investigation it is something to know that your client is in close contact with someone who, for good or evil, has an exceptional nature. My interest is already awakened in the case. If you are ready we will start at once for Woking and see this diplomatist who is in such evil case and the lady to whom he dictates his letters."

We were fortunate enough to catch an early train at Waterloo, and in a little under an hour we found ourselves among the fir-woods and the heather of Woking. Briarbrae proved to be a large detached house standing in extensive grounds within a few minutes' walk of the station. On sending in our cards we were shown into an elegantly appointed drawing room, where we were joined in a few minutes by a rather stout man who received us with much hospitality. His age may have been nearer forty than thirty, but his cheeks were so ruddy and his eyes so merry that he still conveyed the impression of a plump and mischievous boy.

"I am so glad that you have come," said he, shaking our hands with effusion. "Percy has been inquiring for you all morning. Ah, poor old chap, he clings to any straw! His father and his mother asked me to see you, for the mere mention of the subject is very painful to them."

"We have had no details yet," observed Holmes. "I perceive that you are not yourself a member of the family."

Our acquaintance looked surprised, and then, glancing down, he began to laugh.

"Of course you saw the 'J H' monogram on my locket," said he. "For a moment I thought you had done something clever. Joseph Harrison is my name, and as Percy is to marry my sister Annie I shall at least be a relation by marriage. You will find my sister in his room, for she has nursed him hand and foot this two months back. Perhaps we'd better go in at once, for I know how impatient he is."

The chamber in which we were shown was on the same floor as the drawing room. It was furnished partly as a sitting and partly as a bedroom, with flowers arranged daintily in every nook and corner. A young man, very pale and worn, was lying upon a sofa near the open window, through which came the rich scent of the garden and the balmy summer air. A woman was sitting beside him, who rose as we entered.

"Shall I leave, Percy?" she asked.

He clutched her hand to detain her. “How are you, Watson?” said he cordially. “I should never have known you under that moustache, and I daresay you would not be prepared to swear to me. This I presume is your celebrated friend, Mr. Sherlock Holmes?”

I introduced him in a few words, and we both sat down. The stout young man had left us, but his sister still remained with her hand in that of the invalid. She was a striking-looking woman, a little short and thick for symmetry, but with a beautiful olive complexion, large, dark, Italian eyes, and a wealth of deep black hair. Her rich tints made the white face of her companion the more worn and haggard by the contrast.

“I won’t waste your time,” said he, raising himself upon the sofa. “I’ll plunge into the matter without further preamble. I was a happy and successful man, Mr. Holmes, and on the eve of being married, when a sudden and dreadful misfortune wrecked all my prospects in life.

“I was, as Watson may have told you, in the Foreign Office, and through the influence of my uncle, Lord Holdhurst, I rose rapidly to a responsible position. When my uncle became foreign minister in this administration he gave me several missions of trust, and as I always brought them to a successful conclusion, he came at last to have the utmost confidence in my ability and tact.

“Nearly ten weeks ago—to be more accurate, on the twenty-third of May—he called me into his private room, and, after complimenting me on the good work which I had done, he informed me that he had a new commission of trust for me to execute.

“‘This,’ said he, taking a gray roll of paper from his bureau, ‘is the original of that secret treaty between England and Italy of which, I regret to say, some rumours have already got into the public press. It is of enormous importance that nothing further should leak out. The French or the Russian embassy would pay an immense sum to learn the contents of these papers. They should not leave my bureau were it not that it is absolutely necessary to have them copied. You have a desk in your office?'

"'Yes, sir.'

"'Then take the treaty and lock it up there. I shall give directions that you may remain behind when the others go, so that you may copy it at your leisure without fear of being overlooked. When you have finished, relock both the original and the draft in the desk, and hand them over to me personally tomorrow morning.'

"I took the papers and—

"Excuse me an instant," said Holmes. "Were you alone during this conversation?"

"Absolutely."

"In a large room?"

"Thirty feet each way."

"In the centre?"

"Yes, about it."

"And speaking low?"

"My uncle's voice is always remarkably low. I hardly spoke at all."

"Thank you," said Sherlock Holmes, shutting his eyes; "pray go on."

"I did exactly what he indicated and waited until the other clerks had departed. One of them in my room, Charles Gorot, had some arrears of work to make up, so I left him there and went out to dine. When I returned he was gone. I was anxious to hurry my work, for I knew that Joseph—the Mr. Harrison whom you saw just now—was in town, and that he would travel down to Woking by the eleven o'clock train, and I wanted if possible to catch it.

"When I came to examine the treaty I saw at once that it was of such importance that my uncle had been guilty of no exaggeration in what he said. Without going into details, I may say that it defined the position of Great Britain towards the Triple Alliance, and foreshadowed the policy which this country would pursue in the event of the French fleet gaining a complete ascendency over that of Italy in the Mediterranean. The questions treated in it were purely naval. At the end were the signatures of the high dignitaries who had signed it. I glanced my eyes over it, and then settled down to my task of copying."

"It was a long document, written in the French language, and containing twenty-six separate articles. I copied as quickly as I could, but at nine o'clock I had only done nine articles, and it seemed hopeless for me to attempt to catch my train. I was feeling drowsy and stupid, partly from my dinner and also from the effects of a long day's work. A cup of coffee would clear my brain. A commissionaire remains all night in a little lodge at the foot of the stairs and is in the habit of making coffee at his spirit-lamp for any of the officials who may be working over time. I rang the bell, therefore, to summon him.

"To my surprise, it was a woman who answered the summons, a large, coarse-faced, elderly woman, in an apron. She explained that she was the commissionaire's wife, who did the charing, and I gave her the order for the coffee.

"I wrote two more articles, and then, feeling more drowsy than ever, I rose and walked up and down the room to stretch my legs. My coffee had not yet come, and I wondered what the cause of the delay could be. Opening the door, I started down the corridor to find out. There was a straight passage, dimly lighted, which led from the room in which I had been working, and was the only exit from it. It ended in a curving staircase, with the commissionaire's lodge in the passage at the bottom. Halfway down this staircase is a small landing, with another passage running into it at right angles. This second one leads by means of a second small stair to a side door, used by servants, and also as a short cut by clerks when coming from Charles Street. Here is a rough chart of the place:"

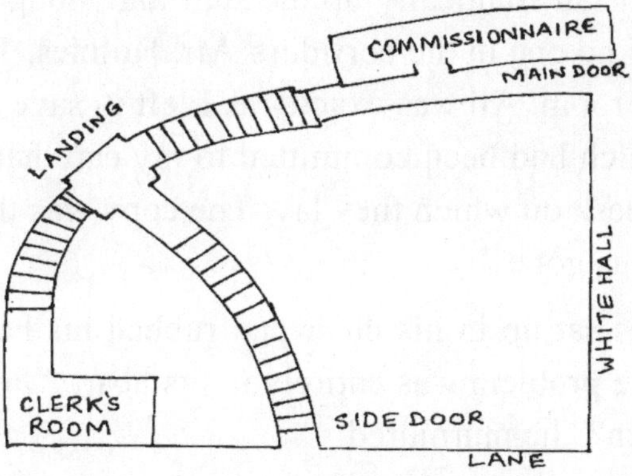

"Thank you. I think that I quite follow you," said Sherlock Holmes.

"It is of the utmost importance that you should notice this point: I went down the stairs and into the hall, where I found the commissionaire fast asleep in his box, with the kettle boiling furiously upon the spirit-lamp. I took off the kettle and blew out the lamp, for the water was spurting over the floor. Then I put out my hand and was about to shake the man, who was still sleeping soundly, when a bell over his head rang loudly, and he woke with a start.

"'Mr. Phelps, sir!' said he, looking at me in bewilderment.

"'I came down to see if my coffee was ready.'

"'I was boiling the kettle when I fell asleep, sir.' He looked at me and then up at the still quivering bell with an ever-growing astonishment upon his face.

"'If you was here, sir, then who rang the bell?' he asked.

"'The bell!' I cried. 'What bell is it?'

"'It's the bell of the room you were working in.'

"A cold hand seemed to close round my heart. Someone, then, was in that room where my precious treaty lay upon the table. I ran frantically up the stair and along the passage. There was no one in the corridors, Mr. Holmes. There was no one in the room. All was exactly as I left it, save only that the papers which had been committed to my care had been taken from the desk on which they lay. The copy was there, and the original was gone."

Holmes sat up in his chair and rubbed his hands. I could see that the problem was entirely to his heart. "Pray, what did you do then?" he murmured.

"I recognized in an instant that the thief must have come up the stairs from the side door. Of course I must have met him if he had come the other way."

"You were satisfied that he could not have been concealed in the room all the time, or in the corridor which you have just described as dimly lighted?"

"'It is absolutely impossible. A rat could not conceal himself either in the room or the corridor. There is no cover at all."

"Thank you. Pray proceed."

"The commissionaire, seeing by my pale face that something was to be feared, had followed me upstairs. Now we both rushed along the corridor and down the steep steps which led to Charles Street. The door at the bottom was closed but unlocked. We flung it open and rushed out. I can distinctly remember that as we did so there came three chimes from a neighbouring clock. It was a quarter-to-ten."

"That is of enormous importance," said Holmes, making a note upon his shirt-cuff.

"'The night was very dark, and a thin, warm rain was falling. There was no one in Charles Street, but a great traffic was going on, as usual, in Whitehall, at the extremity. We rushed along the pavement, bare-headed as we were, and at the far corner we found a policeman standing.

"'A robbery has been committed,' I gasped. 'A document of immense value has been stolen from the Foreign Office. Has anyone passed this way?'

"'I have been standing here for a quarter of an hour, sir,' said he, 'only one person has passed during that time—a woman, tall and elderly, with a Paisley shawl.'"

"'Ah, that is only my wife,' cried the commissionaire; 'has no one else passed?'

"'No one.'

"'Then it must be the other way that the thief took,' cried the fellow, tugging at my sleeve.

"But I was not satisfied, and the attempts which he made to draw me away increased my suspicions.

"'Which way did the woman go?' I cried.

"'I don't know, sir. I noticed her pass, but I had no special reason for watching her. She seemed to be in a hurry.'

"'How long ago was it?'

"'Oh, not very many minutes.'

"'Within the last five?'

"'Well, it could not be more than five.'

"'You're only wasting your time, sir, and every minute now is of importance,' cried the commissionaire; 'take my word for it that my old woman has nothing to do with it and come down to the other end of the street. Well, if you won't, I will.' And with that he rushed off in the other direction.

"But I was after him in an instant and caught him by the sleeve.

"'Where do you live?' said I.

"'16 Ivy Lane, Brixton,' he answered. 'But don't let yourself be drawn away upon a false scent, Mr. Phelps. Come to the other end of the street and let us see if we can hear of anything.'

"Nothing was to be lost by following his advice. With the policeman we both hurried down, but only to find the street full of traffic, many people coming and going, but all only too eager to get to a place of safety upon so wet a night. There was no lounger who could tell us who had passed.

"Then we returned to the office and searched the stairs and the passage without result. The corridor which led to the room was laid down with a kind of creamy linoleum which shows an impression very easily. We examined it very carefully, but found no outline of any footmark."

"Had it been raining all evening?"

"Since about seven."

"How is it, then, that the woman who came into the room about nine left no traces with her muddy boots?"

"I am glad you raised the point. It occurred to me at the time. The charwomen are in the habit of taking off their boots at the commissionaire's office, and putting on list slippers."

"That is very clear. There were no marks, then, though the night was a wet one? The chain of events is certainly one of extraordinary interest. What did you do next?"

"We examined the room also. There is no possibility of a secret door, and the windows are quite thirty feet from the ground. Both of them were fastened on the inside. The carpet prevents any possibility of a trapdoor, and the ceiling is of the ordinary whitewashed kind. I will pledge my life that whoever stole my papers could only have come through the door."

"How about the fireplace?"

"They use none. There is a stove. The bell-rope hangs from the wire just to the right of my desk. Whoever rang it must have come right up to the desk to do it. But why should any criminal wish to ring the bell? It is a most insoluble mystery."

"Certainly the incident was unusual. What were your next steps? You examined the room, I presume, to see if the intruder had left any traces—any cigar-end or dropped glove or hairpin or other trifle?"

"There was nothing of the sort."

"No smell?"

"Well, we never thought of that."

"Ah, a scent of tobacco would have been worth a great deal to us in such an investigation."

"I never smoke myself, so I think I should have observed it if there had been any smell of tobacco. There was absolutely no clue of any kind. The only tangible fact was that the commissionaire's wife—Mrs. Tangey was the name—had hurried out of the place. He could give no explanation save that it was about the time when the woman always went home. The policeman and I agreed that our best plan would be to seize the woman before she could get rid of the papers, presuming that she had them.

"The alarm had reached Scotland Yard by this time, and Mr. Forbes, the detective, came round at once and took up the case with a great deal of energy. We hired a hansom, and in half an hour we were at the address which had been given to us. A young woman opened the door, who proved to be Mrs. Tangey's eldest daughter. Her mother had not come back yet, and we were shown into the front room to wait.

"About ten minutes later a knock came at the door, and here we made the one serious mistake for which I blame myself. Instead of opening the door ourselves, we allowed the girl to do so. We heard her say, 'Mother, there are two men in the house waiting to see you,' and an instant afterwards we heard the patter of feet rushing down the passage. Forbes flung open the door, and we both ran into the back room or kitchen, but the woman had got there before us. She stared at us with defiant eyes, and then, suddenly recognizing me, an expression of absolute astonishment came over her face.

"'Why, if it isn't Mr. Phelps, of the office!' she cried.

"'Come, come, who did you think we were when you ran away from us?' asked my companion.

"'I thought you were the brokers,' said she, 'we have had some trouble with a tradesman.'

"'That's not quite good enough,' answered Forbes. 'We have reason to believe that you have taken a paper of importance from the Foreign Office, and that you ran in here to dispose of it. You must come back with us to Scotland Yard to be searched.'

"It was in vain that she protested and resisted. A four-wheeler was brought, and we all three drove back in it. We had first made an examination of the kitchen, and especially of the kitchen fire, to see whether she might have made away with the papers during the instant that she was alone. There were no signs, however, of any ashes or scraps. When we reached Scotland Yard she was handed over at once to the female searcher. I waited in an agony of suspense until she came back with her report. There were no signs of the papers.

"Then for the first time the horror of my situation came in its full force. Hitherto I had been acting, and action had numbed thought. I had been so confident of regaining the treaty at once that I had not dared to think of what would be the consequence if I failed to do so. But now there was nothing more to be done, and I had leisure to realize my position. It was horrible. Watson there would tell you that I was a nervous, sensitive boy at school. It is my nature. I thought of my uncle and of his colleagues in the Cabinet, of the shame which I had brought upon him, upon myself, upon everyone connected with me. What though I was the victim of an extraordinary accident? No allowance is made for accidents where diplomatic interests are at stake. I was ruined, shamefully, hopelessly ruined. I don't know what I did. I fancy I must have made a scene. I have a dim recollection of a group of officials who crowded round me, endeavouring to soothe me. One of them drove down with me to Waterloo, and saw me into the Woking train. I believe that he would have come all the way had it not been that Dr. Ferrier, who lives near me, was going down by that very train. The doctor most kindly took charge of me, and it was well he did so, for I had a fit in the station, and before we reached home I was practically a raving maniac.

"You can imagine the state of things here when they were roused from their beds by the doctor's ringing and found me in this condition. Poor Annie here and my mother were broken-hearted. Dr. Ferrier had just heard enough from the detective at the station to be able to give an idea of what had happened, and his story did not mend matters. It was evident to all that I was in for a long illness, so Joseph was bundled out of this cheery bedroom, and it was turned into a sickroom for me. Here I have lain, Mr. Holmes, for over nine weeks, unconscious, and raving with brain-fever. If it had not been for Miss Harrison here and for the doctor's care, I should not be speaking to you now. She has nursed me by day and a hired nurse has looked after me by night, for in my mad fits I was capable of anything. Slowly my reason has cleared, but it is only during the last three days that my memory has quite returned. Sometimes I wish that it never had. The first thing that I did was to wire to Mr. Forbes, who had the case in hand. He came out, and assures me that, though everything has been done, no trace of a clue has been discovered. The commissionaire and his wife have been examined in every way without any light being thrown upon the matter. The suspicions of the police then rested upon young Gorot, who, as you may remember, stayed over-time in the office that night. His remaining behind and his French name were really the only two points which could suggest suspicion; but, as a matter of fact, I did not begin work until he had gone, and his people are of Huguenot extraction, but as English in sympathy and tradition as you and I are. Nothing was found to implicate him in any way, and there the matter dropped. I turn to you, Mr. Holmes, as absolutely my last hope. If you fail me, then my honour as well as my position are forever forfeited."

The invalid sank back upon his cushions, tired out by this long recital, while his nurse poured him out a glass of some stimulating medicine. Holmes sat silently, with his head thrown back and his eyes closed, in an attitude which might seem listless to a stranger, but which I knew betokened the most intense self-absorption.

"Your statement has been so explicit," said he at last, "that you have really left me very few questions to ask. There is one of the very utmost importance, however. Did you tell anyone that you had this special task to perform?"

"No one."

"Not Miss Harrison here, for example?"

"No. I had not been back to Woking between getting the order and executing the commission."

"And none of your people had by chance been to see you?"

"None."

"Did any of them know their way about in the office?"

"Oh, yes, all of them had been shown over it."

"Still, of course, if you said nothing to anyone about the treaty these inquiries are irrelevant."

"I said nothing."

"Do you know anything of the commissionaire?"

"Nothing except that he is an old soldier."

"What regiment?"

"Oh, I have heard—Coldstream Guards."

"Thank you. I have no doubt I can get details from Forbes. The authorities are excellent at amassing facts, though they do not always use them to advantage. What a lovely thing a rose is!"

He walked past the couch to the open window and held up the drooping stalk of a moss-rose, looking down at the dainty blend of crimson and green. It was a new phase of his character to me, for I had never before seen him show any keen interest in natural objects.

"There is nothing in which deduction is so necessary as in religion" said he, leaning with his back against the shutters. "It can be built up as an exact science by the reasoner. Our highest assurance of the goodness of Providence seems to me to rest in the flowers. All other things, our powers, our desires, our food, are all really necessary for our existence in the first instance. But this rose is an extra. Its smell and its colour are an embellishment of life, not a condition of it. It is only goodness which gives extras, and so I say again that we have much to hope from the flowers."

Percy Phelps and his nurse looked at Holmes during this demonstration with surprise and a good deal of disappointment written upon their faces. He had fallen into a reverie, with the moss-rose between his fingers. It had lasted some minutes before the young lady broke in upon it.

"Do you see any prospect of solving this mystery, Mr. Holmes?" she asked with a touch of asperity in her voice.

"Oh, the mystery!" he answered, coming back with a start to the realities of life. "Well, it would be absurd to deny that the case is a very abstruse and complicated one, but I can promise you that I will look into the matter and let you know any points which may strike me."

"Do you see any clue?"

"You have furnished me with seven, but of course I must test them before I can pronounce upon their value."

"You suspect someone?"

"I suspect myself."

"What!"

"Of coming to conclusions too rapidly."

"Then go to London and test your conclusions."

"Your advice is very excellent, Miss Harrison," said Holmes, rising.

"I think, Watson, we cannot do better. Do not allow yourself to indulge in false hopes, Mr. Phelps. The affair is a very tangled one."

"I shall be in a fever until I see you again," cried the diplomatist.

"Well, I'll come out by the same train tomorrow, though it's more than likely that my report will be a negative one."

"God bless you for promising to come," cried our client. "It gives me fresh life to know that something is being done. By the way, I have had a letter from Lord Holdhurst."

"Ha! what did he say?"

"He was cold, but not harsh. I dare say my severe illness prevented him from being that. He repeated that the matter was of the utmost importance, and added that no steps would be taken about my future—by which he means, of course, my dismissal—until my health was restored and I had an opportunity of repairing my misfortune."

"Well, that was reasonable and considerate," said Holmes. "Come Watson, for we have a good day's work before us in town." Mr. Joseph Harrison drove us down to the station, and we were soon whirling up in a Portsmouth train. Holmes was sunk in profound thought and hardly opened his mouth until we had passed Clapham Junction.

"It's a very cheery thing to come into London by any of these lines which run high and allow you to look down upon the houses like this."

I thought he was joking, for the view was sordid enough, but he soon explained himself.

"Look at those big, isolated clumps of building rising up above the slates, like brick islands in a lead-coloured sea."

"The board-schools."

"Lighthouses, my boy! Beacons of the future! Capsules with hundreds of bright little seeds in each, out of which will spring the wiser, better England of the future. I suppose that man Phelps does not drink?"

"I should not think so."

"Nor should I, but we are bound to take every possibility into account. The poor devil has certainly got himself into very deep water, and it's a question whether we shall ever be able to get him ashore. What do you think of Miss Harrison?"

"A girl of strong character."

"Yes, but she is a good sort, or I am mistaken. She and her brother are the only children of an iron-master somewhere up Northumberland way. He got engaged to her when travelling last winter, and she came down to be introduced to his people, with her brother as escort. Then came the smash, and she stayed on to nurse her lover, while brother Joseph, finding himself pretty snug, stayed on, too. I've been making a few independent inquiries, you see. But today must be a day of inquiries."

"My practice—" I began.

"Oh, if you find your own cases more interesting than mine—" said Holmes with some asperity.

"I was going to say that my practice could get along very well for a day or two, since it is the slackest time in the year."

"Excellent," said he, recovering his good-humour. "Then we'll look into this matter together. I think that we should begin by seeing Forbes. He can probably tell us all the details we want until we know from what side the case is to be approached."

"You said you had a clue?"

"Well, we have several, but we can only test their value by further inquiry. The most difficult crime to track is the one which is purposeless. Now this is not purposeless. Who is it who profits by it? There is the French ambassador, there is the Russian, there is whoever might sell it to either of these, and there is Lord Holdhurst."

"Lord Holdhurst!"

"Well it is just conceivable that a statesman might find himself in a position where he was not sorry to have such a document accidentally destroyed."

"Not a statesman with the honourable record of Lord Holdhurst?"

"It is a possibility and we cannot afford to disregard it. We shall see the noble lord today and find out if he can tell us anything."

"Meanwhile I have already set inquiries on foot."

"Already?"

"Yes, I sent wires from Woking station to every evening paper in London. This advertisement will appear in each of them."

He handed over a sheet torn from a notebook. On it was scribbled in pencil:

£10 reward. The number of the cab which dropped a fare at or about the door of the Foreign Office in Charles Street at quarter to ten in the evening of May 23d. Apply 221B, Baker Street.

"You are confident that the thief came in a cab?"

"If not, there is no harm done. But if Mr. Phelps is correct in stating that there is no hiding-place either in the room or the corridors, then the person must have come from outside. If he came from outside on so wet a night, and yet left no trace of damp upon the linoleum, which was examined within a few minutes of his passing, then it is exceedingly probable that he came in a cab. Yes, I think that we may safely deduce a cab."

"It sounds plausible."

"That is one of the clues of which I spoke. It may lead us to something. And then, of course, there is the bell—which is the most distinctive feature of the case. Why should the bell ring? Was it the thief who did it out of bravado? Or was it someone who was with the thief who did it in order to prevent the crime? Or was it an accident? Or was it –?" He sank back into the state of intense and silent thought from which he had emerged; but it seemed to me, accustomed as I was to his every mood, that some new possibility had dawned suddenly upon him.

It was twenty past three when we reached our terminus, and after a hasty luncheon at the buffet we pushed on at once to Scotland Yard. Holmes had already wired to Forbes, and we found him waiting to receive us—a small, foxy man with a sharp but by no means amiable expression. He was decidedly frigid in his manner to us, especially when he heard the errand upon which we had come.

"I've heard of your methods before now, Mr. Holmes," said he tartly. "You are ready enough to use all the information that the police can lay at your disposal, and then you try to finish the case yourself and bring discredit on them."

"On the contrary," said Holmes, "out of my last fifty-three cases my name has only appeared in four, and the police have had all the credit in forty-nine. I don't blame you for not knowing this, for you are young and inexperienced, but if you wish to get on in your new duties you will work with me and not against me."

"I'd be very glad of a hint or two," said the detective, changing his manner. "I've certainly had no credit from the case so far."

"What steps have you taken?"

"Tangey, the commissionaire, has been shadowed, He left the Guards with a good character, and we can find nothing against him. His wife is a bad lot, though. I fancy she knows more about this than appears."

"Have you shadowed her?"

"We have set one of our women on to her. Mrs. Tangey drinks, and our woman has been with her twice when she was well on, but she could get nothing out of her."

"I understand that they have had brokers in the house?"

"Yes, but they were paid off."

"Where did the money come from?"

"That was all right. His pension was due. They have not shown any sign of being in funds."

"What explanation did she give of having answered the bell when Mr. Phelps rang for the coffee?"

"She said that her husband was very tired and she wished to relieve him."

"Well, certainly that would agree with his being found a little later asleep in his chair. There is nothing against them then but the woman's character. Did you ask her why she hurried away that night?"

"Her haste attracted the attention of the police constable."

"She was later than usual and wanted to get home."

"Did you point out to her that you and Mr. Phelps, who started at least twenty minutes after her, got home before her?"

"She explains that by the difference between a 'bus and a hansom.'"

"Did she make it clear why, on reaching her house, she ran into the back kitchen?"

"Because she had the money there with which to pay off the brokers."

"She has at least an answer for everything. Did you ask her whether in leaving she met anyone or saw anyone loitering about Charles Street?"

"She saw no one but the constable."

"Well, you seem to have cross-examined her pretty thoroughly. What else have you done?"

"The clerk Gorot has been shadowed all these nine weeks, but without result. We can show nothing against him."

"Anything else?"

"Well, we have nothing else to go upon—no evidence of any kind."

"Have you formed any theory about how that bell rang?"

"Well, I must confess that it beats me. It was a cool hand, whoever it was, to go and give the alarm like that."

"Yes, it was a queer thing to do. Many thanks to you for what you have told me. If I can put the man into your hands you shall hear from me. Come along, Watson."

"Where are we going to now?" I asked as we left the office.

"We are now going to interview Lord Holdhurst, the cabinet minister and future premier of England."

We were fortunate in finding that Lord Holdhurst was still in his chambers in Downing Street, and on Holmes sending in his card we were instantly shown up. The statesman received us with that old-fashioned courtesy for which he is remarkable and seated us on the two luxuriant lounges on either side of the fireplace. Standing on the rug between us, with his slight, tall figure, his sharp features, thoughtful face, and curling hair prematurely tinged with gray, he seemed to represent that not too common type, a nobleman who is in truth noble.

"Your name is very familiar to me, Mr. Holmes," said he, smiling. "And of course I cannot pretend to be ignorant of the object of your visit. There has only been one occurrence in these offices which could call for your attention. In whose interest are you acting, may I ask?"

"In that of Mr. Percy Phelps," answered Holmes.

"Ah, my unfortunate nephew! You can understand that our kinship makes it the more impossible for me to screen him in any way. I fear that the incident must have a very prejudicial effect upon his career."

"But if the document is found?"

"Ah, that, of course, would be different."

"I had one or two questions which I wished to ask you, Lord Holdhurst."

"I shall be happy to give you any information in my power."

"Was it in this room that you gave your instructions as to the copying of the document?"

"It was."

"Then you could hardly have been overheard?"

"It is out of the question."

"Did you ever mention to anyone that it was your intention to give anyone the treaty to be copied?"

"Never."

"You are certain of that?"

"Absolutely."

"Well, since you never said so, and Mr. Phelps never said so, and nobody else knew anything of the matter, then the thief's presence in the room was purely accidental. He saw his chance and he took it."

The statesman smiled. "You take me out of my province there," said he.

Holmes considered for a moment. "There is another very important point which I wish to discuss with you," said he. "You feared, as I understand, that very grave results might follow from the details of this treaty becoming known."

A shadow passed over the expressive face of the statesman. "Very grave results indeed."

"And have they occurred?"

"Not yet."

"If the treaty had reached, let us say, the French or Russian Foreign Office, you would expect to hear of it?"

"I should," said Lord Holdhurst with a wry face.

"Since nearly ten weeks have elapsed, then, and nothing has been heard, it is not unfair to suppose that for some reason the treaty has not reached them."

Lord Holdhurst shrugged his shoulders.

"We can hardly suppose, Mr. Holmes, that the thief took the treaty in order to frame it and hang it up."

"Perhaps he is waiting for a better price."

"If he waits a little longer he will get no price at all. The treaty will cease to be secret in a few months."

"That is most important," said Holmes. "Of course, it is a possible supposition that the thief has had a sudden illness—"

"An attack of brain-fever, for example?" asked the statesman, flashing a swift glance at him.

"I did not say so," said Holmes imperturbably. "And now, Lord Holdhurst, we have already taken up too much of your valuable time, and we shall wish you good day."

"Every success to your investigation, be the criminal who it may," answered the nobleman as he bowed us out at the door.

"He's a fine fellow," said Sherlock Holmes as we came out into Whitehall.

"But he has a struggle to keep up his position. He is far from rich and has many calls. You noticed, of course, that his boots had been resoled. Now, Watson, I won't detain you from your legitimate work any longer. I shall do nothing more today unless I have an answer to my cab advertisement. But I should be extremely obliged to you if you would come down with me to Woking tomorrow by the same train which we took yesterday."

I met him accordingly next morning and we travelled down to Woking together. He had had no answer to his advertisement, he said, and no fresh light had been thrown upon the case. He had, when he so willed it, the utter immobility of countenance of a red Indian, and I could not gather from his appearance whether he was satisfied or not with the position of the case. His conversation, I remember, was about the Bertillon system of measurements, and he expressed his enthusiastic admiration of the French savant.

We found our client still under the charge of his devoted nurse, but looking considerably better than before. He rose from the sofa and greeted us without difficulty when we entered.

"Any news?" he asked eagerly.

"My report, as I expected, is a negative one," said Sherlock Holmes. "I have seen Forbes, and I have seen your uncle, and I have set one or two trains of inquiry upon foot which may lead to something."

"You have not lost heart, then?"

"By no means."

"God bless you for saying that!" cried Miss Harrison. "If we keep our courage and our patience the truth must come out."

"We have more to tell you than you have for us," said Phelps, reseating himself upon the couch.

"I hoped you might have something."

"Yes, we have had an adventure during the night, and one which might have proved to be a serious one." His expression grew very grave as he spoke, and a look of something akin to fear sprang up in his eyes. "Do you know," said he, "that I begin to believe that I am the unconscious centre of some monstrous conspiracy, and that my life is aimed at as well as my honour?"

"Ah!" cried Holmes.

"It sounds incredible, for I have not, as far as I know, an enemy in the world. Yet from last night's experience I can come to no other conclusion."

"Pray let me hear it."

"You must know that last night was the very first night that I have ever slept without a nurse in the room. I was so much better that I thought I could dispense with one. I had a night-light burning, however. Well, about two in the morning I had sunk into a light sleep when I was suddenly aroused by a slight noise. It was like the sound which a mouse makes when it is gnawing a plank, and I lay listening to it for some time under the impression that it must come from that cause. Then it grew louder, and suddenly there came from the window a sharp metallic snick. I sat up in amazement. There could be no doubt what the sounds were now. The first ones had been caused by someone forcing an instrument through the slit between the sashes, and the second by the catch being pressed back.

"There was a pause then for about ten minutes, as if the person were waiting to see whether the noise had awakened me. Then I heard a gentle creaking as the window was very slowly opened. I could stand it no longer, for my nerves are not what they used to be. I sprang out of bed and flung open the shutters. A man was crouching at the window. I could see little of him, for he was gone like a flash. He was wrapped in some sort of cloak which came across the lower part of his face. One thing only I am sure of, and that is that he had some weapon in his hand. It looked to me like a long knife. I distinctly saw the gleam of it as he turned to run."

"This is most interesting," said Holmes. "Pray what did you do then?"

"I should have followed him through the open window if I had been stronger. As it was, I rang the bell and roused the house. It took some little time, for the bell rings in the kitchen and the servants all sleep upstairs. I shouted, however, and that brought Joseph down, and he roused the others. Joseph and the groom found marks on the bed outside the window, but the weather has been so dry lately that they found it hopeless to follow the trail across the grass. There's a place, however, on the wooden fence which skirts the road which shows signs, they tell me, as if someone had got over, and had snapped the top of the rail in doing so. I have said nothing to the local police yet, for I thought I had best have your opinion first."

This tale of our client's appeared to have an extraordinary effect upon Sherlock Holmes. He rose from his chair and paced about the room in uncontrollable excitement.

"Misfortunes never come single," said Phelps, smiling, though it was evident that his adventure had somewhat shaken him.

"You have certainly had your share," said Holmes. "Do you think you could walk round the house with me?"

"Oh, yes, I should like a little sunshine. Joseph will come, too."

"And I also," said Miss Harrison.

"I am afraid not," said Holmes, shaking his head. "I think I must ask you to remain sitting exactly where you are."

The young lady resumed her seat with an air of displeasure. Her brother, however, had joined us and we set off all four together. We passed round the lawn to the outside of the young diplomatist's window. There were, as he had said, marks upon the bed, but they were hopelessly blurred and vague. Holmes stooped over them for an instant, and then rose shrugging his shoulders.

"I don't think anyone could make much of this," said he. "Let us go round the house and see why this particular room was chosen by the burglar. I should have thought those larger windows of the drawing room and dining room would have had more attractions for him."

"They are more visible from the road," suggested Mr. Joseph Harrison.

"Ah, yes, of course. There is a door here which he might have attempted. What is it for?"

"It is the side entrance for trades-people. Of course it is locked at night."

"Have you ever had an alarm like this before?"

"Never," said our client.

"Do you keep plate in the house, or anything to attract burglars?"

"Nothing of value."

Holmes strolled round the house with his hands in his pockets and a negligent air which was unusual with him.

"By the way," said he to Joseph Harrison, "you found some place, I understand, where the fellow scaled the fence. Let us have a look at that!"

The plump young man led us to a spot where the top of one of the wooden rails had been cracked. A small fragment of the wood was hanging down. Holmes pulled it off and examined it critically.

"Do you think that was done last night? It looks rather old, dose it not?"

"Well, possibly so."

"There are no marks of anyone jumping down upon the other side. No, I fancy we shall get no help here. Let us go back to the bedroom and talk the matter over."

Percy Phelps was walking very slowly, leaning upon the arm of his future brother-in-law. Holmes walked swiftly across the lawn, and we were at the open window of the bedroom long before the others came up.

"Miss Harrison," said Holmes, speaking with the utmost intensity of manner, "you must stay where you are all day. Let nothing prevent you from staying where you are all day. It is of the utmost importance."

"Certainly, if you wish it, Mr. Holmes," said the girl in astonishment.

"When you go to bed lock the door of this room on the outside and keep the key. Promise to do this."

"But Percy?"

"He will come to London with us."

"And am I to remain here?"

"It is for his sake. You can serve him. Quick! Promise!"

She gave a quick nod of assent just as the other two came up.

"Why do you sit moping there, Annie?" cried her brother. "Come out into the sunshine!"

"No, thank you, Joseph. I have a slight headache and this room is deliciously cool and soothing."

"What do you propose now, Mr. Sherlock Holmes?" asked our client.

"Well, in investigating this minor affair we must not lose sight of our main inquiry. It would be a very great help to me if you would come up to London with us."

"At once?"

"Well, as soon as you conveniently can. Say in an hour."

"I feel quite strong enough, if I can really be of any help."

"The greatest possible."

"Perhaps you would like me to stay there tonight?"

"I was just going to propose it."

"Then, if my friend of the night comes to revisit me, he will find the bird flown. We are all in your hands, Mr. Holmes, and you must tell us exactly what you would like done. Perhaps you would prefer that Joseph came with us so as to look after me?"

"Oh, no, my friend Watson is a medical man, you know, and he'll look after you. We'll have our lunch here, if you will permit us, and then we shall all three set off for town together."

It was arranged as he suggested, though Miss Harrison excused herself from leaving the bedroom, in accordance with Holmes's suggestion. What the object of my friend's manoeuvres was I could not conceive, unless it were to keep the lady away from Phelps, who, rejoiced by his returning health and by the prospect of action, lunched with us in the dining room. Holmes had a still more startling surprise for us, however, for, after accompanying us down to the station and seeing us into our carriage, he calmly announced that he had no intention of leaving Woking.

"There are one or two small points which I should desire to clear up before I go," said he. "Your absence, Mr. Phelps, will in some ways rather assist me. Watson, when you reach London you would oblige me by driving at once to Baker Street with our friend here, and remaining with him until I see you again. It is fortunate that you are old schoolfellows, as you must have much to talk over. Mr. Phelps can have the spare bedroom tonight, and I will be with you in time for breakfast, for there is a train which will take me into Waterloo at eight."

"But how about our investigation in London?" asked Phelps ruefully.

"We can do that tomorrow. I think that just at present I can be of more immediate use here."

"You might tell them at Briarbrae that I hope to be back tomorrow night," cried Phelps, as we began to move from the platform.

"I hardly expect to go back to Briarbrae," answered Holmes, and waved his hand to us cheerily as we shot out from the station.

Phelps and I talked it over on our journey, but neither of us could devise a satisfactory reason for this new development.

"I suppose he wants to find out some clues as to the burglary last night, if a burglar it was. For myself, I don't believe it was an ordinary thief."

"What is your own idea, then?"

"Upon my word, you may put it down to my weak nerves or not, but I believe there is some deep political intrigue going on around me, and that for some reason that passes my understanding my life is aimed at by the conspirators. It sounds high-flown and absurd, but consider the facts! Why should a thief try to break in at a bedroom window where there could be no hope of any plunder, and why should he come with a long knife in his hand?"

"You are sure it was not a house-breaker's jimmy?"

"Oh, no, it was a knife. I saw the flash of the blade quite distinctly."

"But why on earth should you be pursued with such animosity?"

"Ah, that is the question."

"Well, if Holmes takes the same view, that would account for his action, would it not? Presuming that your theory is correct, if he can lay his hands upon the man who threatened you last night he will have gone a long way towards finding who took the naval treaty. It is absurd to suppose that you have two enemies, one of whom robs you, while the other threatens your life."

"But Holmes said that he was not going to Briarbrae."

"I have known him for some time," said I, "But I never knew him do anything yet without a very good reason," and with that our conversation drifted off on to other topics.

But it was a weary day for me. Phelps was still weak after his long illness, and his misfortunes made him querulous and nervous. In vain I endeavoured to interest him in Afghanistan, in India, in social questions, in anything which might take his mind out of the groove. He would always come back to his lost treaty, wondering, guessing, speculating as to what Holmes was doing, what steps Lord Holdhurst was taking, what news we should have in the morning. As the evening wore on his excitement became quite painful.

"You have implicit faith in Holmes?" he asked.

"I have seen him do some remarkable things."

"But he never brought light into anything quite so dark as this?"

"Oh, yes, I have known him solve questions which presented fewer clues than yours."

"But not where such large interests are at stake?"

"I don't know that. To my certain knowledge he has acted on behalf of three of the reigning houses of Europe in very vital matters."

"But you know him well, Watson. He is such an inscrutable fellow that I never quite know what to make of him. Do you think he is hopeful? Do you think he expects to make a success of it?"

"He has said nothing."

"That is a bad sign."

"On the contrary, I have noticed that when he is off the trail he generally says so. It is when he is on a scent and is not quite absolutely sure yet that it is the right one that he is most taciturn. Now, my dear fellow, we can't help matters by making ourselves nervous about them, so let me implore you to go to bed and so be fresh for whatever may await us tomorrow."

I was able at last to persuade my companion to take my advice, though I knew from his excited manner that there was not much hope of sleep for him. Indeed, his mood was infectious, for I lay tossing half the night myself, brooding over this strange problem and inventing a hundred theories, each of which was more impossible than the last. Why had Holmes remained at Woking? Why had he asked Miss Harrison to remain in the sickroom all day? Why had he been so careful not to inform the people at Briarbrae that he intended to remain near them? I cudgelled my brains until I fell asleep in the endeavour to find some explanation which would cover all these facts.

It was seven o'clock when I awoke, and I set off at once for Phelps's room to find him haggard and spent after a sleepless night. His first question was whether Holmes had arrived yet.

"He'll be here when he promised," said I, "and not an instant sooner or later."

And my words were true, for shortly after eight a hansom dashed up to the door and our friend got out of it. Standing in the window we saw that his left hand was swathed in a bandage and that his face was very grim and pale. He entered the house, but it was some little time before he came upstairs.

"He looks like a beaten man," cried Phelps.

I was forced to confess that he was right. "After all," said I, "the clue of the matter lies probably here in town."

Phelps gave a groan.

"I don't know how it is," said he, "but I had hoped for so much from his return. But surely his hand was not tied up like that yesterday. What can be the matter?"

"You are not wounded, Holmes?" I asked as my friend entered the room.

"Tut, it is only a scratch through my own clumsiness," he answered, nodding his good morning to us. "This case of yours, Mr. Phelps, is certainly one of the darkest which I have ever investigated."

"I feared that you would find it beyond you."

"It has been a most remarkable experience."

"That bandage tells of adventures," said I. "Won't you tell us what has happened?"

"After breakfast, my dear Watson. Remember that I have

breathed thirty miles of Surrey air this morning. I suppose that there has been no answer from my cabman advertisement? Well, well, we cannot expect to score every time."

The table was all laid, and just as I was about to ring Mrs. Hudson entered with the tea and coffee. A few minutes later she brought in three covers, and we all drew up to the table, Holmes ravenous, I curious, and Phelps in the gloomiest state of depression.

"Mrs. Hudson has risen to the occasion," said Holmes, uncovering a dish of curried chicken. "Her cuisine is a little limited, but she has as good an idea of breakfast as a Scotchwoman. What have you there, Watson?"

"Ham and eggs," I answered.

"Good! What are you going to take, Mr. Phelps—curried fowl or eggs, or will you help yourself?"

"Thank you. I can eat nothing," said Phelps.

"Oh, come! Try the dish before you."

"Thank you, I would really rather not."

"Well, then," said Holmes with a mischievous twinkle, "I suppose that you have no objection to helping me?"

Phelps raised the cover, and as he did so he uttered a scream and sat there staring with a face as white as the plate upon which he looked. Across the centre of it was lying a little cylinder of blue-gray paper. He caught it up, devoured it with his eyes, and then danced madly about the room, pressing it to his bosom and shrieking out in his delight. Then he fell back into an armchair, so limp and exhausted with his own emotions that we had to pour brandy down his throat to keep him from fainting.

"There! there!" said Holmes soothingly, patting him upon the shoulder. "It was too bad to spring it on you like this, but Watson here will tell you that I never can resist a touch of the dramatic."

Phelps seized his hand and kissed it. "God bless you!" he cried.

"You have saved my honour."

"Well, my own was at stake, you know," said Holmes. "I assure you it is just as hateful to me to fail in a case as it can be to you to blunder over a commission."

Phelps thrust away the precious document into the innermost pocket of his coat.

"I have not the heart to interrupt your breakfast any further, and yet I am dying to know how you got it and where it was."

Sherlock Holmes swallowed a cup of coffee and turned his attention to the ham and eggs. Then he rose, lit his pipe, and settled himself down into his chair.

"I'll tell you what I did first, and how I came to do it afterwards," said he. "After leaving you at the station I went for a charming walk through some admirable Surrey scenery to a pretty little village called Ripley, where I had my tea at an inn and took the precaution of filling my flask and of putting a paper of sandwiches in my pocket. There I remained until evening, when I set off for Woking again and found myself in the highroad outside Briarbrae just after sunset.

"Well, I waited until the road was clear—it is never a very frequented one at any time, I fancy—and then I clambered over the fence into the grounds."

"Surely the gate was open!" ejaculated Phelps.

"Yes, but I have a peculiar taste in these matters. I chose the place where the three fir-trees stand, and behind their screen I got over without the least chance of anyone in the house being able to see me. I crouched down among the bushes on the other side and crawled from one to the other—witness the disreputable state of my trouser knees—until I had reached the clump of rhododendrons just opposite to your bedroom window. There I squatted down and awaited developments.

"The blind was not down in your room, and I could see Miss Harrison sitting there reading by the table. It was quarter-past ten when she closed her book, fastened the shutters, and retired.

"I heard her shut the door and felt quite sure that she had turned the key in the lock."

"The key!" ejaculated Phelps.

"Yes, I had given Miss Harrison instructions to lock the door on the outside and take the key with her when she went to bed. She carried out everyone of my injunctions to the letter, and certainly without her cooperation you would not have that paper in your coat-pocket. She departed then and the lights went out, and I was left squatting in the rhododendron-bush.

"The night was fine, but still it was a very weary vigil. Of course it has the sort of excitement about it that the sportsman feels when he lies beside the watercourse and waits for the big game. It was very long, though—almost as long, Watson, as when you and I waited in that deadly room when we looked into the little problem of the Speckled Band. There was a church-clock down at Woking which struck the quarters, and I thought more than once that it had stopped. At last, however, about two in the morning, I suddenly heard the gentle sound of a bolt being pushed back and the creaking of a key. A moment later the servants' door was opened, and Mr. Joseph Harrison stepped out into the moonlight."

"Joseph!" ejaculated Phelps.

"He was bare-headed, but he had a black cloak thrown over his shoulder, so that he could conceal his face in an instant if there were any alarm. He walked on tiptoe under the shadow of the wall, and when he reached the window he worked a long-bladed knife through the sash and pushed back the catch. Then he flung open the window, and putting his knife through the crack in the shutters, he thrust the bar up and swung them open.

"From where I lay I had a perfect view of the inside of the room and of everyone of his movements. He lit the two candles which stood upon the mantelpiece, and then he proceeded to turn back the corner of the carpet in the neighbourhood of the door. Presently he stooped and picked out a square piece of board, such as is usually left to enable plumbers to get at the joints of the gas pipes. This one covered, as a matter of fact, the T joint which gives off the pipe which supplies the kitchen underneath. Out of this hiding-place he drew that little cylinder of paper, pushed down the board, rearranged the carpet, blew out the candles, and walked straight into my arms as I stood waiting for him outside the window.

"Well, he has rather more viciousness than I gave him credit for, has Master Joseph. He flew at me with his knife, and I had to grasp him twice, and got a cut over the knuckles, before I had the upper-hand of him. He looked murder out of the only eye he could see with when we had finished, but he listened to reason and gave up the papers. Having got them I let my man go, but I wired full particulars to Forbes this morning. If he is quick enough to catch his bird, well and good. But if, as I shrewdly suspect, he finds the nest empty before he gets there, why, all the better for the government. I fancy that Lord Holdhurst, for one, and Mr. Percy Phelps for another, would very much rather that the affair never got as far as a police-court."

"My God!" gasped our client. "Do you tell me that during these long ten weeks of agony the stolen papers were within the very room with me all the time?"

"So it was."

"And Joseph! Joseph a villain and a thief!"

"Hum! I am afraid Joseph's character is a rather deeper and more dangerous one than one might judge from his appearance. From what I have heard from him this morning, I gather that he has lost heavily in dabbling with stocks, and that he is ready to do anything on earth to better his fortunes. Being an absolutely selfish man, when a chance presented itself he did not allow either his sister's happiness or your reputation to hold his hand."

Percy Phelps sank back in his chair. "My head whirls," said he,"your words have dazed me."

"The principal difficulty in your case," remarked Holmes in his didactic fashion, "lay in the fact of there being too much evidence. What was vital was overlaid and hidden by what was irrelevant. Of all the facts which were presented to us we had to pick just those which we deemed to be essential, and then piece them together in their order, so as to reconstruct this very remarkable chain of events. I had already begun to suspect Joseph from the fact that you had intended to travel home with him that night, and that therefore it was a likely enough thing that he should call for you, knowing the Foreign

Office well, upon his way. When I heard that someone had been so anxious to get into the bedroom, in which no one but Joseph could have concealed anything—you told us in your narrative how you had turned Joseph out when you arrived with the doctor—my suspicions all changed to certainties, especially as the attempt was made on the first night upon which the nurse was absent, showing that the intruder was well acquainted with the ways of the house."

"How blind I have been!"

"The facts of the case, as far as I have worked them out, are these:

This Joseph Harrison entered the office through the Charles Street door, and knowing his way he walked straight into your room the instant after you left it. Finding no one there he promptly rang the bell, and at the instant that he did so his eyes caught the paper upon the table. A glance showed him that chance had put in his way a State document of immense value, and in an instant he had thrust it into his pocket and was gone. A few minutes elapsed, as you remember, before the sleepy commissionaire drew your attention to the bell, and those were just enough to give the thief time to make his escape.

"He made his way to Woking by the first train, and, having examined his booty and assured himself that it really was of immense value, he had concealed it in what he thought was a very safe place, with the intention of taking it out again in a day or two, and carrying it to the French embassy, or wherever he thought that a long price was to be had. Then came your sudden return. He, without a moment's warning, was bundled out of his room, and from that time onward there were always at least two of you there to prevent him from regaining his treasure. The situation to him must have been a maddening one. But at last he thought he saw his chance. He tried to steal in, but was baffled by your wakefulness. You may remember that you did not take your usual draught that night."

"I remember."

"I fancy that he had taken steps to make that draught efficacious, and that he quite relied upon your being unconscious. Of course, I understood that he would repeat the attempt whenever it could be done with safety. Your leaving the room gave him the chance he wanted. I kept Miss Harrison in it all day so that he might not anticipate us. Then, having given him the idea that the coast was clear, I kept guard as I have described. I already knew that the papers were probably in the room, but I had no desire to rip up all the planking and skirting in search of them. I let him take them, therefore, from the hiding-place, and so saved myself an infinity of trouble. Is there any other point which I can make clear?"

"Why did he try the window on the first occasion," I asked, "when he might have entered by the door?"

"In reaching the door he would have to pass seven bedrooms. On the other hand, he could get out on to the lawn with ease. Anything else?"

"You do not think," asked Phelps, "that he had any murderous intention? The knife was only meant as a tool."

"It may be so," answered Holmes, shrugging his shoulders. "I can only say for certain that Mr. Joseph Harrison is a gentleman to whose mercy I should be extremely unwilling to trust."

Chapter 11

THE ADVENTURE OF THE FINAL PROBLEM

It is with a heavy heart that I take up my pen to write these the last words in which I shall ever record the singular gifts by which my friend Mr. Sherlock Holmes was distinguished. In an incoherent and, as I deeply feel, an entirely inadequate fashion, I have endeavoured to give some account of my strange experiences in his company from the chance which first brought us together at the period of the 'Study in Scarlet', up to the time of his interference in the matter of the 'Naval Treaty'—an interference which had the unquestionable effect of preventing a serious international complication. It was my intention to have stopped there, and to have said nothing of that event which has created a void in my life which the lapse of two years has done little to fill. My hand has been forced, however, by the recent letters in which Colonel James Moriarty defends the memory of his brother, and I have no choice but to lay the facts before the public exactly as they occurred. I alone know the absolute truth of the matter, and I am satisfied that the time has come when no good purpose is to be served by its suppression. As far as I know, there have been only three accounts in the public press: that in the *Journal de Genève* on May 6th, 1891, the Reuter's dispatch in the English papers on May 7th, and finally the recent letters to which I have alluded. Of these the first and second were extremely condensed, while the last is, as I shall now show, an absolute perversion of the facts. It lies with me to tell for the first time what really took place between Professor Moriarty and Mr. Sherlock Holmes.

It may be remembered that after my marriage, and my subsequent start in private practice, the very intimate relations which had existed between Holmes and myself became to some extent modified. He still came to me from time to time when he desired a companion in his investigations, but these occasions grew more and more seldom, until I find that in the year 1890 there were only three cases of which I retain any record. During the winter of that year and the early spring of 1891, I saw in the papers that he had been engaged by the French government upon a matter of supreme importance, and I received two notes from Holmes, dated from Narbonne and from Nimes, from which I gathered that his stay in France was likely to be a long one. It was with some surprise, therefore, that I saw him walk into my consulting room upon the evening of April 24th. It struck me that he was looking even paler and thinner than usual.

"Yes, I have been using myself up rather too freely," he remarked, in answer to my look rather than to my words; "I have been a little pressed of late. Have you any objection to my closing your shutters?"

The only light in the room came from the lamp upon the table at which I had been reading. Holmes edged his way round the wall, and, flinging the shutters together, he bolted them securely.

"You are afraid of something?" I asked.

"Well I am."

"Of what?"

"Of air guns."

"My dear Holmes, what do you mean?"

"I think that you know me well enough, Watson, to understand that I am by no means a nervous man. At the same time, it is stupidity rather than courage to refuse to recognize danger when it is close upon you. Might I trouble you for a match?" He drew in the smoke of his cigarette as if the soothing influence was grateful to him.

"I must apologize for calling so late," said he, "and I must further beg you to be so unconventional as to allow me to leave your house presently by scrambling over your back garden wall."

"But what does it all mean?" I asked.

He held out his hand, and I saw in the light of the lamp that two of his knuckles were burst and bleeding.

"It's not an airy nothing, you see," said he, smiling. "On the contrary, it is solid enough for a man to break his hand over. Is Mrs Watson in?"

"She is away upon a visit."

"Indeed! You are alone?"

"Quite."

"Then it makes it the easier for me to propose that you should come away with me for a week to the Continent."

"Where?"

"Oh, anywhere. It's all the same to me."

There was something very strange in all this. It was not Holmes's nature to take an aimless holiday, and something about his pale, worn face told me that his nerves were at their highest tension. He saw the question in my eyes, and, putting his fingertips together and his elbows upon his knees, he explained the situation.

"You have probably never heard of Professor Moriarty?" said he.

"Never."

"Ay, there's the genius and the wonder of the thing!" he cried. "The man pervades London, and no one has heard of him. That's what puts him on a pinnacle in the records of crime. I tell you Watson, in all seriousness, that if I could beat that man, if I could free society of him, I should feel that my own career had reached its summit, and I should be prepared to turn to some more placid line in life. Between ourselves, the recent cases in which I have been of assistance to the royal family of Scandinavia, and to the French republic, have left me in such a position that I could continue to live in the quiet fashion which is most congenial to me, and to concentrate my attention upon my chemical researches. But I could not rest, Watson, I could not sit quiet in my chair, if I thought that such a man as Professor Moriarty were walking the streets of London unchallenged."

"What has he done, then?"

"His career has been an extraordinary one. He is a man of good birth and excellent education, endowed by nature with a phenomenal mathematical faculty. At the age of twenty-one he wrote a treatise upon the binomial theorem, which has had a European vogue. On the strength of it he won the mathematical chair at one of our smaller universities, and had, to all appearances, a most brilliant career before him. But the man had hereditary tendencies of the most diabolical kind. A criminal strain ran in his blood, which, instead of being modified, was increased and rendered infinitely more dangerous by his extraordinary mental powers. Dark rumours gathered round him in the university town, and eventually he was compelled to resign his chair and to come down to London, where he set up as an army coach. So much is known to the world, but what I am telling you now is what I have myself discovered.

“As you are aware, Watson, there is no one who knows the higher criminal world of London so well as I do. For years past I have continually been conscious of some power behind the malefactor, some deep organizing power which forever stands in the way of the law, and throws its shield over the wrong-doer. Again and again in cases of the most varying sorts—forgery cases, robberies, murders—I have felt the presence of this force, and I have deduced its action in many of those undiscovered crimes in which I have not been personally consulted. For years I have endeavoured to break through the veil which shrouded it, and at last the time came when I seized my thread and followed it, until it led me, after a thousand cunning windings, to ex-Professor Moriarty, of mathematical celebrity.

“He is the Napoleon of crime, Watson. He is the organizer of half that is evil and of nearly all that is undetected in this great city. He is a genius, a philosopher, an abstract thinker. He has a brain of the first order. He sits motionless, like a spider in the centre of its web, but that web has a thousand radiations, and he knows well every quiver of each of them. He does little himself. He only plans. But his agents are numerous and splendidly organized. Is there a crime to be done, a paper to be abstracted, we will say, a house to be rifled, a man to be removed—the word is passed to the Professor, the matter is organized and carried out. The agent may be caught. In that case money is found for his bail or his defence. But the central power which uses the agent is never caught—never so much as suspected. This was the organization which I deduced, Watson, and which I devoted my whole energy to exposing and breaking up.

“But the Professor was fenced round with safeguards so cunningly devised that, do what I would, it seemed impossible to get evidence which would convict in a court of law. You know my powers, my dear Watson, and yet at the end of three months I was forced to confess that I had at last met an antagonist who was my intellectual equal. My horror at his crimes was lost in my admiration at his skill. But at last he made a trip—only a little, little trip—but it was more than he could afford, when I was so close upon him. I had my chance, and, starting from that point, I have woven my net round him until now it is all ready to close. In three days—that is to say, on Monday next—matters will be ripe, and the Professor, with all the principal members of his gang, will be in the hands of the police. Then will come the greatest criminal trial of the century, the clearing up of over forty mysteries, and the rope for all of them; but if we move at all prematurely, you understand, they may slip out of our hands even at the last moment.

"Now, if I could have done this without the knowledge of Professor Moriarty, all would have been well. But he was too wily for that. He saw every step which I took to draw my toils round him. Again and again he strove to break away, but I as often headed him off. I tell you, my friend, that if a detailed account of that silent contest could be written, it would take its place as the most brilliant bit of thrust-and-parry work in the history of detection. Never have I risen to such a height, and never have I been so hard pressed by an opponent. He cut deep, and yet I just undercut him. This morning the last steps were taken, and three days only were wanted to complete the business. I was sitting in my room thinking the matter over when the door opened and Professor Moriarty stood before me.

"My nerves are fairly proof, Watson, but I must confess to a start when I saw the very man who had been so much in my thoughts standing there on my threshold. His appearance was quite familiar to me. He is extremely tall and thin, his forehead domes out in a white curve, and his two eyes are deeply sunken in his head. He is clean-shaven, pale, and ascetic-looking, retaining something of the professor in his features. His shoulders are rounded from much study, and his face protrudes forward and is forever slowly oscillating from side to side in a curiously reptilian fashion. He peered at me with great curiosity in his puckered eyes.

"'You have less frontal development than I should have expected,' said he at last. 'It is a dangerous habit to finger loaded firearms in the pocket of one's dressing gown.'

"The fact is that upon his entrance I had instantly recognized the extreme personal danger in which I lay. The only conceivable escape for him lay in silencing my tongue. In an instant I had slipped the revolver from the drawer into my pocket and was covering him through the cloth. At his remark I drew the weapon out and laid it cocked upon the table. He still smiled and blinked, but there was something about his eyes which made me feel very glad that I had it there.

"'You evidently don't know me,' said he.

"'On the contrary,' I answered, 'I think it is fairly evident that I do. Pray take a chair. I can spare you five minutes if you have anything to say.'

"'All that I have to say has already crossed your mind,' said he.

"'Then possibly my answer has crossed yours,' I replied.

"'You stand fast?'

"'Absolutely.'

"He clapped his hand into his pocket, and I raised the pistol from the table. But he merely drew out a memorandum-book in which he had scribbled some dates.

"'You crossed my path on the fourth of January,' said he. 'On the twenty-third you incommoded me; by the middle of February I was seriously inconvenienced by you; at the end of March I was absolutely hampered in my plans; and now, at the close of April, I find myself placed in such a position through your continual persecution that I am in positive danger of losing my liberty. The situation is becoming an impossible one.'

"'Have you any suggestion to make?' I asked.

"'You must drop it, Mr. Holmes,' said he, swaying his face about.

"'You really must, you know.'

"'After Monday,' said I.

"'Tut, tut!' said he. 'I am quite sure that a man of your intelligence will see that there can be but one outcome to this affair. It is necessary that you should withdraw. You have worked things in such a fashion that we have only one resource left. It has been an intellectual treat to me to see the way in which you have grappled with this affair, and I say, unaffectedly, that it would be a grief to me to be forced to take any extreme measure. You smile, sir, but I assure you that it really would.'

"'Danger is part of my trade,' I remarked.

"'This is not danger,' said he. 'It is inevitable destruction. You stand in the way not merely of an individual but of a mighty organization, the full extent of which you, with all your cleverness, have been unable to realize. You must stand clear, Mr. Holmes, or be trodden under foot.'

"'I am afraid,' said I, rising, 'that in the pleasure of this conversation I am neglecting business of importance which awaits me elsewhere.'

"He rose also and looked at me in silence, shaking his head sadly.

"'Well, well,' said he at last. 'It seems a pity, but I have done what I could. I know every move of your game. You can do nothing before Monday. It has been a duel between you and me, Mr. Holmes. You hope to place me in the dock. I tell you that I will never stand in the dock. You hope to beat me. I tell you that you will never beat me. If you are clever enough to bring destruction upon me, rest assured that I shall do as much to you.'

"'You have paid me several compliments, Mr. Moriarty,' said I. 'Let me pay you one in return when I say that if I were assured of the former eventuality I would, in the interests of the public, cheerfully accept the latter.'

"'I can promise you the one, but not the other,' he snarled, and so turned his rounded back upon me and went peering and blinking out of the room.

"That was my singular interview with Professor Moriarty. I confess that it left an unpleasant effect upon my mind. His soft, precise fashion of speech leaves a conviction of sincerity which a mere bully could not produce. Of course, you will say: 'Why not take police precautions against him?' The reason is that I am well convinced that it is from his agents the blow would fall. I have the best of proofs that it would be so."

"You have already been assaulted?"

"My dear Watson, Professor Moriarty is not a man who lets the grass grow under his feet. I went out about midday to transact some business in Oxford Street. As I passed the corner which leads from Bentinck Street on to the Welbeck Street crossing a two-horse van furiously driven whizzed round and was on me like a flash. I sprang for the footpath and saved myself by the fraction of a second. The van dashed round by Marylebone Lane and was gone in an instant. I kept to the pavement after that, Watson, but as I walked down Vere Street a brick came down from the roof of one of the houses and was shattered to fragments at my feet. I called the police and had the place examined. There were slates and bricks piled up on the roof preparatory to some repairs, and they would have me believe that the wind had toppled over one of these. Of course I knew better, but I could prove nothing. I took a cab after that and reached my brother's rooms in Pall Mall, where I spent the day. Now I have come round to you, and on my way I was attacked by a rough with a bludgeon. I knocked him down, and the police have him in custody; but I can tell you with the most absolute confidence that no possible connection will ever be traced between the gentleman upon whose front teeth I have barked my knuckles and the retiring mathematical coach, who is, I daresay, working out problems upon a black-board ten miles away. You will not wonder, Watson, that my first act on entering your rooms was to close your shutters, and that I have been compelled to ask your permission to leave the house by some less conspicuous exit than the front door."

I had often admired my friend's courage, but never more than now, as he sat quietly checking off a series of incidents which must have combined to make up a day of horror.

"You will spend the night here?" I said.

"No, my friend, you might find me a dangerous guest. I have my plans laid, and all will be well. Matters have gone so far now that they can move without my help as far as the arrest goes, though my presence is necessary for a conviction. It is obvious, therefore, that I cannot do better than get away for the few days which remain before the police are at liberty to act. It would be a great pleasure to me, therefore, if you could come on to the Continent with me."

"The practice is quiet," said I, "and I have an accommodating neighbour. I should be glad to come."

"And to start tomorrow morning?"

"If necessary."

"Oh, yes, it is most necessary. Then these are your instructions, and I beg, my dear Watson, that you will obey them to the letter, for you are now playing a double-handed game with me against the cleverest rogue and the most powerful syndicate of criminals in Europe. Now listen! You will dispatch whatever luggage you intend to take by a trusty messenger unaddressed to Victoria tonight. In the morning you will send for a hansom, desiring your man to take neither the first nor the second which may present itself. Into this hansom you will jump, and you will drive to the Strand end of the Lowther Arcade, handing the address to the cabman upon a slip of paper, with a request that he will not throw it away. Have your fare ready, and the instant that your cab stops, dash through the Arcade, timing yourself to reach the other side at a quarter-past nine. You will find a small brougham waiting close to the curb, driven by a fellow with a heavy black cloak tipped at the collar with red. Into this you will step, and you will reach Victoria in time for the Continental express."

"Where shall I meet you?"

"At the station. The second first class carriage from the front will be reserved for us."

"The carriage is our rendezvous, then?"

"Yes."

It was in vain that I asked Holmes to remain for the evening. It was evident to me that he thought he might bring trouble to the roof he was under, and that that was the motive which impelled him to go. With a few hurried words as to our plans for the morrow he rose and came out with me into the garden, clambering over the wall which leads into Mortimer Street, and immediately whistling for a hansom, in which I heard him drive away.

In the morning I obeyed Holmes's injunctions to the letter. A hansom was procured with such precautions as would prevent its being one which was placed ready for us, and I drove immediately after breakfast to the Lowther Arcade, through which I hurried at the top of my speed. A brougham was waiting with a very massive driver wrapped in a dark cloak, who, the instant that I had stepped in, whipped up the horse and rattled off to Victoria Station. On my alighting there he turned the carriage, and dashed away again without so much as a look in my direction.

So far all had gone admirably. My luggage was waiting for me, and I had no difficulty in finding the carriage which Holmes had indicated, the less so as it was the only one in the train which was marked 'Engaged'. My only source of anxiety now was the non-appearance of Holmes. The station clock marked only seven minutes from the time when we were due to start. In vain I searched among the groups of travellers and leave-takers for the lithe figure of my friend. There was no sign of him. I spent a few minutes in assisting a venerable Italian priest, who was endeavouring to make a porter understand, in his broken English, that his luggage was to be booked through to Paris. Then, having taken another look round, I returned to my carriage, where I found that the porter, in spite of the ticket, had given me my decrepit Italian friend as a travelling companion. It was useless for me to explain to him that his presence was an intrusion, for my Italian was even more limited than his English, so I shrugged my shoulders resignedly, and continued to look out anxiously for my friend. A chill of fear had come over me, as I thought that his absence might mean that some blow had fallen during the night. Already the doors had all been shut and the whistle blown, when—

"My dear Watson," said a voice, "you have not even condescended to say good morning."

I turned in uncontrollable astonishment. The aged ecclesiastic had turned his face towards me. For an instant the wrinkles were smoothed away, the nose drew away from the chin, the lower lip ceased to protrude and the mouth to mumble, the dull eyes regained their fire, the drooping figure expanded. The next the whole frame collapsed again, and Holmes had gone as quickly as he had come.

"Good heavens!" I cried, "how you startled me!"

"Every precaution is still necessary," he whispered. "I have reason to think that they are hot upon our trail. Ah, there is Moriarty himself."

The train had already begun to move as Holmes spoke. Glancing back, I saw a tall man pushing his way furiously through the crowd, and waving his hand as if he desired to have the train stopped. It was too late, however, for we were rapidly gathering momentum, and an instant later had shot clear of the station.

"With all our precautions, you see that we have cut it rather fine," said Holmes, laughing. He rose, and throwing off the black cassock and hat which had formed his disguise, he packed them away in a handbag.

"Have you seen the morning paper, Watson?"

"No."

"You haven't seen about Baker Street, then?"

"Baker Street?"

"They set fire to our rooms last night. No great harm was done."

"Good heavens, Holmes, this is intolerable!"

"They must have lost my track completely after their bludgeon-man was arrested. Otherwise they could not have imagined that I had returned to my rooms. They have evidently taken the precaution of watching you, however, and that is what has brought Moriarty to Victoria. You could not have made any slip in coming?"

"I did exactly what you advised."

"Did you find your brougham?"

"Yes, it was waiting."

"Did you recognize your coachman?"

"No."

"It was my brother Mycroft. It is an advantage to get about in such a case without taking a mercenary into your confidence. But we must plan what we are to do about Moriarty now."

"As this is an express, and as the boat runs in connection with it, I should think we have shaken him off very effectively."

"My dear Watson, you evidently did not realize my meaning when I said that this man may be taken as being quite on the same intellectual plane as myself. You do not imagine that if I were the pursuer I should allow myself to be baffled by so slight an obstacle. Why, then should you think so meanly of him?"

"What will he do?"

"What I should do."

"What would you do, then?"

"Engage a special."

"But it must be late."

"By no means. This train stops at Canterbury; and there is always at least a quarter of an hour's delay at the boat. He will catch us there."

"One would think that we were the criminals. Let us have him arrested on his arrival."

"It would be to ruin the work of three months. We should get the big fish, but the smaller would dart right and left out of the net. On Monday we should have them all. No, an arrest is inadmissible."

"What then?"

"We shall get out at Canterbury."

"And then?"

"Well, then we must make a cross-country journey to Newhaven, and so over to Dieppe. Moriarty will again do what I should do. He will get on to Paris, mark down our luggage, and wait for two days at the depot. In the meantime we shall treat ourselves to a couple of carpet-bags, encourage the manufactures of the countries through which we travel, and make our way at our leisure into Switzerland, *via* Luxembourg and Basle."

At Canterbury, therefore, we alighted, only to find that we should have to wait an hour before we could get a train to Newhaven.

I was still looking rather ruefully after the rapidly disappearing luggage-van which contained my wardrobe, when Holmes pulled my sleeve and pointed up the line.

"Already, you see," said he.

Far away, from among the Kentish woods there rose a thin spray of smoke. A minute later a carriage and engine could be seen flying along the open curve which leads to the station. We had hardly time to take our place behind a pile of luggage when it passed with a rattle and a roar, beating a blast of hot air into our faces.

"There he goes," said Holmes, as we watched the carriage swing and rock over the points. "There are limits, you see, to our friend's intelligence. It would have been a *coup-de-maître* had he deduced what I would deduce and acted accordingly."

"And what would he have done had he overtaken us?"

"There cannot be the least doubt that he would have made a murderous attack upon me. It is, however, a game at which two may play. The question now is whether we should take a premature lunch here, or run our chance of starving before we reach the buffet at Newhaven."

We made our way to Brussels that night and spent two days there, moving on upon the third day as far as Strasburg. On the Monday morning Holmes had telegraphed to the London police, and in the evening we found a reply waiting for us at our hotel. Holmes tore it open and then with a bitter curse hurled it into the grate.

"I might have known it!" he groaned. "He has escaped!"

"Moriarty?"

"They have secured the whole gang with the exception of him. He has given them the slip. Of course, when I had left the country there was no one to cope with him. But I did think that I had put the game in their hands. I think that you had better return to England, Watson."

"Why?"

"Because you will find me a dangerous companion now. This man's occupation is gone. He is lost if he returns to London. If I read his character right he will devote his whole energies to revenging himself upon me. He said as much in our short interview, and I fancy that he meant it. I should certainly recommend you to return to your practice."

It was hardly an appeal to be successful with one who was an old campaigner as well as an old friend. We sat in the Strasburg *salle-à-manger* arguing the question for half an hour, but the same night we had resumed our journey and were well on our way to Geneva.

For a charming week we wandered up the valley of the Rhone, and then, branching off at Leuk, we made our way over the Gemmi Pass, still deep in snow, and so, by way of Interlaken, to Meiringen. It was a lovely trip, the dainty green of the spring below, the virgin white of the winter above; but it was clear to me that never for one instant did Holmes forget the shadow which lay across him. In the homely Alpine villages or in the lonely mountain passes, I could still tell by his quick glancing eyes and his sharp scrutiny of every face that passed us, that he was well convinced that, walk where we would, we could not walk ourselves clear of the danger which was dogging our footsteps.

Once, I remember, as we passed over the Gemmi, and walked along the border of the melancholy Daubensee, a large rock which had been dislodged from the ridge upon our right clattered down and roared into the lake behind us. In an instant Holmes had raced up on to the ridge, and, standing upon a lofty pinnacle, craned his neck in every direction. It was in vain that our guide assured him that a fall of stones was a common chance in the springtime at that spot. He said nothing, but he smiled at me with the air of a man who sees the fulfilment of that which he had expected.

And yet for all his watchfulness he was never depressed. On the contrary, I can never recollect having seen him in such exuberant spirits. Again and again he recurred to the fact that if he could be assured that society was freed from Professor Moriarty he would cheerfully bring his own career to a conclusion.

"I think that I may go so far as to say, Watson, that I have not lived wholly in vain," he remarked. "If my record were closed tonight I could still survey it with equanimity. The air of London is the sweeter for my presence. In over a thousand cases I am not aware that I have ever used my powers upon the wrong side. Of late I have been tempted to look into the problems furnished by nature rather than those more superficial ones for which our artificial state of society is responsible. Your memoirs will draw to an end, Watson, upon the day that I crown my career by the capture or extinction of the most dangerous and capable criminal in Europe."

I shall be brief, and yet exact, in the little which remains for me to tell. It is not a subject on which I would willingly dwell, and yet I am conscious that a duty devolves upon me to omit no detail.

It was on the third of May that we reached the little village of Meiringen, where we put up at the Englischer Hof, then kept by Peter Steiler the elder. Our landlord was an intelligent man and spoke excellent English, having served for three years as waiter at the Grosvenor Hotel in London. At his advice, on the afternoon of the fourth we set off together, with the intention of crossing the hills and spending the night at the hamlet of Rosenlaui. We had strict injunctions, however, on no account to pass the falls of Reichenbach, which are about halfway up the hills, without making a small detour to see them.

It is, indeed, a fearful place. The torrent, swollen by the melting snow, plunges into a tremendous abyss, from which the spray rolls up like the smoke from a burning house. The shaft into which the river hurls itself is an immense chasm, lined by glistening coal-black rock, and narrowing into a creaming, boiling pit of incalculable depth, which brims over and shoots the stream onward over its jagged lip. The long sweep of green water roaring forever down, and the thick flickering curtain of spray hissing forever upward, turn a man giddy with their constant whirl and clamour. We stood near the edge peering down at the gleam of the breaking water far below us against the black rocks, and listening to the half-human shout which came booming up with the spray out of the abyss.

The path has been cut halfway round the fall to afford a complete view, but it ends abruptly, and the traveller has to return as he came. We had turned to do so, when we saw a Swiss lad come running along it with a letter in his hand. It bore the mark of the hotel which we had just left and was addressed to me by the landlord. It appeared that within a very few minutes of our leaving, an English lady had arrived who was in the last stage of consumption. She had wintered at Davos Platz and was journeying now to join her friends at Lucerne, when a sudden hemorrhage had overtaken her. It was thought that she could hardly live a few hours, but it would be a great consolation to her to see an English doctor, and, if I would only return, etc. The good Steiler assured me in a postscript that he would himself look upon my compliance as a very great favour, since the lady absolutely refused to see a Swiss physician, and he could not but feel that he was incurring a great responsibility.

The appeal was one which could not be ignored. It was impossible to refuse the request of a fellow-countrywoman dying in a strange land. Yet I had my scruples about leaving Holmes. It was finally agreed, however, that he should retain the young Swiss messenger with him as guide and companion while I returned to Meiringen. My friend would stay some little time at the fall, he said, and would then walk slowly over the hill to Rosenlaui, where I was to rejoin him in the evening. As I turned away I saw Holmes, with his back against a rock and his arms folded, gazing down at the rush of the waters. It was the last that I was ever destined to see of him in this world.

When I was near the bottom of the descent I looked back. It was impossible, from that position, to see the fall, but I could see the curving path which winds over the shoulder of the hills and leads to it. Along this a man was, I remember, walking very rapidly.

I could see his black figure clearly outlined against the green behind him. I noted him, and the energy with which he walked, but he passed from my mind again as I hurried on upon my errand.

It may have been a little over an hour before I reached Meiringen. Old Steiler was standing at the porch of his hotel.

"Well," said I, as I came hurrying up, "I trust that she is no worse?"

A look of surprise passed over his face, and at the first quiver of his eyebrows my heart turned to lead in my breast.

"You did not write this?" I said, pulling the letter from my pocket. "There is no sick Englishwoman in the hotel?"

"Certainly not!" he cried. "But it has the hotel mark upon it! Ha, it must have been written by that tall Englishman who came in after you had gone." He said.

But I waited for none of the landlord's explanation. In a tingle of fear I was already running down the village street, and making for the path which I had so lately descended. It had taken me an hour to come down. For all my efforts two more had passed before I found myself at the fall of Reichenbach once more. There was Holmes's Alpine-stock still leaning against the rock by which I had left him. But there was no sign of him, and it was in vain that I shouted. My only answer was my own voice reverberating in a rolling echo from the cliffs around me.

It was the sight of that Alpine-stock which turned me cold and sick. He had not gone to Rosenlaui, then. He had remained on that three-foot path, with sheer wall on one side and sheer drop on the other, until his enemy had overtaken him. The young Swiss had gone too. He had probably been in the pay of Moriarty and had left the two men together. And then what had happened? Who was to tell us what had happened then?

I stood for a minute or two to collect myself, for I was dazed with the horror of the thing. Then I began to think of Holmes's own methods and to try to practise them in reading this tragedy. It was, alas, only too easy to do. During our conversation we had not gone to the end of the path, and the Alpine-stock marked the place where we had stood. The blackish soil is kept forever soft by the incessant drift of spray, and a bird would leave its tread upon it. Two lines of foot marks were clearly marked along the farther end of the path, both leading away from me. There were none returning. A few yards from the end the soil was all ploughed up into a patch of mud, and the brambles and ferns which fringed the chasm were torn and bedraggled. I lay upon my face and peered over with the spray spouting up all around me. It had darkened since I left, and now I could only see here and there the glistening of moisture upon the black walls, and far away down at the end of the shaft the gleam of the broken water. I shouted; but only that same half-human cry of the fall was borne back to my ears.

But it was destined that I should, after all, have a last word of greeting from my friend and comrade. I have said that his Alpine-stock had been left leaning against a rock which jutted on to the path. From the top of this boulder the gleam of something bright caught my eye, and raising my hand I found that it came from the silver cigarette-case which he used to carry. As I took it up a small square of paper upon which it had lain fluttered down on to the ground. Unfolding it, I found that it consisted of three pages torn from his notebook and addressed to me. It was characteristic of the man that the direction was as precise, and the writing as firm and clear, as though it had been written in his study.

My Dear Watson [it said]:

I write these few lines through the courtesy of Mr. Moriarty, who awaits my convenience for the final discussion of those questions which lie between us. He has been giving me a sketch of the methods by which he avoided the English police and kept himself informed of our movements. They certainly confirm the very high opinion which I had formed of his abilities. I am pleased to think that I shall be able to free society from any further effects of his presence, though I fear that it is at a cost which will give pain to my friends, and especially, my dear Watson, to you. I have already explained to you, however, that my career had in any case reached its crisis, and that no possible conclusion to it could be more congenial to me than this. Indeed, if I may make a full confession to you, I was quite convinced that the letter from Meiringen was a hoax, and I allowed you to depart on that errand under the persuasion that some development of this sort would follow. Tell Inspector Patterson that the papers which he needs to convict the gang are in pigeonhole M., done up in a blue envelope and inscribed 'Moriarty'. I made every disposition of my property before leaving England and handed it to my brother Mycroft. Pray give my greetings to Mrs. Watson, and believe me to be, my dear fellow,

Very sincerely yours,

Sherlock Holmes.

A few words may suffice to tell the little that remains. An examination by experts leaves little doubt that a personal contest between the two men ended, as it could hardly fail to end in such a situation, in their reeling over, locked in each other's arms. Any attempt at recovering the bodies was absolutely hopeless, and there, deep down in that dreadful cauldron of swirling water and seething foam, will lie for all time the most dangerous criminal and the foremost champion of the law of their generation. The Swiss youth was never found again, and there can be no doubt that he was one of the numerous agents whom Moriarty kept in his employ. As to the gang, it will be within the memory of the public how completely the evidence which Holmes had accumulated exposed their organization, and how heavily the hand of the dead man weighed upon them. Of their terrible chief few details came out during the proceedings, and if I have now been compelled to make a clear statement of his career, it is due to those injudicious champions who have endeavoured to clear his memory by attacks upon him whom I shall ever regard as the best and the wisest man whom I have ever known.

THE END